"Oh, my God. Look," Nisha said, nudging Jordan. "Can you believe Tara's actually letting *Victor* hold her precious iPhone? I mean, the girl has a panic attack every time I even *think* about touching it."

"Maybe it's iLove," Jordan joked as Tara flitted around the chaotic store with Victor following close behind.

Nisha laughed. "He kind of reminds me of a little puppy."

"No, not a puppy," Jordan said, watching them. "Victor's a very well-groomed, picture-perfect prom date. He's exactly what Tara set out to achieve with the makeover." Jordan had to admire her friend's drive. *Tara figures out what she wants, sets herself a goal and just . . . does it. Every. Single. Time. Me? I'd be happy if I could get past the "figure out what she wants" part.*

Read all the **Prom** books!

**ONCE UPON A PROM #1**
*dream*

**ONCE UPON A PROM #2**
*dress*

**ONCE UPON A PROM #3**
*date*

Also by Jeanine Le Ny

**I ♥ BIKINIS: ISLAND SUMMER**

# ONCE UPON A PROM
# *dress*

JEANINE LE NY

Point

ISBN-13: 978-0-545-03181-3
ISBN-10: 0-545-03181-8



Text design by Steve Scott

12 11 10 9 8 7 6 5 4 3 2 8 9 10 11 12 13/0

Printed in the U.S.A.
First printing, March 2008

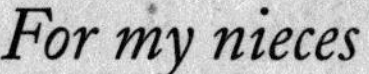

*For my nieces*

## *Acknowledgments*

A big thanks goes to Sonya Singh for the helpful information on *Kathak* and Hindu; Segal Manoj for sharing her wisdom on growing up Indian in America, and to Aimee Friedman for her boundless encouragement and guidance.

# ONCE UPON A PROM
# *dress*

*3 weeks, 3 days, 19 hours, and 42 minutes till Prom . . .*

# CHAPTER *One*

*Recipe for (Prom) Success*

1) *A gown — ANY gown (that makes me look like a goddess).*
2) *One (classy) limousine. No electric blue Hummers.*
3) *Lots of good friends (to share classy limo).*
4) *One fantasy date (preferably cute, preferably personable, preferably Nate — hey, it's a FANTASY, OK?).*
5) *Beautiful sunset (to incite romance).*
6) *Awesome venue, awesome theme, awesome food, awesome band (natch).*

Tara Macmillan rested her hands lightly on the marble banister of the Fairmont Hotel's grand terrace, drinking in the sunset's glorious palette of purples, yellows, and reds. A warm breeze carrying the scent of lavender kissed her skin and teased her senses. Below her, classmates pulled onto the circular drive — one limousine after another — arriving in beautiful gauzy dresses and elegant tuxedos, excited and chatty and definitely ready to party.

*The prom. It's finally here,* Tara thought, her stomach fluttering with excitement. A jazzy cover of her favorite song wafted through the hotel's entrance into the evening air, calling out for her to dance. What was she waiting for?

By now the couples had drifted into the hotel and Tara was alone, except for two red-jacketed valet guys chatting at the bottom of the steps. Turning to go inside, she noticed the tall one steal one glance her way, then another. Which Tara thought was very cool, if a little unusual. Most boys weren't so obvious about their appreciation of the female form. Not hers anyway.

*Hmm. A beautiful sunset . . . a good-looking boy's attention without any effort on my part?* Tara wasn't one to believe in the power of astrology, but if she *were*, she'd have no choice but to think that the stars had aligned themselves just for her. She swiped her sleek French twist with her fingertips, not one strand out of place. Even her naturally wavy hair was behaving tonight.

The valet boy peeked at her again, and Tara gave him a smile and her best sorry-I've-got-a-prom-date-to-meet shrug before turning to enter the hotel. She had gone to all the trouble of transforming her date, Victor Kaminski, from goofy mullet-haired mascot to enviable hunk. Okay, maybe not *quite* a hunk, but definitely cute enough to dance with. And that was what she intended to do. Dance with him. Where *was* Victor anyway?

Determined to find him, Tara breezed through the hotel lobby and came across an easel holding a black pinboard that read WELCOME TO YOUR STARRY NIGHT, EMERSON HIGH SCHOOL SENIORS! Tara shook her head. *The hotel got our theme wrong. It's supposed to be "Once Upon a Time."* Not that she was complaining. She loved the idea of having a "Starry Night" prom, but she also recalled fighting about it with fellow committee member, Jenny Brigger. And losing.

*Whatever.* Tonight Tara was all about going with the flow. Turning over a new leaf. Starting a fresh page. It was the new Tara. The relaxed Tara. The Tara who didn't care (as much) if everything wasn't perfect.

Moments later though, after stepping into the Fairmont Hotel ballroom, she let out an involuntary gasp — because everything *was* perfect. Instead of a ballroom decorated with a Disney-like castle as expected, Tara entered a room draped whimsically in golds and greens, inspired by Van Gogh's famous *Starry Night* painting.

The tables bordering the dance floor were adorned with sparkly navy linen, fine china, and spectacular centerpieces of wild curling branches and exotic greenery that mimicked the unruly brush strokes for which the artist was known. The band was in full swing now and the crowd on the dance floor grooved underneath a blanket of twinkling globe-like lanterns.

Tara spotted Jenny Brigger standing at a nearby table, directing students to their seating, and she cruised over to her.

"Tara was right about *everything*," she overheard Jenny telling Stuart Fullman, another prom committee member. "'Starry Night' is the most amazing theme ever. I mean, the girl is seriously brilliant." Jenny fluffed out the skirt of her taupe bubble dress as she gabbed. "I just hope we did her vision justice. Think she'll be surprised?"

*Who is this person giving me all the credit?* Tara wondered. *Definitely not the Jenny I know and loathe.* She touched her fingertips to her lips to hold back a giggle. Not only was Jenny acting weird, she was wearing the 1980s retro monstrosity that Tara's best friends, Jordan Taylor and Nisha Khubani, had convinced Tara *not* to buy for the prom. Apparently it made Tara's butt look like a gigantic upside-down mushroom cap. Unfortunately it did the same for Jenny, who chose to pair it with one of her signature scrunchies — a taupe one that happened to match the fabric of her dress perfectly. *I wonder if she had that thing custom made,* Tara thought just as Jenny spotted her.

"Hey, you!" Jenny cried, immediately dumping Stuart to head for Tara. "Oh, my God. You look *soooo* amazing," she gushed. "Like a total prom queen!"

"Yeah, right," Tara said with a roll of the eyes. Jordan was going to be prom queen, not her. "Um, you look nice, too," she added since Jenny seemed to have forgotten her regular personality at home and was being almost, um, *sweet.*

"I *sooooo* like your dress," Jenny added, admiring it.

Actually, Tara was liking the new Jenny. "Thanks," she said, glancing down at herself: one-shouldered, shimmering white silk, a high slit up the right side. The dress seemed familiar . . . but not because she'd bought it. Then Tara realized the problem.

*Okay, Tara. What, exactly, are you doing in Jordan Taylor's prom gown?* Tara forced herself not to hyperventilate in front of Jenny. There had to be an explanation . . . why couldn't she remember it? Had the stress of planning the prom destroyed her last brain cell? She had to find Jordan. "Well, see you on the dance floor, Jenny."

Tara's heart beat in time with the pulsating music as she searched for her friend. She tried to cross the room but was stopped midway by Billy and Sam from the baseball team. Then two cheerleaders that Tara sort of knew grouped around her.

"Ooh. I *have* to get a picture!" one said and snapped her camera at Tara.

"Don't forget to stop by our table later, okay?" the other girl told her. "Awesome job, by the way. We knew you could do it. See ya!"

Tara smiled. All the attention was flattering. *It's nice that they appreciate the work that goes into a great prom.* She glanced at the kids mingling, taking photos, and rocking out to the music. Her eyes traveled to the edge of the dance floor where she spotted Nisha, in her beautiful lemon-colored gown, holding hands with her boyfriend, Brian. The two of them were talking to Victor, but Jordan was nowhere to be found. *Maybe they know where she is.*

Tara waved, heading over. Victor looked very handsome in his black tuxedo. When she got there she surprised him with a hug. "Nice tux," she remarked.

"Yeah, my *date* picked it for me," Victor said and gave her a friendly nudge. "You don't look so bad yourself."

"Totally," Nisha agreed.

Tara was beginning to feel better about her dress. If it *was* Jordan's, wouldn't Nisha have flipped out already?

She was about to ask if Nisha knew where Jordan and Nate were hiding when Nisha leaned in and said, "Looks like they're getting ready to announce the prom king and queen."

*Good,* Tara thought and turned toward the clearing dance floor. *I'll talk to Jordan after the ceremony.*

The crowd settled to a low murmur as Principal Harris crossed in front of the band and grabbed a microphone from the lead singer. "Ladies and gentlemen," he said into the mike. "Can I have your attention, please? I'd like to announce our Emerson High School royalty." He cued the band for a drumroll. "For this year's prom queen, winning by a landslide . . ." He paused for dramatic effect. "I give you . . ."

*Come on,* Tara thought. *Jordan Taylor. Say it. Say it!*

"Jorrrrdaaaaaan Taaaaaallllllorrr!" he cried.

The house erupted in applause and Tara

joined right along, clapping wildly and searching the crowd for her friend.

"Hey, congrats," Victor said, giving her a friendly hug.

Nisha and Brian did the same.

What could Tara say? She *had* run an excellent campaign to elect Jordan prom queen, but Tara wasn't the one who deserved the credit. Jordan was. Mr. Harris was still on the dance floor alone and was beginning to look confused as he waited for Jordan to show.

Tara noticed several people staring at her as if they expected her to pull Jordan out of her tiny sparkly evening bag. *Hello? I don't know where she is either?*

After a few minutes, Victor leaned in. "You think maybe you should go up there and get the crown?" he asked her.

*Me?* Tara thought. "Uh, no thanks."

"Come on. We can't wait all night. Just go and get it," Victor said, giving her a little nudge.

"Hey!" Tara tripped onto the dance floor and glared at Victor, who shot her an encouraging thumbs-up. *Fine,* she thought. Feeling awkward, she clicked across the shiny wood, still looking for Jordan's pretty face and shoulder-length blond hair in the crowd . . . and getting annoyed. *How can Jordan blow off being prom queen? I feel like an idiot standing in for her like this.*

Tara could feel the eyes of her classmates bore into her skin as she approached Mr. Harris. It seemed like an eternity before he called out the name of the prom king.

"Nate Lombaaaarrrrrddddooooo!"

Nate made the grand gesture of raising both his arms in the air. "Yes!" he cried, pumping his right fist enthusiastically and waving to the other students.

The more Tara watched, the more she felt sorry for him. *Look how adorable he is, playing to the crowd as if his girlfriend didn't just ditch him in front of everybody.* He was doing a pretty decent job of it, too. And Tara was beginning to think that maybe, just maybe, her best friend didn't deserve a boyfriend as sweet as Nate — and not just because Tara had a tiny crush on him either. How could Jordan do this to him? Where *was* she?

Finally, Nate strode up next to Tara and took her hand.

Tara tried to ignore her tingling palm. "What should I do?" she whispered. "What should I say to everybody?"

"Forget it," he assured her. "Just let them put the crown on your head, and then we'll dance. We don't have to say anything."

So she did. And when the band began to play a gentle ballad, Nate turned to her, smiled shyly, and took her into his arms. "I'm so glad you're here. I wouldn't want to do this with any other person," he whispered, pulling her so close that Tara thought she could feel Nate's heart beating through his tuxedo jacket. Or was that her heart?

"Really?" Even though Nate was Jordan's boyfriend, Tara allowed herself to enjoy the moment. She wrapped her arms around Nate's shoulders and rested her head lightly on his chest as they swayed to the music. Tara tried not to freak when Nate nuzzled closer. It felt good being this near to him, so natural, almost as if he were . . . her boyfriend.

After a minute, Nate broke away a bit and gazed intensely into Tara's brown eyes. "You're so beautiful," he told her.

*Beautiful? Me?* Tara's heart swelled as she took in his words. *I, Tara Macmillan, am considered beautiful by Nate Lombardo?* "Yeah, well . . . you know," she said, pretending as if she heard it all the time.

"Seriously," Nate went on. "I've never seen you *more* beautiful, Jordan."

*Wait. Jordan?*

"What did you just call me?" Tara asked.

"I called you beautiful, Jord." Nate smiled. "Want me say it again?"

*Nate thinks I'm Jordan?* She glanced at the crowd watching them dance. *Does everybody?* It took about four seconds for her to stop caring. Because now Nate was leaning toward her, eyes closed. *Oh. My. God. He's going to kiss me. Or Jordan. Or . . . who cares!*

She closed her eyes too, wondering what his lips were going to feel like. Was he as good a kisser as she expected? *Kiss me, Nate,* she thought. *Kiss me . . .*

*Da, da, da, dummmmmmmmmm . . . Da, da, da, dummmmmmmm.*

The band's ballad suddenly switched from sultry R&B to a tinny version of Beethoven's Ninth Symphony, breaking the mood — and ruining what was surely meant to be the best moment of Tara's high school career.

*Da, da, da, dummmmmmmmmm . . . Da, da, da, dummmmmmmm.*

Tara groaned. *Why, why,* why *did I let Jenny Brigger pick this sucky band?* She opened her eyes.

But when she did, she was not at the prom, *not* looking into the face of the boy she'd been secretly dreaming about for months. She was underneath her fluffy purple duvet. In her purple bedroom. Alone. With her cell-phone–slash–handheld-computer chirping that annoying ring tone from atop her nightstand.

*Da, da, da, dummmmmmmmmm . . . Da, da, da, dummmmmmmm.*

*Why do I* always *wake up right before the best part of the dream?* Tara rolled over and closed her eyes again, desperate to get back to the part where she and Nate were about to make lip contact.

*Da, da, da, dummmmmmmmmm . . . Da, da, da, dummmmmmmm.*

It was no use. Tara flicked open her eyes, resisting the urge to throw her pillow at the phone. She answered it instead. "Hello?"

"Hey, Tara. It's me. What's up?"

Me meaning *Jordan,* Tara realized. She swallowed hard, feeling a pit form in her stomach. What was she supposed to tell her friend? *"Oh, hey, Jord! I was just dreaming about having your prom gown, your hot boyfriend, and your all-around charmed life?"*

*I don't think so.* Instead she replied, "What's *up*? Not me. I was *sleeping*, Jordan." Maybe it came out a little harsh.

"No need to be a grump, sleepyhead," Jordan replied in that breezy tone of hers. "Nisha and I were thinking of doing brunch later. Want to meet up? I thought we'd do Joes. You know, that funky teahouse I've been talking about nonstop?"

"You mean that place where you went on your nondate with Emo Boy Supreme?" Tara couldn't help herself. She found it hard to believe that Jordan was sort-of-friends with a boy who sported Black Satin nail polish on a regular basis. *Why does she want to hang out with that weird guy when she has Nate?* It was all too bizarre.

"Sorry. Can't make it. I'm meeting Victor," Tara added, which was the truth. Except for the sorry part. Tara wasn't in the mood to listen to Jordan complain about her perfect life. The girl had absolutely no clue how easily things came to her: like that white silk prom dress, for instance. One shopping trip. *One!* Tara had been searching for weeks and *still* nothing.

She waited for Jordan to protest, but got an awkward silence instead.

"If we're going to take back the prom from Jenny Brigger and her posse, we've got a lot of planning to do," she added for good measure. Unlike in her dream, Tara knew that Jenny wasn't about to go along with any of Tara's ideas — even though, officially, Tara was head of the prom committee. Wasn't it Jenny who'd gone behind Tara's back and organized a prom mutiny? "Believe it or not, Victor agreed to do it over prom dress shopping." Tara was all about multi-tasking.

"Prom planning *and* shopping?" Jordan repeated. "Wow, that's really nice of him. I do believe our school mascot has it *bad* for you."

Was that a dig? Tara wondered. Was Jordan making fun of her because Tara had to give Victor a geek-to-chic makeover? Did Jordan even *know* how *cute* he looked now?

"You know, Victor's a really good guy, Jordan. And he'll be a really good prom date, too," Tara replied testily. *But I'd still rather be kissed by Nate Lombardo,* she added silently.

Words she hoped Jordan would *never* hear.

*3 weeks, 3 days, 17 hours, and 33 minutes till Prom . . .*

# CHAPTER *Two*

"It was only a kiss. One stupid kiss. No big deal," Jordan said firmly from her perch on an overstuffed chair at Joes. She uttered the words with such conviction that she surprised herself. To the naked ear it might have sounded as if Jordan actually *believed* what she was talking about. As if she *hadn't* been up most of last night, cheeks tear-stained from worry and guilt and feeling totally jerk-like for kissing Shane Dresden — a boy who was a friend, yes, but who was, most certainly, *not* Jordan's boyfriend. The lovable Nate Lombardo had held that title for the past year and a half.

Nisha was sitting cross-legged on a yellow loveseat, wearing her favorite vintage jeans with the perfect holes in the knees, a crisp white tee, and a pair of cute metallic ballet flats. Jordan squirmed as she watched her friend's exotic almond-shaped eyes go from wide to narrow. "Yeah. Uh-huh. I don't believe you," Nisha said. Apparently the girl did not have a naked ear; she had those supersonic best friend ears that could detect the slightest tone of doubt.

Not knowing how to reply, Jordan took a long sip of her spicy chai, letting her eyes wander to the old claw-foot bathtub filled with yellowing paperbacks for the taking. She noticed two scruffy-looking boys lounging a couple of seats over — one in black-framed glasses and baggy, paint-splattered jeans, the other with a guitar case slung over a wingback chair. The guy with the guitar had a cute shaggy haircut, the color of sand, which was how Jordan always imagined Nate's might look if he let it grow out a little.

*Nate.* Another pang of guilt pinched her chest.

"Kissing Shane was nothing, all right?" Jordan said. Why couldn't Nisha just believe it? If she did, then maybe, little by little, Jordan could believe it too. "Don't people kiss all the time?" she added with a wave of her chai for emphasis. "Like that foreign-exchange student, Paolo. He kisses people twice to say 'hi' then does it again to say 'bye' or whatever. That's, like, four kisses in passing alone. So why does kissing Shane *once* have to be such a big deal?"

Nisha tilted her head, seeming to consider it. "Okay, first of all, Paolo doesn't count. He's *Italian.* His kissing is either totally cultural . . . or he's doing it because he's got a cute accent so he knows he can get away with it. And second? I thought you said kissing Shane *wasn't* a big deal."

"Oh, it's not," Jordan assured her. "*So* not. Really, really, not."

"Hmm." Nisha placed her enormous cup of peach tea lemonade on a metal end table and leaned forward. "I guess that's why you can't stop talking about it, huh?"

"Fine," Jordan replied. "From this moment forward I'll refrain from ever mentioning Shane Dresden and/or his lips again. See?" She pretended to close an invisible zipper over her mouth. But the truth was, Jordan wanted to go on forever about how kissing Shane wasn't a big deal because she knew that when she was finally quiet she'd have to deal with reality: that last night she may have accidentally flushed her relationship with Nate down the toilet.

Voted "Most Likely to Live Happily Ever After" in the yearbook, she and Nate were their high school's favorite couple. To the students at Emerson High, she and Nate were like Oreos and milk, sun and sand, Dolce and Gabbana; they were just good together, no questions asked. Nate was on the football *and* baseball teams, while Jordan had led the cheerleading squad to national victory. They were so popular it was a given that they'd be crowned prom king and queen in a couple of weeks. And Jordan adored Nate's boyish charm, not to mention the fact that he was completely gorgeous and caring and, oh yeah, *loyal.*

"Oh, Nisha, I feel *awful,*" Jordan moaned. What was the point of still pretending? She wasn't fooling anyone. "I mean, there Nate was, being all super-boyfriendy in my den, munching on microwave popcorn and watching a movie that I'd picked out. And where was I? I was kissing Shane right in front of my house." She covered her face with her hands, feeling the familiar sting of tears behind her eyes. "God, could I be any more evil?"

"You're *not* evil, Jord. You didn't go out there intending to kiss the guy," Nisha reminded her. "He said he wanted his jacket back and you went to return it *and* to tell him to get the hint — that you're with Nate."

It was true. And Jordan *wanted* to be with Nate, but there was something about Shane that stirred her every time she saw him. The boy may have been unconventional looking with his uneven jet-black hair and nail polish to match, but he was also poetic and intense. Jordan found herself strangely attracted to him — which was why she'd stopped returning his calls.

Nisha leaned forward, putting a hand on Jordan's knee. "Things happen, Jord. People make mistakes." She handed her a brown paper napkin. "Here."

Jordan dried her eyes, grateful to have such a good friend. Ever since second grade, right or wrong, Nisha had always had her back. But Jordan knew she had to make this situation good again somehow. Should she pour her heart out to Nate and beg his forgiveness? Hold it all inside and hope that he never found out?

Or break up with him?

"Look, maybe it's like you said," Nisha went on, "one kiss shouldn't be a big deal."

"It *shouldn't* . . ." Jordan trailed off as she remembered Shane's soft, cherry-colored lips — a warm contrast against his pale skin and mysterious dark eyes. How she'd welcomed the feel of his arms as they lingered in an embrace long after the kiss had ended. Jordan's heart had felt as if it might have thumped right out of her chest from beating so hard.

"Oh, boy," Nisha said. "By the look on your face, I gather Shane's lip-lock was pretty good?"

"Unforgettable," Jordan admitted. "That's the problem." *Was it worth giving up Nate for?*

"So what are you going to do?" Nisha asked.

"I have to choose," Jordan replied, though it sounded strange saying it out loud. Choose whom? There was only one choice: the boy who'd been there since junior year. The one who *knew* her and liked her friends. She couldn't imagine slow dancing at the prom with anyone else.

"Nate?" Nisha asked hopefully, and Jordan nodded.

"Right now, I can't see myself without him, and I don't think I want to."

"Not to mention that the whole school would probably riot if you guys broke up right before prom," Nisha half-joked.

"Yeah, there's that, too," Jordan said. "Maybe we should keep what happened with Shane between us. Telling Nate will only hurt him, and for what?" She paused, reflecting. "I was probably just infatuated with Shane because he's so different from the other the guys I know. Anyway, now that I've kissed him, it's like he's out of my system, right? So I'm over it."

Nisha raised her eyebrows. "You sure about that?"

*I know I want to be,* Jordan thought. "I'm sure," she said. "And what harm could one little secret do?"

Nisha stared at Jordan as if she'd just sprouted an extra head. "You're asking this of the girl whose mother so kindly arranged for *a nice Indian boy* named Raj to take her to the prom because said mother has *no idea* her daughter's been *secretly dating* a nice American boy named *Brian* for *months*?"

"Um, yes?" Jordan gave Nisha a weak smile. Okay, so her friend's life was just as complicated as her own, if not more so.

Nisha's Indian-born parents were notoriously conservative and didn't allow Nisha to date — especially boys of the non-Indian persuasion. They'd never met Brian — and probably never would — which was a shame because he and Nisha made an adorable couple.

"Listen, I thought I could handle the whole secret boyfriend thing, but now . . ." Nisha raked back her long dark brown hair in frustration. "I'm having a hard enough time hiding my relationship with Brian from my parents. How am I supposed to keep it together with this new addition?" She fiddled with the heart on the pretty silver charm bracelet that Brian had given her to mark their six months of dating. "Not only that. Brian and I planned to celebrate our anniversary tonight, but my mom and dad set up this get-to-know-you dinner with Raj and his parents . . . also *tonight.*" She sighed and shook her head. "I'm stuck."

Jordan tried to think of a way to help but all she could come up with was the lame, "You could . . . play sick?"

"Thanks, but I think that excuse is a tad overused. Only to be applied as a last resort." Nisha sighed again. "I'm at a total blank. I hope Tara can help think of something. She's usually good for a devious plan or two." Nisha turned her head to look at the front door, where a black-clad girl with long blond dreads was entering, then glanced at her watch. "Where is she, anyway?"

"Oops. I forgot. Tara couldn't make it. Something about shopping with Victor — and conspiring to take back the prom from the infamous Jenny Brigger?" Jordan laughed.

"Oh." Nisha seemed disappointed, possibly bordering on desperate. "Did she give you any input on the Shane thing, at least?"

"I didn't have time to mention it when I called her this morning," Jordan said. *But I would have, if I hadn't hung up so fast.* For some reason everything Jordan had said to Tara seemed to be the absolute *wrong* thing to say, so Jordan had ended the conversation after only a few minutes. "Nisha, is it me or has Tara been kind of weird lately?"

"Weird, how? Like coming to school in her bathrobe weird?" Nisha asked with a grin.

Jordan rolled her eyes. "I did that *once.* On senior prank day. It was supposed to be funny!"

"Oh, it was," Nisha said, teasing her. "But whatever, I wouldn't worry about Tara. You know how cranky she gets when she's stressed. Maybe all the prom planning finally pushed her over the edge."

"Yeah," Jordan agreed, though that didn't make it okay. Like that time Tara was annoyed because Jordan found the perfect prom gown on her first day of shopping. So what if she was stressed that day? And then there were the numerous snarky comments about Shane, which had nothing at all to do with prom. *Which is why I'm not upset about her being MIA today. If Tara knew I kissed Shane, I'd* never *hear the end of it.*

"I have a brilliant idea," Nisha piped up. "I think we need to partake in some retail therapy. If we can't feel good, then we might as well *look* good. And who knows? We could get lucky and find me a prom gown." She gathered her stuff and stood. "Maybe we'll run into Tara and Victor at the mall. I'll bet you a pair of Steve Madden stilettos she's in a better mood."

*Oh, joy,* Jordan thought. But she couldn't go anyway. "I still have that photography project hanging over me," she explained with a sigh. "I should head over to Rocky Point and take some thought-provoking pictures." Her teacher, Mr. Davidson, had given her a second chance to improve the D on her introspective series, which, according to him, lacked depth. "I'll walk you out, though."

Jordan grabbed her leather tote, dumped her garbage, and then headed out of Joes with Nisha.

Only someone was heading in at the same time and blocking the doorway — a tall boy with a fringe of black hair half-hiding one of his dark eyes.

"Shane?" Jordan asked, her heart suddenly racing. She was pretty sure it was due to panic. Now that he saw her, there was no way she could send him the wimpy our-kiss-was-a-huge-mistake e-mail that she was planning on, could she?

"Jordan!" Shane smiled brightly, and Jordan couldn't help but return the gesture. "I can't believe you're here. I was just calling you," he said, holding up his cell phone mid-dial. "Tell me you're not leaving."

"I'm not leaving," she replied automatically, trying hard to ignore the openmouthed stare from Nisha and trying *really hard* not to stare at Shane's lips. How come she never noticed they were so plump before? *Quit it, Jordan.* Right. She had to let Shane down. Over e-mail. "Actually, I *am* leaving." She shook her head. "To work on my photography project."

"Cool." Shane casually leaned against the weathered brick wall of the entryway.

"Uh, *ahem*?" Nisha cleared her throat.

Jordan blushed. "Oops! Shane, this is Nisha. Nisha, Shane."

"Hey," Shane said.

"Hi." Nisha gave a little wave then said, "Well, I'm out. I've got important business to attend to — *at the mall.*"

Shane laughed. "Yeah, I've got business at the tea bar. Nice meeting you, Nisha." He turned to Jordan and said, "Wait for me, okay? So we can talk a minute?" Then he headed to the back counter.

Nisha squeezed past Jordan, giving her a wry smile. "He's nice. No wonder you're not over it," she said. "Good luck dumping him."

"What? Hey! I am *so* over it!" Jordan called to Nisha, who was by now opening the door to her blue Jetta parked at the corner. Nisha waved, then climbed into the driver's seat.

"You're so over what?" Shane asked, startling Jordan. He was holding some sort of frozen green concoction.

"Oh, um, nothing," she said. "Just a private joke." She supposed she could have simply said *"I'm over you"* then stormed out, but that would have been a bit on the psychotic side, not to mention tacky. And maybe dumping him over e-mail was a little tacky, too. "Want to come to Rocky Point with me?" she blurted out. This way, *he* could do his talking and she could break the bad news to him in a civilized adult manner.

Jordan ran a variety of scenarios through her head on the way to the park but once there, she couldn't seem to start the conversation. Before she knew it, she'd pulled her mom's Nikon F from her leather tote and was snapping photos. Of anything:

daffodils poking out of the grass in the green meadow, kids squealing on the swings in the playground. Then she turned the camera on herself, since this was supposed to be an introspective, and clicked a bunch of self-portraits from odd angles. Which, on second thought, might have seemed a little too MySpace.

Shane came up with the idea of setting the shutter speed so they could take action shots. "Okay, now do something cheerleaderish," he said, holding the camera steady for her.

Soon Jordan was backflipping across the lawn, straddle splitting off of picnic tables, jumping high with her arms overhead as the shutter clicked frame after frame. She felt at once foolish but also liberated as Shane laughed and shouted encouragements. Finally she ended the shoot by leaping into a corkscrew then landing in a one-kneed position on the grass with a silly grin on her face. "Ta da!" Then she fell dramatically into the grass, breathing heavily and glowing with sweat.

Shane laughed and sat next to her with the camera in his hands. "Wow. I had no idea what an athlete you are."

"Thanks." Jordan wiped her hair off her forehead and nodded appreciatively. "Most people think cheerleading is about looking cute in a ponytail and supporting a team, and maybe to some degree it is, but it's also a major sport. You have to be fit if you want to be competitive." She gave Shane's skinny arm a slight pinch.

"Are you saying that I can't flip around the park like an Energizer bunny, too?" he asked, giving her a good-natured poke in the ribs.

Jordan regarded his lean frame. "Maybe I am."

"Ohhhhh, I smell a challenge." Shane grinned and handed her the camera. "You may want to capture this feat of greatness on film." He jumped up and strode to a nearby picnic table. "Watch and learn, my friend," he said, climbing on top.

*My friend.* Why did that sting?

Jordan focused the camera on Shane as he leapt off the table, attempting an awkward straddle split. On the way down, his legs tangled and he sprawled out onto the grass.

Jordan giggled. "Sorry, but I have to cut you from the squad. You're just not cheerleader material!" she called.

Shane didn't respond, didn't even flinch.

"Shane?" *He didn't land that hard, did he?* Jordan rushed to his side and kneeled over him, her heart starting to pound. "Shane!" she repeated, shaking him lightly.

Shane opened his eyes suddenly and smirked, and Jordan squealed when he grabbed her by the waist and pulled her down next to him.

"Faker!" she cried, swatting him on the chest, and he responded by tickling her ribs.

"No, no! I'm too ticklish!" She erupted into giggles as they wrestled playfully on the grass, gasping for air from their laughter. Surprised by Shane's strength, there was only one thing for Jordan to do. "Stop! I give in. I can't take it anymore!" A second after Shane released his grip, Jordan pushed full force with her body and flipped him onto his back. "Sucker!" she said devilishly, pinning his hands over his head, though she knew very well that he could probably tackle her right then if he wanted to.

Instead, he stayed still, panting from the exhaustion of laughing and tumbling.

Jordan found herself growing serious as Shane regarded her. She released his hands and they moved from over his head to her arms, sending a gentle shiver up her spine. And Jordan felt an imaginary string tugging at her, pulling her closer to Shane, until their faces were only inches apart.

"Jordan . . ." he whispered.

*I want to kiss him*, she realized, her heart pounding even faster in her chest. *But* . . . "I can't," she murmured, pulling away from him and rolling onto her back. "This can't happen. I have a boyfriend. I can't see you anymore." Jordan said the words quickly, afraid she might stop herself if she didn't. She covered her eyes with her right arm. *I love Nate,* she reminded herself. *I love him . . . so why does it feel as if my heart is being torn apart?*

She uncovered her eyes to find Shane sitting up. "I just thought . . ." he began then stopped. "Okay," he said, and looked away from her. "I mean, it's not that big of a deal," he added with a shrug. "Really."

But Jordan knew it was an act. "I'm sorry," she told him, and they leaned in for one last hug. A long hug. Jordan found herself holding on to him for dear life. *Why don't I want to let go? I barely know this boy.*

Jordan pulled back and searched Shane's eyes — eyes so dark and sad. "Jordan, I don't want to say good-bye," he told her.

"Me, neither," Jordan admitted. To Shane. To herself.

A moment later she felt Shane's soft lips touch hers, and she closed her eyes. There was no time to think about Nate and the prom.

All Jordan knew was she liked this boy. She liked him a lot. And this time, she would kiss him more than once.

*3 weeks, 2 days, 23 hours, and 28 minutes till Prom . . .*

# CHAPTER *Three*

Several shopping hours later, Nisha flopped onto her white bedspread, frustrated, as she tried to think of an excuse for why she couldn't go to dinner with her boyfriend. She wanted something sharp, something ingenious, but, at this point, she'd settle for something *believable*.

Jordan hadn't been much help this morning, Tara hadn't returned her call yet, and although Nisha's retail therapy expedition had resulted in one *killer* pair of leopard print platform heels, two pairs of cute — yet sensible — Havaiana flip-flops, and a tube of chocolate-flavored lip gloss, she still had zero excuses for Brian — zero good ones, that is.

For the millionth time, she proceeded to run through some possible illnesses. *Stuffy nose? Too common. Swollen glands? Too vague. Horrible virus of unknown origin that keeps me chained to my toilet? Too . . . ew.* Nisha frowned and rolled onto her back, resentful for having to lie — again. *I don't* want *to come up with an excuse. Tonight's a special night. I want to be with my boyfriend! Why can't my parents appreciate where I'm coming from? Just once?*

Probably because her parents were born in India. They grew up believing in *marriage,* not dating. And maybe, in some weird way, setting her up with an acceptable prom date was their attempt at being . . . what? Modern?

Her mom and dad meant well, Nisha knew that much. She just really, *really* wished they'd get a clue. Hadn't they been living in Selina, Illinois, since Nisha was six years old? That was more than half her life. It was only natural that she'd feel more American than Indian at times. *Most* times.

Aside from the girls in her *Kathak* class at the Todi Studio for Indian Classical Dance, all of Nisha's friends were American. Her two best friends, Jordan and Tara, certainly were. When Nisha wasn't spending countless hours texting them or gabbing on the phone, she was online, updating her Facebook profile, downloading singles onto her iPod, or watching her favorite TV shows. *American* TV shows. She wore jeans and cute tees, and, much to her mother's horror, Nisha enjoyed fast food. A lot.

Your typical American girl.

Of course, Nisha would always have a bond with her homeland, too. She adored her Indian heritage — the delicious delicacies, the warm people, the rich history. But when it came to matters of the heart, well, Nisha wanted nothing to do with Indian culture. She wanted to experience love on her *own* terms. Just because an arranged marriage seemed right for her older sister, Kali, didn't mean it was right for Nisha, too, did it? Nisha wanted to be free to fall madly, deeply, passionately in love with whomever she wanted . . . like *Brian,* for instance.

*Why does my love life have to be so complicated?* Nisha sighed, gazing at the lacy canopy hanging above her bed, filtering the early evening sun. Then she glanced at the digital clock on her nightstand. Two hours until she was supposed to meet Brian at the Coral Café — and thirty minutes before she and her parents had to leave to go to her supposed prom date's house.

"Okay, I'm *beyond* desperate," she murmured.

Her cell phone chirped. Nisha slid it from her jeans pocket and saw that it was Brian. *Oh, God.* She was hoping she'd have a last momentary surge of inspiration, but all she kept thinking was, *swollen glands.*

*It'll just have to do,* she thought then answered the phone. Weakly. "H-hello?"

"My sister is *driving. Me. Nuts,*" Brian said immediately.

In the background Nisha could hear a squeal of laughter then a girl's voice saying, "I'm not touching you. I'm not touching you!" Then Brian saying, "Cut it out, Sarah. Geez!"

"You've got to help me out here, Nisha," he told her. "Let's head over to Coral Café early. Before I kill my sister, get thrown in jail, and have to miss the prom."

*Early?* Nisha froze with panic. She coughed twice to buy some time.

"Whoa," Brian said. "You sound awful. You okay?"

"Well . . . not really," Nisha said. "My glands are, um, kind of *swollen,* I guess." She winced as the words came out.

"Swollen?" Brian repeated. "How'd that happen?"

*How?* Nisha hadn't gotten that far in the excuse department. Luckily her call waiting beeped. "Oh, Tara's on the other line, Brian. Be right back." She clicked to the other line.

"Tara, you've got to help me. Quick, why would I have swollen glands?"

"You told him your *glands* are *swollen*?" Tara asked, incredulous. "Really, Nisha. It's a miracle you've been able to hide Brian from your parents for so long."

"*Tara*," Nisha urged her. "*Please.*"

"Okay, okay. Let's think. Ummmm," Tara paused. "I know! Tell him you're having female problems. That's always a good one."

"What about my *glands*?" Nisha demanded.

"Nisha?" Tara said slowly. "Trust me on this one, okay? Mentioning *female* and *problems* in the same sentence can pretty much guarantee he won't ask about your glands. He's a guy. He'll want to hang up."

Nisha nodded. "Right. Thanks, Tara. I'll call you later." She clicked over to Brian.

"I swear, Sarah! If you don't quit it right now, I'm gonna —"

"Brian?" Nisha asked.

"Oh, hey," Brian said. "So, you ready for the restaurant? Like, now? Please say yes."

"Well, that's the thing. I'm kind of having, um, *female problems,*" Nisha said, drawing out the last two words. "Like, severe ones. Can we do it next week? I promise I won't be sick."

Just as Tara had predicted, Brian grunted out what seemed to be a "Yeah, no problem, feel better." A minute later Nisha was hanging up the phone, feeling totally disappointed. She'd been looking forward to celebrating with Brian all week and now she had to spend their six-month anniversary with some guy named Raj.

"*Beta*? Are you almost ready?" Nisha's mother asked, knocking on the door then opening it. *Beta* was her parents' pet name for Nisha. Roughly translated, it meant "sweetheart" in English. Mrs. Khubani entered the room, looking regal in a blue silk sari edged in paisley. Her long dark hair was braided then twisted into a bun at the nape of her neck, showing off her gold earrings, which matched the two bangles adorning her right wrist. She turned pale when she caught sight of Nisha's clothes. "Why aren't you dressed?"

Nisha glanced at the outfit she'd been wearing all day minus the bracelet Brian had given her, which was safely tucked away in her jewelry box so her parents wouldn't ask her about it. She propped herself up on an elbow, letting her long tresses fall messily around her shoulders. Why should Nisha take the time to look special? It wasn't as if she was getting ready for a date. "I *am* dressed," she replied.

"In *that*?" Her mom pointed to the holes at Nisha's knees. "Why do you wear such things? People will think your father and I cannot dress you properly. Are you not embarrassed, *Beta*?"

Nisha rolled her eyes. *Embarrassed? Me? You're the one who shops for clothes in a fabric store.* "Mommmmm," she moaned.

"Do not 'Mom' me," Nisha's mother continued. "Mrs. Dixit might take one look at you and change her mind about letting Raj go to that prom party of yours. Then what?" She paused before answering her own question. "You will not have a prom date, that is what!"

Nisha brightened as she stared at the frayed knees of her jeans. *Correction: I'll have only* one *prom date,* she thought with a devious smile.

"Don't worry, Mommy. It's fine. People pay top dollar for jeans like these." *Yeah, for the ones you buy in a department store. Not the ones you buy at a vintage shop in town.* Nisha had spent most of the drive to the Dixit home reassuring her mother that her well-worn outfit was no big deal, though she was counting on the odd chance that it would be.

Raj and his parents had seemed nice enough when she'd met them yesterday afternoon, but who knew? Maybe they were snobby clothes hounds allergic to vintage. Which was why she had even changed into an old-school concert tee. This one was black, and it featured a guy with long ratty blond hair who was in some ancient rock band called Van Halen.

"Leave it alone, Shovana," her father had finally said as they pulled into the Dixits' driveway next to a white Saab convertible. "There is nothing we can do about it now."

*Nope,* Nisha thought happily. She smiled widely when Mrs. Dixit greeted them at the door, and she handed her the tin of syrupy *jalebis* her mother had made for the occasion. The woman wasn't wearing a sari, like Nisha's mom, but had on a black outfit with a pretty print scarf pinned elegantly over one shoulder.

"I don't believe it," Mrs. Dixit said with a slight giggle, giving Nisha the obvious once-over as she entered.

*What?* Nisha shifted in place. Her outfit might have been a little grunge-meets–hair-band, but it wasn't *laughable.* Without looking, Nisha could feel the I-*told*-you glare coming from her mother.

Mr. Dixit appeared through a doorway, in a pair of khakis and a polo shirt. He took one look at Nisha and started laughing as well. "I guess Raj was right," he said to his wife between chuckles.

Nisha didn't like this one bit. Disdain she could deal with — she *welcomed* it — but this? This was downright rude. And why was Raj talking about her when he barely *knew* her? "What's so funny?" she asked, trying not to sound as irritated as she felt.

"Come," Mrs. Dixit said, showing them to the living room. Raj stood when they entered. He was wearing a drapey white linen shirt, sleeves rolled, tucked into a pair of Diesel jeans with various holes strategically worn into the fabric. "See? He's wearing the same holey jeans!"

"Come on now, Mum," Raj said.

*Right. His jeans are probably from Bloomingdale's,* Nisha thought, feeling suddenly less clever and more underdressed. *And what's up with the weird fake accent? Did he have it the first time we met? Kind of*

*British, but not quite? Because he goes to school abroad? Does he think he's fooling anybody?*

*"I guess they're a match made in . . . denim,"* Mr. Khubani added with a quick wink in Nisha's direction.

*Oh . . . God,* Nisha thought, not sure which was more embarrassing: being the butt of the stupid joke, or her *father,* for telling it.

The parents had a good laugh — they obviously thought it was the most hilarious thing ever — while Nisha and Raj exchanged commiserating glances. He was nice looking: tall, with wavy black hair and cocoa-colored skin. His brownish-green eyes were friendly and his smile, confident. *Cute,* Nisha thought, but she still wished she could be at the Coral Café with Brian.

Despite Nisha's initial misunderstanding, Mr. and Mrs. Dixit turned out to be lovely hosts. Mrs. Dixit led the group to the dining room to an absolute feast. Nisha took bite after delicious bite of sweet and savory lamb *keema,* tangy chicken *tandoori,* and spinachy *saag paneer.* Her mouth watered over the sautéed okra, *channa masala,* and *kadhi pakora* vegetables with warm yogurt sauce — all served with basmati rice and delicious *roti* bread.

The parents exchanged old stories of India as they ate, and Nisha was fascinated by their tales of living within the hustle and bustle of Mumbai, back when it was called Bombay.

She closed her eyes for a moment, trying to visualize what life had been like before her family moved to America but couldn't recall much. Only bits and pieces: a modest, yet homey, apartment . . . grasping her mother's hand in a crowded outdoor market . . . some kind of curry simmering all day on the stove. Mostly Nisha remembered her grandmother — her father's mother — who would hug her endlessly and sometimes sneak her salty fried lotus roots as a treat when Kali was at school and her mom wasn't looking. Each time she'd say that it was their little secret.

But now that India was so far away, Nisha didn't know her grandmother well anymore. She'd seen her only four or five times since coming to America, and when her father called home, Nisha was always too shy with her halting Hindi to say anything more than "How are you?" or "I miss you."

*I wonder what* Daadii *would think of life here in America? What would she have to say about holey jeans and high school proms and anniversary dates?*

Perhaps if her grandmother had moved with them to America, she and Nisha would still be sharing secrets. Nisha could tell her grandmother stories about Brian — how her heart skipped a beat every time he held her hand in the movies, and how he left adorable, cute "chocolate-grams" in her locker when she was having a bad day, and how, for the very first time in her life, Nisha felt she was falling in love with somebody.

Maybe *Daadii* would be so touched that she'd convince Nisha's parents to allow

Nisha to attend the prom with Brian and not Raj?

*Yeah, right,* she thought. *In my dreams.*

"Isn't that right, Nisha?" she heard her mother saying. About what she had no idea.

"Mmm," Nisha said, hoping it sounded nondescript enough to answer the question without knowing what it was.

"Nisha is very modest," Mrs. Khubani told Raj and his parents, smiling. "But she is quite an accomplished *Kathak* dancer."

Nisha felt her cheeks flush. She'd been a student of the ancient art form for the past eleven years. She was considered talented, but did her mom have to brag about it?

"Just like you, Mum," Raj said with that accent again, yet his words still piqued Nisha's interest.

"You're a *Kathaki* too, Mrs. Dixit?"

"I used to be," the woman admitted. "I haven't performed in a while, but I still love it, and I still practice my *navras* on occasion." The *navras* were the nine facial expressions that *Kathaki* used to help recount the stories of Hindu mythology to an audience.

Nisha and Mrs. Dixit branched into an animated conversation about the evolution of Indian Classical Dance and the thrill of performing on the stage. It turns out that Mrs. Dixit used to dance on the same circuit with Nisha's guru, Gargi Kumar, before she retired and started the Todi Studio. And before Nisha knew it, her parents were inviting the Dixits to Nisha's recital on Saturday and the Dixits were accepting.

"Raj, why don't you show Nisha the garden?" Mrs. Dixit asked after a delicious dessert of her mom's warmed *jalebis.* "You two should get to know each other before the big night, don't you think?" She gave Mrs. Khubani a smile and a conspiring wink.

Nisha held her eye roll for when she was out of the parents' sight and following Raj to the kitchen. They poured two fresh mango *lassies* from the fridge then headed out the sliding glass doors and onto a wooden deck. The garden wasn't very big, so, after the twenty-second tour, they wound up sitting in a pair of low teak chairs on the grass and sipping their drinks.

"Where are you going to college, again?" Raj asked.

"Emory." Nisha remembered from their first visit that he was a year older and attended the Sorbonne in Paris, France. "I can't believe you go to the Sorbonne," she said, turning in her seat to face him. "It's weird enough to know I'll be leaving for Georgia in a couple of months. I can't imagine taking classes in another country — not to mention in another language. Pretty impressive."

Raj smiled. "Thanks, but I promise you it is not," he said. "My father worked for this company that had him relocating every few years. My parents were living in France when I was born, so French is kind of my first language — after Hindi and Punjabi, of course. Then we spent a few years in England, then Germany, then finally we settled in America. And now, here we are."

"So you're, like, a citizen of the world?" Nisha said. *No wonder he has a strange accent. He speaks a zillion languages.* "Sorry, still impressed."

Raj laughed. "Citizen of the world, huh? I never thought about it that way. When I was a kid I spent a lot of time upset over having to leave friends that I'd just made. I hated traveling back then. I love it now, though."

"Yeah, well, just be glad that you're good with languages," Nisha replied. "The running joke in my family is that I speak *broken* Hindi perfectly. I'm taking Spanish in school, but I don't know if I'd be able to communicate if I lived in Spain."

"You'd get the hang of it after a while. It's tough to live in a foreign country but it's the only way to *really* learn a language — to be fluent," he said, casually crossing his legs. For the first time, Nisha noticed that Raj was wearing a pair of expensive Prada *man*dals.

*Brian wouldn't be caught dead in those things,* she thought. *Thank God.* Not that she had anything against mandals — *on Raj.* They just weren't the kind of footwear you'd find on an American boy. And Nisha's boyfriend was definitely the sneaker-wearing, apple-pie–eating, baseball-playing type. That was for sure.

Nisha glanced at Raj, wondering if she should tell him about Brian. He seemed like a nice guy, and he was so worldly. Maybe if she just explained the situation to him — tell him that she was seeing someone — he'd be cool about it. Who knew? Maybe Raj could somehow help her introduce Brian to her parents and she'd get to go to the prom with her boyfriend without drama.

*I'll go for it,* Nisha decided. *But I have to be smart. I can't just blab it out.* She glanced at Raj again, deciding how to test the waters. "So. Raj. I was wondering. Since you *are* technically French, does that make you a hopeless romantic?" she asked, praying that it didn't sound as if she was flirting with him.

Raj ran a hand though his thick hair. "Oh, definitely," he said. "In fact, I think romance is kind of underrated. *Real* romance is, anyway."

Nisha felt a flutter of hope. *Keep going,* she thought. "And your definition of 'real romance' is . . . ?" she prompted him.

Raj tilted his head, seeming to formulate an answer. "Okay, it's like this," he said, turning and leaning closer. "Today you see guys and girls dating, holding hands, maybe kissing in public . . . am I right?"

"Uh-huh." Nisha nodded excitedly. She could totally relate since she'd had done all of the above with Brian. *Go on,* she thought.

"Well, these people *say* they're in love but they break up after a few months or years and then it's done. A lot of times it's over something minuscule that ends in a major fight. That kind of romance can't be real," he declared.

"Okaaaaaay," Nisha said slowly, not sure what he was driving at. "So what *is*?"

"Real romance is what our parents have," Raj told her. "It's about making a big commitment to *one* person, not weak promises to many," he explained. "Look, my parents didn't even like each other when they first met, and now, after all these years of marriage, they love each other. They have fun together. *That's* real romance, don't you think?"

"Oh. Yeah. Of course." Nisha said as her heart quickly sank to her feet. She knew the mandal-wearing citizen of the world couldn't be trusted. So she could never tell Raj about her boyfriend — not without risking her parents finding out. And Nisha couldn't tell Brian about the setup with Raj either. It would totally hurt Brian's feelings, rightfully so, and that was the *last* thing Nisha wanted to do.

What she *wanted* was to go to the prom with her boyfriend. Period.

*So how do I get what I want?* Nisha wondered.

*3 weeks, 2 days, 1 hour, and 29 minutes till Prom . . .*

# CHAPTER *Four*

*Top Ten Things You Might Hear Out of Jenny Brigger's Mouth*

1) *Committee meeting — pronto!*
2) *"Once Upon a Time" is the most original theme ever 'cause I'm the one who originally thought of it.*
3) *Tara's the head of the prom committee? Tara–Schmara.*
4) *Of course, my boyfriend, PrinceStudly007, is a real prince. That's why he can't make it to the prom.*
5) *Excuse me. Does this scrunchie match my eye shadow?*

6) *Who needs music, decorations, or **FOOD** at the prom when we can have a beautiful replica of the Disney castle?*
7) *It was all Tara's fault.*
8) *A date for the prom? I've got seven. They came with my Snow White costume.*
9) *Oh, no! I just realized that all my prom ideas suck!*
10) *Fine. Tara's the kindest, smartest, most amazingly gorgeous girl this side of the equator. **Now** will you help me fix this mess?*

"Tell me again why *we're* the ones snazzing up the 'Student Newz' bulletin board to look 'Once Upon a Time-y?'" Tara asked as she tore off an old flyer for the spring musical. "Isn't this theme Jenny's idea?"

It was Monday afternoon. She and Victor were redesigning the bulletin board outside the principal's office.

Victor was on the opposite end removing a scalloped green border stapled around the edges. "*You're* doing it as a gesture of solidarity — to show Mr. Harris that you and Jenny can work together — remember?"

Tara nodded. "Right. Solidarity."

"And *I'm* here out of the goodness of my heart — to help a prom date in need." Victor swung his index fingers in her direction. "That'd be you, T-Bone."

"Victor, *why*," she asked, "do you insist on calling me that? Do I look like a steak?"

"Aw, come on, let me call you T-Bone," Victor begged. "I promise not to say it in front of anybody. And it's much better than T-rex, which is the only alternative I could come up with. Right?"

Tara didn't know why he couldn't just call her by her *real* name. "Okay. But only because you're saving my life by joining the committee, and my kindness ends when the prom does," she said, helping him yank off the faded yellow background paper on the board. "Seriously, though. You know how much I appreciate this, right?"

Last week Jenny Brigger had somehow

managed to turn all of Tara's plans for the prom upside down as well as turn the prom committee against Tara. She'd even convinced the principal to nix Tara's "Starry Night" theme for her own "Once Upon a Time" idea at the very last minute. With no one left in her corner, Tara had wanted to throw in the towel, but Victor wouldn't let her — he said that she had a duty to save the Emerson prom from Jenny's cheesy sense of taste — and he joined the committee to help.

*Who knew such a great guy was lurking inside that cougar costume?* When Tara had reluctantly agreed to go to the prom with the school mascot on the condition that she gave him a makeover, she never imagined he'd turn into a friend. And she certainly never imagined he'd transform into a major cutie, but that's what had happened.

Tara peeked at Victor out of the corner of her eye as he dumped the crumpled yellow paper into a nearby trash can. With his former mullet and unibrow a distant memory, Victor's brown hair was cropped close in the back and sides but was longer and tousled on top. Now that he was making an effort to wear his contacts, Tara (and the world) could see his very nice hazel eyes.

A shopping expedition had garnered him the loose khakis and graphic, non–Star Trek, T-shirt he wore, both of which now looked as if they'd been picked from a crumpled ball at the bottom of his closet. *Oh, well. Nobody's perfect.* She noticed Victor making a beeline for his backpack against the wall. "What's up?" she asked.

"I almost forgot," Victor said, digging deep into his bag. "Jenny asked me to give this to you in homeroom this morning. It's a list of her *recommended suggestions* for the bulletin board." He pulled out a sheet of pale blue notepaper with fuzzy black-and-white cats at the top and held it up for Tara to see:

1) **Make the board sparkly, but NOT glitzy. It's supposed to be soft and powdery. More**

***Wish-Upon-a-Star than Weekend-in-Vegas. Tara, call me ASAP if you don't know the difference.***

*Call her ASAP? Is she kidding me?* Taking a sharp breath, Tara stopped reading and turned to Victor. "Hey, Victor. You know where I've always wanted to go?" she asked him with vinegar in her voice.

"Let me guess," Victor said with a sly smile. "Vegas, baby?" He crumpled Jenny's list in his fist and tossed it over his shoulder into the trash can. "I'm with you."

They started decorating with a background collage of prom dresses and tuxes that Tara had cut out from the magazines she had lying around her room at home. Then they arched big glossy silver letters that spelled out "Once Upon a Time" at the top of the board. Tara attached graphics of storybooks and a castle and clinking glasses to appease Jenny. Meanwhile, Victor stapled up important information that they'd saved from the old board — stuff about prom tickets, the fashion show and upcoming raffle, as well as prom queen nominations.

Tara thought of Jordan and of her troubling dream, then quickly shook it from her mind. She put the finishing touches on the board and stepped back for a quick review. "It's definitely missing something," she said, squinting at it. "It's got to be flashier if it's going to say 'Fairy Tale in Vegas.'"

"I know just the thing," Victor said, backing down the hall. "Be right back." He turned and broke into a run. A few minutes later he returned holding a rolled-up tube of white Christmas lights. "I'm sure Coach Myers won't mind if we borrow these from his office," he said.

"Perfect!" Tara quickly helped Victor affix the lights around the border of the bulletin board then plugged them into the outlet underneath. The lights flashed on all at once then began to chase around the board.

"And now for the *pièce de résistance,*" Victor said, sliding something out of his back pocket. It was a cardboard cutout of Elvis Presley in his infamous white jumpsuit complete with cape and enormous belt. "I had this taped on the inside door of my locker. It may not say prom, but it definitely says Vegas." He pinned it up next to the prom king nominations.

Tara laughed. "It's perfect. Jenny's going to hate it," she said. Then she cut out a tiny crown from some silver paper and pinned it onto Elvis's head so it looked as if he really was a king. She cut out another crown, made a "prom queen" out of a magazine clipping of a girl in a short fuchsia dress, and stapled it next to the prom queen nominations. "There. Done."

Tara was giving the board one last inspection when her eyes fell on the list of names up for nomination — or rather *Jordan's* name. Last time Tara looked, her best friend was running unrivaled and had seventy-six adoring fans when she only needed three nominations to qualify. But now, as she peered closer, Tara was surprised to see that someone else was up for prom queen.

*Me?* Tara stared at her name in the nominee slot at the top of the form, hardly able to believe it. *Wow,* she thought, her lips curling into a smile as her stomach jumped in disbelief. *Three people actually nominated me?* Eddie Mathews, Sabrina Sawyer, and Toby Gantos. Tara didn't know who they were and she didn't care. "Victor, come here. You've got to see this!"

"What?" Victor crossed the hallway and scanned the list. "That's awesome. Congrats, T-Bone!" He pulled a pen from the back pocket of his pants and signed his name too, bumping up her total to four nominations.

Tara was too thrilled to lecture Victor on how it wasn't a good idea to keep a pen that might leak in the pocket of his new pants. "There's so much to do," she gasped. "Like posters and meet-and-greets and I have to write an essay . . ." She paused, her excitement suddenly turning to panic. "What am

I saying? I can't compete against Jordan. I'm supposed to be her campaign manager. Besides, nobody will vote for me. It'll be a landslide, and I'll be completely humiliated!" She grabbed Victor's pen, about to cross her name off the list.

"Tara, chill," Victor said, stopping her with his hand. "Why are you freaking out like this? You're just as pretty as Jordan is and you're smart and cool and you have a good heart. You'll get a ton of votes . . . people love you!" His face turned a bright shade of pink. "Uh, I mean people like you. Definitely *like.*"

*More than Jordan?* Tara wondered. *That's doubtful.*

"What I'm trying to say is, you can be prom queen if you want to," Victor went on. "You can do anything, Tara. I truly believe that."

Tara smiled. "Thanks, Victor." Clearly the boy was delusional, but he was sweet all the same, which made her realize something else. "And thanks for getting those guys to nominate me, too."

"Huh?" Victor said, suddenly unable to peel his gaze off of his sneakers. "Me? I didn't. Why would you think that?"

Tara shrugged. "No reason," she said, but she had a feeling it was true. "Should we head over to the committee meeting?"

"Looks like the committee is coming to us," Victor said with a sigh.

Tara turned to see Jenny Brigger marching purposefully down the hallway, her curly brown ponytail pulled high with her signature scrunchie. The other two members, Stuart and George, lagged behind her.

Jenny took one look at the blinking "Fairy Tale in Vegas" extravaganza, gasped, and then immediately scowled at Tara. "You did this on purpose, didn't you?" she snarled.

Tara blinked innocently. "Did what?" she asked, not exactly hiding her smile. "You don't like it?"

Mr. Harris emerged from his office carrying a stack of folders.

"Look what Tara did to the bulletin board," Jenny complained, gesturing to it. "Does that say 'Once Upon a Time' to you?"

Tara held her breath as the principal glanced at the lights, the prom wear, and the crowned Elvis. "Well, it's a definite eye-catcher . . . and it does say 'Once Upon a Time' at the top, doesn't it?" he admitted. "I like it. Good job, Tara."

Tara beamed. "Oh, it wasn't all me. It was a *team effort*," she said as graciously as she could. "Right, Jenny?"

"Yup." Jenny replied, glaring intensely at Tara. If her beady eyes could have burned two holes into Tara's temple, they would have.

Tara found a certain satisfaction in that. She turned to the other committee members. "Let's start our meeting, shall we?" She led the way down to the classroom that they used in the basement.

Surprisingly, Jenny had nothing more to say about the bulletin board during the meeting. She was oddly agreeable when Tara mentioned that Jenny's choices of pink and blue linen might be a little too "baby shower" then suggested silver and blue instead. George produced three DJ samples, and the committee chose the best one with barely a peep of contest from Jenny. Stuart showed the group the ticket design, and they all agreed that they'd go to the printer tomorrow.

*Why is Jenny being so cooperative all of a sudden?* Tara was suspicious but decided to think positively. *We don't have much time to get this thing rolling. Maybe she just wants the process to run smoothly from now on. Just like I do.* As a peace offering, Tara asked Jenny to choose the photographer, and she approved Jenny and Stuart's idea of taking keepsake photos in front of an enormous storybook backdrop to go along with the theme. They also settled on an ice sculpture of a castle, also to go with the theme, rather than constructing a giant replica of one. *I still hate the castle idea,* Tara thought, *but hey, there's got to be give and take somewhere. Maybe I shouldn't have been so demanding in the beginning. Maybe we just started off on the wrong foot.*

Tara checked each item off her list as the meeting progressed. It was going so well that she probably could have handled it without Victor at her side.

Finally, Tara was ready to give her report on the project she'd been handling — the annual prom-wear fashion show. Every year the committee worked with a local merchant to put on a fashion show featuring prom gowns and tuxedos in the school's auditorium. Raffle tickets were sold at the door with a chance at a free dress or a tux of the winner's choosing from the store. The event built pre-prom excitement, and the proceeds from it would be put toward the senior carnival on the last day of school.

"I've been talking to the people over at Papillion and they're providing the fashions this year," Tara informed the group. "I'm taking the models for their fittings tomorrow after school. As you know, the show will be held during the eighth period special assembly on Friday," she said. "And I guess that's all for today. Thanks for the great work, everybody."

Jenny raised her hand.

"Yes, Jenny?" Tara asked.

"Yeah. Number one: We didn't agree as a committee about this partnership with Papillion. I've never heard of them. Number two: Who are these supposed models? I never saw anyone's book. And number three: Why are we even bothering with a fashion show? We have enough to do for, you know, the *prom*."

Tara rolled her eyes and glanced at Victor, who gave her a sympathetic shrug. *So much for smooth sailing.* "To answer your questions," she said calmly, "Papillion is a cute boutique downtown that carries all the latest. The models are girls from the senior class, not professionals, so they don't *have* model books. And the reason we're doing this show? *One,* because it's a tradition. *Two,* some of the students don't have dresses or tuxes picked out and might need some ideas. And *three,* it gets the school into the fun spirit of prom, which, quite frankly, is lacking in this room at the moment." Tara could feel her face getting hot.

"Oh, really?" Jenny asked. "Well, I think *you're* lacking in *team* spirit. You were so willing to share glory for that hideous bulletin board. How come you're not doing the same with this?" She stood up and marched to the front of the room where Tara was standing. "*I* want to pick out all the dresses for the fashion show *and* I want to see if these models you chose are up to standard."

"It's only fair," Stuart squeaked from his chair.

George was in his own world, bobbing his head to the music playing on his iPod.

Tara surveyed Jenny's saggy jeans and tired plaid blouse, which had the front flaps of a corduroy vest sewn into it. A corduroy vest was bad enough, but a *fake* one? No *way* was she going to let this *Fashion Don't* run the prom-wear show. She crossed her arms over her chest and said, "And what if I say no?"

Jenny pulled her cell phone from her front pocket, her gaze glued to Tara's. "Should I call Principal Harris and ask *him*? It won't take a minute. I've got him on speed dial."

*Figures.* "Go ahead," Tara snapped, daring her. She was pretty sure the principal wouldn't appreciate a call on his cell after school hours.

"Ladies, ladies!" Victor popped out of his seat. "I'm sure we can find a solution to this. After all, Tara, Jenny does deserve to be a part of the fashion show."

Tara's jaw dropped. Uh, *whose* side was Victor supposed to be *on*? "But —"

"Why does Jenny want to be behind the scenes when her talents lie elsewhere?" Victor asked. "That's exactly what I was thinking, too, Tara."

Jenny shifted her weight to one foot and

planted a hand on her hip. "What are you blabbering about?"

Victor turned to her. "It's just that a pretty girl such as yourself shouldn't waste her time backstage when she needs to be . . . on the runway."

"Me?" Jenny blushed. "You think?"

"Of course." Victor nodded. "Don't you?"

"Well, I — I guess I could be a model," she said with a timid smile. Then she glared at Tara, who at that moment realized she was staring. "What? Do you have a problem with that?" Jenny asked.

"No. Oh, no. No problem here. Definitely not," Tara replied, holding her hands up in surrender, completely floored by how Victor had just wrapped Jenny around his finger, before her very eyes.

*The boy definitely has people skills.* She grinned to herself, proud and grateful and impressed by her prom date in more ways than one. *I wonder how his skills are on the dance floor.*

*3 weeks, 1 day, 1 hour, and 10 minutes till Prom . . .*

# CHAPTER *Five*

Jordan emerged from her dressing stall, into the main area of Papillion Boutique, and into the excited buzz of guys and girls getting fitted for the upcoming fashion show.

"Jorrrrrdaaaaan!" Moose, the burly catcher from the baseball team, yelled from the other side of the room. He was wearing a snug white shirt and tuxedo pants that were too short.

"Mooooooose!" Jordan cried back, and laughed.

Tara was kneeling at Moose's feet, tape measure dangling around her neck, tugging uselessly at the bottom of his trousers. "Madeline, we have an issue!" she called, standing and brushing off her black pencil pants. The owner of the boutique rushed over to correct the problem.

Meanwhile, Jordan turned to a mirror to study the black strapless gown with the small train at the bottom she was wearing. "Does this look okay, Nisha?"

"Not bad . . . but not as good as the white one you bought for the prom," Nisha commented, still in her jeans and flipping through a nearby rack of dresses. She pulled out a short and swingy coffee-colored one, examined it briefly, then shoved it back with a sigh.

"That was cute. Why don't you try it on?" Jordan suggested. After all, time was ticking and Nisha had yet to find her ideal prom dress. She'd come close with a sweet lemon-colored empire gown, but couldn't seem to make up her mind about it no matter how many times she went back to the mall to try it on.

Nisha shrugged. "Not in the mood, I guess."

"You're *not* in the mood to shop?" Jordan asked. Nisha was always in the mood to shop. She crossed over to her and placed a hand on her friend's shoulder. "Okay, tell me."

"It's my mom," Nisha admitted. "She won't stop talking about . . . *you know who.*" She glanced behind them to make sure Brian wasn't within earshot. "Yesterday she was all, 'Isn't Raj handsome? Isn't he smart? Why don't you give him a call tonight, *Beta*? Invite him over for some *gobi paratha,*'" Nisha whispered, imitating her mother's accent. "Why can't she be like that with Brian?"

Jordan tilted her head. "Wait. You *told* your parents about Brian?"

"You think I'm *crazy*? No, I just know my parents, that's all." Nisha looked around again. "Where's Nate? You haven't talked to him about *you know what* yet, have you?"

Nisha was still the only one who knew the whole illicit story between Jordan and

Shane, including their latest kissing session. "I think Nate's getting into his tux," Jordan replied, then toned her voice down to a murmur. "And I'm trying to hold off on *the talk* until after the fashion show, you know? I don't want my drama to spoil things for Tara."

That wasn't the only reason.

The thing was, Jordan didn't *want* to say good-bye to Nate; she still really loved him. However, last weekend's romantic moment in the park had only proved that she couldn't trust herself to stay away from Shane. Cheating on your boyfriend was bad enough, but holding on to him when you knew there was a good chance of it happening again was even worse.

And although Jordan didn't want to admit it, there was a *very* good chance of it happening again. Her head kept telling her to just forget about Shane but somehow her heart wouldn't let it happen.

*How would I feel if the situation were reversed?* Jordan wondered. *What if Nate had instant chemistry with some girl . . . and couldn't help cheating on* me*? What would* I *want?*

The answer was clear.

Maybe some chicks were cool with sharing a boyfriend but Jordan definitely wasn't one of them. No matter how much it hurt, in the end she'd have to be free. Because she deserved more — she deserved respect.

*And so does Nate,* Jordan knew, a thick lump forming in her throat at the thought of life without him.

"Oh, my God. Look," Nisha said, nudging Jordan. "Can you believe Tara's actually letting *Victor* hold her precious iPhone? I mean, the girl has a panic attack every time I even *think* about touching it, yet she gives *him* the honor of smudging up the screen? I don't get it."

"Maybe it's iLove," Jordan joked, glad for the distraction. She watched as Tara flitted around the chaotic store, examining outfits and making sure everything was moving along on schedule. Victor was following close behind, looking adorable in a black tux with a blue shirt and no tie, when Tara turned suddenly, bumping into him. Victor accidentally dropped her handheld-computer–slash–cell-phone onto the floor, resulting in Tara's horrified scream as she snatched it up off the carpet.

Nisha laughed. "He kind of reminds me of a little puppy trying to help, but always getting in the way."

"No, not a puppy," Jordan said, watching them. "Victor's a very cute, well-groomed, picture-perfect prom date. He's exactly what Tara set out to achieve with the makeover." Jordan had to admire her friend's drive. *Tara figures out what she wants, sets herself a goal and just . . .* does *it. Every. Single. Time. Me? I'd be happy if I could get past the "figures out what she wants" part.*

Tara spotted Jordan and Nisha and headed over to them, leaving Victor to deal with a tall guy from the basketball team and his too-short sleeves. "Hey guys," Tara sang.

Jordan spun carefully, modeling the glovelike gown for Tara. "Well?"

"Oh, stop fishing for compliments. You know you look flawless," Tara said with a wave of the hand.

*Fishing?* Jordan thought. She couldn't decide if the comment was rude on purpose, due to stress, or some failed attempt at dry humor. So she let it go.

Tara focused on Nisha. "Where's your dress?"

Nisha was about to answer when, "It's here! It's here!" Madeline cried, carrying a pale yellow cocktail number in her arms. "I found just the one for this beautiful young lady." She presented it to Nisha, then went to check on someone else.

Jordan, Tara, and Nisha gazed at the gauzy chiffon gown and burst out laughing. It was the exact one that Nisha had been trying on, putting on hold, and *not* buying at Nordstrom for weeks!

"Gee, that looks familiar," Jordan said

with a snort. "Maybe it's a sign that you should — I don't know — *get it*?"

"You think?" Nisha asked, fingering a delicate satin spaghetti strap with tiny bows on it. She entered a changing room with the dress in her arms. Minutes later she emerged and twirled in front of the mirror, layers of filmy material swinging gracefully around her.

At the same time, Brian came out of his stall in a classic double-breasted tux and a long skinny tie meant to give the suit a modern twist. His jaw dropped when he spotted Nisha.

"What do you think?" she asked him.

"I — I —" he stuttered.

"I think he likes it," Tara finished for him.

"Uh-huh," Brian said, swallowing hard. "You — you —"

"You think she looks beautiful?" Jordan prompted him.

Brian nodded. "Uh-huh."

"Nisha, for God's sake, buy the dress

already. Most girls can only dream about rendering their boyfriends speechless." Jordan gestured to Brian, trying not to think of Nate when she spoke the word *boyfriend*.

"Better yet, purchase a few raffle tickets," Tara suggested. "Maybe you'll *win* the dress. If you don't, *then* you can buy it."

Nisha exchanged a glance with Brian then with her friends. "Okay," she said, nodding. "I'll do it." Then her face broke into a smile as she let out a tiny squeal. "Eeeeee! I've got a prom dress! I've got a prom dress!" she cried, doing that happy clap thing she did whenever she got excited. Jordan grinned. "How about you?" she asked Tara. "Find anything you like here?"

"Nothing that really wows me," Tara confessed, looking stressed. "Madeline says she's got something for me to wear the day of the fashion show, but I haven't —"

"No! I am *not* taking my hair out of this ponytail," Jenny Brigger grumbled a few mirrors down, breaking into their conversation.

She was wearing a pale blue sleeveless dress with a high neckline and delicate rhinestone detailing. She was looking surprisingly elegant, aside from the hair.

"Just *try* it," Madeline pleaded, reaching for Jenny's scrunchie. "The dress is too formal for a ponytail."

"Ow! Stop it! Don't touch me!" Jenny cried, shooing Madeline away with her hands.

Tara rolled her eyes. "The fun never ends with that one," she murmured and headed over to help.

*I had no idea what Tara was dealing with,* Jordan thought after watching her friend argue with a balking Jenny for a full ten minutes, then finally getting the girl to let down her hair. *Now I understand why she's in a snappy mood sometimes. I'd be rude, too, if I had to deal with that.*

"Okay, people! Let's get together for a final review!" Tara said, clapping her hands.

The models gathered at the front of the boutique and Tara ran through everything that was supposed to happen on the day of the show. Then she partnered up the guys and girls. "Moose and Ally, Nisha and Brian, Jenny and Tim . . ." Finally she called Jordan and Nate's names.

Jordan stepped forward. When Nate didn't, she looked around, spotting his white-panted legs poking out from underneath a changing stall door.

So did Victor. "He's in there," he said, pointing to the stall. "I can see his feet."

"Nate?" Jordan asked. "You coming out?"

Nate peeked over the top of the door. "Nope. Sorry," he said. "No can do."

Jordan gazed back to Tara, who shrugged. "Somebody had to wear the white tuxedo. Madeline says it's a classic."

"Come on out, Nate. I'll bet it's not as bad as you think it is," Jordan assured him.

The door to the stall slowly squeaked open and Nate emerged red-faced and wearing a white tuxedo: white shirt and pants, white vest, white jacket with tails, and shiny white shoes.

Despite the unfortunate outfit, Jordan thought he actually looked . . . "You're adorable!" she cried before she could stop herself. She cringed when the rest of the guys in the shop began to tease him.

"Isn't he sweet!"

"He looks like an angel!"

"The dude's so pretty it's breakin' my heart!" Moose said with fake tears as he pounded his chest with a fist.

"Shut up," Nate told the guys. "You're just jealous because I look like a dude in a Snoop Dogg video. Only without the furs. Or the gold. Or the hot video chicks dancing around me."

Jordan smiled. Nate could be so funny.

Madeline stepped forward from the circle surrounding Nate. "You forgot this," she said, holding up a shiny white top hat. "It makes the whole outfit."

"Great!" Nate said sarcastically and popped it onto his head. Someone flipped on the sound system and Nate did an exaggerated strut to the beat of the bass pulsing through the shop. He stopped to strike a pensive pose every few seconds, making Jordan and the others laugh. Nate strolled over to Jordan and extended a hand. "Come on, Jord, you can be my number one video chick," he said. Jordan instinctively shook her head.

"If she won't, then I will!" Tara offered, giggling so hard that her eyes were tearing. "We can work it on Friday," she added, bopping to the music.

"I don't think so," Jordan said, taking Nate's hand and laughing, too, but she was only half joking. She knew Tara was talking about the fashion show, but her words made Jordan think about who her replacement might be after she and Nate were over.

Jordan knew that if Nate dated a friend, it would be all weird all the time — for *her*. She preferred he start dating someone she didn't know — even better, a girl who lived in a different state. A foreign country would be perfect. That way, there'd be almost zero possibility of running into the happy couple and having to deal with the uncomfortable conversation that would surely follow — that is, if Nate decided to ever speak with Jordan again after she broke up with him.

Whatever. Even if Tara were desperate for a prom date, which she wasn't anymore, she'd never break the unwritten moral code of best friend ethics and set her sights on an ex-boyfriend. None of Jordan's friends would.

"You're such a goofball," Jordan told Nate when the song ended and they stopped dancing.

Nate casually slung his arm around Jordan's shoulders and gave her a peck on the cheek. "Come on, you know you love it," he said with a twinkle in his eye.

"My boyfriend, the superfreak!" As the words left her mouth, Jordan felt her body stiffen, suddenly aware again that Nate might not be her boyfriend for much longer. *Am I doing the right thing?* she wondered.

What was wrong with her? Could she really say good-bye to someone who made her laugh all the time? Somebody who was caring and secure?

Shane wasn't nearly as outgoing as Nate, but he *was* poetic and mysterious. And his intensity made her nervous in that delicious, excited-to-see-you-anything-can-happen sort of way.

Standing in the middle of the shop, Jordan felt her head spin in confusion, but deep down, she knew she had to listen to her heart.

Letting go of Nate would be completely devastating.

But it had to be done.

Later.

*3 weeks, 5 hours, and 50 minutes till Prom . . .*

# CHAPTER *Six*

***A Prom Queen's Secret Weapons***

*1) Tooth whitener (for a bright and cheery smile)*
*2) Lightbulb (hold up and twist to perfect wave)*
*3) Victor Kaminski (emotional and poster support)*
*4) Tinted moisturizer (w/SPF 30)*

"Are you *sure* you don't need any help grading those tests, Mr. Blanca?" Tara asked at the end of her AP European History class. "I really don't mind missing lunch. It's not as if I'm hypoglycemic or anything."

"I appreciate the offer, Tara." Mr. Blanca slipped the papers into his briefcase and snapped it closed. "But like I said, I've got it covered." He picked up the attaché and headed for the door. "Oh, and good luck with your prom queen campaign," he added just before exiting the classroom.

"Thanks." Tara sagged her shoulders, slid her leather satchel off her desk in the front row, and slinked to the door. If *Mr. Blanca* observed that she was running for prom queen — a man who failed to notice that he wore the same blazer every day in a different color — *Monday: navy, Tuesday: tan, Wednesday: brown, Thursday: gray, Friday: black* — then that meant Jordan *had* to have heard the news too. Which, incidentally, was why Tara was so willing to donate her lunch period to an unworthy cause.

*Of* course *Jordan knows about it,* Tara said to herself as she entered the crowded hallway and was greeted by six enormous pink-and-purple sparkly "Tara for Prom Queen" posters, courtesy of Victor Kaminski. *How could she not?*

"Hi, Tara!" A chunky girl she recognized from the marching band waved to her.

Tara waved back and was surprised to see that the girl had a button pinned to her backpack with Tara's smiling face and the words "Queen Tara" printed on it. *Victor sure doesn't waste any time,* she thought.

Tara knew she should be ecstatic about the impressive amount of publicity he'd created. It was fantastic. She just wished he'd waited until *after* she'd had a chance to talk to Jordan before beginning the media blitz. Especially since now that Tara was in the running, she wouldn't be able to contribute to Jordan's campaign.

*I hope Jordan isn't too mad about it,* Tara thought as she pushed through a swinging door and headed downstairs to the cafeteria. But she wouldn't blame Jordan for being angry. If the situation was reversed Tara wasn't so sure if *she'd* be in a forgiving mood.

Entering the lunchroom, she spotted Jordan and Nisha deep in conversation at their usual table by the center aisle. *What are they talking about? Me?* she wondered, feeling a sudden spark of paranoia. She took a deep breath and headed over.

"Hey, what's up?" she said, making eye contact with nothing but the white tabletop as she sat.

Jordan pushed a Queen Tara button across the table. "Nice pin," she said.

Tara gulped. *The moment of truth.* "Yeah. About that. I was going to tell you . . ." she began.

"No, really," Jordan said. "It's a nice pin. That's a great picture of you."

Tara worked up the nerve to look at Jordan, whose face was as open and pretty as usual. Her blue eyes glistened without a hint of sarcasm.

"So you're not mad at me?" Tara asked.

"Nope," Jordan said plainly. She took a bite of her turkey sandwich.

"Not even a little mad?" Tara asked, surprised. Why *wasn't* she mad? Tara knew that Jordan was gorgeous, popular, and had the cutest boyfriend in school, but she didn't know her friend was also a saint!

"Well *I'm* mad at you," Nisha piped up. "How come I didn't get any buttons? I have this ginormous pink backpack, and it's totally naked," she said, trying to lift said backpack, but it was too heavy.

Tara laughed. "I'll speak to Victor about it," she told Nisha. "He didn't even give *me* a button, and my face is on it." She turned back to Jordan. "Thanks for being so cool about this, Jord. Victor got these kids to nominate me, and then he started the campaign before I had a chance to talk to you," she said. "I wanted to tell you yesterday at the fitting, but it was too crazy at the boutique. I just feel bad because now I won't be able to help you."

"Please." Jordan waved a hand. "Don't worry about it. It'll work itself out. Actually, now that you're running, the pressure is kind of off me a little."

*It's official. She* is *a saint.* "Let's make a

vow," Tara said, "that whatever happens, we won't let the prom queen thing come between us, okay?" Not that Tara thought it ever would. She just wanted to say it out loud.

"Totally." Jordan nodded. "May the best woman win." She held out her hand for a shake and Tara took it.

"It's a deal," Tara said, "though I doubt I'll even come close to winning since you and Nate are sure to snag both titles."

"Oh . . . my God. *Jordan,*" Nisha said, her eyes wide. "I can't believe you didn't tell her."

"Tell me what?" Tara asked, her gaze switching between Jordan and Nisha, but neither of them looked back.

"What are you talking about, Nisha? There's *nothing* to tell," Jordan said, but the I-can't-believe-you-just-blabbed-that-out glare she shot to Nisha gave away the lie.

Tara stared at Jordan, who was now strangely preoccupied with getting the last scraps of her yogurt out of the plastic cup, then at Nisha, who was busy staring at Jordan. And for the first time since the second grade, Tara felt like . . . an outsider.

"You mean, my two best friends have a secret and I'm not a part of it?" she asked, her voice suddenly small. The lump in her throat had grown so large she could barely utter the words.

"Jordan. *Tell* her," Nisha said, snatching away the girl's yogurt. "This is ridiculous."

"Look, if she doesn't want to tell me then I'm not going to force her," Tara said, trying not to seem as hurt as she was. *Why won't she tell me? Should I leave so that she and Nisha can talk about whatever problem she has in private?* She didn't want to go, but now she felt weird being there. "You know, I forgot," she began icily. "There's somewhere I've got to be and —"

"I kissed Shane," Jordan blurted out.

"What?" Tara asked.

"I kissed him, okay?" Jordan said.

"On two separate occasions," Nisha offered. "Nail Polish Boy has nice lips.

I've seen them up close. I mean, I met him once."

"Nisha!" Jordan groaned and covered her face with her hands.

Tara's mind went numb as she tried to process the information. "You mean to tell me that you're cheating on Nate?" she asked. "You're . . . *cheating* on the most perfect boyfriend you've ever had? With, like, some emo *loser* you met in line at the movies? That is low. No, it's lower than low. It's heartless! How could you do this to Nate?" she demanded, her anger building.

Jordan glanced briefly at where Nate and the other jocks were sitting by the window. "Why don't you say it a little louder, Tara? I'm not sure he heard you," she snapped. "*Now* do you see is why I didn't want to say anything to her, Nisha?"

"Why? Because I think it's wrong?" Tara asked.

"No. Because I knew you'd make me feel even worse than I already do, okay? I know it's not right. I'm not *heartless*,"

Jordan said, her voice cracking on the word. "It's just . . ." She glanced up, seeming to search for the right words. "When I'm with Nate, I think I should be with him, but then when I'm with Shane, I think the only choice is . . . to break it off with Nate." Her eyes began to fill with tears and she lowered her head.

"Jord," Nisha said and put an arm around her. Tara hated to see her best friend cry, but she couldn't bring herself to comfort her.

"It's so confusing," Jordan went on. "How can I like them both? But I do. I don't want to lose either of them, but I'm not cut out to date two guys," she said. "I don't want to hurt anybody — especially Nate — but it's going to happen no matter what."

Tara couldn't recall ever seeing Jordan this upset. In fact, it was a rare event to see her without a smile brightening her face. Now as Tara watched her friend, red-nosed and hiding her tears from the rest of the cafeteria, she wished she could take back her words. Jordan had clearly been struggling with her feelings for a while, and Tara could tell that her friend was truly torn. "I'm sorry, Jord," she said, grabbing her hand. "I didn't mean to be so harsh."

Jordan nodded as she swiped at her tears, her mascara running down her now-ruddy cheeks.

But still, Tara couldn't help feeling sorry for Nate. And she couldn't help thinking that maybe her best friend wasn't such a saint after all.

By the time Tara had met Victor in the student parking lot after school so they could go shopping together, she had come to a conclusion. *I'm going to support my friend,* she'd thought. *It's Jordan's life and she's got to make her own decisions. If she chooses Shane and he breaks her heart, she'll need me. And I'll be there.*

Now that she and Victor were sifting through the racks at T.J. Maxx, Tara had to focus her mind completely on the task at hand: finding the perfect prom dress. Apparently Mr. Maxx wasn't about to make it easy.

"I can't believe that we've resorted to this," she moaned, gesturing to the rows and rows of miscellaneous clothing. "Nothing is in order. Dresses are mixed in with pants, blouses are with the bikinis. . . . Remember those cute shoes I pointed out on display? You know what was inside the only shoebox that had my size on it? Underwear! How are we supposed to find a prom gown in this mess? Do they even *sell* prom gowns here?"

Victor pulled out a periwinkle strapless dress with a sash that could be tied into a bow in the back. "Here's one," he said, showing her.

Tara gasped and examined it. "Hey, not bad, Kaminski." The fabric was an understated matte taffeta, the design a simple cocktail length A-line. *Pretty,* she thought. She glanced at the label inside the dress.

"Jessica McClintock? For sixty-three bucks? Unbelievable!"

"Who's Jessica McClintock?" Victor asked.

"I'll try it on," Tara said, tossing it into a red plastic shopping cart, "but let's look for more."

With newfound hope, Tara and Victor began the hunt, rooting through the racks. *I have a good feeling about this,* Tara thought, finding a silky emerald number and tossing it into the cart. She peeked at Victor who was surveying a supershort black tube dress with a ton of ruching up the sides.

He held it up. "Hey, T-Bone. Want to be my number one video chick?" he teased, making fun of Nate's joke from the day before.

Tara wrinkled her nose. "Ummmm. Too trashy."

"That's the whole point," he said, grinning and hooking it back into the rack. He flipped through a few more pieces then said, "So, I was thinking about the prom queen campaign and I came up with a few ideas. Want to hear 'em?"

"Sure." Tara chucked a sequined wrap dress into the cart. She wasn't sure if it was her style or not, but it was only twenty dollars so it couldn't hurt to try it on.

"Well, Jordan's so popular . . ." he began. "You are, too, but in a different way," he added quickly. "I figure we need to be strategic and target specific voters, you know?"

This was interesting. Tara stopped sifting to listen. "Like who?"

Victor leaned his arm on a rack. "Definitely not the cheerleaders or the jocks. Jordan's got those votes for sure, so it'd be a waste of time," he said. "Instead we need to focus our energy on the intellectual and/or creative types. The math-letes, marching band, theater people . . ."

"That girl who tattooed herself with a safety pin and a marker in the art lab?" Tara added.

"*Exactly,*" Victor said. "She may not be attending the prom, but she can still vote for the queen. And something tells me she's not too fond of cheerleaders. She needs an option on her ballot, Tara. And *you* could be that option."

Tara pondered it. "I think you have something," she said slowly. "It could work." She gazed at the small pile of dresses in her cart and her stomach flipped with anxiety. This made finding an amazing prom dress even more of a priority. She had to look incredible if she was going to wear a crown. "Let's go to the dressing room," Tara announced. "I need to try this stuff on — right now."

Tara slipped into dress after dress while Victor waited outside. The green one was too short, the red one too tight, and the rest of them were all way too blah. *Why can't I pick out a decent gown?* Tara wanted to scream. *Jordan and Nisha found beautiful dresses. How come nothing looks good on me?*

Tara had one last dress to try — the

periwinkle one that Victor had picked out. She removed it from the hanger and stepped into it from the top. The soft material felt nice against her skin and the color made her pale cheeks suddenly seem rosy. *I like it,* Tara thought, getting excited. *I actually like it!* She reached back to close the zipper, but she couldn't do it herself. She needed help.

Holding the dress up with one hand, Tara raced out of the dressing room. "Victor, would you zip me up?" she asked him, taking a place in front of a three-way mirror.

Victor's eyes widened momentarily. "Uh, sure." He cleared his throat before attempting to fasten the garment. "Uh, let's see how this works." He gently tugged on the material.

Tara could feel him jiggling the zipper, but it wasn't closing. She could also tell by his reflection in the mirror that there was a problem.

"I think the zipper is broken," he said after a few more tries. "I can't close it."

“Seriously?” she asked. “The one dress that has potential and it’s damaged?” Was somebody playing a cruel joke on her?

Tara sulked as she returned to the dressing room. As she passed the rack of unwanted items, a long white dress caught her eye. It was one-shouldered and silk and beautiful. It was also the same dress that Jordan had bought. Tara glanced at the price. *Only one twenty-five? Jordan got ripped. She paid two fifty for hers.*

With a hand still on the dress, Tara hesitated before going back to her changing stall. *I wonder what Jordan’s dress would look like on me.* Tara knew she could never buy it, but what hurt would it do just to . . . try it on?

She snatched it off the rack, brought it back to her stall, and quickly slipped it on over her head. Tara stared at her reflection in the mirror. *It looks so good!* she thought, shoulders sagging, lips pouting. She pinned her wavy brown hair atop her head with both hands and stood on her tiptoes, trying to imagine what the dress might look like with heels. "Why does it have to be perfect?" she murmured. But what she really meant to say was, *Why does it have to be Jordan's?*

Tara stepped out of the dressing room to show Victor the dress. "What do you think? Don't you just love it?" she asked him.

"It's okay," Victor said with a shrug. "But I think the purple one looked much better on you."

"Well the *purple* one has a *broken zipper*," she spat out, then immediately regretted it. "Sorry, Victor. I didn't mean to be nasty. I'm just seriously bummed," she said then went back into the dressing room to change.

Tara gazed at her reflection one last time before taking off the dress. *Victor's right. This gown doesn't suit me at all. And it doesn't look nearly as good as it did on Jordan. Something's missing.* And as she pulled the dress over her head, she realized something else. It *wasn't* the exact same dress that Jordan owned, but a designer knockoff. *It figures,* Tara thought, *a cheap imitation. I can never compare to Jordan. Why do I even try?*

"Want to look around some more?" Victor suggested when Tara exited the dressing room. "Maybe they have another one of those purple dresses in your size."

The thought of rummaging through that mess again gave Tara a headache. "I think I'm all T.J. Maxx–ed out," she admitted, and they headed for the exit in silence.

Victor glanced at her. "I know. You can teach me how to dance," he said. "I could sure use a lesson before the prom."

"Maybe another time," Tara replied, not in the mood.

"Come on, T-Bone," Victor said. "Please. I really need your help. Look." He proceeded to do a ridiculous jig to the tinny Muzak playing over the store's speakers. He raised his arms in the air and began moving his hips in a ridiculous manner. "Got any pointers?" he asked, grooving around in a circle.

Two preteens by the jewelry case peeked

at him from behind a display of earrings and giggled. A lady sniffing perfumed soaps stared with wonder.

Tara covered her eyes with one hand. "Ahh! Make it stop! Make it stop!" she said, laughing hard. Only Victor would think of humiliating himself in the middle of a store to make her feel better. *And it worked!*

"How can you say that?" Victor stopped suddenly, hands on his hips, pretending to be insulted.

Tara linked her arm in his. "It's okay, Victor," she said as they left the place behind. "I don't care if my prom date has moves like a chicken."

Maybe a few weeks ago the sight would have horrified her, but not anymore. Tara had a good feeling about attending the prom with this boy. Even if she wore an ugly dress and their feet never touched the dance floor, she knew they'd have an awesome time talking and laughing all night.

Wouldn't they?

*2 weeks, 6 days, 1 hour, and 33 minutes till Prom . . .*

# CHAPTER *Seven*

"So now that you know what you're wearing to the prom, maybe we'll have time to go see a movie?" Brian suggested on Thursday after school.

"Are you kidding me?" Nisha replied. "There are shoes to be found, evening bags to be bought, and hairstyles to be tried. Who has time for the movies?"

"So Sunday afternoon?" he asked, taking her hand in his.

"Okay," Nisha told him. Her hand clasped in his, she swung their arms happily as they strolled down Main Street, her silver charm bracelet glinting in the hazy afternoon sunlight.

Sipping smoothies, they gazed into the windows of the cute canopied shops that bordered the street. It felt good to have a few hours with Brian. Alone. Between school, prom stuff, *Kathak* practice, and her parental obligations, it had been days since she and Brian could just be together. Nisha hadn't had even a free moment to buy Brian an anniversary gift yet. And here she was, wearing the one he'd gotten her every day for a week.

*I'd have more time if my parents didn't make me hang out with Raj.* She forced the bitter notion out of her head. *Think happy thoughts,* she said to herself. *Like limousines, and corsages, and dancing on a moonlit terrace with your boyfriend. . . .*

*Yes, that's better.* Today was Brian's day. She didn't want to think about some nice-enough Indian guy she wasn't even into.

"What are you thinking about?" Brian asked.

"Oh, the usual," she admitted. "Prom."

Brian nodded knowingly. "So what's the deal with Tara and the mascot guy?" he asked. "Are they going out or something? They're always together."

"Victor and Tara? No, they're just friends," Nisha said. "For *now,*" she added. "Tara would never admit it to me, but I think she's starting to like him."

"That's cool. So then I guess it's me and you, Tara and Victor, Jordan and Nate at the table so far?" Brian asked.

"I think so," Nisha said but the truth was that she didn't know *who* was going to show up at their table on prom night. She hoped she was wrong, but the way things were going with Jordan, it looked as though she and Nate wouldn't be dating for much longer. And Nisha still hadn't figured out how to deal with Raj. Ironically, the only sure thing was Tara and Victor.

And then there was the fresh crop of weirdness between Tara and Jordan. Nisha didn't really understand how or why it had started, but out of all the drama surrounding her lately it was the one thing that worried her the most. She squeezed her eyes shut, trying to think happy thoughts again, only this time they didn't pop into her head so easily.

"Nisha? What's up?" Brian asked. "You're never this quiet."

"Nothing," Nisha answered. It was like a reflex. Brian gazed at her with concerned blue eyes. *I should tell him. At least about my friends. Maybe he can help.* "Okay, maybe there *is* something. . . . I have a feeling there's a huge storm brewing between Jordan and Tara," she confessed. "And it's going to get ugly. Like, an enormous zit on your nose ugly. Only worse." It was the first time she'd said it out loud. It felt good to get it out in the open.

"This sounds serious," Brian said. He led Nisha to a bench and they sat down. "Talk to me," he said, wrapping an arm around her.

"Well," she began, "Jordan keeps

confiding in me about stuff, but she makes me promise not to tell Tara. Tara's been complaining to me about Jordan lately, too. And I'm totally caught in the middle."

"Wait. Rewind," Brian said. "Why does Jordan want to keep secrets from Tara? Aren't you all best friends? And what is Tara saying about Jordan that's got you so upset?"

Nisha hesitated, not sure she should expose Jordan's secret. "Promise you won't tell *anybody?*" she asked sternly.

"Of course." Brian nodded.

Trusting that Brian wouldn't repeat it, she took a deep breath and explained the whole sordid love triangle between Nate, Jordan, and Shane. About how Jordan and Shane met at a movie theater and became friends — and Tara made it known that she didn't like the new friendship. About how the secrets began after Jordan and Shane's relationship morphed from platonic to romantic. "She didn't want it to happen. It caught her by surprise," Nisha explained, "and now Jordan is seriously tortured about it. She kept it hidden because she thought Tara was going to judge her, and that's exactly what Tara did when she found out about it."

"So what's going on now that everybody knows?" Brian asked.

Nisha shrugged. "I thought the secrets were over, but they're not," she said. "Jordan hung out with Shane after school yesterday, but Tara has no idea. And Tara keeps telling me that she feels sorry for Nate, but she wouldn't dare say it to Jordan." She sighed. "I'm trying to be a good friend, but I don't know what to say to either of them. And besides, I've got my own issues to worry about."

Brian pulled back to look at her. "You've got issues?" he asked. "What kind of issues? How come you never told me about them?"

*Stupid! How could I let that slip?* "Um, well, they're not *serious,*" Nisha began, with no idea where she was going with this. "And now that I, uh . . . *found my prom dress* everything is hunky-dory. So there's no real issue anymore." *Except that I'm a habitual liar. Who says stuff like hunky-dory.*

"Let's walk," Nisha said and stood. She had to do something to keep her mouth from running.

Brian took her hand again. He was quiet as they ambled down the sidewalk past a vintage dress shop and an office supply store then stopped at the corner. "You know, I don't like to take sides," he said as they waited for the light to change so they could cross the street. "But I think Tara's right about this one. Cheating is cheating."

"Even if there are extenuating circumstances?" Nisha asked. *Like, for instance, if your parents are making you spend time with an Indian boy just because they approve of him?* she added silently.

"What circumstances? It doesn't matter if Jordan 'wants' to be cheating on Nate or if she 'meant' to kiss Shane. In the end she's still lying to him. That's the bottom line."

"I see." Nisha wondered if Brian would consider her times with Raj cheating. *They're not actual dates and I'd never kiss him . . . but I have been lying to Brian.*

The WALK signal flashed. Nisha and Brian were about to cross the street, hand in hand, when Nisha noticed a familiar white Saab stopped at the light. Inside was an elegant Indian woman who was fiddling with the radio.

*Mrs. Dixit!* Nisha realized.

"Oh!" Panicking, she quickly released Brian's hand, turned on her heel, and headed for the nearest display window so that she could stare at some random object until the woman drove away. *Please, don't let her see me with Brian,* she silently prayed. *Please!*

A few seconds later, the light changed and the cars progressed down Main Street. Brian appeared at her side. "What was that all about?" he asked, his voice low.

"What? Nothing," Nisha said then gasped when he held up her bracelet. "Oh, no! Is it broken?"

"You dropped my hand so fast the clasp came loose. It's a little bent, but it should be okay," Brian said as she held out her bare wrist and he clipped the bracelet back on. "So what happened back there? See an old boyfriend or something?" he joked, but Nisha could tell that he wanted answers.

"Cut it out," Nisha said. "You know you're my first boyfriend." That part was the truth. The next part, not so much. "It was just that I saw this really cool, uh . . ." She scanned the display window. *Why, why,* why *do I have to be in front of an office supply store?* ". . . *thing* in the window and I had to check it out," she finished.

"Ohhhhhh," Brian nodded knowingly. "*I* get it."

"Get what?" Nisha wasn't sure — until she followed his gaze to a fancy drafting pen resting in an open box. At least she *thought* he was staring at the pen; he wouldn't be drooling over the case of printer paper *next* to the pen, right? And Brian would be starting his architecture major in the fall at

Georgia State — conveniently located only a few hours from Emory — so it made sense. *Bingo!* she thought. *Now I know what to buy him for our anniversary! I'll get it engraved to make it personal.*

"Come on," she said, dragging him away from the display. "You'll get it at our anniversary dinner."

"Get *what*? You're getting me something?" Brian asked with a wide grin. He slung an arm around Nisha's shoulders as she rolled her eyes. Then they crossed the street and headed for Brian's red Civic.

"Hey, Diablo. Did you miss us?" Brian asked, patting the car's hood. Nisha giggled as he pulled her close to him. "By the way," he said, "everything's set up for dinner on Saturday. I couldn't get reservations for the Coral again, but I planned something even better. Let's meet as six, okay?"

"On Saturday?" Nisha repeated, feeling queasy. Brian had gone to all the trouble of planning their special anniversary dinner *again* and she couldn't make it. *Again.* "I've got a recital at the Todi Studio that day. I thought we'd go out on Sunday. You know, after the movie."

"You have a dance recital?" Brian asked, surprised. "Why didn't you tell me about it? I'd like to see it."

Nisha had a few reasons for not telling Brian:

1) She had a habit of keeping her Indian and American lives separate.
2) Her parents would be there and they still had no clue who he was.
3) Her guru had caught Nisha and Brian kissing and threatened to tell Nisha's parents *unless* she ended it with Brian. Clearly she hadn't. And . . .
4) Hel-*lo*? Nisha's other prom date was going to be there, too!

"It's a very small event," she said, feeling guilty and avoiding Brian's eyes. "There's limited seating in the studio so I could only get tickets for my parents. Otherwise I would have definitely invited you." *Liar.*

"Mmm," Brian murmured. "I wish I would've cleared the date with you before I went and planned everything. But it has to be Saturday or else it's all messed up." He seemed to be thinking. "What about after the recital?" he suggested. "Like eight o'clock? Would that work?"

Nisha didn't see anything wrong with that. The recital was at four. She should be done way before eight. She slid her arms around her boyfriend's waist and smiled. "It's a date."

"Well, that worked out," Brian said, leaning in for a kiss.

*Barely,* Nisha thought as she hugged her boyfriend close. If going to *dinner* with Brian seemed difficult, how in the world would they make it to the prom?

*2 weeks, 6 days, and 58 minutes till Prom . . .*

# CHAPTER *Eight*

"Eight ball, corner pocket," Jordan said, leaning over the pool table in Shane's basement and squinting as she took aim. She slid the pool stick between her fingers, made the shot . . . and missed.

"Yes!" Shane said, raising both arms over his head in victory, his black hair flopping over one eye. "I win!"

"By *default*." Jordan grinned, rested her pool stick on the table, and sat on the edge of the blue floral couch near the table. It wasn't quite the decor she'd imagined when picturing Shane's house. The wood-paneled walls, Thomas Kinkade prints, enormous flat-screen TV, and the wet bar all seemed so . . . suburban. Which didn't seem to mix with Shane's black skinny jeans and red Ramones T-shirt. *Where did you expect him to live? In a dark leather-padded cave?*

"Hey, I'll take it." Shane circled the table and sat beside her. "Seriously. If you'd made the shot, I would've freaked. I thought you said you weren't good at pool?"

"I'm not. Just better than *you,* I guess," Jordan said, teasing him.

Shane tilted his head and smiled slightly. "Oh, you *are*, are you?"

With his face only inches from hers and his dark eyes sparkling, Jordan felt the pull to kiss him.

So she did.

A few soft pecks led to a longer, more serious embrace that made her body shiver. Jordan still hadn't figured out how to talk to Nate, how to handle Tara's disapproval, or how to convince Shane that this was wrong. All she knew was that, right then, she wanted to be exactly where she was. With Shane. Kissing him.

When they broke apart, Shane was beaming.

"What?" she asked, feeling unusually shy, now that his gaze was lingering.

"Nothing. Just happy," he said then kissed her softly on the cheek. "So what do you want to do? Music? Video games? A movie?" He stood and crossed over to the enormous entertainment center against the wall.

"Music," Jordan answered, joining him by the CD player. She quickly scanned his collection, which consisted mostly of punk bands that she'd never heard of. Rancid, Jawbreaker, A Global Threat. . . . Then her eyes caught sight of a familiar name. "*Shakira*?" Jordan asked, holding up the CD and raising her eyebrows.

"Definitely. Not. Mine," Shane said lifting both hands in defense. "My older sister's. But we can play it if you want."

"Okay," Jordan said. "Pop it in." A minute later she was bopping her head and swiveling her body to the frothy tune of "Hips Don't Lie." Feeling comfortable, she danced back to the couch, then flopped down into it.

Shane grabbed two Cokes from the mini-fridge and brought them over. He handed Jordan one before sitting next to her. "So, how's the photography project going?" he asked.

Jordan rolled her eyes. "Going? It's not," she admitted. "I don't know what my problem is. You'd think it'd be easy since it's about *me.* I've got a lot of great shots now, but they're all so different: cheerleading photos, pictures dancing in that club we went to in Chicago, the shots we took in the park, pictures of this fashion show fitting I did the other day. . . . But I have no clue how to connect them in a series."

"You need a hook," Shane said, knowingly. "You'll think of something."

"I hope so." Jordan raked a hand through her hair. "My photography teacher, Mr.

Davidson, is getting pretty impatient. He thinks I'm giving him the runaround, but I'm not."

"*What* is going on down here?" a voice sounded.

Jordan turned to see a boy with spiky platinum hair and black roots thundering down the stairs to the basement.

Another boy with a shaggy brown cut followed him down, "Shane, man. What is *up* with the *Shakira*?" he asked, snickering. "Dude." Then he spotted Jordan. "Oh. Hey."

"Hey, yourself," Jordan said, smiling at the boys and figuring that they were friends of Shane's.

Shane introduced them. "Gavin, Apollo, this is Jordan. Jordan, this is Apollo," he gestured to the guy with the white hair then to the shaggy-haired boy, "and that's Gavin."

"So *this* is the infamous Jordan," Apollo said, striding over and taking a seat in an armchair next to her. "Can I just say that our friend has been talking about you nonstop for weeks?"

"Now we can see why," Gavin said, making himself comfortable in the chair across from Apollo and thumping his black Converse-clad feet onto the coffee table. "Not bad, Dresden. She's pretty cute, even if she does have poor taste in music."

"Gee. Thanks," Jordan said.

"Guys, what are you doing here?" Shane asked.

"What? We can't drop by our good friend's house just to say hi?" he asked, giving Jordan a wink. "And maybe to see what his new friend is like? What did you call her, Shane?" He looked up, thinking. "A goddess?"

*Shane told his friends I'm a goddess?* Jordan held back a smile as she watched Shane's pale skin turn pink. Clearly his friends were there to give him a hard time.

"Man, I can't think with this junk invading my eardrums. Hold on." Apollo jumped up and traded a perfectly good Shakira song for some guy screaming over an acoustic guitar in the background. Then he went over to the mini-fridge and grabbed himself a Coke. "That's better," he said when he'd flopped back into his chair.

"Make yourself at home," Shane said sarcastically.

"Thanks." Apollo cracked open the Coke and took a sip. "Dude, something really messed up is going on over at Joes."

Gavin rolled his eyes. "We were just there and it's like, invasion of the Emerson cheerleaders. There must have been ten of them in there." He gave an exaggerated shudder. "*So* not cool."

"How'd they even find out about the place?" Apollo wanted to know. "They don't usually venture far from the food court at the mall."

"Guys . . ." Shane said with a warning tone.

Jordan winced. She knew how the

cheerleaders had found out. She'd told her friends from the squad about the place last week. *But so what?* "Who cares if a few cheerleaders go to Joes?" she said briskly, trying hard not to feel insulted. "It's good for business."

"Are you kidding me?" Apollo replied. "Cheerleaders are, like, peppy little monsters. Evil is not good for any business."

"Hey. *Guys* . . ." Shane repeated.

"And they're like cockroaches," Gavin added. "When you see a few, you know that there are hundreds of them just waiting for you to turn the lights off before they swarm the place and ruin it."

*Okay. Now I'm insulted,* Jordan thought.

"Guys! *Enough,*" Shane said. "Jordan's a cheerleader. And she goes to Emerson. So shut up."

Gavin and Apollo exchanged a glance, then burst into a fit of laughter.

"You're seeing a cheerleader? What's next? Prom queen?" Apollo asked in between sniggers.

"So?" Shane said, clearly getting annoyed. "You have a problem with that?

"She's a prom queen, *too*?" Gavin said. "You're going out with a cheerleader *and* a prom queen?" He doubled over.

"Dude, first it's Shakira, then before you know it, you're buying corsages and wearing a tux to the prom," Apollo snorted, shaking his head. "Out of all the people I know, I never expected *you* to sellout to that mainstream garbage, man," Apollo said, shaking his head. He looked at Jordan. "No offense."

"'No *offense*?'" Shane repeated. "You think you can talk smack about my girlfriend, tag 'no offense' on the end of it, and that makes it okay?"

*Did he just call me* his girlfriend*?*

Jordan held up a hand to stop Shane. She turned to Apollo. "What do you have against cheerleaders and proms or whatever?"

"Uh-oh. The prom queen is getting angry," Gavin piped in. "Watch out."

Jordan shot Gavin a dirty look as the other boy formulated an answer.

"I don't like oppressive and elitist cliques, for one thing," Apollo told her. "But not only that, you people go around flaunting your stupidity. Bouncing around school in your uniforms or your expensive clothes. You watch music videos and movies that are disguised as entertainment, but are really all about the corporations trying to sell you a lifestyle. In fact, the whole spring frenzy over the prom is just another example of the suits yanking your chain to buy a whole load of useless stuff. You're all a bunch of misguided drones and you don't even have a clue about any it, do you?"

"*I'm* the one without a clue? *I'm* the one in an elitist clique?" Jordan asked, seething. "That's funny, because didn't I just hear *you* talk about how cheerleaders aren't cool enough to hang out at Joes?" She gestured to his dyed hair and punkish attire. "And if you're such an individualist, why is it that you and your buddy over here are dressed almost exactly alike?" Jordan strode to the entertainment center and picked up a CD jewel case to prove her point further. "Interesting. Did you get the idea to wear skinny jeans and bleach your hair from these guys?" She held out the CD. "But you're not trying to emulate a certain, um, *lifestyle,* are you?" she asked, then pointed out his shoes. "Oh, and if you don't think Converse is making *a killing* off of *non-mainstream* people like you who like to wear their sneakers, then you are clearly an idiot, my friend . . . *no offense.*"

Apollo's jaw went slack.

"The prom queen pegged you, man," Gavin said, pointing at Apollo.

Jordan shot him a look. "You, too," she said. "And you can stop being sarcastic about the prom. It may not be your thing, but I'm looking forward to going," she added with a flip of her hair.

But then she thought of something. *Once I work up the nerve to talk to Nate, I won't have a date. And Shane and I won't be attending my prom or his prom or* any *prom together,* she realized.

Jordan had always known that Shane wasn't a fan of the prom, but it hadn't hit home until just then. It was disappointing, to say the least, but she wasn't about to let that stop her from having a special night. Prom may not have been a huge deal for her before, but she suddenly saw it in a new light.

"You know, maybe you think prom is all about limos and tuxes and pretty dresses," Jordan continued. "It's true, that's part of it. But it's also about spending time with your friends. It's about savoring the last moments of high school and celebrating with the kids you grew up with. In a few short weeks, it'll all be over. What's so wrong with wanting to enjoy the last moments of now before closing the chapter and moving on to college?"

There. She said all she had to say on the subject. And she meant every word.

"That was awesome," Gavin said, clapping slowly and sarcastically, clearly making fun of her.

Apollo joined in. "Yeah, she should use it in her queen of the prom essay," he said with a snort.

*What jerks,* Jordan thought. *If these guys are Shane's close friends, then maybe I should rethink hanging out with Shane.* "Okay, I'm done." She grabbed her purse off the coffee table and headed up the steps.

"Jordan!" Shane called, then muttered something to the guys that she didn't hear. She was already out of the basement, through the living room and opening the front door, out onto the porch and down the path to the sidewalk. . . . "Jordan, wait! Please!"

Jordan stopped by the gate and turned. "Why didn't you say anything?" she asked. "And why are you smiling? Do you think something's funny?"

"No way." Shane shook his head earnestly. "And you didn't need my help back there. You were incredible," he said. "Apollo is so arrogant sometimes he can't admit it when he's wrong. But, believe me, he knows it. He's down there, right now, going through my CD covers and feeling like a hypocrite." Shane looked down, then laced his fingers though Jordan's. "Please don't be mad at me because my friends are morons," he said. "They're harmless once you get to know them. I promise."

Jordan found herself softening. It wasn't as if she had to hang out with Apollo and Gavin 24/7, anyway.

"And just for the record, I won't hold your weird obsession with the prom against you," Shane added with a teasing smile.

"What? Me?" Jordan playfully swatted his chest with her hand. "Hardly. I think your *friends* are the ones obsessed . . . with *hating* it."

Shane grinned. "Well, also for the record — just so you know — I'd go to a prom with you any day. If you wanted me to."

Jordan paused, stunned. "Are you serious?" she asked him. "You'd do that for me?"

"I think you're worth a little hypocrisy,"

Shane said, gazing at the ground at first, then into her eyes.

"That's so cool of you. Thanks!" Jordan hugged him, overcome by the gesture. She knew that his opinion was similar to his friends'. In fact, it was only a couple weeks ago that Shane had told her that the prom went against everything he believed in.

"So . . . does this mean you'll ignore Gavin and Apollo and give me a second chance?" he asked softly.

"It does," Jordan replied, pulling back to smile at him.

"Good," Shane said. He tilted his face toward hers, and Jordan knew he was about to kiss her. She closed her eyes, her head swirling as their lips touched and she gently kissed him back.

When they parted Jordan opened her eyes and was greeted by Shane's intense stare. He seemed to have something important to ask her. "So, uh, how did Nate take it when you told him about us? Did he give you a hard time when you broke up with him?"

"Um," Jordan swallowed, hardly knowing what to say. "About that . . ." she began.

Shane stepped back to survey her face. "You *did* break up with Nate, didn't you?" he asked.

"Well, I haven't *exactly* broken up with him yet," she admitted. "But I will," she added quickly. "I'll do it."

"Well . . . *when*?" Shane wanted to know.

It was a good question.

*2 weeks, 5 days, 3 hours, and 12 minutes till Prom . . .*

# CHAPTER *Nine*

*Tara Macmillan's Prom Dress/Limo Etiquette*

1) *Think before you stink: Take it easy on the perfume, ladies.*
2) *Avoid unwanted flashing of underwear: Sit first, then swing both legs into vehicle.*
3) *Ask self: Do I really want to be sucked into a shiny creamsicle-colored corset-dress with poufy sleeves and six layers of crinoline? (If so, ask again.)*
4) *Remember: All embarrassing pics WILL end up on the Internet . . . eventually. (Can also be applied to rule #3.)*

"Oh, Madeline! It's sooo beautiful!" Tara cried as she viewed her reflection in the full-length mirror backstage at the prom-wear fashion show. She was wearing a deep purple-colored halter dress with delicate beading hand sewn into the fabric. The bodice was a formfitting Italian satin, while the skirt was a bit fuller with layer after layer of the finest tulle Tara had ever seen and with cute little pockets sewn into the side seams. She swung the skirt left and right. "I feel like a princess," she said, slipping into a pair of pointy-toed satin heels, dyed to match. "I love every bit of it!"

"This dress is my own, one-of-a-kind, creation," the owner of Papillion told her, beaming. "I wanted an exceptional girl to wear it in the fashion show." She adjusted one of the tiny purple florets that circled Tara's waist. "And it fits you perfectly."

Tara blushed at the compliment. "Is it for sale?" she asked, hoping it was. She *had* to have it for the prom.

"Of course," Madeline told her.

"Great!" Tara said, feeling giddy inside. After all the countless hours of searching, she'd found a dress, and she hadn't even picked it out herself! *This is the one,* she knew. *My prom dress. Finally!* "I'll see you in a few, Madeline. I have to go show my friends!"

Feeling giggly, Tara carefully lifted the hem of her skirt and hurried out of the wings of the stage. She emerged into the connecting hallway, crowded with girls and guys in prom attire waiting anxiously for the show to begin.

Her smile dropped when she noticed Nisha in her yellow empire dress and Jordan in her black strapless gown huddled, deep in conversation, just outside the entrance of the girls' dressing room.

*Oh, no. Jordan looks upset,* Tara thought and quickened her pace.

When Jordan spotted Tara approaching she quickly tapped Nisha on the arm, whispered something, and the two girls immediately stopped talking.

"What's going on?" Tara demanded, noticing the exchange. "What's the big secret?" Her stomach felt cold.

"Oh, no secret," Jordan said, trying to seem casual but coming off as tense. "So I guess the show is going to run without a hitch, huh?" she added. "Everyone looks great. I heard you got Jenny out of her scrunchie again. Good work."

Tara pursed her lips. Jordan wasn't getting off that easily. "Way to change the subject," she replied stormily. "So I take it you're *not* going to tell me what you guys were just talking about." She didn't say it as a question.

"It wasn't about you," Nisha assured her quickly. "I promise."

"I didn't think it was," Tara said. By the way her friends were acting she knew exactly what — or more precisely *whom* — they were talking about. Mr. *I-thought-I-was-blind-in-one-eye-but-eventually-realized-my-hair-was-covering-it* Dresden. "Whatever."

"Do you need us to do something?" Nisha offered, her eyes wide.

*Yeah. How about being my friend. How about cluing me in on what's going on with Jordan. How about noticing that I am wearing the most fabulous dress in the history of fabulous dresses and that all we used to talk about was the prom!*

"Nope," Tara said. "Later." She turned on her heel and headed back the way she had come. *Why won't Jordan include me? What's the big deal? I told her I was sorry about the other day. Now she's acting like we're not even friends anymore.* The last thought pinched Tara's heart. *Don't even think that,* she said to herself. *Focus on the show.*

She crossed the hallway and made a left back into the wings of the stage where there was plenty of action to keep her mind off of Jordan. Two theater tech guys were pushing the podium, from which Tara would emcee the show, downstage, while the lighting guys did a final run-through.

Jenny was marching around holding a clipboard and barking orders, about what, Tara didn't know and didn't care to know.

Then she noticed Victor climbing a ladder set in front of the backdrop of a silver castle, about to fix the blue "Once Upon a Time" banner than had fallen down on one side. "Victor, let me help you," she said, clicking across the shiny stage floor and taking hold of the ladder.

Victor grunted and struggled to tie up the banner. "This isn't working," he said after several tries.

"Let me try," Tara suggested and they switched places.

"So, where are Nisha and Jordan?" Victor asked as she reached up to fasten the banner. "I haven't seen them. Are they here yet?"

"They're in the hall with the other models," Tara told him, an ache resurfacing in her chest. *Maybe I should talk to Victor about what's going on with Jordan. Get his take on the situation*, she thought, and then decided against it. Being the mascot for the athletic teams, Victor was sort-of-friends with Nate, and Tara didn't want to risk Jordan getting into trouble, no matter how wrong she thought her friend was about seeing Shane.

Tara tied a knot in the string that held the banner up. "Got it," she said, just as her pointy purple satin shoe slipped off a rung on the ladder!

Before she even had a chance to say, "Help! Save the dress!" she felt Victor's arms grab hold of her waist. He lowered her safely to the stage floor.

"My dress . . ." Tara gasped, petting herself down. "I didn't rip it, did I?" *Thank goodness, no.* She turned to face Victor, who was directly behind her. "Oh," she said, startled, not realizing that he was standing so close.

Tara's heart pounded, though now that she was face-to-face with Victor, she couldn't decide if it was due to the excitement of the accident or because of . . . him.

"Those shoes are dangerous, T-Bone," he

said softly, regarding her with his hazel eyes. "You okay?"

Unable to speak — something she never thought would happen in her lifetime — Tara swallowed and nodded. Victor had gone from social experiment, to major cutie, to good friend, to . . . what was she feeling now? Tara couldn't describe it. All she knew was that she wanted Victor Kaminski to kiss her.

*Does he want* me *to kiss* him? Tara wondered.

There was only one way to find out.

Closing her eyes and pursing her lips, she angled her head toward Victor. Her breath quickened when she felt the closeness of his lips to hers, then . . .

"Time check!" Jenny Brigger shouted.

Instantly Tara opened her eyes as she and Victor sprang apart.

Jenny swarmed by in her blue gown and her clipboard, looking surprisingly pretty now that her curly hair was falling loose around her shoulders. "What are you guys doing just standing there? The theater is filling up and the show is going to start in a few minutes. Let's go! We've got to move that ladder — *pronto*!"

*No way! Can't you see we were having a moment here?* Tara wanted to shout. But of course she didn't. Instead she helped Victor carry the ladder to an out-of-the-way place in the wings. Victor was acting so casual that Tara wondered if maybe *she* was the only one who had had the moment.

"Good luck," Victor said as she took her place at the podium. Tara nodded, quickly flipping through her speech on the cue cards that she'd left there earlier, trying to ready herself on the show. Then, just as the curtain was opening, Victor gave her a quick kiss on the cheek.

Tara blushed as she touched her face with her hand. *Was that a friend kiss or a more-than-a-friend kiss?* She couldn't wait to find out, but first things first. She had to focus.

Tara gazed into the sea of upperclassmen in the auditorium, feeling only a small bolt of nervousness before plunging ahead. "Welcome to the fifth annual Emerson High School prom-wear fashion show!" she cried, and the audience responded with loud applause. "Today's fine fashions are courtesy of Papillion Boutique located on Main Street in beautiful downtown Selina. At the end of the show, you'll have a chance to win a dress or tuxedo of your choosing, so hold on to your raffle tickets. Now, let's get started!"

The music pulsed, lights flashed, and Nisha and Brian appeared on opposite ends of the stage. Then they both strode to the middle and when they met, Brian offered Nisha his arm. Nisha slid her hand in the crook of his elbow, and the two walked downstage to the beat of the music.

"You can look storybook perfect in this lemon chiffon empire dress with satin bow detailing . . . and even the wartiest frog will seem like a total prince in a double-breasted classic black tux . . ." *If we're doing 'Once Upon a Time' . . . might as well do it one hundred percent,* Tara thought. She hoped Brian wasn't offended by the term "warty frog."

Next Jenny came out in her blue gown and was escorted by Joe from the basketball team. Then Moose lumbered down the catwalk with a cheerleader named Ally who was wearing a swingy silver lamé sheath and four-inch rhinestone sandals.

Tara announced couple after couple, gown after gown. Sweetheart necklines, gowns with straps and without, off-the-shoulder and one-shouldered, high waists and low backs, simple ones, ornate ones, and one puffy red dress that was completely hideous (though she'd never tell Madeline that). . . . Finally, it was time for the last couple to come out.

"Whether your look says fairest of the land or you're in a tux as white as snow, it doesn't matter as long as you rock it like you own the Enchanted Forest."

Which was exactly what Jordan and Nate did. Jordan smiled and waved at the audience in her formfitting black gown. Nate, in his white tails and top hat, met her center stage, did a little spin, and tipped his hat before extending his arm. The audience laughed as Jordan tried to keep up with Nate, who'd chosen to perform a hammy dance toward the edge of the stage rather than simply walk.

Tara leaned closer to the microphone. "Isn't he the most adorable thing you've ever seen?" she said, ad-libbing, which was followed by a sharp glance from Jordan. *Now what did I do wrong?* Tara wondered, then decided that this time she didn't care.

The models did a final circle around the stage then lined up at the edge to take a bow.

"And there you have it, folks," Tara said, ending the show. "Thanks to our models and a big thanks to Madeline from Papillion!"

As the audience applauded, Madeline appeared from the wings waving to the students and holding a large box of tickets.

Tara stepped aside so that Madeline could take the podium.

"Okay, everyone, it's time for the raffle drawing," Madeline said into the microphone. "So take out your tickets and let's see who the winner is!" She dipped her hand into the box. "Are you ready?" she asked, swishing it around the tickets.

"Yeah!" Tara called along with the rest of the senior class and quickly slipped her ticket from a pocket in her dress and checked the number: 098453. She was thrilled to finally know what dress she was wearing to the prom but she'd be even *more* thrilled if she got it for free! Anxiously, she waited for Madeline to call the winner.

"And the winner is . . ." Madeline said as she dramatically whipped a ticket from the box. "0 . . . 9 . . . 8 . . . 4 . . ."

*Oh, my God. I might win!* Tara thought, her heart pumping fast as she gripped her ticket and stared at matching numbers.

". . . 5 . . . 8!" Madeline finished.

Tara's shoulders sagged. Not a winner.

She lost by one number! *Oh, well,* she thought, not too disappointed. *So I'll have to buy my dress. At least I finally know what I want. Plus how many people can say that they're wearing a one-of-a-kind Papillion to the prom?* She searched the audience for a winner but heard a happy squeal sound onstage instead.

"I won! I won!" Jenny cried, her curls bouncing as she held up her ticket and skipped in her blue gown toward Madeline.

*It figures,* Tara thought, rolling her eyes. She stepped up to the mike again. "Well, that concludes the show. Thanks for coming, everybody. See you at the prom!"

The music played as the curtain closed.

"Great job, people!" Tara called backstage, thrilled that the show was such a success, but she had something else on her mind, too. *Now. Where were we?* she thought, searching for Victor through the throng of buzzing models and excited congratulations. She had to find out what had happened just before the show. *Was it a real moment I felt back there? Did Victor feel something too?*

Instead of running into Victor, though, she came across Jenny. Feeling in a team-player mood, Tara decided to thank her for a job well done. "You were awesome out there, Jenny. And congrats on the raffle win."

"Thanks," Jenny said. "It was a fantastic show. I can't believe *you* actually pulled it off but you did. Nice dress, by the way."

Tara blinked. *Was that a compliment* and *an insult?* She gave Jenny a tight smile and decided to keep it moving. She spotted Victor by the doorway to the hall and started to cross toward him. She stopped when she realized he was chatting with Moose and Brian. *I can't ask him if he felt the moment — not in front of those guys. I'll wait until we're alone.* Then Tara noticed Nisha pouring herself a cup of water from the cooler, so she switched course and headed to her friend. Maybe Nisha would tell her what the deal was with Jordan.

"Hey," Tara said and grabbed a cone-shaped cup from the dispenser on the cooler.

"Hey," Nisha replied, sipping her water.

*Okaaaaaay,* this *is uncomfortable,* Tara thought, glancing around. She decided to just go for it. "Nisha, what is going *on* with Jordan?" she blurted out. "It's like she totally hates me all of a sudden."

"This is so hard. I *want* to talk about it, but I promised Jordan that I wouldn't," Nisha said, looking forlorn. "I *will* say that I don't think Jordan's weirdness has to do with you. Not really."

"Then who?" Tara asked.

"Who do you *think*?" Nisha muttered.

*Shane. Who else?* Tara thought. She didn't understand any of this. Why was Jordan making the last few weeks of school weird just because of some guy?

Just then Madeline approached with a few prom gowns slung across her arm. "Tara, would you bag up your gown and give it to Jenny so she can take it home? Be extra careful not to get lipstick on it when you take it off, all right?"

Tara stared at her, her stomach twisting in knots. "Madeline?" she asked slowly. "Why is Jenny taking my dress home?"

"Actually, it's Jenny's dress now," Madeline replied. "She chose it as her raffle prize."

Tara froze, horror washing over her. *No! This can't be happening. This is* my *perfect prom dress, not Jenny's!* "But you *can't* give it to her, Madeline," Tara pleaded. "*I* wanted to wear it to the prom. I was going to buy it."

"Oh, no," Madeline said, biting her lip. "I wish you'd mentioned it to me earlier, Tara, then I wouldn't have promised it to Jenny. I'm sorry but I can't go back on my word now."

*Why not?* Tara thought bitterly, trembling. *I deserve a one-of-a-kind Papillion more than that fashion-disaster does.*

Madeline scanned the wing of the stage.

"Have you seen you friend Jordan?" she asked. "I can't seem find her anywhere and one of the prom chaperones wants to get a closer look at the black gown."

"Jordan?" Tara scoffed and rolled her eyes. "Oh, she probably ran off to make out with her secret boyfriend, Shane, again," she said snidely. She glanced at Nisha, whose jaw was hanging open, shocked, and whose eyes were filled with horror.

"What?" Tara asked. "Madeline doesn't care if Jordan's cheating on her boyfriend."

"But *I* do," an angry boy's voice said from behind her, and Tara suddenly realized why Nisha was so upset. Gulping, she slowly turned to find a red-faced Nate glaring at her, completely livid.

"*Who* . . . is Shane?" he demanded.

*2 weeks, 4 days, 5 hours, and 25 minutes till Prom . . .*

# CHAPTER *Ten*

OMG. The BF wants 2 tlk 2 me ASAP. WHAT did Tara tell him?! Nish, does he know?

Nisha stood in her flowing red-and-gold *lahenga-choli* with matching silk *dupatta* at the Todi Studio for Indian Classical Dance, staring at the screen of her phone as she read and reread the text she'd just received from Jordan.

*I can't respond to it,* she thought, knowing that the storm, which had been brewing between Jordan and Tara for weeks, was about to arrive. *Jordan will find out what*

*Tara accidentally said to Nate soon enough, and then all heck will break loose.*

Seriously.

Nisha also knew that she had to let what was about to come take its course. *What if it gets so nasty that I can't fix it? Forget about having a blast at the prom. There'll be no pre-prom salon visits or picture-taking or even sharing a table at the party.*

Even more frightening to imagine were the scenarios *after* the prom. After graduation. After the summer. After Nisha, Tara, and Jordan all left for separate colleges. *Will they force me to choose between them? How could I? What happens if I can't? Will any of us stay friends?*

"Miss Nisha, I can't hold my foot up here forever!" six-year-old Anjani said, looking so cute in her pretty blue *lahenga* and holding up her skinny leg in its matching *churidar* pants. She was waiting for Nisha to help put on her *ghunghroos.*

"Oops." Nisha smiled at the sight. "I guess I forgot what I was doing," she said, trying to shake off her worries as she tied a band of bronze bells around each of the little girl's ankles.

Anjani hopped to her feet when Nisha had finished. "It's okay. Just as long as it doesn't happen *in there.*" She pointed to the large studio across the hall where friends and family were gathered to watch the Todi students perform.

"That's right," Nisha agreed.

A moment after Anjani had jingled barefooted over to her classmates, Nisha's guru, Gargi Kumar, popped her head into the dressing room. "Nisha, we're ready for the six-year-olds."

Nisha nodded, prepared the girls, and led them into the studio to perform the dance of the fishermen. She tried to concentrate on the girls' *mudras,* or hand gestures, as they went through their routine but her mind kept drifting back to her friends. Several dances later her thoughts wandered to a more pleasant topic: Brian and their anniversary dinner, which was only a few hours away, but even that was tinged by Jordan and Tara's forthcoming blowout.

Assuming that Nisha and Brian actually *made it* to the prom together, which couple would they hang out with? Would they have to spend the entire party ping-ponging between the two girls so that neither would feel slighted, leaving Nisha and Brian absolutely zero time to experience the magic and romance of the night together? That didn't seem exactly fair.

Before long Nisha heard her guru introduce her to the audience. "Last but not least, we have Nisha Khubani performing a technical piece for us."

*I'm on,* Nisha thought as the sound of the flute and sitar filled the studio. Although her mind was still anxious, she smiled as she raised an arm overhead and pranced through the door of the studio. Her *ghunghroos* jangled as she stepped rhythmically on the floorboards, making her dramatic *amad,* or arrival, into the performance area. She spun one, two, three, four, five times before ending with a flourish just as the music halted.

The crowd surrounding her on all sides clapped wildly. Nisha spotted her mother and father sitting on pillows in the third row, smiling proudly and exchanging whispers with Raj and his parents, as the audience prepared for enchantment.

Lowering her gaze, she positioned her red alta-stained fingertips in the *dola mudra* — hands at her hips, palms outward — exposing the large spot left by the vegetable dye she'd used to mark each palm.

The sweet song of the flute entered Nisha's body. *Focus on the hands; the mind will follow,* she thought as the *tabla* drums pulsed out the first rhythm.

Nisha listened carefully to the *bol* then took a deep breath and began the dance. She stomped her bare, alta-outlined feet on the floor, mimicking the beat the musician had set. She lifted her *lahenga* slightly, exposing the 150 jangling bells tied to each ankle at the bottom of her *churidar* pants.

The *tabla*'s rhythm grew slightly faster. Nisha released the skirt and followed the beat by stomping her heels and adding movement of the arms and hands and several spins. She ended with a flirty glance and a smile as if to say, *Is that all you've got?*

Gradually the tempo grew faster and faster, seven, ten, fourteen beats. Nisha felt as though she had the power of *Durga*, the goddess of strength, on her side as she volleyed back and forth with the musicians, reciting their *bols* verbally and then performing them effortlessly with flawless footwork and meaningful hand gestures and facial expressions. She ended her piece with a series of spins, her *lahenga* floating high, like a sea of red-and-gold silk around her waist, as she turned around and around. She ended the piece abruptly with a sudden halt of a spin, one arm reaching to the gods and the other outstretched to the audience, and the music ended.

The crowd burst into applause as Nisha breathed heavily and smiled. She placed her fingertips together and cupped her hands in the *kapota mudra*, as a sign of humility and respect. She bowed her head to the audience, to the musicians, and, of course, to her guru. Then she spun once again and exited the studio feeling exhilarated and rejuvenated — as if she could take on the world!

All the students of the Todi entered the studio once again for a final bow, then circled back to the dressing room to change out of their costumes.

*I'll never stop dancing!* Nisha thought as she switched into a denim mini and a sherbet-colored blouse with cap sleeves. Battling the *tabla* in fourteen-beat *bols* made her feel as though she could handle anything that came her way. The tension between her friends . . . finding a way to attend the prom with Brian . . . Nisha knew she would make it all work out somehow. Not only that, she'd do it with confidence and grace.

Nisha finished dressing, then found her parents, and Raj and his parents, among the crowd outside of the studio.

"Your technique was beautiful," Mrs. Dixit told her, glowing, "your spinning, superb." She turned to Mrs. Khubani. "I'll bet she's good enough to be in an international dance festival."

Nisha blushed. "Thank you," she said. The compliment meant a lot coming from a fellow *Kathaki*.

"How about we all go out to dinner to celebrate?" Mr. Khubani suggested, which made Nisha's heart skip a beat. She couldn't. She had to meet Brian at eight.

"Oh, why don't we let the kids go off on their own?" Nisha's mother piped up. "They're young. They don't want to spend their time with old fogies like us."

Raj coughed and turned pale.

Nisha stared at her mother. "You want me to go out with Raj — alone," she repeated, just to make sure she had heard right.

"Well, we have to cut the apron strings sometime, don't we, Nisha?" she answered lightly, as if this *wasn't* a momentous occasion that should be recorded for the annals of history.

It also meant that Nisha could pretend to feel tired after an hour or so and skip out of the date with Raj to meet Brian.

"Okay," Nisha said, and Mr. Dixit handed Raj the keys to the Saab.

Once they were out of their parents' sight Nisha slipped the lovely charm bracelet that Brian had given her out of her purse and fastened it to her wrist. Why not? Raj wouldn't know it was from her boyfriend anyway.

Raj coughed again when they'd reached the car.

"You okay?" Nisha asked, getting inside. "Because we don't have to go if you're not feeling well." Could she really be this lucky?

"No, I'm fine, thanks. Want to get

some stuffed *paratha*?" Raj asked. "I know this tiny hole in the wall that rolls out a ton of them a day. Any kind you want."

"Ooh, I looooove *paratha*!" Nisha's mouth watered at the thought of eating the unleavened bread filled with curried vegetables or cheeses or meats. "Let's go," she said, but she'd have to remember not to eat too much.

On the drive there, Nisha's mind wandered back to Brian. She wondered if he'd like *paratha* — once she'd explained to him what it was. He wasn't into eating anything too exotic so she wasn't sure if he'd like curried food. Actually, now that she thought about it, it was kind of nice to spend time with someone who already knew what *Kathak* and *paratha* were without the standard explanations.

Nisha glanced at Raj, who was concentrating on the road. He had a strong, Bollywood movie star kind of profile — very handsome and sophisticated, to say the least — and hanging out with him was so easy. For a moment, she imagined what it would be like to date him for real. After all, they grew up in the same culture, liked the same foods, and most of all, he had the stamp of approval from her parents.

*It'd be less stressful, that's for sure, and I guess he's nice enough but . . .*

*But what?*

*He's not Brian,* Nisha thought. *Maybe Raj and I can be friends, but he'd never hold the special place in my heart that Brian does.*

A few minutes later, Raj pulled to a curb and Nisha realized that he wasn't kidding about the *paratha* place being a hole in the wall. The restaurant was so tiny that it could fit only a grill, two people behind the counter, and maybe one or two customers inside — which was why a long line had snaked out onto the sidewalk and down the block. "I guess the place must be good." She surveyed the people, wondering if the food was really delicious enough to wait that long.

"It is," Raj said, coughing again. This time he groaned a little and rested his head in his left hand.

*He doesn't look so hot,* Nisha thought. "Raj, you know, I won't be mad if you want to go home and get some rest," she said. "You seem like you're getting sick. We can always do this another time. It's no problem. Really." *Plus I can get out of here sooner than expected.*

Raj turned his head and looked at her with glassy eyes. "Are you sure?" he asked. "Our parents are out, and I feel bad leaving you alone."

"Oh, don't worry about me," Nisha said, with a casual wave of her hand. *I won't be alone,* she thought. *I'll be with my boyfriend!*

"Are you sure you're not peeking?" Brian asked Nisha later that night.

Blindfolded, Nisha clutched Brian's arm as he led her down a path. "I'm sure. Are we almost there?" she asked, walking gingerly with no idea where they were headed.

After Raj had dropped Nisha at home, Nisha had quickly wrapped Brian's anniversary gift, freshened up, and rushed to meet him at his house. She found Brian waiting for her on his porch and looking so sweet in his tan cotton pants and a blue button-down, which strayed slightly from his usual uniform of jeans and a plain tee. Then, after getting into his car, Brian had asked her to wear a blindfold to make their destination date a surprise. Now she was dying to find out where they were!

"You ready?" Brian gently slipped the blindfold off of Nisha's eyes to reveal . . .

*His backyard?* Nisha thought. It certainly looked like his backyard, only different.

Brian had constructed a large white tentlike gazebo in the center of the lawn, the inside decorated with leafy green plants, making the place look like a tropical paradise. A table was set beautifully with a crisp white cloth, candles, wine glasses, and two plates with metal lids on top, keeping whatever food inside warm. Next to one of the plates was an enormous bouquet of long-stemmed red roses wrapped with pretty paper and a curly pink bow. Soft, romantic music played from an iPod station set up by the table.

*He did this all for me?* Nisha thought, her heart bursting with happiness.

"I hope you're not too disappointed about dinner being here," Brian said. "I couldn't get us another reservation at the Coral Café, so I tried to make it seem like an adventure with the blindfold *and* . . ." He led Nisha around the inground swimming pool dotted with pink-and-white water lilies and into the gazebo. ". . . I got us the next-best thing. Takeout." He pulled off a plate's lid to reveal the café's famous pineapple-glazed chicken — the meal they'd shared on their very first date.

Nisha was speechless.

"Me? Disappointed?" she finally said. "Brian, how could I be? This is so . . . dreamy!" And so was her boyfriend. She wrapped her arms around his neck and kissed him again and again. "You're the best boyfriend ever," she said. "I love it!"

Brian smiled and hugged her tightly. "Good," he said, and swayed her to the music.

Nisha closed her eyes, breathing in his fresh soapy scent as they barely danced. She wished that she'd had the nerve to tell him how she really felt. That she loved being in his arms, and kissing him, and hanging out, and talking, and dancing. . . . She wanted to tell him how sweet and thoughtful he was and that he was funny and cute. But most of all Nisha wanted to say . . .

*I love you, Brian.*

But something was holding her back. She sensed that he loved her, too. So why was she so afraid to say it first?

Brian stopped dancing and Nisha looked up into his serious face. "Nisha, I really have to tell you something," he began. "Something that I've been wanting to say for a long time. . . ."

"What is it?" Nisha asked, her heart

pounding. Would he be the one to say it first? Right here, right now?

Brian reached around his neck and slid Nisha's hands down so that he was holding them in front of her. "Nisha, I . . ." He looked at her wrist and stopped. "How come you're not wearing the bracelet I gave you?" he asked her.

"What do you mean?" Nisha spotted her bare wrist and gasped. "Oh, no. The clasp. I bet it came loose again!" she cried, trying desperately to remember the last time she saw it on her wrist.

When she did it was no consolation.

*It must have fallen off in Raj's car,* Nisha realized. *And if he finds it, he'll read the inscription and know that I have a boyfriend.*

But that wasn't the worst part.

The worst part was, he'd tell her parents.

*2 weeks, 3 days, 3 hours, and 57 minutes till Prom . . .*

# CHAPTER *Eleven*

Jordan stood on the porch of Nate's house trying to come up with an excuse, an explanation, *something* that she could say to make this easier, but she couldn't. All she kept thinking was, *I didn't mean for it to happen this way.*

Which was the truth.

Jordan hadn't mean to fall for Shane in the first place, but she did. She also didn't mean for Nate to find out about it through someone else, but *he* had.

*Maybe it's better this way,* Jordan thought. *At least I don't have to agonize over how to tell Nate about Shane.* Drawing in a deep breath, she prepared herself for the yelling and all the awful names that Nate would surely call her. *You just have to get it over with. Let him get it all out and then go,* she told herself, then rang the doorbell.

Nate's mother opened the door. "Oh, hi, Jordan! Come on in," she said, smiling and ushering her inside. "Nate's in his room. Go on up."

*She has no clue,* Jordan realized as she passed through the living room, heading for the stairs. *Mrs. Lombardo wouldn't be so nice to me if she knew that I broke her son's heart.* She climbed the steps slowly, pausing to gaze at the wall-o'-sports, as Nate called it, pictures chronicling the athletic achievements of Nate and his three older brothers. Basketball, baseball, football, soccer, swimming, lacrosse . . . from the time they were tots, the Lombardo brothers had managed to excel in almost every activity imaginable.

Even Jordan had managed to make it onto the wall in a candid shot taken by

Nate's father during junior year. Jordan was in her cheerleader uniform hugging a toothy Nate after he'd just made a touchdown. She doubted that picture would be up for much longer. *A year and a half,* she thought sadly. *Over.*

Nate's room was to the right of the stairs. When she reached the door she could hear the low volume of the television playing. She hesitated, then knocked, not quite ready for what was about to happen. Nate didn't respond, so she cautiously pushed open the door to find him lying on his plaid bedspread and flipping channels with the remote. "Hey," she said, entering.

Nate stayed silent, his gaze on the television, his jaw clenched.

Jordan crossed over to him and sat on the edge of the bed. "Nate," she said, touching his arm. Nate glanced at his arm then stared coldly into her eyes, and Jordan knew to remove her hand.

"Who is he?" he asked, turning back to the television.

"A boy I met," Jordan replied. "You don't know him."

"Then it's true." He said it as if they were talking about two people they didn't know.

"What's true?" Jordan asked. "What did Tara tell you?"

"Nothing," Nate replied calmly. "Anyway, this isn't about Tara. You're the one who's messing around with someone behind my back. Right?" He didn't raise his voice, didn't even look at her.

Jordan nodded as tears pushed their way to the edge of her lower lids. "I'm sorry," she whispered. "I didn't mean for it to happen this way," she added, but it came off sounding lame rather than heartfelt.

"Don't be," Nate told her. "We both knew that this would happen eventually. It just happened a little sooner than I'd planned, but it's okay. I'll get over it."

*Planned?* Jordan was stunned. "Are you serious?" she asked. "You had a plan?" She couldn't tell if he'd really had one or if he was saying it just to hurt her.

This time Nate looked at her. "Jordan. You didn't really think we'd be together after the summer. In *college*?" he asked.

*Well . . . yes. Before Shane, I did.* She searched his eyes, which were still beautiful, still brown, but different. Distant. He seemed almost . . . bored. *I can't believe he's not upset,* she thought. Jordan wasn't sure why that hurt her so much. Did she secretly hope to find him a blubbering mess or tearing his hair out in grief over their breakup?

Maybe.

Jordan's tears finally spilled over and she lowered her head as she swiped them quickly with her fingers. Staring at her lap, she took a deep breath preparing for Nate's impending barrage of questions. It would be tough to tell him about Shane, but he deserved to know the truth.

Silence.

Jordan glanced back at Nate, who was now staring at the television again. If she didn't know better, she'd think he was giving her the signal to leave.

*Why isn't he asking me anything?* she wondered after a few minutes. If the situation were reversed she'd want to know everything — and she'd expect Nate to tell her. Where they'd met . . . if there was an instant connection of if the relationship had started from a friendship. . . . Most of all, she'd want to know when, exactly, Nate decided he liked the new girl better than he liked her. Jordan knew she'd feel awful hearing all the painful details, but she'd go crazy with wonder if she didn't.

"Shane and I . . . we, um, met in line at the old indie theater downtown. You know, that day we were supposed see that movie, *Vert et Vrai*, together," she offered.

Nate responded with a cold glare. "Are you saying that it's *my* fault you cheated? Because I didn't go to a movie with you?"

"No — that's not it," Jordan said quickly. "I feel horrible about it and —"

"Oh, *I* get it." Nate cut in. "You're trying to make yourself feel better by sharing all the gory details." He nodded and turned his attention back to the television.

"No — it's not like that," Jordan began to explain, but then stopped herself. Clearly, Nate had no interest in hearing about Shane. So what was the point?

And what was left to say?

"Nate, you were my first serious boyfriend," Jordan told him. "You'll always have a special place in my heart. You know that right?" It sounded totally cheesy, but it was true.

"Yup," Nate replied. "Your stuff is over there." He pointed to a box of all the things she'd ever given him that was sitting on the edge of his desk.

"My stuff?" Jordan stared at the box. Clothes, pictures, notes, a little stuffed bear in a football uniform. He'd saved all of it and now it was junk? Jordan couldn't process any of this. "Do you want all your stuff back too?" Her hand immediately went to the tiny diamond pendant necklace she was wearing, which Nate had given her last Christmas. She *loved* that necklace.

Nate eyed it too. "Nah. Keep it. Or trash it. Do whatever you want. It doesn't matter." He hopped off the bed to hand her the box. "Well . . . bye," he said, then flopped back onto his bed and grabbed the remote.

Jordan watched him flip through the channels as if she were already gone. *That's it?* she thought. *A year and a half together and that's all he's going to say? It's like he doesn't even care.* Which made her wonder if he ever really did.

Nate may not have cared that they had broken up, but on Monday morning, Jordan found out that the rest of Emerson High School did.

A lot.

Holding her books close to her chest, Jordan tried to keep her chin up as she marched though the student parking lot and entered the school's courtyard. She crossed the path to the front doors, catching bits and pieces of gossipy whispers and stares.

"Oh, my God" . . . "Nate" . . . "she cheated" . . . "dumped before prom" . . . "thinks she's too good . . ."

*Do they think I can't hear them?* Jordan wondered, barely holding back a flood of tears. *No crying at school,* she vowed, though she wasn't sure she'd make it through the day without breaking down. *Why won't they stop looking at me?*

Finally she saw some friendly faces, Ally, Brie, and C.J. from the cheerleading squad, hanging out in a tight circle by the double doors to the school. Jordan quickened her pace but stopped short when she spotted Nate walking toward them from the opposite direction. He greeted the cheerleaders with a slight wave and stopped to chat — probably about the breakup, Jordan assumed, since the girls seemed to be intensely focused on what Nate was saying. What was he telling them? Ally shook her head and looked to the sky, then C.J. gave him a sympathetic pat on the back.

*Are they taking his side?* Jordan watched the girls and Nate enter the school together, her heart aching. She wasn't sure she had the nerve to even ask them — or if she'd have any friends left by the end of the day. *Maybe I'll just skip school today.* She wanted to skip the rest of the year, but one day would have to do. She spun around and was hurrying back down the path toward the parking lot when she spotted Mr. Davidson, her photography teacher, headed her way. *Oh, great,* she thought. *Just what I need. He's going to ask me about my project.*

"Ms. Taylor, the school is *that* way," Mr. Davidson said, pointing toward the building located in the opposite direction.

"I know. I just forgot something in my car," Jordan replied, hoping he'd buy it.

"Well unless it's your *photography project,* I suggest you leave it there. You're going to be late for homeroom," Mr. Davidson said. "You know, you need to hand in your new introspective before the grading period is over," he reminded her. "You don't want me to give you a D, Jordan. Colleges *do* look over your final grades — even if you've already been accepted."

"Right." Jordan nodded. "I'm working on it," she told him. "Well, gotta go. Don't want to be late." She turned and practically ran into the building, only to find Tara and Victor handing out flyers in front of the auditorium.

"Tara, for prom queen!" Tara called, delivering hot pink papers into the hands of the crowd passing through the hall. "Queen Tara!"

Fuming at the sight, Jordan rolled her eyes. *Great. First Nate, then Mr. Davidson. Now Tara. Anybody else I don't want to see going to jump out in front of me?* She tried to pass by unnoticed, but then heard Tara call her name.

"Jordan. Wait." Tara shoved her flyers into Victor's hands and jogged to catch up with Jordan.

Jordan looked back but kept walking. "I really don't want to do this right now, Tara. Not in front of the whole school."

"Jordan, it was an accident!" Tara cried.

Jordan stopped in front of the first floor girls' room. "It wasn't an accident," she snapped. "You made it very clear that you don't like me seeing Shane. I'll bet you said that stuff about him just *hoping* that Nate would find out. Well, he did. Happy now?"

"No." Tara said. "Jordan, I'm sorry. Please. You have to let me explain."

Jordan sighed. "Fine. In here." She pushed open the door. "Out," she told the three sophomore girls who were crowded around the mirror, applying makeup. As the girls collected their stuff and scurried through the doorway, Jordan checked the stalls, which were empty. She turned to Tara. "Okay, go," she said.

"Jordan, I didn't mean it," Tara told her. "It just stupidly came out of my mouth. But

I never would have said it if I thought Nate would hear it. I swear!"

"You shouldn't have even *said* it in the first place," Jordan told her, hands trembling with anger.

"I knew I shouldn't —" Tara admitted. "But there's this weirdness between us, and I guess I was upset over that. And then Jenny won the raffle and took the dress that *I* wanted to wear to the prom . . . so when the first opportunity to say something snarky came up, I totally grabbed it. And I said something mean and it was wrong and I'm sorry. *Really sorry,* Jordan. Please don't hate me. You have to forgive me. You have to talk to me, Jordan. We don't talk anymore. Say something. *Please.*"

Jordan wanted to say something. As she watched her friend, close to tears, pouring her heart out, she wanted to say that she was mad but she didn't hate Tara. That maybe the way Nate found out about the truth wasn't all Tara's fault. And maybe Jordan didn't talk to Tara about Shane because she was afraid that Tara might think less of her — wasn't Tara the one outraged over this whole thing in the first place? — and Jordan couldn't bear that. Because they were best friends and a best friend's opinion meant a lot. More than a parent's or teacher's or boyfriend's. . . . A best friend's opinion was sacred.

But the only words Jordan could get past the sticky lump in her throat were, "I miss you."

"Me, too!" Tara cried and hugged her friend.

Jordan hugged her back, relieved that the silent war was over. Things may have ended badly with Nate, but her friendship with Tara would eventually heal. Tara hadn't tried to hurt her on purpose. Jordan knew that now.

"So are you okay?" Tara asked when they had parted. "Do you think that maybe you and Nate can be friends at some point?"

Jordan thought back to her icy conversation with Nate in his room on Saturday. "It's over. Everything. That includes friendship." A familiar ache began to creep into her chest and her eyes welled up again. *Don't cry,* she scolded herself. *He barely cared when you broke up with him. Who needs a friend like that? And don't forget — you have Shane.*

Tara leaned against a sink. "Whoa," she said shaking her head. "That's so awful. I'd die if I couldn't talk to him."

Something in the way she said it pricked the hairs at the back of Jordan's neck. "Why? What do you care? He wasn't *your* boyfriend," she said.

"I *know* that," Tara said, her cheeks growing pink. "What I meant to say was that *if* he were my boyfriend I'd die. But he's not. I mean, you guys have been through so much together. It's such a shame."

Jordan watched as her friend shifted her satchel over to one shoulder then decided to put it back on the other. *Why is Tara so nervous all of a sudden?* she wondered, then decided to ask a question.

*"Tara?"* Jordan began. "You don't . . . *want* Nate to be your boyfriend, do you?"

"Jordan, no! Oh, my God, I can't believe you just asked me that!" Tara cried, but she was looking at the sink instead of Jordan. "Of *course* not. I'd *never*," she added. "I mean, I won't even talk to him if you don't want me to, though that'll be a little tough because we're in a couple of the same classes." She lifted her gaze off the sink. "Should we go? I think we might miss homeroom."

"Sure," Jordan said, her mind whirring. *Does Tara have a crush on Nate?* Now that Jordan thought about it, it kind of made sense. There were some signs. Like how she laughed extra loud whenever Nate told a joke. And how Tara would always find a reason to touch Nate when she talked to him. And she never missed a chance to tell Jordan — or the entire senior class — how adorable Nate was. Jordan had thought Tara was only being friendly, but maybe it was more than that. Combine those things with the major outrage over Shane and the cruel comments about him . . .

But even if Tara *did* have a crush on Nate, Jordan could never believe that Tara would try to break up the relationship on purpose. No way. Tara's slip of the tongue on Friday really *was* an accident just like she said it was.

Wasn't it?

*2 weeks, 2 days, 5 hours, and 13 minutes till Prom . . .*

# CHAPTER *Twelve*

**The Mission**

***(should you choose to accept it . . . and you should!)***

1) ***Talk to Nate***
2) ***Talk about Jordan***
3) ***Fix things between them***

"What do you mean, you want *me* to lead the meeting?" Jenny said to Tara outside of prom committee headquarters after school.

"Just do it, Jenny, okay?" Tara replied. "I have something really urgent to take care of." She could hardly believe it herself, but *for once* something in her life was more important than dresses and fashion shows and prom. She turned and headed purposefully down the hall to the double doors that led to the courtyard — to where Nate had agreed to meet with her.

Tara was thankful that she and Jordan had finally said their pieces in the bathroom this morning, but there was one part of the conversation that would not leave her head. *Maybe Jordan's right,* she thought. *Maybe deep down,* I did *make that comment about Shane hoping that Nate would hear it.*

Tara would never admit it out loud, but she'd always been kind of jealous of Jordan and Nate's relationship. What did Jordan have that Tara didn't? Why did she get all the great guys . . . and Tara didn't? Well, except for Victor, but that was beside the point. Now that Jordan and Nate were over, Tara felt completely awful about it. Maybe if she had kept quiet about Shane, Jordan could have ended things with Nate on a better note. Now the two of them weren't even friends, and Tara felt partly responsible for that.

Which was why she had to do something to make things right again.

Tara found Nate lying in the grass, resting his head on his backpack at the far end of the courtyard, and she went over to join him. "Hey," she said, sitting next to him. "Thanks for meeting me."

"What's up?" Nate asked.

"I just wanted to talk to you about what you heard at the fashion show on Friday," Tara replied, picking nervously at the grass. "I know it may have sounded like Jordan was seeing some guy named Shane, but I was really talking about *me.* So you probably shouldn't be so mad at her."

Nate rolled his eyes. "That was weak, Tara. Did Jordan put you up to this?"

"No! Of course not," she said. "And it's not weak." *Okay, it is, but it's all I've got.*

"Right," Nate replied. "Well you can tell Jordan — or not — that I meant what I said about wanting to dump her after the summer. So I don't care if she cheated or not. The way I see it, she did me a favor."

"You don't *care* if your girlfriend *cheated* on you?" Tara asked, examining his face. "Now who's being weak?"

"Whatever you say, Tara." Nate sat up, stretched and yawned.

"Look. I'm not buying the I'm-too-cool-for-this routine," Tara told him. "You and Jordan were great together. I watched you. And I *know* for a *fact* that you were *not* planning to break up with her. You were voted 'Most Likely to Live Happily Ever After,' for God's sake."

Nate looked away. "Yeah. Whatever. That was a long time ago," he said softly.

"It was last month!" Tara replied. "You still love her, don't you?" she added, but he didn't answer. "Nate, if you love her, you shouldn't roll over like a hurt little puppy. Fight for her!"

"Why?" Nate shook his head. "She made me feel like a loser, Tara. I had no clue she was hanging out with another guy. I don't feel like fighting, okay?" He grabbed his backpack and rose, getting ready to leave.

Tara stood, too. "I think you're making a mistake," she said. "I haven't met the guy, but I bet he's nothing compared to you. Maybe she just needs a little time to get her head together."

"Thanks, Tara," Nate said, taking her hand. "But if Jordan really wanted to be with me, she'd be begging to get back with me herself. She wouldn't have sent you." He leaned over and gave Tara a soft kiss on the cheek. "You're a good friend," he told her then headed for the parking lot.

*If I'm such a good friend,* Tara thought, *why do I feel like I totally messed up?* She touched the cheek where Nate had just kissed her. It was funny. Tara had had the occasional daydream about Nate kissing her. Now that she finally knew what it felt like, she didn't care.

Filled with the sudden urge to talk to Victor, Tara turned back toward the school building. Then she noticed two girls on the pathway staring at her, jaws dropped.

Jordan and Nisha. *Did they just see Nate kiss me?* "I can see how that might not look so good," Tara said, chuckling as she crossed the grass toward them. "But it's *so* not what it seems."

Jordan turned to Nisha. "It never is with her, is it? Guess I was right about the crush," she said, then glared at Tara. "Gee, Tara, you sure don't waste any time."

"No, it wasn't like that, Jordan," Tara explained, panic rising in her. "We were talking and he told me —"

"Was that before or after you tricked him into kissing you?" Jordan asked snidely. "Come on, Nisha. Let's go."

"Wait," Nisha said. "Maybe there's a perfectly good explanation."

"Nisha! I can't believe you're taking *her* side on this," Jordan said. "I just broke up with my boyfriend and she already has her claws into him. It's so pathetic."

"I'm not taking —" Nisha began.

*Oh, no she didn't,* Tara thought. *"Pathetic?"* she interrupted Nisha, glaring at Jordan. "The cheater who thinks she's too good to have only *one* boyfriend is calling *me* pathetic? Hmm. That's interesting," she said. "Here I was trying to save your friendship with Nate, and this is the thanks I get? Nisha, do you seriously want to hang out with a lowlife like that over me?"

"No, I —"

"Were you trying to save the friendship before or after you begged Nate to kiss you?" Jordan asked angrily. "I'm out of here." She began to stalk away, then turned. "Nisha, are you coming?"

"No, she's not," Tara replied for her, then waved at Jordan. "Buh-bye."

"Stop it!" Nisha shouted. "I can't take it anymore!" She looked between Jordan and Tara. "You guys are ridiculous. I am *not* choosing between you. So just leave me out of it! I'm taking the bus home."

Tara watched her friend storm across the courtyard and out the front gate. Nisha did have a point, but Tara wasn't about to apologize to Jordan when she had done nothing wrong.

Jordan stared at her with her arms folded across her chest.

"What?" Tara asked.

"You know, I feel sorry for Victor," Jordan said, shaking her head. "He let you give him a makeover and he puts up with your crazy moods because he *likes* you, Tara. Who knows why, since you haven't been very nice to him. And now you're going to dump him for Nate. Nice."

"I am not," Tara said. "I like Victor, too! A lot!" *And you'd know that if you weren't so self-absorbed in your little drama.*

"Right, uh-huh," Jordan said. "I *know* you, Tara. You like to set goals and Nate's been on your list for a *long* time. Well, if you want my leftovers, go for it," she added. "Poor Victor." She turned to leave, her perfect blond hair swinging.

"Poor Victor? You have no clue about me and Victor," Tara said through gritted teeth, seething as she watched Jordan stalk down the path looking all high-and-mighty. Who did Jordan Taylor think she was? Just because she was a cheerleader did not mean she had the right to walk all over Tara. *She's not better than me,* Tara thought. *If anything, I'm better than her!* "At least I'm not a two-faced witch who cheated on her boyfriend!" *Oops.*

Jordan halted mid-stride and glared over her shoulder. "By the way, Tara, if you think for *one second* that a *two-faced witch* like me is going to let you win prom queen after this . . . you are *sooo* wrong."

"*Let* me win?" Tara asked. "Oh, it's on. I don't need you to *let* me win anything! I'll win on my own. And it'll be a landslide!"

"Fine. Bring it," Jordan said. "And consider this friendship officially over!"

*I already do,* Tara thought.

*2 weeks, 23 hours, and 56 minutes till Prom . . .*

# CHAPTER *Thirteen*

On Tuesday evening, Nisha anxiously paced the halls of the Todi Studio for Indian Classical Dance as she waited for Raj to arrive. He had called her yesterday about the charm bracelet, which he'd found underneath the passenger seat of his mother's Saab. Nisha had asked him to meet her at the studio to return it.

Nisha tiptoed into the dance space, flicking on the lights to reveal the mirrored studio. She slipped off her flats and left them by the door, walking barefoot to the center of the room. The *alta* from the recital last Saturday still faintly stained her hands and feet. Instead of her beautiful silk *lahenga*, though, she was wearing jeans and a brown short-sleeved blouse with cream-colored polka dots, which in a weird way sort of matched the spots on her palms.

She stared at herself in the mirror as she considered the complications of her existence of late.

*How did things get so messed up?*

Only a few short weeks ago, she, Jordan, and Tara were excited and happy, shopping for dresses together, planning hairstyles, gossiping about dates and limos and going to the prom. Now the three of them were torn apart. Over what? A boy? A misunderstanding? Maybe it was more than that. But what could she do?

Nisha bent her knees and lifted her left leg at an angle, pointing her toes and longing to hear the sound of her *ghunghroos*. She lowered her leg then spun silently on her heels, forming the shape of a soaring bird with her hands as she gazed upward. She wished she could fly away right now. Fly back to a place where life was simpler. Or at least back to Saturday — to when her performance had left her feeling so confident. Before Jordan and Tara began this silly prom-queen war. And before Nisha realized she'd left her heart-shaped charm bracelet in Mrs. Dixit's car. She couldn't bring herself to return any of Brian's calls until she got it back.

"Nisha?"

She turned, heart jumping with anxiety, to view Raj's tall, lanky frame leaning in the doorway of the studio. She took a deep breath as he entered, bracing herself for a critical speech on the evils of dating.

Raj entered the studio, his wavy hair dripping loose ringlets onto his forehead. When he reached Nisha, he pulled out her bracelet from the pocket of his chinos. "I think this is yours?" he asked with a smile.

Nisha accepted the bracelet, which, she saw, now had a broken clasp. "Thanks," she said, slipping it into the pocket of her jeans and feeling increasingly uncomfortable under Raj's self-righteous gaze.

"So, you have a boyfriend," Raj said, knowingly.

But would he tell her parents? Nisha couldn't risk anything.

"What gives you that idea?" she said, feeling her hands quiver. "I mean, I do have a boy who's a friend, but he's not my boyfriend or anything. I don't date, remember?" Then Nisha felt too awful denying it. "Wait. That's a lie," she said, looking Raj in the eye. "I *do* have a boyfriend. His name is Brian. And we're in love. And I don't care if you think it's *real* love or fake love or whatever. I know what it is. I love him."

If only she could say those words to Brian!

Raj kept eyeing her. "Oh, well . . . I guess I see you in a whole different light," he said with that smug grin still on his face, which was really beginning to irritate her.

Nisha didn't care how he saw her anymore, so there was no sense in keeping up the charade. "Did you tell your parents I'm seeing someone?" she asked plainly.

"No," Raj replied.

Nisha rolled her eyes. "Are you *going* to?" she asked him.

Raj took his time answering. He smug grin turned into a smile, which turned into a chuckle, which turned into a full-blown deep-bellied guffaw. At her!

"I don't know what so funny about that question," she snapped, folding her arms across her chest.

"No . . . I'm sorry. It's not funny. I'm not laughing anymore," he said, trying to stop and covering his mouth with a hand. When he did, Nisha noticed a flicker of red peek out from underneath his right rolled-up sleeve.

"Is that a tattoo?" Nisha asked, reaching for his arm.

"What? No," Raj said, pulling away. "I don't have a tattoo. Why do you think I have a tattoo?"

Nisha squinted at the boy, who seemed

rather nervous for someone who didn't have a tattoo. "Oh, I don't know," she told him. "Maybe it because you're always wearing long-sleeved shirts when it's, like, two hundred degrees outside?" She quickly grabbed hold of his right sleeve and pushed it up to reveal . . .

. . . a red rose with the name Pallavi written elegantly down the stem.

"Nice," Nisha commented. "Who's Pallavi? Your *girlfriend* perhaps?"

Raj nodded sheepishly. "She lives in Paris. We go to the same school. My parents don't know about her yet."

"Really? But what about all that arranged marriage stuff you said?" Nisha teased him. "Making a commitment to one person, not promises to many?"

"That's the line my father is always giving me. I couldn't tell if you were following tradition or not, so I threw it out there to see what you'd say," Raj explained, looking sincere. "You agreed with it, so I knew I couldn't risk letting you know about Pallavi. I plan on telling my parents, but not until after graduation, when we're ready to get married."

Nisha thought back to her pseudo-date with Raj and smirked. "You weren't by any chance faking being sick on Saturday, were you?" *I guess it's the universal bad excuse to get out of a date . . . and I bought it!*

Raj coughed and held his head. "Ohhh . . . I don't feel soooo gooooood," he moaned.

"Wow. You're good," Nisha said. "You even got me to suggest we end the date. Really good." She laughed at the irony of it all. "Thanks for returning my bracelet. I guess I have to be nice to you from now on," she added. "Since you can totally blackmail me."

"And vice versa," he added with another chuckle.

Nisha sighed, feeling enormously relieved. Now that there was no chance of her parents — or Raj's parents — finding out about Brian she could concentrate on getting to the prom with her *real* boyfriend. "Thanks again, Raj," she said, and, impulsively, leaned over to give him a friendly hug.

That was when she noticed Brian standing in the doorway of the studio. Nisha instantly jerked away from Raj.

"When you didn't return my call, I figured you'd be here," Brian told Nisha coolly, then gave Raj an unfriendly once-over. "Who's this?"

"This is Raj," Nisha said, striding over to take Brian's hand so that he wouldn't get the wrong idea. "Come in. I want you to meet him."

The two boys nodded at each other, and Nisha began to tell the funny story about their traditional parents and how they'd arranged for Raj to take her to the prom, not knowing that Raj and Nisha both had secret dating lives. "Raj and I just found out about it now," Nisha explained to Brian, still feeling nervous — though she wasn't sure why. "But everything is cool. We can totally go to the prom together and my mom and dad will never know. Right, Raj?"

Raj held up a hand, his expression solemn. "Your secret is safe with me."

"So it all works out!" Nisha said, turning to Brian. "Isn't that awesome?"

Brian surveyed Nisha's face, then Raj's, and then said, "No, Nisha. It's *not* awesome."

*Oh . . . no,* Nisha thought.

Brian gave Raj a look that said *get lost,* and Raj mumbled a brief good-bye, hurrying out of the studio.

Nisha watched him make a quick exit. *Maybe Brian's mad about Raj,* she thought. *I guess I don't blame him.* Nisha took his hands and looked him seriously in his blue eyes. "There's *nothing* going on between me and Raj, Brian. You can trust me on that one."

"Trust you?" Brian dropped her hands and stepped away from her. "You don't get it, Nisha, do you?"

She shook her head, frightened for what was coming.

"All this time you've been lying to me," Brian said, running a hand through his short blond hair. "All this time you've been making excuses when you had to be with Raj and making more excuses so that I couldn't meet your parents. . . . Did you really think I didn't know you were lying to me?" he demanded, his eyes full of pain.

"But I *had* to lie, Brian," Nisha pleaded. "I *want* to tell my parents — and I will — but I need more time. I can't do it now with the prom so close. I'm afraid that they'll get upset and they won't let me go to the prom at *all*."

But Brian wasn't listening. "I thought if I just gave you enough space, you'd find a way to bring our relationship out in the open," he went on, shaking his head. "But now I know that it's *never* going to happen. . . ."

"So now what?" Nisha asked him, her whole body trembling. "What are you saying?"

"I'm saying that you either tell your parents that we're going to the prom together . . . or we're *not* going together."

***1 week, 6 days, 23 hours, and 39 minutes till Prom . . .***

# CHAPTER *Fourteen*

"So you've got Apollo rethinking his entire existence. He even downloaded a few Shakira songs off iTunes," Shane said to Jordan as they hiked through the grand meadow of Rocky Point Park. "And *paid* for them."

"No, he did *not*!" Jordan said, surprised, as she snapped a picture of the pond in the distance, framed by a gathering of trees on either side.

"Okay, no, but wouldn't it be interesting if he did?" Shane joked. His hand brushed Jordan's slightly, sending a rush of tingles up her arm, and instinctively they laced their fingers together.

Jordan smiled up at him, noticing how the late evening sun cast an orangey hue over his pale angular face and how Shane's dark intense eyes seemed to brighten as he smiled back at her. At the last moment, Jordan had decided to take some photos of the park at sunset, and she was glad for the company.

Jordan had told herself that she was going to finish her photography project once and for all, but underneath that she was really trying to get her mind off Tara, Nisha, and Nate.

*I feel so betrayed,* she thought as yesterday's awful scene came rushing back at her — of Nate holding Tara's hand and kissing her in the Emerson High School courtyard. It was only a peck on the cheek, yes, but Jordan knew what Tara was doing. Jordan had had a feeling for a while now that Tara had had a crush on Nate, and now she was trying to get him to like her back. Maybe she'd succeed.

The funny thing was that now that she

and Nate were broken up, Jordan felt a sense of relief. She wanted to see where this thing with Shane was going, and she didn't want Nate back.

But the fact that Tara had told Nate about Shane in the first place, then was hitting on Nate only days after Jordan had ended it with him — only *hours* after Tara had said she'd never do something like that — was killing Jordan inside. *We were supposed to be best friends. And now she's jumping into my shoes so quickly?*

And then there was the serious drama about the prom queen. Jordan hadn't really cared about Tara being in the running, but now that Tara had stabbed her in the back, and tried to steal Nate, she couldn't *possibly* let her take away the prom queen title, too, could she?

Maybe not, but Jordan didn't have to do what she did right *after* her argument with Tara. Or rather, she *shouldn't* have.

Her stomach twisted remembering how

she'd marched from the courtyard into the student parking lot, angry and upset. As soon as Jordan had spotted Victor by his orange car, she knew just what she could do to hurt Tara right back — give her a taste of what it felt like to be betrayed by a best friend.

So she went over to Victor, made a little small talk at first, then told Victor that she saw Nate and Tara kissing in the courtyard. It wasn't exactly a lie, but Jordan knew it wasn't the whole truth either.

And the hurt look in Victor's eyes was enough to make her wish that she'd never done it. He didn't say much after that — just got into his car and drove away — and Jordan had no idea if he'd talked to Tara or not, since she hadn't spoken to either Tara or Nisha since yesterday.

*Did Nisha find out what I did? Is she mad at me, too?* Jordan wondered. This whole thing was way out of hand, but there was nothing Jordan could do to fix it. And why should she be the one to take the first step anyway? It was Tara who'd started all the hostility, not the other way around.

"Jordan?" Shane asked her. "You okay? You're so quiet. What are you thinking about?"

Jordan shrugged and sighed. "Friends," she said, "or lack thereof. Everything sort of blew up when I broke up with Nate."

"Oh." Shane nodded. He was quiet for a moment then said, "I can't say that I'm sorry you broke up with Nate," he told her. "But I *am* sorry about your friends. I'm sure they'll come around eventually."

Jordan wasn't as confident about that as Shane was.

"So . . . does this mean that I'll be renting a tux for the Emerson prom?" he asked her, and for the first time Jordan had to stop and consider the answer.

The prom was about celebrating the last moments of high school with your friends. That was what Jordan had so passionately told Shane's buddies, Apollo and Gavin.

*But what happens if you don't have friends anymore?* she wondered. *What's the point of celebrating alone?*

*There is no point,* Jordan realized. *Not really. So why should I bother going to the prom?*

Take a sneak peek at the

final book in the

***ONCE UPON A PROM***

trilogy in:

Tara Macmillan stifled a yawn, hoping her concealer was still working its magic on the dark circles beneath her chestnut-colored eyes. She was passing out "Queen Tara" buttons to her fellow Emerson High School classmates outside the auditorium before homeroom. She smiled and encouraged everyone to "Vote Tara" for prom queen, but she feared that her lack of pep was showing through.

She'd spent the last two nights not even coming *close* to the eight hours of recommended shuteye. At least the insomnia wasn't a total waste. Instead of aimlessly counting sheep, Tara spent the wee hours of the morning creating her online prom presence by: 1) updating her MySpace and Facebook accounts to include her campaign agenda, 2) adding links to a newly created website dedicated solely to promoting Tara's prom queen-iness to the world, and 3) recording a video blog, stating what prom queen means to her and posting it to the Student Shout Out page of the school's website.

But the real reason for Tara's sleeplessness was that she was feeling horribly guilty for calling her best friend, Jordan Taylor, a two-faced witch.

Tara knew she'd said it only in anger. How could Jordan believe that Tara would come onto Nate, Jordan's ex? Okay, maybe Tara had had a *slight* crush on the boy — and maybe she'd been a *tiny* bit jealous of her friend's relationship with him — but the truth was that last Monday Jordan caught Tara trying to *mend* Nate and Jordan's relationship.

It wasn't *Tara's* fault if Nate had given her an appreciative peck on the cheek right after he'd said that he wanted nothing to do with Jordan.

But all that still didn't erase the fact that Tara had to talk to Jordan at some point. *We can't let this go on much longer . . . can we?* she wondered as a familiar pain stabbed her temple — the one that invaded her head every time she thought about the fight. *Push through it, Tara.* She commanded herself to perk up and flipped her chocolate-colored hair over her shoulders.

"Don't forget to vote for Tara Macmillan for prom queen!" she called, giving away a few more buttons of her smiling face. She noticed a senior from the cheerleading squad, Ally, holding out her hand for one, which was a major surprise since Jordan was the cheerleaders' captain. Wasn't Ally supposed to be supporting her teammate? "You really want one of these?" Tara asked.

"Totally." Ally nodded. "I am *so* not voting for Jordan after what she did to Nate. So I guess it's all you."

"Um, thanks?" Tara replied, handing her a button. It wasn't exactly a vote of confidence, but she'd take it.

"Whatev." Ally's gaze shifted beyond Tara and she gasped. "Oh, my God. He's coming over here," she said in a panicky whisper. She began frantically pawing through her enormous leather tote. "Please, God, *please* let me find my lip gloss. I think he might ask me to the prom!"

"Who?" Tara held back a laugh. It wasn't long ago that *she'd* been just as anxious as Ally about finding a date for the big event. The school's mascot, Victor Kaminski, hadn't been the ideal candidate at first but Tara had accepted his invitation anyway — on the condition that she give him a makeover. After a wardrobe do-over, a cool haircut, and a little eyebrow wax she was pleasantly surprised to find that Victor not only had an awesome personality, he was really cute too! They'd become great friends along the way. *Maybe a little more?* Tara hoped so, but she wasn't sure.

Ally never answered Tara, but her crush was revealed when Nate Lombardo strolled by with his backpack casually slung on one shoulder and a baseball cap hiding his sandy-colored hair. "Hey, what's up, T?" he said.

"Just chillin'" Ally answered, smiling wide, her cherry-colored lips now perfectly glossed.

Nate nodded at Ally. "Cool." He turned back to Tara. "How's the campaign going?"

Jordan shrugged. "Well —"

"*I'm* voting for her, that's for sure," Ally broke in. "And I bet a most of the other seniors on the squad are too."

"Nice," Nate said then hesitated before adding, "You know, I kind of have to ask Tara something. In private. You don't mind, Ally, do you?"

Ally's smile faded. "Oh. No. Go right ahead. You guys have your little talk." She shot Tara an icy glare before pivoting and heading down the hall.

Tara gave a mock shiver. "Something tells me Ally's minutes away from drawing a mustache on that 'Queen Tara' pin I gave her. She likes you, you know."

"Ally's a nice girl," Nate remarked, "but she needs to ease up on the lip gloss. I'm more into the natural look."

"Like Jordan," Tara said, knowingly, forgetting for a second that they'd broken up. Why couldn't she keep her big mouth shut?

"Or you," Nate added. His brown eyes sparkled mischievously.

Clearly the boy had no clue how much product was in Tara's hair at the moment. But still, she could feel a hot blush creep onto her cheeks as she let out an awkward chuckle. *No way. Is Nate flirting with me?*

"So where's Victor?" he asked, focusing on Tara again. "Didn't you say he was helping you with the prom queen thing?"

Tara scanned the hall of wall-to-wall students. "He's supposed to be here handing out promo materials with me, but I guess he blew it off," she said, disappointed.

Nate tossed the "Queen Tara" pin between his hands. He seemed to want to say something else. "Did you . . . talk to Jordan yet?"

"No," Tara responded with a sigh. "And I have no clue when it's going to happen. We both said some pretty mean things to each other." Would they *ever* talk? They had to — before their silly dispute ruined the whole prom. Right? Her head began to throb again.

"Oh, man." Nate's face softened when he noticed how upset Tara was. He placed an arm around her shoulders. "I'm sorry. I feel like this is my fault," he said. "I tried to explain things to Jordan yesterday, but she started arguing with me."

"Don't worry about it," she told him. "This is between me and Jordan. It's not your fault." She looked around, observing that the crowd of students was beginning to thin. "Maybe we should get to homeroom."

"Yeah," Nate said, backing away. "See you in the lunchroom?" He was usually parked at the jock table, while Tara sat with Nisha . . . and Jordan.

"I'll be there," Tara replied as he strode away, though she wasn't sure who she'd be eating with today. She bent down to gather her leather satchel and the box that held her overload of "Queen Tara" buttons and noticed a pair of blue suede Vans approaching. She gazed up, knowing exactly to whom they belonged.

"Hey, if it isn't my prom-date-slash-campaign-manager-extraordinaire," she said, rising to greet him. "You missed the entire morning PR session, Victor. What happened?"

Victor stood there, emotionless, holding a box of hot pink handouts for Tara's campaign. "You know what happened," he said. "I don't have to spell it out for you." He held out the box for her to take. "Here. I'm done with your campaign."

"What? Why?" she asked, her heart pounding. Tara glanced at the box but wouldn't accept it. She looked at her friend, confused. "Please, Victor, you can't just quit without telling me what I did."

"Fine." Victor's hazel eyes narrowed. "Jordan told me how you and Nate Lombardo were all over each other in the courtyard the other day," he replied. "Do you really think you can pretend to like me so I'll help you with your prom queen campaign? I don't think so."

"But it's not true, Victor," she responded quickly. "And I *do* like you." She liked him more than he knew.

A flash of anger surged deep inside Tara as she grasped what Jordan had done. *Jordan knew that I was starting to like Victor as more than a friend and a prom date, so she exaggerated the story so that Victor would feel used and leave me flat.*

Tara had no idea that Jordan could be so cruel. She'd done it simply to hurt Tara, and Victor was an innocent bystander. Maybe Tara had hurt Jordan, too, but it wasn't on purpose — and she didn't *lie.*

*Of all the sneaky, conniving, horrible . . . I can't believe, I even* considered *being the bigger person and apologizing first!*

"So why would your best friend say something like that if it *weren't* true," Victor asked, arms folded over his chest, waiting for an explanation.

"Because we're not friends anymore," Tara replied, wondering now if they ever really were.

# BLACK ROBE

"An exemplary act of imagination in which Brian Moore has brought vividly to life a radically different world and populated it with men and women wholly unlike us. His novel's achievement, however, is that, through the course of its shocking narrative, these strangers become first figures of great sympathy and finally images of our own humanity. By the end of BLACK ROBE, we recognize its fierce, awful world as the one we live in. We put Mr. Moore's novel down and look at ourselves and our places differently."

James Carroll
*The New York Times Book Review*

"WE'VE LEARNED TO EXPECT THE UNEXPECTED FROM MOORE . . . *BLACK ROBE* IS ONE OF HIS MOST POWERFUL BOOKS."

Walter Clemons
*Newsweek*

"What Moore has given us here is an authentic, historically accurate and both shocking and moving account . . . A stark, cruel story emerges as the priests try desperately to survive and carry out their mission to the Indians."

Barbara A. Bannon
*The Chicago Sun-Times*

"A LEAN, POWERFUL, THEOLOGICAL NOVEL . . . Like the strongest work of Graham Greene, Shusaku Endo, and other restless Catholic novelists: disturbing, haunting storytelling—bringing the period background to life with raw, bold strokes."

*The Kirkus Reviews*

Another Fawcett Crest Book
by Brian Moore:

COLD HEAVEN

# BLACK ROBE

Brian Moore

FAWCETT CREST • NEW YORK

A Fawcett Crest Book
Published by Ballantine Books
 Published in the United States by Ballantine Books, a division of Random House, Inc.

Library of Congress Catalog Card Number: 84-21222

ISBN 0-449-20947-4

This edition published by arrangement with E. P. Dutton, Inc.

Manufactured in the United States of America

First Ballantine Books Edition: March 1986

For Jean

# AUTHOR'S NOTE

A FEW YEARS AGO, IN GRAHAM GREENE'S *COLLECTED ESSAYS,* I came upon his discussion of *The Jesuits in North America,* the celebrated work by the American historian Francis Parkman (1823–1893). Greene quotes this passage:

> [Father] Noel Chabanel came later to the mission for he did not reach the Huron country until 1643. He detested the Indian life—the smoke, the vermin, the filthy food, the impossibility of privacy. He could not study by the smoky lodge fires, among the noisy crowd of men and squaws, with their dogs and their restless, screeching children. He had a natural inaptitude to learning the language, and labored at it for five years with scarcely a sign of progress. The Devil whispered a suggestion in his ear: Let him procure his release from these barren and revolting toils and return to France where congenial and useful employments awaited him. Chabanel refused to listen: and when the temptation still beset him he bound himself by a solemn vow to remain in Canada to the day of his death.

*A solemn vow.* A voice speaks to us directly from the seventeenth century, the voice of a conscience that, I fear, we no longer possess. I began to read Parkman's great work and discovered that his main source was the *Relations,* the voluminous letters that the Jesuits sent back to their superiors in France. From Parkman I moved on to the *Relations* themselves, and in their deeply moving reports discovered an unknown and unpredictable world. For, unlike the English, French, and Dutch traders and explorers, the Jesuits came to North America not for furs or conquest, but to save the souls of those whom they called "the Savages."*

To succeed, they had to learn the "Savages' " often scatological tongues and study their religious and tribal customs. These letters, the only real record of the early Indians of North America, introduce us to a people who bear little relationship to the "Red Indians" of fiction and folklore. The Huron, Iroquois, and Algonkin were a handsome, brave, incredibly cruel people who, at that early stage, were in no way dependent on the white man and, in fact, judged him to be their physical and mental inferior. They were warlike; they practiced ritual cannibalism and, for reasons of religion, subjected their enemies to prolonged and unbearable tortures. Yet, as parents, they could not bear to strike or reprove their unruly children. They were pleasure-loving and polygamous, sharing sexual favors with strangers as freely as they shared their food and hearth. They despised the "Blackrobes" for their habit of hoarding possessions. They also held the white man in contempt for his stupidity in not realizing that the land, the rivers, the animals, were all possessed of a living spirit and subject to laws that must be respected.

From the works of anthropologists and historians who have established many facts about Indian behavior not known to the early Jesuits, I was made doubly aware of the strange and gripping tragedy that occurred when the Indian belief in a world of night and in the power of dreams clashed with the Jesuits' preachments of Christianity and a paradise after death. This novel is an attempt to show that each of these beliefs inspired in the other fear, hostility, and despair, which later would result in the destruction and abandonment of the Jesuit missions, and the conquest of the Huron people by the Iroquois, their deadly enemy.

*In the early part of the seventeenth century the native people of Canada were not known to the French as "Indians," but by the names of their tribal confederacies, and were referred to collectively as "Les Sauvages" (the Savages). The natives, for their part, spoke of the French as "Normans" and of the Jesuit fathers as "Blackrobes." As for the obscene language used by the natives at that time, it was a form of rough banter and was not intended to give offense. I am aware that I have taken a novelist's license in the question of Algonkian understanding of Iroquoian speech.

* * *

While much of the information contained in this novel on the mores, beliefs, and language of both "Savages" and Jesuits comes from the *Relations,* I am also indebted to other sources. I would like to thank James Hunter, Research Curator of Sainte Marie Among the Hurons, and also Bill Byrick, Professor Bruce Trigger of McGill University, and Professor W. J. Eccles of the College of William and Mary for assistance on various points.

I am indebted to Le Conseil des Arts du Canada for making it possible for me to visit places in Canada where records are kept of Iroquois, Algonkin, and Huron history and customs, and the sites of early Iroquois and Huron settlements, in particular, the village of Midland, Ontario, where the Ontario government has accurately reconstructed longhouses, a village, and the original Jesuit mission established there.

# ONE

# 1

LAFORGUE FELT HIS BODY TREMBLE. WHAT CAN BE keeping them? Has the Commandant refused? Why has he not sent for me? Is this God's punishment for my lie about my hearing? But it wasn't a lie; my intention was honorable. Or is that a sophistry? Am I now so mired in my ambition that I can no longer tell truth from falsehood?

For what seemed the hundredth time, the sentry on duty outside the Commandant's quarters turned and marched along the ramparts of the fort. Laforgue heard voices. He looked down the steep path which led to the wooden buildings of the settlement. Two men were coming up. One was an officer, his slouch hat tilted over his forehead, his uniform whitened by dust. When Laforgue saw the face of the second man, he felt a sudden disquiet. A month ago, this man, a fur trader named Massé, had run from the stinking wineshop where the traders drank to yell obscene insults at Laforgue. The insults concerned a Savage girl Massé had been sleeping with, a girl Laforgue had lately tried to instruct in the faith.

Now, seeking to avoid further taunts, he moved closer to the shadow of the ramparts. And as he did, he looked up at the Commandant's quarters. Framed in a window was the face of Champlain.

The Commandant, sitting at his window, saw a wide-brimmed clerical hat tilt up to reveal the pale, bearded visage of Father Laforgue. He looked past the lonely figure of the priest to the settlement of Québec, a jumble of wooden buildings, three hundred feet below. As in a painting, his eye was led toward the curve of the great river where four French ships lay at anchor. In a week they would be gone.

Behind him, he heard the Jesuit Superior cough, a small reminder, deferential yet impatient. "You were saying, Commandant?"

"I said it is late in the year. Tell them that."

The Jesuit, Father Bourque, translated for the Savages. Chomina, the elder Savage, had shaved his head bald except for a ridge of hair, which bristled across the crown like the spine of a hedgehog. His face was a mask of white clay. The younger, a leader called Neehatin, had ornamented himself for this occasion by drawing rings of yellow ochre around his eyes and painting his nose a bright blue. Both watched Champlain as they might a large and unpredictable animal. When the Jesuit had finished, the younger Savage spoke. Champlain turned to him as a deaf man toward moving lips. In all these years, he, the founder of this land, had not mastered the Savage tongue.

"He asks if Agnonha no longer wishes them to carry the French," Father Bourque said.

"Why would he ask that?"

"I think they are worried that you will not give them the six muskets they have requested," the Jesuit said.

"As you know, your Excellency, this is the real reason they have offered to help us."

Champlain smiled at the Savage. "Tell him Agnonha is grateful for his offer of help. Tell him that for once Agnonha may be willing to offer muskets as presents. But tell him my concern is this. To succeed, the journey should have started three weeks ago."

"With respect," Father Bourque said, "I think there is still time to reach the Ihonatiria mission. As you know, I have twice made this journey myself."

Champlain looked at the priest's black cassock and thought, irreverently, that it reminded him of a schoolboy's smock. When you were still a boy in school, Father, I made and mapped the journey of which you speak. What do you know of that time? Why do you think these Savages want muskets? It is not to hunt but to kill their enemies.

"It is not just the onset of winter," he told the Jesuit. "There is the other, the greater danger. We have not spoken of that."

The Jesuit bowed his head. "The journey, like our lives, is in God's hands."

"But what if there is no mission? What if Laforgue arrives to find the two Fathers dead?"

"We will cross that bridge when we come to it."

Champlain fingered his graying beard in a gesture which semaphored his irritation. "Not *we,*" he said. "It is Father Laforgue who must cross it. I do not know him well, but certainly he has no experience of these hardships."

"Would you wish to question him, your Excellency? I have brought him with me. He waits outside."

"What can I learn from that? I have said he has no experience of the great river."

"In my opinion," the Jesuit said, "he is adequate to the task. He is an ordained member of the Society of Jesus and, as such, his capabilities have been carefully assessed by the Order."

"You are talking of assessments which were made in

France. I am talking of dangers and sufferings the Society of Jesus has not dreamed of."

"With respect," Father Bourque said. "There are few hardships not envisaged or experienced by our members in different lands."

Champlain looked at the Savages, who squatted on the floor, their knees as high as their heads. The Savages considered it ill-mannered to parley while standing. While he had been careful to remain seated, the Jesuit carelessly paced the room. "The young man you are sending with him is a boy, not yet twenty," Champlain said.

"True. But he is an exceptional young man."

"In what way is he exceptional, Father?"

"He was sent out as a workman, but with the highest recommendations. He is devout and diligent. His uncle, a priest, instructed him in Latin, and he studied with the Récollet Fathers in Rouen."

"Latin will not help him on the great river."

"No. But he is highly intelligent and adaptable. When I discovered his talent for languages, I sent him off to spend time with the Algonkin at their eel fishery. In a year he has mastered Algonkian and Huron speech."

Champlain heard a sudden noise. It was the noise of a wooden bowl striking against the floor. The Savages had begun to gamble, shaking the bowl and examining the plum stones in it. The stones were painted white on one side, black on the other. The gamble was to guess which color predominated. "Father," he said. "We have talked too long in our tongue. They are weary of us."

"True. My apologies."

Again, the bowl banged on the floor. Champlain felt a familiar numbness move up his arm. Will this be my last winter? Will I never again see the red flame of Richelieu's robe come toward me in the long gallery of the Palais de Justice, passing all those who seek his ear? I bend to kiss his ring; he smiles at me, a smile that tells nothing of the smiler's thought. Who will he send here to replace me? And what would he say to this request? The journey to almost certain death of a priest and a boy, against the chance to save a small outpost for France and for the Faith. In the conquest of a nation, lives are currency.

He had his answer. He smiled at the painted faces. "Tell them six muskets. No more."

Laforgue, watching, at last saw the Superior and the Savages emerge from the Commandant's quarters.

Is it yes or no? Why did he not send for me? Quickly, he walked along beneath the ramparts, controlling his desire to break into a run. The Superior, passing the guard, turned to the Savages, but the Savages, whose custom it was not to utter formal farewells, simply walked away. They did not use the path which led down to the settlement, but went across the rougher terrain which led to their encampment.

Father Bourque looked back when he heard Laforgue's footstep. "Ah, there you are," he said. "Come. We must hurry."

He moved past Laforgue, going down the path. Laforgue, trained in the rule of obedience, did not ask the question which consumed his thoughts, but fell in a pace behind him. They passed by the officer and Massé, who, coming up, bowed respectfully to the Superior. Massé did not look at Laforgue. In silence, the two priests continued down to the jetty, where their canoe was moored. Father Bourque waited while Laforgue untied the rope and, draping his wooden clogs around his neck so as not to damage the thin bark bottom, stepped neatly into the birch-bark craft, and held it steady against the mooring place. Father Bourque, also removing his clogs, got into the front of the canoe as Laforgue, kneeling precisely as the Savages had taught him, carefully moved the craft out onto the river. He heeled it toward a tributary which led downstream to the Jesuit residence. Father Bourque took up his paddle. Steadily they stroked toward the far bank of the tributary, where a rectangle of wooden palisades enclosed two buildings which formed the residence. Laforgue, aware that the Superior was judging his skills, rose up at the precise moment the swift canoe glided to shore and leaped onto the landing place, neatly catching the prow and guiding it in.

"Where is Daniel?" Father Bourque asked, as he disembarked.

"I believe they are all working up at the storehouse."

"All of them?" The Superior did not wait for a reply but set off along the narrow track which led to the residence. As they entered the long-grassed meadows surrounding the palisades, a miasma of mosquitoes clouded about them, causing them to slap their faces, duck and proceed, half running, toward the gate. "Find Daniel and bring him to me," the Superior said.

Inside the gate they separated, Father Bourque entering the principal building, a one-story construction of wooden planks, plastered with mud and thatched with grasses. Laforgue hurried on to the second building, half burned some years back by the English, a building the Jesuits' workmen were now repairing. As he approached, he heard the sound of hammering and laughter; someone shouted something in the Breton tongue. Escaping the mosquito cloud, he ducked under the hanging which served for a door. As he did, the laughter and hammering ceased and from their perches and workbenches the men looked down at him in silence.

"What news, Father?"

The head carpenter had asked the question, but Laforgue looked at Daniel Davost, who stood, holding a plank, his mouth full of nails.

"No news yet," Laforgue said. "But Father Bourque wants to see Daniel at once."

"Then you're going," the carpenter said. The other workmen exchanged glances. All of them disapproved of the priests' sending a young boy on this dangerous journey. And now, as Daniel left with Laforgue, angry voices were raised, speaking Breton, which Laforgue did not understand.

"What did they say, Daniel?"

"Nothing, Father. Some joke."

Outside, in the choking swarm of insects, they ran toward the main residence. As they entered they passed through the chapel, a small bare room with a wooden altar on which were two cloth hangings; one represented the Holy Spirit in the form of a dove, the other an image of the Virgin. The chapel opened into the refectory, which the priests used also as their workroom. In this room twelve Savage men and women squatted on the ground in a semicircle, just inside the doorway. They did not move when Daniel and Laforgue entered but kept their eyes on a clock which sat on the refectory table. The smell of their unwashed bodies and greasy hair filled the room with a pungent sickly odor. Two other priests, Fathers Bonnet and Meynard, were in the adjoining kitchen together with a lay brother.

"I have brought Daniel, Father," Laforgue said.

The Superior, who was working at the refectory table, turned and pointed to the clock. The hands stood at two minutes to four. Laforgue nodded to show he understood. All waited in silence, watching the clock.

These Savages, unlike those who had attended on the Commandant, wore no paint. They were in their normal summer garb, the men naked except for a breech clout, the women covered modestly enough in long tunics made of animal skins. All were filthy, their hair matted with food particles, their skin greased to keep off flies and mosquitoes. And yet, despite this, their slender bodies, their lack of facial hair, and an absence of physical deformities made them seem more handsome and of a higher species than the priests of the residence.

Now, as the hands of the clock moved toward four, one of the male Savages rose and walked around it, then went into the chapel to see if anyone was hiding there. Satisfied, he returned, nodding to the others. In the kitchen, the priests ceased their labors and fell silent. All waited in a quiet in which the only sound was the ticking of the clock.

The clock chimed: *Dong! Dong! Dong! Dong!* At the stroke of four, the Superior cried out, "Stop!"

The chime died. The clock's steady ticking was heard. The Savages gave a cry of astonishment and delight, turning to each other with the amazement of people who have witnessed a miracle. The eldest male Savage began to speak to the others. "You see, it's just as I fucking well told you. The Captain is alive. The Captain spoke. I told you. He spoke."

The Savages smiled and exchanged glances of pleasure. An old woman laughed. "Shit," she said. "What did he say?"

All turned to the Superior, who now raised his head from the writing of his letter. In the Savage tongue, Father Bourque replied, "He says it is time to go. He says, 'Get up and go home.' "

At once, chattering among themselves, the deputation of Savages rose. They approached the clock shyly, peering at it, not daring to touch it. Then, obedient to its command, they filed out of the refectory, going through the chapel to the front door, which Father Bonnet held open as he bade them farewell.

Daniel Davost heard the slap of the bolt in the lock as Father Bonnet shut the door: a jailer sound. He saw the priests come from their tasks to gather in the refectory. Now it will be told. He shivered, as though the locked door had shut him into a prison from which there was no escape. What will I do if the journey is canceled? The Algonkin will gather by the river and slip away at dawn. She will be among them; she kneels in Chomina's canoe, head bent, plying a paddle. She will not look back. There are no farewells in their lives. Last night in our stifling room, twelve snoring workmen above and around me, I spat in Jesus' face, I who once was pure, who now desire to go on this journey not for God's glory but for the most base and sinful reason.

He turned to look at the Superior, who still penned his letter. His alarm turned to panic. *What if the journey is canceled? I will run away.*

Father Bourque wrote on, his quill pen covering page after page in haste, for this report must be made as full as possible. That was what the Order wished. In the past few days he had labored on it in every spare moment, for it must leave with the ships next week. This report Father Provincial in France would distribute widely among the faithful and powerful as an inspiration for funds and volunteers to aid in the work of saving souls. In his neat hand, Father Bourque set down the subject of his greatest concern.

*Two weeks ago there came here from the country of the Hurons a Savage, baptized in the faith by Father Brabant. This Savage, by name Ihongwaha, brought to us a letter from Father Brabant, who ministers to the Savages in the region of Ossossané. It is a request that we send as soon as possible a replacement for Father Jerome, who is ill in the northern part of that country in a place called Ihonatiria. Father Brabant also writes that there is a sickness or fever now general in the whole region and that the sorcerers of the Huron people have accused the "Blackrobes" (our Fathers) of bringing this illness. Father Brabant writes that a Savage of the Ihonatiria region, baptized a Christian, arrived at Ossossané with news that the chiefs, after a council, sent word to Father Jerome that if their young warriors decided to put a hatchet in his head and in the head of Father Duval, his assistant, they would have nothing to say about it. Father Brabant writes that, plagued as his own region is with this fever, he will not find it possible to visit the northern region to ascertain the Fathers' fate. He asks that we send at once a priest to carry on the mission at Ihonatiria in the event that the illness of Father Jerome has proved fatal, or in the event that he and Father Duval have been martyred. We have been much disturbed by this news and have asked the help of the Sieur de Champlain in persuading a party of Algonkian hunters to take one of our Fathers with them on the annual journey to their winter hunting grounds, and, further, to provide paddlers to take the Father on to the top of the Great Rapids, whence the Allumette people will help him proceed. And so, with the good offices of the Sieur de Champlain we have decided—*

"Father Bourque?"

The Superior looked up. He saw that the refectory was now filled with the priests of the mission and that the youth, Daniel Davost, was also present. The Superior shook some sand on his writings, then stood and, turning to the company, made the sign of the cross. "Let us pray," he said, and began, in Latin. When the prayer was finished, he again made the sign of the cross. "We have given thanks because it has pleased God to grant our request."

At once, the room filled with excited murmurings. "Yes," said Father Bourque. "The Commandant has agreed to the Savages' requests for presents, including six muskets and some powder and shot. He will also give the customary departure feast. Father Bonnet?"

"Yes, Father?"

"We will make some contribution to this feast. You will discuss it with the cook of the garrison. Now, sit down, everyone."

Obediently the company took their places around the refectory table. "We must decide now what must be got ready and what can be carried in the canoes," the Superior said. "As, at best, you will travel with only two canoes from the point at which the Algonkin leave you at the head of the rapids, we must choose carefully. You will take clothing for the mission and, in addition, a chalice, a monstrance, four missals, two sets of mass vestments, writing materials, and two gallons of altar wine. You will also take trading goods: tobacco, awls, beads, knives, hatchets. As for food, we will prepare enough corn meal for their sagamité gruel to feed the entire party for the twenty days it will take to reach the top of the rapids. You will take a change of clothing and cloaks for the winter ahead. All these things, with the exception of the food, must not be more than can be placed in one canoe in the event that the Savages desert you. At the worst, you must be able to paddle and portage one canoe and its contents."

"What about snowshoes, Father?" Laforgue asked.

There was laughter. Everyone had watched Laforgue practice daily in the long grasses of the meadows, his feet attached to the strange thong and wooden *raquettes* with which the Savages traveled the winter snows, lifting his legs like some strange seabird in a marsh.

"Yes, take them," Father Bourque said. "Oh, and Daniel? When we are finished here I want to see you for a moment."

The talk went on, but Daniel no longer heard what was said. *I want to see you for a moment.* Someone, one of the Algonkin up at the fishery, must have said something in a joke to one of the fur traders, who may have told one of the priests, who would at once be in duty bound to tell the Superior, who now will confront me. And he will know that I have lied, and I have not confessed, that I have sinned and sinned and cannot stop. Which of the priests was responsible? Father Laforgue? No, he would have shown it in his manner as we came here today.

And now, ending the discussion, the Superior beckoned Daniel to follow him. In panic, his mouth dry, he rose and followed Father Bourque out of the residence, going toward a small storage shed where the priests sometimes heard confessions. The choice of this shed as a place to parley could only mean that he had been discovered. They entered. The Superior shut the door. He gestured to Daniel to take the solitary stool, sat himself down on an upended plow, shipped from France eight years ago but not yet used in this inhospitable climate, and hitched up his cassock, revealing bare ankles, cruelly swollen by mosquito bites.

"Tell me, Daniel, why do you want to make this journey?"

The question hung in the air. Daniel forced himself to look at the Superior. *Someone has told him. He must know.* "Why do you ask, Father?" He heard his voice waver as he spoke.

"Because I must decide. When I spoke today with the Sieur de Champlain, he warned me of the great dangers and mentioned your youth. It is true that you are very young."

"I do not feel young," Daniel said. Relief made him want to burst out laughing. *He knows nothing. He knows nothing, after all!*

But it was Father Bourque who laughed, throwing back his head and showing carious teeth. "That proves you are still a boy. But you haven't answered my question. *Why* do you want to make this journey?"

Daniel hesitated, then said, as a child says its catechism. "For the greater glory of God."

*I spit on Jesus' face as I tell that lie.*

"But you are not a Jesuit."

"I wish to serve God. That is why I asked to be sent to New France."

"Yes. Of course. Of course." The Superior bent down and scratched his bitten ankles. "Well then, I will make you a promise. If, at the end of a year, you still have this wish, we will do what we can to help you. We will bring you back from Ihonatiria and send you to France to study for the priesthood. Would that please you, Daniel?"

"Yes, Father." He knows nothing. He sees me black-robed, devout, his younger self, prostrate before the altar as I take my priestly vows. As last year I saw myself, when I knelt in the Church of the Blessed Virgin in Honfleur, my arms outstretched in adoration of my Savior, making my vow to spend two years serving God in a distant land.

"Are your parents alive?" Father Bourque asked.

"No, Father. My nearest relative is my uncle, the priest I told you about."

"The one who taught you Latin. So if anything happens to you, which God forbid, he is the one I must write to?"

"Yes, Father."

"God bless you, then," the Superior said. "Oh, and Daniel? Send Father Laforgue to me. I will wait for him here."

Savage drumbeats punctuated drunken Breton songs. Mosquitoes and tiny midges moved in separate clouds as they sought out blood. The day had been warm but an evening coolness came in from the river, bringing relief to the Commandant and the Savage leaders, who sat in a circle on the riverbank; Champlain upright in an armchair, wearing a cloak made of beaver skins. Outside this circle, the Jesuits of the mission huddled as though beleaguered, drab figures in long black cassocks, their wide-brimmed hats looped up at the sides. Farther down the riverbank, the majority of the population of New France, some one hundred colonists, artisans, fur company employees and soldiers, strolled about among the remaining Savages of the Algonkian band, who were now eating their share of the Commandant's feast. These, the younger men, together with the women and children, crowded around a bank of smoking fires on which were placed cooking kettles containing a stinking mess of bear meat, fat, fish, and sagamité. The Savages ate gluttonously from the kettles, stopping from time to time to wipe their greasy fingers on their hair or on the coats of their dogs, which ran barking around the fires in search of discarded scraps.

In the center of the council circle, Samuel de Champlain looked to his interpreter, who gave a slight nod, warning that the time had come for him to speak. He rose, bowed to the leaders, then settled himself again in his armchair and beckoned to the group of priests. At once, Father Paul Laforgue rose and came to the Commandant's side, a slight, pale man, thin-bearded, intellectual, but with a strange determination in the eyes and narrow mouth. Champlain turned to the Savage leaders and pointed to Father Bourque and the other Jesuits. "These are our Fathers," Champlain said. "We love them more than we love ourselves. The whole of the French nation loves them. They do not go among you for your furs. They have left their friends and their country to show you the way to heaven. If you love the French as you say you love them, then love and honor these, our Fathers. And, in particular, I, Agnonha, commend to you Father Laforgue, who is going far into the land of the Hurons. I say to those of you who will accompany him on his journey, guard him well. And now I place this beloved Father in your care."

As the speech was translated, sentence by sentence, the assembly of Savages uttered the customary ejaculations of approval. The guttural sounds reminded Champlain of animals groaning in pain, but he smiled contentedly. They also meant the journey had been approved.

Two leaders rose and squatted before him. One began to speak. In the traditional manner of the Savages, he first repeated what Champlain had said and then summarized what had been said on this subject on previous occasions. The Savages, having no written language, conducted all their affairs in this manner, constantly astonishing the French by their remarkable feats of recall. The leader went on to proclaim Algonkian fealty to the French in general and to Champlain in particular.

His speech recalled the time, more than twenty-five years before, when Champlain, whom the Savages called Agnonha, or "Iron Man," had buckled on his steel armor and gone forth with the Algonkin and Huron to fight against and kill the Iroquois, their traditional enemy.

When the speech was finished, Champlain uttered some words of gratitude, then rose to signal an end to the parley. At once, Chomina and Neehatin, the leaders of the hunting party that would accompany Laforgue, went to the priest and embraced him as a sign that he had been given into their trust.

Satisfied, Champlain signaled to his officers and left the gathering. As he walked under the balcony of the trading post of the Company of One Hundred Associates of New France, Martin Doumergue, the chief clerk of the post, rose and bowed to his Excellency. Behind Doumergue, Pierre Tallevant, his assistant, newly arrived from France, concealed a half-filled bottle of brandy behind his back as he bowed in turn. Both men watched as the Commandant and his officers set off up the steep path in the direction of Champlain's fort.

"Why is the Commandant dressed like a Savage?" Tallevant asked, as he again produced the bottle and filled his superior's glass.

Doumergue laughed. "You mean the fur robe? It's a present from the chiefs. Anyway, it's symbolic, isn't it?"

"What do you mean?"

"I mean, without the fur trade none of us would be in this colony."

"Colony?" Tallevant said. "Why do they call it a colony? Look at that mob out there. Where are the colonists? Where are the families who're going to settle this place? The English have colonists, the Dutch have colonists, but what do we have? Fur traders and priests."

Doumergue drank, then placed his glass on the railing of the balcony. "Do you blame us?" he asked. "I mean, would you bring a woman out here? I want to show you something."

Unsteady in drink, Tallevant rose and went to the railing.

"Look over there," Doumergue said. "See that Savage with a musket on his back?"

"The one eating from the kettle?"

"Right. Know who that is? It's Jean Mercier."

"What are you talking about?"

"That's Mercier, I tell you," Doumergue said. "He's just been up-country with one of their hunting parties, buying pelts. See? He dresses like them now. He even eats their food."

Tallevant stared uneasily at the almost naked figure biting into a piece of bear meat, the animal hair still on the half-cooked flesh. The man wore European hunting boots, not the soft shoes made of skins which a real Savage would use. Could this be the Rouennais fur trader whose accounts Tallevant had seen entered in the Company's ledgers in Caen? He turned to Doumergue. "What happened to him? Is he drunk or mad?"

"No, no. He likes the life."

"But how can he? That stinking food, the flies, the smells, the way they live."

"The way they live?" Martin Doumergue laughed. "They live for their pleasure, for a full belly. They live to hunt and fish. They do no work, the Algonkin. And, most important, they let him fuck their young girls. He likes that. He likes to hunt, he likes to get away from the life the priests would have us live here, praying and fasting and all that. He's free up there. And he's not the only one. I have twenty-one traders on my books. In five years, if they stay here, most of them will be like Mercier."

"I don't believe it," Tallevant said.

"And if we do bring in colonists," Doumergue said, "the same thing will happen to them. Do you think I'd bring a woman out and marry her and settle here? What for? So that my sons will grow up half savage, running naked in the woods, then dying of starvation when the snows come?"

Uneasily, Tallevant looked back at the tall figure of the trader, the lank greasy hair, the thin loins, the buttocks bare beneath the breechclout. Doumergue is wrong; it must be drink or madness. To go from all that we know and are back to that brutish state? "It makes no sense," he said aloud.

"Doesn't it? It makes sense to me. We're not colonizing the Savages. They're colonizing us. Even the Commandant in that smelly fur robe is happier here than he ever was in France."

Tallevant refilled his glass and drank. The brandy fumes rose in his head. "Well, not me," he said. "When my contract is up, I'm going home."

Martin Doumergue looked at him. "Will you? I wonder. Will any of us?"

The two Savages who had risen to embrace Paul Laforgue at the conclusion of the Commandant's feast now led him to the temporary encampment of the Algonkin, their brightly painted faces grinning in a manner which made him think of medieval masquers on feast days in his native Normandy. As he entered the encampment he was surrounded by a crowd of Savage women, the married ones prematurely aged and worn by toil, the young girls shamefully loose in their clothing, brazen and carefree as the gleeful, unruly Savage children who ran behind him, pinching and pulling him as though he were a toy for their amusement. Straining to hear through the dull ringing of his infected left ear, Laforgue understood that the Savage women were asking what food he would bring on the journey, would he have tobacco, did he have brandy to give them. Faces crowded close, white teeth set off by sun-browned skin, handsome, merry dark eyes, long dark hair: these faces, these people will be my only companions, save Daniel, when tomorrow we set out upriver.

Laforgue had never lived in an encampment of Savages. With the exception of Father Bourque, none of the priests now in the Québec residence had traveled as he would travel, sleeping outdoors or in Savage shelters, eating only Savage food. "It is travel of the most difficult sort," the Superior had warned him. "Yet it is also the most advantageous way in which to make the journey. For if you travel with a hunting party of men, women and children, there is always the chance that, if a child or an adult fall ill en route, a soul can be gained for God by a deathbed baptism. Father Brabant and others have written in the *Relations* that each time they journeyed to the Huron lands they had the great privilege of saving at least one soul in this manner. Remember, such a blessing will more than justify all the perils and discomforts you may suffer."

Now, remembering the Superior's words, Laforgue forced a smile as he endured the badgering of the Savage children: one tugging at the beads of his rosary as if to break them; another pulling at his beard and calling him a hairy dog, for the Savages were not bearded and pulled out their own sparse facial hair, considering it to be ugly. A third child, a giggling little girl, kept trying to slip her hand through the buttons of Laforgue's cassock and fondle his genitals. The Savages paid no attention to this, for it was unheard of for them to punish or restrain their children in any way. And so, as the little imp persisted, Laforgue lifted her up and put her aside, then tried to make his way clear of the crowd. But the Savage women laughingly restrained him and now, thinking longingly of his cell, where at this hour he would kneel alone in a time of prayer, he decided to invoke Captain Clock. Raising his hands as if to address the crowd, he shouted, "Wait! Captain Clock says I must go home. Captain says it is time for me to go."

"Where is the Captain?" an old Savage woman asked. "Are you hiding the Captain now?"

"No, the Captain is in our house. But he spoke this morning. Excuse me, I must go now."

*"Dong! Dong! Dong! Dong!"* The old woman, her face a web of tiny creases, imitated the sound of the striking clock in a manner inhuman in its accuracy.

"Stop!" cried a Savage after the fourth sound. All exploded in laughter. Chomina, the leader who had escorted Laforgue into the encampment, took him by the hand and cleared a passage for him among the laughing throng. "Go then, Nicanis," he said, using the name the Algonkin had given Laforgue. "Go home to the Captain and tell him that tomorrow, at first light, we await you here."

"Till tomorrow," Laforgue said. The Savages were still. Even the children ceased their movements. They stood, watching him in silence, as he walked away from their fires, going downriver to the place where the traders lay about drinking. As Laforgue approached this place, he saw Daniel, standing in the shadow of the trees, waiting for him.

"I have a canoe, Father. I will take you back to the residence."

"Good," Laforgue said, then looked at the boy. "Is something wrong?"

"No, Father."

But something *was* wrong, he was sure of it. It was as though Daniel were fearful, and as they continued on he saw that the boy moved high on the riverbank as though to avoid the place between the trees where the traders were. A sensible precaution, no doubt, for one could never be sure of the traders' mood, especially when it was a public holiday and they had been drinking. As though to confirm this thought, male voices shouted and then Laforgue heard a sudden scream. A Savage girl ran out from the trees, long-legged and awkward as a foal about to fall. The girl was tall and slender and dressed for some Savage ceremony, wearing only a short kilt from waist to knee and a collar and necklace of the blue and purple beads which the Savages fashioned from the inside of shells. She ran directly toward Laforgue and Daniel, then swerved as though they were a wall, twisting about to run away downriver. As she did, Laforgue saw a Savage come from the trees in pursuit. The Savage was drunk; he wore hunting boots which were not made for running and now, as he lurched past Laforgue, he skidded and fell, his half-naked body subsiding in a dusty cloud near the soft mud of the river's edge. Laforgue looked at Daniel, who, ignoring the fallen Savage, was staring after the fleeing girl. He took the boy's arm, seeking to hurry him away from these occasions of lust, but as they passed the sprawled figure of the Savage, the man twisted around and caught the skirt of Laforgue's cassock, forcing him to stop. The Savage looked up, his eyes muddied with drink, then said in French, "Bless me, Father, for I have sinned."

"Come, Father," Daniel said. "Pay no attention."

"Wait." Laforgue stared in astonishment at the Savage. "You speak French?"

"Imperfectly," said the Savage. "And I would prefer not to."

At once, Laforgue knelt beside the man and made the sign of the cross, for this Savage must be a Christian. Where did he come from, how did he learn such good French, how did he know, in French, those words which were a request that a priest hear one's confession? "I cannot confess you now, my son," Laforgue said gently. "You are drunk."

The Savage smiled. Suddenly, behind him in the trees, Laforgue heard laughter and knew that he had been played a trick. This Savage was not an Algonkin but one of those renegade French traders, the coureurs de bois, who went in the woods with the Savages and affected their heathen ways. And as Laforgue turned to see who mocked him, half a dozen other men of this sort came from the trees. With them were three half-naked Savage girls. The traders were half-stripped themselves, their hair and bodies decked with Savage feathers and colored beads. All were drunk.

It was no place for a priest. "Come, Daniel," he said, but as he tried to rise from his kneeling position, the false Savage pulled again on his cassock, causing him to stumble before he managed to free himself.

Daniel had already gone ahead, and as Laforgue started after him, the traders' laughter loud in his ears, he saw the boy run in the direction of the Savage girl, who had circled and was coming back. Daniel began calling out to her, and so Laforgue turned his good ear in that direction. But heard, as so often in the past weeks, only a dull, distant sound. What was Daniel saying? He should not speak to her. She might be drunk. In drink, the Savages believed that a devil took possession of them. If a drunken Savage killed another, the Savages did not hold him responsible for his action, and so it was dangerous to go near them when they were in that condition. But as Laforgue drew closer he saw Daniel grip the girl's arm.

"Let her be," he called.

"Go back to your people," Daniel said, and this time Laforgue heard his words. "Go on, go at once." He looked as though he would strike the girl, but at that moment she twisted free of his grip and ran to the renegade trader, who rose, lewdly holding out his arms in welcome, his breechclout awry, his penis erect and sticking up.

"Come away now," Laforgue said, his face hot with anger at the sight of the trader's shame. But Daniel moved ahead of him.

"Let me be," the boy said, but stared open-mouthed at the scene below them on the bank, the trader embracing the girl as she began to fondle his penis, he pulling her short skirt up over her buttocks.

It was a sight the devil had sent, and Laforgue would have none of it. With a strength that surprised him, he caught hold of Daniel and turned him away, saying,

"Let's go back. We must get ready. We are leaving at first light tomorrow."

And saw in the boy's face a stupefaction as though the sight of lust had robbed him of all sense.

"Where is the canoe?" Laforgue asked. "Where did you leave the canoe?"

But the boy pulled back, as though to look again at the scene of lechery.

"Come away," Laforgue said. "Don't look at that. It is a sin to look."

"I *wasn't* looking," the boy said. There were tears in his eyes. "This way," he said, in an angry, strangled voice, and started off at a fast pace, leaving Laforgue behind as they ran to the place where the mission canoe was moored. Why was he crying? But then Laforgue reminded himself that Daniel was a sheltered child brought up by a priestly uncle in a small Norman village. What would a boy like that know of such lewd debauchery?

"You should punish him," the boy said suddenly, as he untied the canoe. "If you tell Father Bourque, Father Bourque will tell the Commandant and he will be put in the stocks. It's what he deserves. Disrespect for religion is a sin and forbidden."

"But Mercier is a Huguenot," Laforgue said. "He is not of our faith."

"Even so. It is forbidden. You should tell the Commandant."

"Yes, yes, it is my duty," Laforgue said. "But we are leaving tomorrow and I have not time—I mean, I cannot find it in my heart. He was drunk. He was confused."

"Mercier confused?" Daniel said, pushing the canoe out into the shallows. He stood, steadying the canoe so that Laforgue could climb in. "Mercier doesn't give a damn, about God or France or anything. We should tell Father Bourque."

"Daniel," Laforgue said. "Father Bourque has enough to trouble him, don't you think?"

The boy, silent, bent over the prow of the canoe, paddling skillfully as a Savage.

"Tomorrow we start our journey," Laforgue said. "That is what we must think of now. Let us ask God's forgiveness for our sins and for this man's sins also. Don't you agree?"

At last, he saw Daniel half turn his head and nod agreement. But his body still shook with sobs. He is still a child, Laforgue reminded himself. It is my duty to protect him.

# 2

"WE ARE READY," CHOMINA SAID.

Neehatin did not answer. He was looking at the Blackrobes. The chief Blackrobe now stood near the water. The Blackrobe Nicanis and the Norman boy went down on their knees before him. The chief Blackrobe raised his right hand, the hand open like a knife. He made a downward movement, then a sideways movement. The two who knelt bowed their heads beneath this movement as the chief Blackrobe spoke some words in their tongue.

"What are they doing?" Chomina asked.

"It is some fucking sorcery," Neehatin told him. "They make that sign to silence their enemies. You have divided their food up among our canoes?"

"I have done it."

"Where are the six muskets?"

"Three in my canoe, three in yours. And I have placed the powder and shot in a skin, as you said."

"We will not use the muskets until we reach the

hunting ground," Neehatin said. "Those Norman pigs have given only half the powder and shot I asked for. Besides, we have to learn how to shoot them."

"The Norman boy knows how."

"Fuck him," Neehatin said. "We will learn ourselves."

He looked at the riverbank. The boy and the Blackrobe had risen from their knees, and now they went forward to put their arms around the chief Blackrobe as though he were some woman. Neehatin looked back at his own people. They waited. There were twenty-six, including women and children. He looked at the sky. The moon sat pale in the clouds as day came out of night. The sky gave no sign against their leaving.

Neehatin walked down to the Blackrobes. He smiled at them. "We are ready," he said.

Laforgue knelt in the narrow canoe, the paddle resting on his knees, his wooden clogs tied around his neck, his head bare to the cool morning breeze. Behind him a Savage woman steadied the canoe with light strokes of her paddle. Three dogs sat on skins which covered the cargo, and at the front a male Savage held the craft in midstream, waiting, looking back to where the other canoes were moving off from shore. On the riverbank, Fathers Bourque, Bonnet and Meynard lined up in a row, waving their hats in a gesture of farewell. There were five canoes in all: the Savages traveled in family groups, the children and dogs sitting on the goods, the women paddling in the middle, the men in front and at the rear, steering and guiding the craft. Laforgue saw Daniel in the canoe behind his own and, ahead, Neehatin, the leader, who now raised his hand in a gesture which at once set all in movement. The canoes, incredibly light and fragile for their heavy burdens, glided swiftly into the slipstream, using the ebb flow to avoid moving against the main current. Laforgue looked back at the huddle of wooden settlements, at the steep cliffs and, above them, at the earth and timber ramparts enclosing the modest stone edifice of Champlain's fort, which was the principal building of New France. As he did, from the ramparts came a puff of smoke and the roar of cannon. Alarmed and astonished, the Savages looked up. Neehatin, standing in his canoe, called out that the cannon fire was an honor, a salute from the Normans for their journey. Delighted, laughing, the Savages bowed to their stroke. The canoes sped on. The Savages, as was their way, fell silent, the only noise now the slap of paddles in quiet waters.

Two years ago, before leaving France, Laforgue had journeyed to his home in Rouen to say an anniversary mass for the repose of his dead father's soul. After the ceremony, he and his mother walked back to her house, passing through the Place du Vieux Marché. It was a wet and windy spring day; rain beat on the roofs of the timbered Norman houses in the square. His mother, holding her cloak over her head, turned from her normal homeward path and crossed the square to that spot, marked by a cross, where, two hundred years before, faggots had been piled high to burn Saint Joan of Arc at the stake. His mother stopped at this holy place and, in the driving rain, knelt in prayer while Laforgue stood, awkward, not wanting to interrupt her devotions, not willing to kneel on the wet cobbles amid passing strangers. When she rose, her skirts wet, her stockings awry, his mother turned to him and said, "I prayed for you, Paul. I prayed for you here. Do you know why?"

"No, *maman.*"

"Because God has chosen you, just as He chose the Maid."

Her words made him blush. Surely it was foolish to compare him with a saint like Joan of Arc, but still it was true that ever since the Order had granted his petition to be sent to New France he had dreamed of the glory of martyrdom in that faraway land.

"Come," he said, taking her arm. "Let's go home. You're soaking. You will get your death of cold."

His mother gripped him tightly as they set off. "Promise me," she said. "Promise that when you go there, you will remember me in your daily prayers."

"Of course, of course," he said. "I always do, *maman.*"

"No, no, listen to me. God will hear your prayer as He will not hear mine. He will hear you as He did the Maid. For He has chosen you to die for Him. I will never see you again."

"*Maman,* please. You mustn't compare me with Saint Joan. I'm not a saint. Come. Let's go home."

Now in the silence of the great river, watching a flock of geese fly over distant treetops, Laforgue heard again his mother's words. In the past two years, living in the residence at Québec, every waking moment had been a preparation for this day: the time spent learning the unwritten Algonkian and Huron tongues, studying the writings of Father Brabant on the customs and language of the Savage peoples, the hours of practice in canoes, a scrupulous diligence in all tasks assigned to him, no matter how onerous or menial, and, above all, constant daily prayer, beseeching Saint Joseph and the Virgin to intercede on his behalf and grant him the honor of some greater danger in a lonely place. From the day the Savage, Ihongwaha, brought Father Brabant's letter telling of sickness in the Huron country, he had prayed in nightly vigils that he would be the chosen one. For, indeed, this was a journey like those he had read of long ago in the Jesuit house in Dieppe, a mission worthy of the Order's heroic martyrs in Paraguay, a mission to the very place where Father Brabant labored, he whom the Hurons revered, whose letters published in the *Relations* were an inspiration to all at home in France. And now his prayers had been answered. Today he set out for that place where martyrdom was more than just a pious hope. This is my hour. This is my beginning.

The day passed. The sun, high in the sky, dipped until it barely cleared the tops of the trees. A wind rippled the water into waves, a wind which numbed Laforgue's cheeks. He remembered what Father Bourque had told him of a second false summer which came in mid-October, bringing a few days of heat at the end of the autumnal season. That false summer was ending. Winter was near.

The sun fell below the tree line. Shadows moved across the surface of the water. Neehatin called out a command and at once the canoes turned, gliding toward a small tributary inlet. There, the Savages disembarked, pulling their canoes clear of the water. Laforgue, his limbs aching from hours of kneeling, walked stiffly up to the clearing where the Algonkin, with the ordered bustle of long practice, had begun to make preparations for camp. Neehatin and Chomina, the captains, assembled the men and then dispersed them among the trees. Some carried bows and arrows, others long spears like javelins, others hatchets and clubs. Daniel, taking his gun, joined one of the groups but called to Laforgue, "Stay here, Father. They say there is a chance of game. We'll be back in an hour or so."

"Will I come with you?"

The boy shook his head. Men and dogs disappeared in the undergrowth. A sudden clamor of voices filled the clearing as women passed by, carrying long poles of spruce saplings which they had just cut down. Laforgue sat for a moment watching the noisy children run about in the open space; then, remembering that it would soon be dark, he began to read his breviary. But the familiar book seemed strange in this place, and the Latin sentences jumbled in his head.

He looked up. In the center of the clearing some of the younger women had raised the long poles to converge in a sort of roof, while older ones brought from the canoes sheets of birch bark, which they unrolled, and then assembled to make the walls of the habitation. Still others dragged green spruce boughs from the nearby forest, spreading them in a vast carpet to provide a bed on which all could sleep. The work was long and arduous. The horizon took on the pale pink blush of the dying sun.

He looked at the words on his page and thought of the Jesuit house in Dieppe at this the hour of the evening office, when priests walked in the cloister, reading their breviaries, silent and absorbed. He had been one of them. But from now on he would read his office in some clearing in a strange forest, or behind the wooden palisades of a distant mission house. He looked again at the rabble of Savage women, emaciated, burdened by years of toil, limbs gnarled, faces worn by sun and wind; at the brown, laughing girls; at the children, wild as the forest which was their home. With these people he would live for years, perhaps for the rest of his life. A sudden sadness came upon him. He looked up at the pink orb of sky. A rush of tiny black birds whirled like commas across the clearing and disappeared among the treetops in a twittering swirl. He heard distant cries and, minutes later, the first male Savages came out of the forest. Their mood was jubilant. They held aloft, for the women's admiration, the slain bodies of hares and quail.

Fires were lit. The large kettles in which the Savages cooked all their food were brought up from the canoes and hung on poles which slanted over the fire. Gradually, as the sky darkened, the rest of the hunters returned. All were empty-handed until Chomina, the hunting captain, appeared with three other men, carrying on a long pole the slung body of a deer. Shouts of joy filled the air. The Algonkin butchered the deer and threw it into the kettles with the other carcasses. Then Laforgue saw Daniel come in empty-handed, stowing his gun in its hide pouch.

"Daniel?"

"Father Paul."

Daniel came over. He seemed distraught. He took

off his beaver cap, and Laforgue noticed that he had braided his long hair in the Algonkian manner.

"They have killed a deer," Daniel said. "That means we will not make an early start tomorrow."

"But we must have an early start," Laforgue said. "I will speak to Neehatin. We must go at first light."

As he spoke, darkness seeped through the crepuscular light in the clearing. The bodies of the Savages became silhouettes, moving around the flame-lit circle of fires. Dogs ran about, barking, chased by children who tormented them. In the light of the fires, the faces of the older Savages seemed inhuman as wooden masks. Then, as the first pieces of half-cooked meat were taken from a pot, Neehatin rose, cut a slice from a haunch of deer, and came to Laforgue, holding it on his knife. "Here, Nicanis," he said. "Eat this. Now you will truly eat."

This was the Savage phrase of hospitality. Laforgue took the greasy meat in his hands. Hair and skin still adhered to it. "Now I will truly eat," he said and, conquering his nausea, bit into the half-cooked flesh. Men came up smiling, as Neehatin took a second piece of meat and gave it to Daniel, saying, "Now, Iwanchou," for this was the name the Algonkin had given the boy.

"Fucking good deer meat," one Savage said.

"Eat, fucking eat," another said.

Laforgue winced at the foul words. "They speak as dogs would speak, if they had tongues," Father Bourque had said about their filthy banter. "Remember it is not meant badly. We must ignore it. They will not change." He watched them eat. "Gluttony is their highest form of happiness," the Superior had told him. "They cannot be made to hoard their food against a time when there is none. Corn for their sagamité is the only food they will save." And Father Brabant, in his letters to Father Provincial, had once joked that the only prayer the Savages would make to God, was "Give us each day elk, beaver, and moose." Laforgue looked at the greasy half-cooked meat. He had been warned that not to eat offered food was, to the Savages, an insult to the one who had offered it, and so he looked for a place where he might dispose of his portion without being seen. Daniel had moved close to the fires, squatting in the Savage fashion, contentedly calling out in the Algonkian tongue to those near him. Laforgue moved into the shadows, going downriver. As he did, a dog ran after him, jumping up, trying to get a scrap of meat. Using this as a solution, he allowed the animal to get its teeth into the flesh, then let go of his portion. The dog at once ran off into the undergrowth with its prize.

It rained. A drizzle became a downpour. The fires hissed. Women ran to the canoes to make sure the bundles were covered. The other Savages, ignoring the rain, ate stolidly until the kettles were empty. Then, soaking wet, they entered the night's habitation. Laforgue, sheltering under a tree, saw Neehatin come toward the forest and, turning his good ear in the leader's direction, heard his name.

"Nicanis? Nicanis?"

"Neehatin, you called me?"

"Nicanis, have you eaten?"

"I have truly eaten."

"Then let us go in," Neehatin said. "It will rain all night."

And so, following his host, Laforgue entered the bark habitation, pulling aside the bearskin covering which served as a door. Inside, on the bed of spruce boughs, were huddled all the Savage families, men, women and children, curled in fetal positions or lying on their backs with knees drawn up. Huddled against them or on top of them were their dogs. Laforgue saw Daniel lying in one of these groups, his cloak drawn up to cover his face as though he already slept.

"Here, Nicanis," Neehatin said, pushing aside a woman to make a place for the priest. "Lie there. You will be well."

Obediently Laforgue curled up, his back to an old woman, his face uncomfortably close to a young male who put his arm around the priest as though they were children in the same bed. Dogs crawled over the bodies of the sleepers, looking for a place to lie. A child cried. Two men conversed in low voices. Rain drummed steadily on the birch-bark roof and dripped into the dwelling from a large hole in the top of the habitation which opened on the night sky. The bed of spruce was surprisingly soft and Laforgue buried his face in the boughs, hoping that the smell of the needles would dull the sickly odor of unwashed bodies. He tried, as was his nightly custom, to direct his last waking thoughts to the crucifixion of Jesus. But the old woman behind him kicked him in the back as she rolled over, snoring. The fetid smell of the Savages' breath lay like a low cloud in the confined space, and gradually he became aware of giggles as young girls and boys crawled about in search of each other. He pulled his hat down over his eyes to shut out that which he should not see, but as he did a girl came close to him and he felt his penis stiffen.

How can I sleep in a place like this? I should go out and sleep under the trees. But what about the nights ahead, when the cold will make it impossible to survive outside and alone? This is a test. It is God's wish that I remain here.

Burrowing his face in the branches, he tried to shut out the sound of the lascivious giggles. He began to pray, automatically at first, but at last the words became prayer. *O Lord, I give Thee thanks. Thou hast brought me here.*

Neehatin woke. The dream filled his mind. He did not know what it commanded, but it must be obeyed. The fact that he had dreamed it on the first night of a journey meant it signaled a danger ahead. But what danger? He must divine what it said. He got up and made his way through the mass of sleeping bodies. As he passed his wife, he kicked her in the small of the back, signaling her to rise and follow him. He went out. The sky was quiet. The rain had stopped. Above the forest, the moon watched him as he walked across the clearing. He looked into the forest. The forest was still asleep. He squatted down on the riverbank, facing the waters.

He heard his wife's footsteps in the clearing. In the Iroquois nation women had power in council, but Neehatin's people treated their wives as they did their dogs. Neehatin did not understand why his people behaved thus. His wife had the gift of sight. He looked at her as she came toward him under the gaze of the moon. She was ugly with many winters and bent with the burdens of carrying, cooking and making shelter. Her children did not help her. All were males. When she came up, she squatted down beside him and he knew that she knew. "Yes," he said. "I dreamed."

She looked at him. "On the first night of a journey," she said. "Shit!"

"It's a warning," he said. "That is good, isn't it?"

She did not answer this. "Tell me your dream."

"I was on a log. I paddled across a river and landed in an open place. I walked up to a meadow, and when I did, this fucking big serpent followed me through the grasses."

"Then?"

"I went back to the river and again sat on the log. As I paddled away, a heavy man jumped onto the log behind me and made it rock. I fell in the water and a fish swam up and told me to follow it. It led me to the farther shore. That is all. What does it mean?"

She bent her head, thinking. "The serpent is a sorcerer. We must find a sorcerer to tell us what is the danger."

"So it is a danger, then?"

She nodded. "Yes. The heavy man is the Blackrobe."

Neehatin was surprised. He had not thought of that. "So it is the Blackrobe who brings us danger?"

"Yes."

"But we have taken him with us. What does the dream say I must do?"

"It says you must find the fish. We must get a sorcerer to tell us what is the fish that will save us."

"Mestigoit is a sorcerer," Neehatin said. "He is the only one between here and the winter hunting place. He lives with the Montagnais in the middle place."

"How many nights?"

"Eight."

"Shit," she said. "Eight nights?"

"We will drive hard. With any fucking luck we might do it in seven."

"You must try," she said. She looked at the forest. "The trees have wakened. It is time to go."

"First I must tell the senior men." He looked at her, then at the forest. A great fear came upon him. "I show no fear," he said. He spoke not to his wife but to the forest.

The trees murmured. He did not hear what they said.

"What will I do now?" he asked them.

*Smile upon the Blackrobe,* the forest said.

"I will do that," Neehatin said.

Laforgue woke. Above him, in the opening of the roof of the Savage habitation, he saw the morning sky. He felt that he would vomit. Shutting his nostrils to the fetid stink of his sleeping companions, he stumbled over to the doorway. When he stepped out into the clearing, all was clean and still. Grass and leaves glittered with dew. In the nearby forest, sunlight struck down through the great aisles of trees, reminding him of the shadows in the nave of the cathedral of Coutances. He looked at the river, at that swift current which carried these waters thousands of leagues to the sea. Near the beached canoes, a small group of Savages squatted in a semicircle, listening to their leader. Laforgue saw Neehatin's lips move but at that distance could not hear what was said. Not wishing to intrude, he walked in the opposite direction, continuing on until he was out of sight of the encampment. Then, alone in the morning silence, he knelt by the current and, undoing the buttons of his cassock, bathed his head and hands in the chill waters. When he had finished he wiped himself dry with tufts of grass, then knelt again to say his morning prayers. As so often, when facing a new trial he invoked the aid of the Virgin Mary.

O Holy Mother, he prayed, I ask for your solemn benediction on this journey. I ask your help in this weakness which has afflicted my ear. Unless this infection abates, I fear I will no longer be able to hear what is told to me. I do not ask your Son to lift this trial from me. I know that these afflictions have a meaning, that God does not allow Himself easily to be conquered and the more one gives, the more one gains, the more one loses, the more one finds. But God sometimes hides Himself, and then the cup is very bitter. When, afflicted by this deafness, I feel unable to carry out His work, I fear in my weakness that He has hidden His face from me. . . .

At that moment a great shadow passed over him, and, looking up, his prayer stillborn on his lips, he saw, high above, a huge eagle of a sort he had never seen in France, its head white, its beak and talons yellow, its great blackish wings rigid as sails, catching the wind eddies as it glided back and forth over the trees. Suddenly, swift as clashing swords, the great wings shut. The eagle plummeted between the trees. And as Laforgue knelt there, his struggles, his deafness, the dangers of his journey were transformed miraculously into a great adventure, a chance to advance God's glory here in a distant land. God was not hidden; He had shown Himself in the eagle's flight. Laforgue saw the eagle rise from the trees, its great wings beating steadily as it carried off its prey. In the beauty of this wild place, his heart sang a *Te Deum* of happiness.

* * *

"The other Norman is now awake," Chomina said.

Neehatin, who had just told his dream to the senior men, looked up and saw the boy Iwanchou come across the clearing. Unlike the Blackrobe, this boy had keen ears. Neehatin made a sign of caution to the others. The boy came up.

"When do we leave?" he asked.

"We leave now."

"Good. Nicanis will be pleased."

Neehatin pointed downriver. "Nicanis is awake and went down there. Find him and tell him we are ready."

"I will do that," the boy said.

The senior men watched him go. "Why did you say we will leave?" one of them asked. "There is good hunting here."

"Because the dream says we must."

"Are you sure of that?" asked Ougebemat, an old man who, years ago, had fought with Agnonha against the Iroquois. The senior man turned to him. Ougebemat was one who read dreams.

"I am sure," Neehatin said, but he felt the sweat of fear trickle from the hair at his neck.

"The man who made you fall off the log is the Blackrobe," Ougebemat said. "Am I right?"

Neehatin looked at him, alarmed. He says what my wife said. "Yes, you are right," Neehatin said.

"Then to obey the dream we should leave these Norman pigs and go on alone."

Neehatin shook his head. "It does not tell me that. Besides, we have made a promise to their leader. Do you not fear his anger, you who fought beside him?"

"I shit upon his anger. I shit upon all Normans," Ougebemat said. "I fear the dream."

"I, too, fear it," Neehatin said. "And I obey it by taking these Norman turds in our canoes. The dream told me that the serpent is a sorcerer, and so we must keep the Blackrobe with us until the sorcerer tells us what to do with him."

He saw at once that his words had won the argument.

There was agreement among the senior men. If the dream said the serpent was a sorcerer, then Ougebemat was overruled.

"If the dream tells you that," Ougebemat said, "then it must be obeyed. For it is not dreamed by some useless prick, but by a leader."

The others made the sound of approval, for of course Ougebemat spoke the truth. The dream of a leader must be obeyed. A dream is more real than death or battle.

"We must leave at once," Neehatin said. "The sorcerer, Mestigoit, is seven nights, maybe eight, from here. We will be in danger until we find him. We must travel as if there is a fire at our back. Agreed?"

All gave the guttural of assent. They rose. The parley was over. Neehatin felt the muscles of his neck tremble with tension and pulled his chin down lest Chomina notice, Chomina who watched other men as a hunter watches for a movement which will tell him when to strike. But Chomina did not know that the dream had told Neehatin nothing, that it was Neehatin's wife who said the serpent meant a sorcerer.

And at that moment, aware that—while these men did not know he had not spoken the truth—the river, the forest, the animals they would hunt all knew his lie, Neehatin looked again at the forest and felt great fear. And again the forest spoke, reassuring him. *Smile upon the Blackrobe,* the forest said.

*I have done so,* Neehatin told the trees. He turned and signaled to the women who had come up. "Take down the birch bark. Load the canoes. Hurry."

# 3

In the next four days, the Savages paddled from dawn to dusk. They did not stop to eat or even to relieve themselves; to Laforgue's disgust, while in the canoes they urinated into the kettles used for cooking food. When Laforgue wished to defecate, the Algonkin who acted as lead paddler in his canoe signaled him to do so off the rear of the craft. And so, in shame among the gibes of the children and to the amusement of the women, he must bare his buttocks to the wind. The Savages, foul-mouthed as always, called out jokes and insults, some of which he did not catch, but those he heard made him wince; one woman yelling, "Look at his white bum," and another, "Show us your prick, Nicanis"; and yet, with all this banter, their paddling did not cease and the canoe was not allowed to fall behind the others. The Savages' strength amazed him; they paddled in relays, never shirking their turn. His shoulders ached and his arms felt as though they had been wrenched on a rack. But he remembered Father

Brabant's warning: "When you take up a paddle in their canoes, do not lay it down until you have done your share. If you do, they will despise you." And so, hour after hour, in pain, he toiled with them, smiling as they insulted him. There was no harm in these insults. They insulted each other ceaselessly but did not take offense. In Québec, when he had first studied their language, he had been warned by Father Bourque of their habit of answering questions about the word "God" or "heaven" by giving as the equivalent some foul word like fuck or cunt. And so, said Father Bourque, we must be constantly on guard against this and learn well all the filthy words they employ. Now, to his shame, these words were often the only part of a Savage sentence which made sense to his failing ears.

Each night at the onset of darkness, the canoes landed. A fire was lit and the foul corn gruel called sagamité was cooked over an open fire. It tasted, to Laforgue, like watery glue, yet he must eat it or starve. The Savages no longer thought of hunting. When they had eaten, they crept into the night's makeshift habitation and slept until the hour before dawn, when they rose, ate some of the cold sagamité left over from the night before and, collecting their belongings, knelt again in the canoe. Laforgue and Daniel, although weary and often faint, quickly accustomed themselves to this rhythm of travel and, like the Algonkin, passed the day mainly in silence, paddling, staring at the lank hair and tawny shoulders of the paddler ahead, traveling through landscapes which, hour after hour, day after day, never seemed to change.

On the evening of the fourth day, shortly before the canoes landed for the night, it began to rain. The Algonkin, on landing, at once put on the garments they wore in cold weather, long tunics and stockings made of moose skin which they tied around them with many thongs. Laforgue, stiff from his day's work, stumbled and fell as he came up the riverbank. Daniel at once ran to him.

"Are you all right, Father Paul?"

Laforgue smiled. "Even though I was trained to kneel for hours in the chapel, it seems I have lost the habit."

As he and Daniel went on they saw, in a small knot near the trees, Chomina, Neehatin and the senior men, a strange sight in their moose-skin garments, their heads close in a parley. Neehatin turned and looked at the priest. His lips moved.

"He is calling you," Daniel said. "Do you not hear him?"

"Yes, yes, I hear him," Laforgue said, but saw only that the Savage moved his lips.

"Come with me," Laforgue told Daniel. "You can help me speak with him."

Neehatin came toward them in the rain, saying something Laforgue could not catch.

"What does he say?"

"He says they have paddled hard so that we will reach the rapids early, as Agnonha wishes. He asks that you give them thank-yous."

"Thank-yous?"

"It's a word they use when they want you to give them a gift."

"What thank-yous do you want?" Laforgue said to the leader.

"You have tobacco," Neehatin said. "We do not. With tobacco we will paddle hard and you will be pleased."

"But we are keeping the tobacco to trade on the Ottawa."

Neehatin smiled. It was not a pleasant smile. "*Khisakhiran,*" he said.

*Khisakhiran* was a phrase the Savages used to criticize the French for not sharing with others. *Khisakhiran* meant "You love it, you love it more than us." The Savages shared everything, even with strangers. But Laforgue remembered the Superior's warning: "If you give to them what you have, they will ask and ask until they have taken all you own."

"What if I give a pipeful to each?" Laforgue asked Neehatin, smiling to show he was not offended at the insult.

But the Algonkin shook his head and said contemptuously, "*Sakhita.*" It meant, "Since you love it, then love it." He walked away.

"He is offended, Father."

"I know he is offended. I am not deaf."

"If we do not share with them," Daniel said, "how can we expect them to share with us?"

Laforgue felt himself flush. Why is it that this boy, barely twenty, feels he can lecture me on how to deal with the Savages? "All right," he said angrily. He called after Neehatin. "Neehatin, forgive me. Please take the tobacco."

The Savage stopped, then turned around, staring at Laforgue. Inexplicably, he burst into laughter.

"I am sorry," Laforgue said again.

"We will smoke," Neehatin said and smiled. He called to the women. "Get the tobacco from Nicanis's canoe. Now we will truly smoke."

Two young girls ran down to Laforgue's canoe and began to undo one of the bundles. "It's the wrong bundle," Laforgue said to Daniel. "What if they find the altar wine?"

At once, Daniel ran to the canoe and, laughing, slapped a tall slender girl, who was undoing the bundle which contained vestments, missals and the altar wine. Laughing, the girl hit Daniel, who caught hold of her and pulled her to the bundle in which the tobacco was stored. Neehatin walked down to the canoe and took possession of the small bale of tobacco which Laforgue had counted on to help them pay the Allumette people for their help in portages on the upper river. A cry of joy went up.

The priest turned, walked away and, under the shelter of the trees, took out his breviary. The rain had almost ceased. As he read his office, his weariness was such that his eyes closed and he fell asleep. When he woke, the fires were lit and the cooked sagamité was being apportioned. The men and the older women lay around smoking their pipes. Laforgue pulled his cloak around him. He was hungry, but the thought of sagamité repelled him. He rose and, taking his knife, began to cut some spruce branches and arrange them in a pallet under the shelter of a large tree. As he did, someone came toward him in the darkness. It was Daniel.

"What are you doing, Father Paul?"

"I thought I would sleep out here for a change."

"Why?"

"I have trouble with my sleep in the habitation. The stink, the noise, the things that go on in there."

"What things?" Daniel stared at the priest.

"Have you not seen? Better you should not. I am not happy that you sleep there either. Especially you."

"Why especially me?"

"The Savages are like dogs. They have no—" He felt himself flush. These were things he did not want to put into words.

"But we cannot sleep outside," Daniel said. "It may rain again. If we fall sick, the Algonkin will not help us."

"They would not leave us."

"But they would not help us. We must fend for ourselves. That is their way. And something is wrong. Haven't you noticed?"

"Wrong?"

"Why are we traveling like this? I heard Chomina's wife say that we must travel like this for three more days."

"Merciful God," Laforgue said. "Can we stand it?"

"We must," the boy said. "Besides, it's what you wanted, isn't it? You told me we are late in starting on the journey."

"By my map," Laforgue said, "in three days we should reach the first falls. Perhaps that is what they have in mind."

"I don't know," the boy said. "But they are worried about something. Look, it's raining again. Let's go in."

And so, in company with Daniel, Laforgue entered the stinking habitation. Within minutes dogs scrambled over him, walking on his stomach. He struck out, crying, *"Aché, aché,"* the words the Savages used to drive dogs off, but it was useless. The Savages did not feed their animals in any regular manner, and these last days, with no hunting, there were no scraps and so, hungry and restless, the dogs stuck their snouts in and out among the sleeping bodies. A child bawled. Laforgue drew his cloak over his face and covered his ears with his hands. As on previous nights, his whole body ached with grievous pain. I will never be able to sleep.

And, at once, he fell asleep.

When he woke again it was pitch dark. He uncovered his face and looked up at the opening which showed the sky. The moon had hidden itself. The habitation now slept the sleep of the predawn hour, the Savages huddled in a cohesive mass, like some great animal, twitching as though dreaming a collective dream. Laforgue moved stiffly, his shoulders in pain from his labors in the canoe. As he did, he saw that Daniel was no longer his sleepmate. In Daniel's place a Savage woman lay, her face within inches of his, her mouth open, her breathing sonorous in a fluttering snore. Laforgue squirmed around and sat up, looking for Daniel. But in the darkness it was impossible to tell one body from another. Again he was nauseated by the smell. Perhaps Daniel went outside? Laforgue rose and, stumbling, trying not to walk on others, made his way to the flap which screened off the entrance.

Outside the night air was fresh as new wine. The great silence, the immensity of the sky, the clean smell of the forest, all were the delicious obverse of the cramped, fetid habitation. Above, amid trailing leaves of cloud, the moon slipped in and out of sight like some plump, mysterious fruit, its cold rays lighting the dark floor of the forest in a steely sheen. He looked around. He was alone.

Slowly, he walked across the open space and faced the river's current. The night was warm. It was as though, after the rain, the summer's heat had stolen back. He turned, half tempted to go and make his bed there among the trees. And then, so close as to make the skin prickle on his neck, a man's voice spoke softly in the Savage tongue. A second voice murmured a reply. His heart pounded. He remembered the Superior's warning about the suddenness of the enemy. They were speaking to each other. They had not seen him. The sound came from directly behind him, in the trees. Bending down foolishly in a half crouch, as though by diminishing his height he lessened his chance of being seen, he turned to face the forest.

He heard new sounds. It was no longer speech but a kind of moaning. He heard, also, the rustle of undergrowth. Moving forward he gently parted a screen of birch leaves and was instantly in full view of two people. But they did not see him.

He crouched down, half closing the screen of leaves but still peering through. He heard himself begin to pant, his breathing an imitation of the sounds ahead. The moonlight slipped clear of all cloud, shining bright as day. He stared at the naked forms, the boy kneeling behind the girl, his hands gripping her waist, the girl bent over, her arms and face on the ground, as he came into her from behind, like dogs coupling. The boy lifted his head as his loins thrust into her. His face was wild with excitement. The boy was Daniel. The moaning sounds were his.

And Laforgue, peering through the leaves, saw it all, saw her nakedness, her pointed breasts almost touching the ground, her face contorted as though in pain.

And as he saw it he tried to still his own agitation. He watched and watched, afraid of being seen, his mind flooded with this vision of lust. He felt his penis swell and stiffen until it hurt. He moved his head a little, peering in, not wanting to miss the next thrust of the boy's loins. And to his shock and excitement it was as though he were the boy, rearing above that Savage girl, the same girl he had seen earlier, the tall slim girl who had run down to get tobacco from the canoe.

The boy gasped in climax, then leaned forward, resting his head on her shoulders. Both eased down onto the improvised nest they had fashioned from branches and clothing. He watched as, slowly, the girl's fingers began to move along Daniel's thigh. She raised herself up and then, to Laforgue's astonishment, her head moved down to his loins. In all his celibate dreams, dreams for which he had scourged himself in his novice cell, he had never imagined such a thing. The girl kissed and sucked on Daniel's penis, and the sight filled him with such a mixture of shame, anger and desire that he felt he would faint. The girl crawled around in the makeshift bed and now, as she kissed Daniel in that place, she presented her narrow girlish buttocks to the Jesuit's avid stare, as though offering him the same delight she had just given to the boy.

And at that, as though possessed, Laforgue began to fumble with the buttons of his cassock. Kneeling, still staring, his breathing harsh as a tearing sheet, he began to jerk furiously until his semen spurted, spilling on the ground. The lovers, kissing each other, began again to rear up, positioning themselves for coitus as their watcher turned away, crawling clumsily on all fours, moving in awkward haste across the clearing until he was close to the riverbank. He rose and, stumbling, in panic, began to run. He ran down the riverbank and along the edge of the current, running until the encampment was far out of sight.

He stopped and looked back. He was alone. It was as though he were the only living thing in this place. He bowed his head and began to sob, in a harsh broken rhythm, the sound oddly loud as it echoed across the moonlit waters of the river. He stood sobbing in that wild place, bereft of all hope, beyond all forgiveness. The moon faded, and gradually a bloody dawn was born in the sky. Laforgue turned away from the river and, taking out his knife, went again into the forest, coming back with some spruce boughs, trimmed and pliant, twisted to form a discipline. Again he faced the river, then lowered his cassock and unbuttoned his undershift, leaving his torso bare. Methodically, as though he used a flail on wheat, he scourged his back, lash after lash, as blood spilt into the folds of his lowered robe, until his flayed back was purpled as the sky above. Only then did he cast the discipline aside and, falling to his knees, try to say the prayers of penance, the prayers of shame.

"Where is Nicanis?" Neehatin called, as the canoes were placed in the water.

Daniel looked around. Where was he? And then he saw the priest come around the bend of the riverbank, walking slowly, as though in thought. "Father Laforgue?" Laforgue looked up and, seeing the Algonkin ready to depart, hurried to join them. Where had he been? Daniel wondered, but then lost interest in the priest for there *she* was, getting into Chomina's canoe, kneeling behind her mother as they moved out into the stream. Daniel paddled, trying to come closer to her, but his paddlers stalled the canoe in the water, signaling him to wait. There was a rule to travel. First Neehatin's canoe, then Chomina's. Then the others. As she passed she did not look at him. He knew she would not look at him. Nor did she want him to look at her. Oonta had told him that was their custom. A suitor must pretend no interest in the girl; he must not look at her or speak to her or stay near her, unless accidentally. Otherwise everyone will make a mockery of him and the girl will feel shame for him.

*Look at me,* he willed her as her canoe glided by. Your canoe will be ahead of mine all day. I will not see you until night.

If she does not want me to look at her, it means she sees me as a suitor. But that's impossible. The Algonkin don't care if we sleep with their girls, but they will never accept me as her husband. They say we are ugly and hairy, that we do not share with others as they do. They believe themselves to be more intelligent than we are.

Yet she *must* see me as a suitor. Otherwise she would laugh and look at me as the other girls do. Oonta and that other little girl at the eel fishery let me do what I wanted. They did not care if I looked at them and spoke to them when others were present. But she does. She tells me I am not ugly as are the other French. Yet she let Mercier put his prick inside her. She kissed him there.

I cannot bear to think of that. When I was fourteen and in the schoolyard of the Récollet Fathers, I saw a boy pass around filthy drawings to the others. I gave him all my money so that I could take the drawings and tear them up. That is how I feel when I think of her and Mercier. Yet why do I feel that way, when I myself think of doing it to her, all day, all night? I am now the opposite of the boy in the schoolyard, the boy I once was.

Does she think of me as a suitor? What would Chomina say? I think he likes me; he says he loves me well. But one cannot believe what they say. They lie to us as they would never lie to each other, because they do not think of us as men but as monsters. Father Bourque said when they first saw our ships and went aboard, we offered them wine and dry biscuit. They went back and told their people that we were devils who lived in a floating wooden island and drank blood and ate dry bones. They believe animals have souls and intelligence. They believe the trees are alive and watching them. Because we do not believe as they do, they think us stupid. They would only accept me if I became as they are. They might adopt me then, as they do some of their prisoners. But Father Bourque said they rarely adopt their prisoners: instead they torture and kill them. To become one of them I would have to torture and kill as they do. Could I? I have tortured my Savior, and for a girl who is not a girl but a wild animal. I give her presents, yes, but it is not just for presents that she sleeps with me. She thinks of me as a suitor. It must be that.

What do I know? I cannot think. I no longer pray, I who once wanted to give my life for God. I think I am in love with her, but how can it be love when it will bring me eternal damnation? If I died tonight I would go straight to hell. Yet even though I know it, I cannot repent. I cannot because I do not wish to lose her. To save my soul I should at once confess to Father Paul. But if I did, he would make it his duty to keep me away from her. I must have her. I will have her tonight. I will be damned for all eternity. She thinks of me as her suitor. I think only of that.

On the sixth day of the race to the sorcerer, it turned cold. High gray clouds dulled the sky as the canoes sped along the great concourse of the river. The Savages pressed on as never before. Even when, ahead of the leading canoe, a family of moose blundered down to the water—the male raising its antlered head to utter a cry of alarm, the females stock-still in the shallows—Neehatin's arm rose in signal, commanding the paddlers to continue.

The rain ceased. Just before dark, soft drifting snowflakes fell like a swarm of moths. Laforgue, his back smarting from his self-inflicted contrition, looked up at the sky. At once he thought of the aide-mémoire written for him by the Superior:

*If a heavy snowfall occurs within two weeks of the start of your journey, the Algonkin may decide not to travel farther but to winter in some place where they can hunt large animals who flounder in the snow. I pray that the snows will not come until you have passed the rapids. It is there the portages are the longest. I must warn you that in the past Father Brabant and Father Gulot were left below the rapids with one canoe and little food, but they still reached their destination with the help of this map. God did not turn from them as He will not turn from you. Your journey is in His hands.*

But this is not a true snowfall, Laforgue reflected as he stared into the mist of snowflakes. And if we are abandoned by the Savages, at least Daniel will be removed from the occasion of sin. What am I to do? It is my duty to ask him to confess and abjure the company of that girl. But how can I speak to him? Who am I to speak to anyone, I who am unspeakable?

When the canoes landed, the snow was thick on the ground. Neehatin called out instructions about the habitation, instructions Laforgue did not hear because at that moment he was looking for Daniel. Where was he, was he with that girl? He went to the place where the women were cutting boughs for the habitation and saw the girl with two others, dragging spruce branches out of the forest. As was the custom, while they worked they exchanged foul words and insults, laughing all the while. When Laforgue looked at her face he felt his cheeks grow warm with embarrassment.

The girl's long black hair was gathered behind her neck and held in place by a disk of native copper. She wore a necklace of beads which fell between her breasts. Like so many of the Savages her skin was light, as though bronzed by the sun, and her teeth were gleaming white. But her tunic, as was usual, was greasy and stained and her arms and legs were blackened with grime from the campfires. He looked at her and had to force himself to look away. The devil uses her against us.

At that moment he saw Daniel come from the forest, his cap filled with wild berries. Daniel came up to him at once.

"Here, Father. Take some."

As Laforgue took a handful he avoided Daniel's eye. Into his mind came the lustful picture that, last night, he had tried to burn into his brain. In silence, he ate the bitter berries.

"How was the day?" the boy asked.

He shrugged awkwardly. He did not feel able to speak. If I speak, I must confront him.

"Something is very wrong," Daniel said.

"Wrong?" Laforgue's voice was hoarse.

"One of the Savages told me they must reach a certain place by tomorrow night. I don't know why."

"A Savage told you? Which one?"

"Chomina's daughter," the boy said. His face showed no concern.

"That one? That girl over there? The one dragging branches?"

Daniel looked to where the three girls were working. "Yes, the tall one," he said. He kept looking at the girl. "They will build a winter habitation tonight," he said. "It's because of the snow."

I must speak to him. I must tell him that I know. But, as before, he could not say the words. Instead, he reached into Daniel's cap and took a few more of the bitter berries. As he munched them, Daniel turned and went across the clearing to where the men were using their snowshoes as shovels to clear a space for the habitation. The tall girl, laughing, began to call out something to the others. Nearby, the older women were cooking the night's meal of sagamité, pushing long branches into the blazing fire.

Laforgue turned away. Tears filled his eyes, tears he did not understand. He went into the woods and, stumbling, found a place where the snow had not fallen.

There, under the trees, he knelt to pray. Tears wet his cheeks as he said, over and over, the words of contrition. *O my God, I am heartily sorry for having offended Thee.* His lips moved but, even as he prayed, the image of last night came into his mind and his penis stiffened. He knelt there for a long time. The darkness came. He heard someone call his name.

"Father Paul?"

He rose and came out of the tree shelter. Daniel stood in the clearing. "Have you eaten?"

"I am not hungry," Laforgue said.

"Neehatin wants us to go in. We will leave at first light."

Because of the cold the habitation was smaller than those built before, and with a lower roof. The Savages must crawl in on hands and knees. A fire burned in its center and the smoke was suffocating, blinding the eyes and causing everyone to cough. Laforgue's nose and throat were assailed in such force by the smoke that he pressed his face into the spruce branches on the ground. Despite the fierce heat of the fire his back froze. In the noise of the coughing and the crying of children, sleep was impossible. Daniel lay near him but when, after a while, Laforgue opened his eyes he could no longer see in the haze. He lay, his mind shipwrecked among snatches of prayer, anguished promises that he would confront the boy, and the troubling and insidious images of lust which again came before him. At last when, the fire dying and the smoke abating, he sensed all were asleep, he managed to raise himself up and peer about for Daniel. But as he had feared the boy was nowhere to be seen. Crawling about amid the grumbles of sleepy Savages, Laforgue at last reached the bearskin which served as a door and, on his hands and knees, came out into the open. The night air was very cold. The moon was not visible. He could barely see ten paces in front of him. As he stood up, a roaring filled his infected ear and for a moment he thought he would lose consciousness. The moon came out from behind a cloud so that, for the first time, he could see his path. He entered the forest. He did not call out Daniel's name, and as he moved cautiously in the undergrowth he realized, with shame, that he had wished to come on them unseen. And if I do, if I see them copulating, will I hide and again become the third actor in this scene? I am not competent to counsel or censure him. I am no longer fit to be a priest.

He turned and left the forest. The night was now freezing cold. At the door of the habitation he crawled in, burrowing himself a place among a huddle of sleeping Savages. At last, warmed by human contact, exhausted, he fell asleep.

# 4

THE SAVAGES SANG. THEY HAD BEEN SINGING SINCE dawn, when they embarked on the river. Their songs were, as always, monotonous chants, without gaiety, attuned to the rhythm of their labors. But this was the first time they had sung in seven days. It was as though the song were a celebration, as though the journey were ending. And indeed, shortly after noon, on a sudden signal from Neehatin, the paddling ceased. As the canoes drifted on the edge of the current, a loon skimmed low over the waters, uttering its lonely call. In the silence which followed, Neehatin seemed to listen. And then, from the trees by the shoreline, some twenty unknown Savages came, waving aloft their javelins and shields. From their dress and decorations they seemed similar to the Algonkin, and at sight of them Neehatin sent his canoes toward shore. As the canoes came in, some of the strangers ran into the shallows, helping to lift them to dry land. Laforgue leaned forward, clumsily rocking his craft. "Who are these?" he asked.

"Montagnais," said his paddler.

As the Savages had no way of greeting strangers, their greeting was simply to accept the strangers' help in disembarking from their craft. The newcomers were all male. When Daniel and Laforgue stepped ashore these men came up, circling them as though they were strange sights. At last, one of the newcomers turned to Ougebemat. "Why does this one wear black stuff?"

"Because he is a fucking demon," Ougebemat said, and some of the Algonkin began to laugh.

"They are covered with hair like a pig," a newcomer said. "Why did you bring us these ugly pigs?"

"Because they are hungry," Ougebemat said. "They wanted to eat us, but we told them they would have to eat you instead. We told them you are shit and you taste sweet."

All were laughing now, Algonkin and Montagnais, but Laforgue, watching, could see that some of the newcomers were still uneasy. He smiled at them and said, "We have come to help you. We are sent by our great God, who is the God of all of us, even of you whom we have never seen."

"This black one cannot speak properly. He barks like a dog," a Montagnais said.

"They are Normans and they also speak their own tongue, which is like birds singing," Chomina said. "They are strange ones. They live on wooden islands in the great water. They are ugly, all right, but they have good presents to give. And we love them because their leader Agnonha fought and won for us, many winters ago, when we killed the fucking Iroquois."

"Then they are Agnonha's men," said one of the newcomers. "They are the shits who love furs."

"They love them more than life," Chomina said, and all laughed.

Neehatin then raised his hand. "Is Mestigoit with you?"

"He is."

"Good. I must speak with him." He turned to his group. "Look for berries and game. I will be back soon."

"There is no hunting in this part," one of the newcomers said. "We are moving on."

"Yesterday we saw moose," Chomina said.

"That was yesterday, you shithead," the newcomer said, laughing. "If you stay here I'll tell you what you will eat. You will eat tree bark."

Neehatin approached Laforgue. "I will not be long, Nicanis. There is someone I must see before we move on."

The newcomers went with him. All disappeared in the trees. "Tell me," Daniel asked Laforgue. "Have you thought what you will do if they abandon us?"

"We will go on alone. But why would they abandon us?"

Daniel did not answer. He took up his musket. "I'll go into the forest," he said. "Maybe I can find some game." He went off. Some of the Algonkian males took their spears and hatchets and also went into the woods. Laforgue looked at the tall girl, who was picking fleas from her mother's hair and eating them. The Savages ate these insects, not from appetite but as a revenge against the fleas for having been bitten by them. That was what Father Bourque had told him. He said it was part of their feelings toward their enemies. An enemy must be shown no mercy. He must be crushed. Laforgue sat down, opened his breviary and began to read his daily office. When he had finished, some children ran up and snatched off his wide-brimmed hat. Running after them to retrieve it, he stumbled and fell.

As he got up, wincing because he had bruised his knee, he saw Neehatin come from the forest, followed by a small figure which, at first, Laforgue took to be a child. But this was no child. It was the only deformed Savage he had yet seen, a small hunchback, his wizened face painted a bright yellow, a strange pigtailed hat perched on his naked skull. He wore an extraordinary garment of old patched fur and carried a loose bag of skins containing his belongings. When the women and children saw this figure, they fell silent. Neehatin, crossing the clearing, made a sign to Chomina, who had not gone into the woods. Chomina got up and, entering the forest, uttered a loud high cry which imitated some animal. It was a signal for the hunters to return. The hunchback, meantime, walked around the clearing, peering at the faces of the women and children like an actor taking his bow, but stopped abruptly when he reached Laforgue. His glittering black eyes narrowed and blinked as though he faced a blinding light. He turned and looked to Neehatin, who nodded, whereupon the hunchback, stepping carefully as though he trod on river ice, moved very close to the Jesuit. Laforgue, holding his wide-brimmed hat in one hand, his breviary in the other, smiled uncertainly at the little man who now stood directly beneath him, immobile, looking up, his painted face dead as a mask, its only sign of life his glittering jewel eyes. There was something about him which caused Laforgue an instant unease so that, forgetting what he had been taught about addressing a strange Savage, he said, "I am Nicanis. What is your name?"

"Ah! Ah! Ah!" The hunchback danced up and down in a sudden rage. "Why do you tell your name? Why do you ask my name? You know you must never do that."

"I am sorry," Laforgue said. "I forgot." For it was true that the Savages did not like to be asked their names and, if asked, would pretend not to understand. Father Bourque had told him, also, that he should not tell his own name unasked.

He stared at the little hunchback, who continued to dance up and down, calling, "Ah! Ah! Ah!" as though he were in pain.

"I said I am sorry." Laforgue tried to smile. "I ask your pardon."

"No, no, no," the hunchback cried. "You lie. I will tell you why you said that name. Because it is not your name. It is the name of the man who was in your body before you crept inside it. You are not Nicanis, whoever that man was. You are a demon."

Laforgue felt himself start. "Why do you say that?" he asked.

"Because *I* am a demon," the hunchback said. "Oh, yes. Everyone knows it. I entered the cunt of an Algonkian woman thirty winters past and was borne by her as a child. And you, Blackrobe, you also are a demon. Now, let me see." He turned away from Laforgue, half bowing, again circling like an actor before his audience. He stopped, facing the forest, and waited, in a pose of total immobility.

At that moment, as though in a play, Chomina's hunters came from the trees. Among them was Daniel. The hunchback pointed to Daniel. For a moment all was still, the figures in the clearing frozen as figures in a frieze.

"Let me look at you," the hunchback cried. "Are you this demon's son? Are you? No, no, I see it now. You are just another Norman pig, a greedy fucker in love with furs."

Daniel smiled. "I am not in love with furs. I am here to help this Father in his work. We are traveling north to the country of the Hurons."

"Father, what Father?" the hunchback shouted, as though he misunderstood. "This Blackrobe is not your Father, I tell you. He is not what he says he is. He is a demon." He bent over, opened his bag of skins and took from it a drum of the sort used by the Savages for their ceremonies and songs, a flat circular drum made of skins with pebbles inside it. He held up the drum and, circling again, shook it as he made his way back to Laforgue. He shook the drum to the right of the Jesuit, then to the left. He began to howl in a loud ferocious manner and ran around Laforgue, still shaking the drum. The Savages stood silent, watching. At the third circling, the hunchback laid down his drum in front of the priest, then, turning, scuttled back across the clearing to Neehatin, who bent to listen as the little man whispered in his ear. When he had finished, the hunchback ran back and picked up the drum. He no longer looked at Laforgue. It was as though the priest had ceased to exist.

"He is a sorcerer," Daniel said to Laforgue.

A sorcerer. Laforgue thought of what Father Brabant had written in the *Relations*.

> *The sorcerers are our greatest enemies. They are cunning and prey on the people's ignorance. But, also, in some way I fear that they may traffic with the devil. I do not know for sure, but when I traveled with the Savages, the sorcerer did his best to impede my efforts to implant the Faith. I felt he was the agent of the Evil One. Day and night he incited others to kill me.*

Neehatin raised his hand. "We will go now," he told the band. "Mestigoit will travel in the canoe of Nicanis. We will find moose upriver. My dream tells me so."

And now, as the canoes slid into the water, the children and the sorcerer climbed into the center of Laforgue's craft. The hunchback arranged himself with his back to the forward paddlers, his legs drawn up underneath him in a squatting position, his glittering eyes fixed on Laforgue, as though he were his jailer. Laforgue, made uneasy by his stare, heard again the strange words of the hunchback. *You are not Nicanis, whoever that man was. You are a demon.* Can it be that this man is the devil's agent and sees the mark of my sin in me? Or can it be that the Evil One is using him to tempt me to despair and doubt and so prevent me from completing my mission?

Now that they had found the sorcerer, the Savages no longer seemed driven. After less than two hours they disembarked in a long meadow, fringed by the omnipresent trees of the forest. At once, Neehatin gave permission to the hunters to go in search of game, while the women, as usual, began to build a habitation. It had not snowed here, but the air was chill.

Laforgue sat alone, reading his breviary, but as he did, he saw the hunchback Mestigoit urinating at the far end of the meadow. He and Laforgue were the only men left in camp. The sorcerer came up and sat cross-legged in front of the priest as Laforgue turned the pages of his breviary. From his bag of skins the sorcerer took his flat drum and shook it. After a few moments he began to howl, accompanying his strange cries with a frantic rattling of the drum. The noise caused Laforgue's head to ring, but he read on. Seeing this, the sorcerer rose and began to dance around the Jesuit, stamping his feet, shaking the drum close to Laforgue's face, howling so horribly that there could no longer be any pretense of ignoring him.

Laforgue shut his breviary. "What's wrong?" he asked. "Why do you do this?"

The hunchback stopped prancing and put his head on one side. "I am driving you out, demon. I am telling you to come out of that man's body and leave this place. You fear noise, demon. You do not like the drum."

"I am not a demon," Laforgue said, whereupon the hunchback shook his drum, resumed his howling cries and danced up and down as before. Laforgue, trying to control his anger, put his breviary in his cassock pocket and walked across the meadow, going toward the woods.

The woods were dangerous. Father Bourque warned that if you did not track your path exactly you could become lost as in a maze. But as he heard the sorcerer's drum at his back, Laforgue entered the forest, penetrating farther and farther into the aisles of trees. As he hurried on, the hunchback's howls grew fainter until, at last, he could no longer hear them. He stopped to listen and heard, far away, the rattling sound of the drum. He went on.

At last there was silence. He looked around. On every side, the forest was the same. Long shafts of light struck down from a great height, increasing the gloom. There was no wind. He decided to remain here until the pestilential hunchback had found some other diversion. He sat down with his back to a tree and looked up at the sky. The afternoon seemed endless. As he gazed around at the undergrowth and its carpet of leaves and mosses, the thought came to him that in this great empty land, so few Savages roamed the woods that he could be the first man in all history to walk into this particular glade.

As this thought struck him, he realized that he did not know which way he had come. Where was the meadow? He looked again at the sky, but the sky gave no clue. He remembered Father Bourque's advice. "If you are lost, do not try to walk out blindly." Surely he was only minutes away from the place where the Savages had beached their canoes. He thought of the hunchback. Perhaps the hunchback was close? He called out, "Mestigoit? Mestigoit, answer me. Sound your drum." But his words echoed as in a cave. He looked left, then right. I will be calm. I will wait quietly until I hear the hunters returning. I may even see them, here among the trees. But what if they do not come back in this direction? Surely they will send men to look for me. I will pray. It may be that the Lord has chosen for me to end here alone in this wilderness. If that be Thy will, I am Thy servant and I give Thee thanks. But even as he prayed he knew that he did not give thanks. Instead, he was gripped by a growing, blinding fear.

He listened again, but all was so still that he asked himself if his failing right ear had now become totally deaf. He stood up, taking a branch, and struck it against the base of a tree. He heard, clearly, the sound it made. Why is it so quiet? I cannot be more than a quarter of a mile from the meadow. If I move off in this direction and walk for a quarter of a mile and do not find the meadow, I will retrace my steps to this point.

He began to walk, looking down to see if he left

tracks. But the leafy undergrowth recorded no imprint. He then used a small branch to score a mark on every third tree and in this way went what seemed to be a quarter of a mile. The sky was darker now. He wondered if he could climb a tree and seek out his bearings. But these trees, tall, with few lower branches, seemed unclimbable. He decided, all at once, that he was going deeper into the forest, moving away from the meadow. He started back. For the first few minutes he managed to retrace his steps by means of the markers, but then, he did not know why, he could no longer find any markers. He was lost.

"Mestigoit? Mestigoit? This is Nicanis." But no one heard. Or perhaps the hunchback lurked somewhere in the trees listening, the hunchback who was a sorcerer in league with the devil, a sorcerer who believed him a demon and would be glad to let him die. He felt sweat on his brow. "Mestigoit?" he called. "Mestigoit, the demon has left me. Help me."

The sky was very dark. It was the edge of night. The hunters would have returned by now. Daniel will ask Neehatin to send out men to look for me. But if the sorcerer says I am a demon and have fled into the woods, perhaps Neehatin will not send men to find me. I must be calm. *De profundis clamavi ad te, Dominum.* Out of the depths have I cried unto Thee, O Lord. O Lord, hear my voice.

Suddenly, he heard a shout. It was the most wonderful sound. His heart hammered. He listened, but again all was silence. I cannot have imagined it. It was a shout.

He set off, hurrying in the direction of the shout. Or *was* it the direction? He must be calm, but he ran faster, stumbling, panting, peering amid the dappled gloom of the trees. "Chomina?" he called. "Chomina, it's Nicanis." Perhaps he was going in the wrong direction. He stopped. His breath sounded spent as though he would collapse. To be so near, yet to miss them. If they had moved on, he might never catch up with them. Again he began to run, but now at an angle to his previous direction, his eyes straining to discern the shapes of men in the gloom of trees, his dulled ears waiting a further shout.

Terror. He gasped as if he had been struck a mortal blow. Ahead of him, like a flashing blur of darkness, a Savage, his spear uplifted, rushed through the trees to kill him. The spear was almost in his chest when the Savage face opened in a grin. "Shit!" the Savage cried. "I thought I had a moose but all I have is this silly prick, Nicanis." At once, three other Savages materialized like ghosts in the murk of trees.

"I am lost," Laforgue told them.

"Come, then," the Savage said. "We are going back to the habitation. Why did you come in here, if you do not know the woods?"

"He's an old woman," a second Savage said, laughing. "The woods are for men."

The Savages, surrounding him, laughed and laughed. Laforgue began to laugh as well. Never had their foul banter amused him until now. Moved in some way he did not understand, he embraced the Savage who had found him, burying his face in the filthy tunic which covered the man's torso. And as he did, his laughter changed to tears. I might have died here, alone in this wilderness. I did not welcome death, as a holy person should. I was afraid.

"What is wrong with you, you silly prick?" the Savage asked. "Why are you weeping? Come on. Let's go back."

He shivered. Like a dog behind its masters, he stumbled in their wake as they moved swiftly through the trackless woods, ignoring the darkness around them. On and on they went, laughing, making their foul jokes, abusing each other as they had abused him until, suddenly, ahead he saw a distant blaze of flame. They emerged into the long meadow. The habitation had been built, the fires were lit. The Savages with their women and children squatted like animals along the rim of the smoking pit, stirring sagamité in their kettles. And Laforgue, coming toward this scene, felt his heart fill with an inexpressible relief. It was as though, walking a long and lonely road, he had come over a hill to the sight of a village, the village where he was born.

That night he awoke with a start. Someone had kicked him in the back. Squirming around among the packed, stinking bodies of his companions, he saw the sorcerer Mestigoit, asleep, curled up like a hedgehog behind him. In the smoking firelight he saw Daniel lying near the door. At once, the thought came to him that, if today he had been lost forever in the woods, Daniel would have continued in a state of mortal sin and might die here among the Savages without benefit of confession. I cannot go on this way, Laforgue told himself. I must confront him. If he tries to go out tonight I must prevent him. Where is the girl?

But he could not see the girl. He crawled closer to Daniel. Dogs yelped and children cried and occasionally he heard furtive sounds which led him to believe that some of the Savages were copulating. He tried to pray. Gradually the sounds of crying children were replaced by an orchestra of grunts and snores. Again, he looked at the place where Daniel lay. He saw Daniel's back but then, with a start, realized that he had been mistaken. At once, he tried to sit up but found that the hunchback had rolled so close that he lay on the fold of his cassock. Carefully he disengaged himself, but as he did the sorcerer opened his glittering eyes and watched him with a minatory stare.

Laforgue moved away, then lay down, feigning sleep. After a few minutes, with great caution, he crawled toward the doorway. When he rose up in the night outside, his heart beat fast. Where are they? If I find them I must not look at them but must call Daniel's name at once. He stared about him, but all he saw was the meadow's emptiness. He went down to the trees at the edge of the meadow and walked along the rim of the forest, calling softly, "Daniel? Daniel?" If Daniel heard, would he answer or would he hide from sight? Laforgue shivered. As he did, he thought he heard a sound, as though someone were in pain. It came from the other end of the meadow, in the direction of the river. Yes, it came from the river. He ran across the meadow, running toward the sound.

She saw the sorcerer curl up behind the Blackrobe. Her father said that the sorcerer would not let the Blackrobe out of his sight until he found the answer. Yet this afternoon the Blackrobe had escaped the sorcerer and, in the forest, had cast a spell on the hunting. That was what Neehatin told the senior men. She was not supposed to listen to such things. Unmarried women and those who were married and had no children were themselves treated as children. Yet she had risked creeping close to the place where Neehatin held council, because she feared for her lover. When Neehatin told the men that the Blackrobe had cast a spell, he said that was why they found no moose today in a place where the forest had promised moose.

When the sorcerer lay down beside the Blackrobe she saw that Iwanchou, her lover, was lying near the door. He had whispered to her that he would wait until the Blackrobe was asleep and then slip out to meet her in the trees. But tonight she feared the forest. The forest would be angry because the Blackrobe had cast a spell on it. Iwanchou was of the Blackrobe's tribe. The forest might revenge itself on him—and on her, if she were with him. But it grieved her that she would not meet him in the forest tonight. She wanted to fuck with him. Every night, she wanted to fuck with him. She did not understand what had happened. She had fucked with other boys and men. Everyone liked to do it, just as everyone liked to eat. The trick was to fuck before marriage and not have children. That was happiness, and she had been happy. But since thirty nights ago when she had first fucked with Iwanchou up at the eel fishery, she wanted only him. And he wanted only her. He became angry if she went with others. She remembered his anger that day on the riverbank when the Norman trader, who had fucked her before, caught hold of her, drunk, and fucked her again. Iwanchou would have killed the trader if the Blackrobe had not been there. Iwanchou was a strange boy. He feared the Blackrobe and did not want the Blackrobe to know that he and she fucked together. The Blackrobes did not fuck at all. Her father, Chomina, said that was because they were sorcerers. But that did not make sense to her. For sorcerers fucked. Even Mestigoit, who was as ugly as a porcupine and claimed to be a demon, had today shown the girls a stiff prick and begged them to let him do it.

When she asked Iwanchou why he feared to let the Blackrobe see him fuck, he said it was because of his god, who was also the Blackrobe's god. He said his god would be angry with him. Why would he be angry, she asked. What is wrong with fucking? Or is it because, as my father says, you Normans have no women of your own? Of course we have women, he said. In our country across the water there are many women. But she wondered if he lied. She remembered that he once said he had never fucked with a woman until he came to the Algonkin.

Now as she lay in the habitation and thought of these things, her eyes burned with tears which were not just tears of the smoke. She wanted to get up and go out with Iwanchou. She did not understand why, now, she wanted only him. Girls her age fucked with many men and received many presents before they married. It was the time of joy. After marriage, women were slaves. She had said all this to Iwanchou. She knew that he, too, had fucked with others, with Oonta and her young sister up at the eel fishery. But that was before I met you, he said. From now on we fuck only with each other. If it is presents you want, I will give you presents you cannot dream of. I will take you to my country, where you will eat every day as much as you want. She did not believe him. There was no place anywhere where one ate every day. She asked her father about that. Her father said it could be true that the Normans ate every day, but that was only because they were greedy pigs who would not share their food with others. They hide it in their habitations and refuse to pass it out when asked, her father said. No one should ever trust them, he said. They told the Hurons that if they embraced their god he would protect them from all harm. But that is shit, her father said. The Hurons who accept the Norman god die and starve like other people. And they practice a water sorcery, her father said. They put drops of water on the heads of sick people and babies, and the people and babies die. When she heard her father say these things she felt afraid. She asked Iwanchou if he would make her serve his god. But he said, "I no longer serve him myself. I serve the manitou."

The manitou was the great demon. Her father said the other Normans, the ones who came for furs, were madmen, bewitched by the manitou. They would give knives, wampum, kettles, awls, clothing, even muskets for the furs of beaver, otter, lynx and wildcat. They did not make ceremonial robes of these furs, as the people did, but instead took them out to their wooden islands in the river. When the snows came the islands disappeared into the wide water beyond and came back empty, many, many nights later when the winters were gone.

"Do not say that you serve the manitou," she told Iwanchou. "If you do, I must run away from you."

"Then we will run away together," he said. He wept when he said that. He said he did not have a plan for them. But they would be together always, he said.

"Why do you say that?" she asked him. "You know very well that when we reach the upper rapids, you and the Blackrobe will journey on to the Huron country, while we will stay here for the winter hunting. You will leave and I will never see you again."

"I won't leave you," Iwanchou said. "I will leave the Blackrobe when we reach the upper rapids. I will ask your father, Chomina, if I can become your husband and live and hunt with the Algonkin. I can teach them how to use their muskets," he said. "And I can get them more powder and shot, when the Blackrobes pay me what is owed me."

Sometimes, when he spoke like this, she remembered that although he was her age he was still a child. Her father would shit on him as a husband. Her father would say, "How can I give you as wife to a Norman? Everyone knows they are stupid as a blind elk. They do not know that this world is alive, that the trees speak, that the animals and fish are possessed of reason and will revenge themselves on us if we do not respect their dead. These stupid Normans feed the bones of beaver to dogs. The beaver does not forgive them," her father would say. "How could you take as husband a hunter the animals will not respect? You will starve."

When she told Iwanchou that he was wrong, that her father would never accept him as her husband, he said, "Then we will run away. Together."

"Why do you keep saying that?" she asked him. "It makes no sense. Where would we run?"

"I will take you to Québec," he said. "I will take you to Agnonha and ask that I be sent back with you to my country."

"In a wooden island?" she said. "No, no, I would be afraid."

"You need not be afraid," he said. "They are just great canoes. And when we reach my country, I will give you presents you have never dreamed of."

But she did not want presents. She did not know what to do. She wanted Iwanchou but she knew that soon, if the sorcerer said so, Iwanchou and the Blackrobe might die. She wept. She did not sleep. As the fire guttered into ashes, she felt Iwanchou tug at her robe. "Come," he said. And she went, crawling out into the cold, looking to see if the sky was angry. Iwanchou took her hand and led her toward the forest. "No," she said. "Not there."

"Why not?"

"The Blackrobe cast a spell on the forest. We must not go there."

Iwanchou smiled in the moonlight. "Who said that?"

"Mestigoit."

"That is shit," Iwanchou said. "Come."

"We will go to the river," she said. "Nicanis did not cast a spell upon the river." She pulled him around and began to run across the meadow, going down to the riverbank. He ran after her in the moonlight. He was laughing. When he was with her at night, he often laughed. During the day she had forbidden him to look at her or come near her. It was the custom for a young man, when he desired a girl as his betrothed one, not to look at her or speak to her or stay near her. She thought of him as her betrothed but did not want to tell him so. Instead she told him that he must stay away because she feared her father's anger. As he, for his part, feared the Blackrobe's anger. And so he did his best not to look on her while others were in view. He did not come near her except at night. But when they did meet, as now in the moonlight, he could not hide his joy. He laughed in happiness as, hand in hand, they went down the riverbank. They found a bed of ferns, well away from the habitation, and he lay on it, opened his breeches and showed her a stiff prick. "I am hungry," he said. "All night I was thinking of food. I asked myself, How can your people go so long without food? And then I thought of you. I had the answer. I no longer thought of food, I thought of you. Look," he said, "see what you have done. Kiss it." She knelt in front of him and kissed it. She shivered in the cold night air, but she was hot under her tunic. He pulled up her tunic and his tongue touched her breasts. She felt her nipples stiffen. She wanted to fuck now but she must ask him about the spell. "Why would Nicanis cast a spell so that we cannot find moose?"

"Shut up," he said. "Kiss me."

"Why would he want us to starve?" she said. "Answer me."

"How can I answer when you talk shit?" he said. "Come on. Lie down."

The bed of ferns was damp but, excited, she stripped off her tunic and her skirt and was naked for him, her only adornment a long necklace of white and purple beads made from the insides of shells. It hung and shook between her breasts as she reared over him and took his prick in her mouth, sucking it. Beneath her, he began to pull off his clothes so that he, too, would be naked. His skin was different from the skin of the people. She called it ghost skin and now, as she looked up along the white column of his belly and chest, it glistened silver in the night. He began to moan loudly and took her head in his hands, pulling her off his prick because he did not want to spend yet. She knelt and was about to turn and present her rear to him when she heard a sound of feet. Enemy? Quickly, she scrambled aside and threw his breeches over to Iwanchou, warning him to silence. As he dressed, the sound was louder; someone was running in their direction. She peered over the tops of the ferns and saw the runner, his long skirts hiked up.

She whispered, "Nicanis!"

Iwanchou crouched down at once in the ferns, but she knew that was useless. The Blackrobe was coming their way; there was no place to hide. And then he appeared at the top of the riverbank and, looking down, discovered them. She heard him speak in the Norman tongue, his voice not angry, as she expected, but pleading and afraid. She saw the Blackrobe go to Iwanchou and try to embrace him. But Iwanchou pushed him away and came to her, helping her to fasten her tunic, his voice angry, speaking the strange Norman sounds. And then she saw the Blackrobe go down on his knees and put his hands together, palms flat against each other. The Blackrobe looked up at the sky and began to chant in the Norman speech.

It came upon her that the Blackrobe was putting a spell on them, because Blackrobes did not fuck and did not want others to fuck. And she said to Iwanchou, "Why do you let him do this? He is making a spell against us."

Iwanchou cradled her head against his chest. "No," he said. "He is speaking to his god. Come. Let us go back inside. I must think. We will have to decide."

"Decide what?" she asked him, but he did not answer. As they turned away from the kneeling Blackrobe, he stopped chanting and called out Iwanchou's Norman name, "Dan-Ya? Dan-Ya?" She saw that there were tears in the Blackrobe's eyes. Why did he weep? She looked at the sky but felt no danger. Night was the time of the dead. In the forest all around them, the dead walked and talked and watched what was happening here. What did the dead think of what they saw now, the Blackrobe, kneeling, casting some spell while she and Iwanchou walked away?

Or was it a spell? Did he, indeed, talk to his god, as Iwanchou said he did? And what did he say to him? And then her breath caught again as she saw that it was not only the dead who watched. Mestigoit stood among the trees. On his face was a smile, a smile she feared. He beckoned to her and to Iwanchou, summoning them to come to him. She would have obeyed, but Iwanchou shook his head and held her close. The sorcerer stepped out from the shelter of the trees and came up to her with his strange dancing step, a man small as a child, his back bunched like an eagle's wings. "You have joined the dead, Annuka," he said to her. "See?" He pointed to the kneeling figure of the Blackrobe. "He has cast the spell of death on you."

"Come away," Iwanchou said to her.

"Where will you go?" the hunchback said, and laughed. "Where will you go?"

* * *

When he saw the girl naked below him on the riverbank, Laforgue averted his eyes. He heard a scuffling sound. When he looked again, Daniel was shielding her as she dressed. "Daniel," Laforgue said. Words would not come. He bent his head.

"Go away, Father," Daniel said. "Go away."

"I cannot." He moved toward the boy, as if to embrace him. "Daniel, let us pray together, for your sin and for mine."

But Daniel pushed him away. "Leave me alone," he said, in a choked, angry voice. "I don't want to pray. I am going to live with this girl."

"No. If you do, your sin will be my sin for all eternity. Listen to me. God will forgive you, as He will forgive us all, if only we ask His forgiveness. Daniel, kneel with me."

And making the sign of the cross, Laforgue went down on his knees in the grass, joining his hands in prayer. "Merciful God, our Savior, we implore Your pardon—"

But as he said the words, the girl spoke loudly in the Savage tongue. "Why do you let him do this? He is making a spell against us."

He heard Daniel say something about him praying to his god. Then, pulling her after him, the boy scrambled up the riverbank. "Daniel?" Laforgue called. "Daniel?" as they fled across the meadow. He stood up and saw them at the rim of the trees, then saw the sorcerer appear. The sorcerer said something Laforgue could not hear. The girl turned and ran away. Laforgue watched Daniel run after her, catch up with her and embrace her. Embracing, they went toward the habitation. I will wait until morning, he told himself. I will wait until morning and then I will speak to him, alone. What does he mean, he is going to live with her? The devil has addled him as he addled me.

He stood, looking down the meadow. The sorcerer

was coming his way. In his left hand the sorcerer held his flat drum, and as he crossed the meadow he began to shake it. He came closer, beginning his shuffling dance. The sound of the drum's pebbles rattled like hailstones in the chamber of Laforgue's infected ear. In the moonlight he saw the sorcerer's glittering eyes.

"Demon," cried the sorcerer. "Are you there? Are you still hiding in the Blackrobe? Answer me."

"Be quiet," Laforgue said. "The others are asleep. There is no demon."

"No!" Shaking his drum, the sorcerer began his horrible howls.

"Stop it!" Laforgue shouted, and to his surprise the sorcerer stopped, his movements arrested as though Laforgue had plunged a javelin into his chest.

"Come then," the sorcerer said quietly. "Come, Nicanis. I will show you something."

Beckoning to Laforgue in his usual theatrical manner, the sorcerer led him to the edge of the trees. "Listen," the sorcerer said. "What do you hear?"

Laforgue heard nothing except the crackling of small branches and the night sighing of swaying boughs.

"Well?" asked the sorcerer.

"I hear nothing. My ears are poor."

"Do you not hear Her voice?"

"What voice? I tell you my ears are poor."

"Look, then. Look over there." The sorcerer pointed, almost timidly, at a dark huddle of trees. "See? She wears a robe of beautiful hair. It is the hair of the men She has killed. Just now, when you were down by the river, I heard Her call your name. 'Nicanis?' She called. I knew then that the demon had left you. Look, now. Can you not see Her?"

"I see nothing," Laforgue said.

"Then come away," the sorcerer said. "Let us go together to the habitation."

Unwillingly, Laforgue followed the hunchback across the moonlit meadow. He felt numbed with the cold. He saw that the sorcerer kept glancing back at the trees.

"Ah," said the sorcerer. "She is gone. But She will be back."

"Who are you speaking of?" Laforgue said.

The sorcerer smiled. "How strange you Normans are. You are deaf and blind as are the dead in daytime. You say you know many things, and yet you speak like small children with few words and no understanding. She called your name. If you were one of us your heart would burst with terror. Yet you hear nothing, you feel nothing."

"Who is this 'she'?" Laforgue asked. "Is it some sorcery, some devil you fear?"

The sorcerer smiled. "I told you, you are as a child; you see nothing, you hear nothing, you know nothing. Poor Nicanis." He held aside the flap of skin at the doorway. "Come. Let us sleep. Even I cannot help you now."

# 5

NEXT MORNING IT SNOWED. WHEN THE SAVAGES emerged from their habitation, a thick fall had weighted the branches of the surrounding forest, whitened and concealed the ground of the meadow and filled the air in a blinding mist. The Savages seemed pleased. Children hurled themselves into this first real snow of winter, rolling like little logs down the slopes of the riverbank. Dogs yelped excitedly and ran about, pissing yellow streams in the white carpet. The women began to tear down the walls of the night's habitation, rolling the bark up and hurrying to pack it in the canoes. Laforgue, seeking Daniel, came upon him as he covered his musket in a deerskin cloth.

"Good morning."

The boy looked at him, his eyes cold. Snow covered his shoulders like a cloak. "There is no time to talk now, Father. We must start at once. Neehatin wants to reach the Isle of Dyes by early afternoon. That means hard paddling."

"Very well," Laforgue said. "We won't speak about last night. But what is this talk of leaving to live with that girl? Father Jerome's life may depend on our reaching Ihonatiria before winter sets in. Without you, I cannot do it."

"We're talking about today, not the future," the boy said. "Come. It's important that we hurry."

Laforgue felt his face flush with anger. "What is more important than your immortal soul?"

"Hurry!" the boy said again.

"Answer me. What could you do now that would be more important than going down on your knees and asking God's forgiveness?"

But as he spoke, the boy turned away and ran toward the canoes.

"Daniel, listen to me."

"You listen to *me,*" the boy called back. "If you care about the life of Father Jerome, get in the canoe. Hurry. They do not like to be kept waiting."

"Don't be impertinent." Laforgue's voice rose in anger. "No matter what you think of me, I am a priest. There is a respect you owe my cloth." But as he said this he felt, suddenly, the foolishness of his words. What respect? What sort of priest was he? Why did he speak to this boy as to a pupil in a schoolroom when he knew, and the boy knew, that they were alone, abandoned here in this land God gave to Cain, the devil's land, living among barbarians who now impatiently pushed their canoes out into the stream?

He ran down to his canoe, throwing in his cloak, pulling off his clogs to wade in the icy water, scrambling over the side of the fragile craft as the Algonkian paddlers watched. The canoes, forming a long snake, moved swiftly out into the great river. Snow blinded Laforgue as he removed his wide-brimmed hat so as not to impede the vision of the paddler behind him. Two dogs clambered over him to nestle in the pile of belongings in the center of the canoe.

When he took up the paddle and began to stroke, his

head felt faint and his ears rang with the familiar deafening noise he had come to fear. He stared ahead into the blinding mist of snow; the chill air formed tiny icicles in the hair of his beard and eyebrows. Someone kicked him from behind, almost unbalancing him in the narrow canoe. He turned, slewing to one side, to let the child who had kicked him pass by and scramble up with the other children on the snow-covered pile of baggage. But as this child settled itself, it turned and looked back at him. Through the veil of snowflakes he saw the wizened face and glittering eyes of the sorcerer, Mestigoit.

All morning the canoes moved upriver. The storm did not abate. At times the wind seemed to shift and the snow beat upon their backs instead of their faces. On either side, the forest, mantled by snow, seemed to blur and disappear into the white woolen cloud of sky, as though the land itself had melted into the desolation of winter. Laforgue, paddling, felt his arms and shoulders ache as though he had been flayed. His knees and thighs froze in their cramped position, and numbness spread down his left leg, often causing him to half topple at the end of his stroke. Try as he might, he could not keep pace with the Savage ahead of him, and there were times when he was forced to let his paddle trail in the water and, panting, dizzy, bow his head, his ears ringing, his body racked with pain.

Early in the afternoon he saw, mistily, in the distance, the shores of a large island in the center of the river, and as he did, the snake of canoes turned left, going toward a landing place. The Island of Dyes, Daniel had called this place, and Laforgue remembered reading in Father Brabant's account of his journey that this was where the Algonkin found a red root with which they dyed their ceremonial robes. The island was heavily wooded. Laforgue, his clogs tied around his neck, his cassock hiked up, scrambled about in the shallows, helping pull his canoe clear of the water, pushing it up onto the snow-covered shore.

The Savages, on landing, at once tied to their feet the large flat disks made of thongs and wood which the French called *raquettes.* Laforgue, undoing his bundle of belongings, took out these snowshoes on which, at Québec, he had spent many hours of practice. Having tied them on, he maneuvered carefully across the snow, but now, in real winter snow, his practice did not stand him in good stead. Reaching a deep drift, he toppled into it. Gleeful children ran around him and one of the Algonkian men helped him right himself, laughing, saying, "Stand up, you silly prick. Have you been drinking the Norman drink that makes you fall down?"

"Thank you," Laforgue said, and smiled. One must always smile and give thanks and never lose one's temper, for the Savages were slow to anger and surprisingly good-humored about their own trials and sufferings.

"Lift your feet up like this, Nicanis," the man said, and demonstrated. Slowly, Laforgue went up the incline. Beside him, adept on a child's set of snowshoes, the hunchback moved with a light, hopping step.

At the top of the incline stood Neehatin and Chomina, both armed for a hunt. "Today you will come with us when we seek moose," the hunchback said. "Neehatin has told me to watch you, Blackrobe. No spells against the hunt, do you hear? Pray to your god. Ask him to send us moose."

"I will do that," Laforgue said. He saw that Neehatin was looking down at him. The Algonkian leader's face made him think of the stone image of a dead Saxon king he had seen carved on a tomb in Bayeux. Neehatin raised his arm and shouted some orders of which Laforgue heard only "Beyond the trees . . . Chomina with five men . . . Ougebemat, the ravine . . ." and then, "Iwanchou, put away your musket and take a javelin. We do not want the noise of your cannon."

"Come," the hunchback said. "Follow me. Lift your feet like this."

And so, moving among sparse trees, plodding on the wide, flat snowshoes, Laforgue followed the hunters into the white unknown. A chill wind caused powdered snow to blow off the tops of drifts in a fine, sugary mist. Laforgue, keeping as close as he could to the hunchback's pace, gradually became aware that the others had gone on ahead and were lost to his sight. Through the trees they came out onto a long snow-covered hillside which stretched down for half a mile to end in a wooded ravine. At the top of this slope, he again saw the hunters. They had cut and fashioned long poles, to which they attached javelins tipped by stone points. Balancing these poles, they went cautiously down the sloping hillside. The hunchback turned and put his filthy hand over Laforgue's mouth, warning him to silence.

The hunters spread out in a wide, wavering line, becoming smaller until their figures were like children's, far down the white slopes. Suddenly, the hunchback tensed and pointed. From a clump of trees, ungainly, floundering in the deep snow, came a male and two female moose. Their long thin legs plunged into the drifts and they staggered, mired as though the snow were a white glue. The hunters, seeing them, advanced, not running but stalking them as though afraid to come too close. Laforgue saw Chomina turn and give a signal to the others. All stopped.

Chomina was closest to the animals. Raising his unwieldy javelin he hurled it, striking a moose in the neck. The animal reared up in the deep snow. The remaining two, frantic, began a slow muddy gallop back toward the trees. At once, other hunters, some hurling their javelins, some jabbing with them like spears, circled and attacked the injured moose. Laforgue saw the animal fall, saw the snow stained by blood. Five hunters now burst from another part of the forest, trying to block off the escape of the two fleeing animals. The javelins flew. One of the moose tripped and fell, and the hunters, swift, sure, incredibly agile on their flat snowshoes, closed in for the kill. The unharmed moose, a doe, had reached higher ground where the snows were not deep and now, at speed, fled to safety along the tree line. At that, the hunters broke their silence with howls of triumph. Two of the large animals lay dead in the snow. The hunchback turned to Laforgue, his glittering eyes filled with joy. "Ho, ho," he cried, uttering the guttural Savage cry of pleasure. "Your god has answered you, Nicanis. Those moose have died for you. I told you the demon had gone out from under your black robe, you lucky old prick. Now, we will eat. Yes, tonight we will truly eat."

But Laforgue was looking about for Daniel. At last he saw the boy standing close to the first-killed moose, as the Algonkin began with their knives to hack the animal into sections. From the area where the canoes were beached, women appeared, pulling behind them the long strips of bark with which they enclosed their habitation. The women went down to the scene of carnage and the hunters loaded pieces of the dismembered animal onto these makeshift sleds. Daniel was helping to skin the hind leg of a moose, and as Laforgue watched the boy, his hands and forearms stained with blood, his long hair flowing down his back, his clothing greasy, he seemed, at a distance, indistinguishable from the young men around him. And again Laforgue thought of other Frenchmen he had seen in this wild and empty land: of the fur trader Mercier, half naked, eating at the kettles; of the young coureurs de bois who went into the woods with the Algonkin in search of furs and came back to Québec, wild, corrupted, sleeping with the Savage girls. How was it that, in a few months of living like animals among these barbarians, they could forget the civilization they had left behind and, with no fear of eternal damnation, embrace the ways of ignorance and filth in which these barbarians lived? Is Belial more beautiful than Jesus? Laforgue asked himself. Impossible. Then how can it be that he is more ardently loved, more promptly obeyed and more devotedly adored?

But now he was given little time to reflect on such matters. For all around him, as though in drunken euphoria, the Savages were bustling about, calling out foul slanders on each other, laughing and cavorting like buffoons as they dragged their catch back to the encampment where the fires were already ablaze in the snow. The kettles were slung and the meat was thrown in. Children and dogs romped in the snowdrifts while the hunters, as though to celebrate their victory, began to gamble among each other, tossing stones in a bowl as they waited for the meat to cook. As the Jesuit warmed his freezing feet and tried to dry the hem of his robe at the flames, Neehatin approached him. The sorcerer, who had been trying to caress a girl little older than a child, stopped his depredations and at once came over, as though to eavesdrop.

"Well, Nicanis," Neehatin said, smiling. "Mestigoit tells me he has pulled that demon out of your asshole. Is that right?"

"There was no demon," Laforgue said, remembering to smile. But he did not hear what Neehatin said next; his ears began their painful ringing. "What was that?" he asked.

"I said, can your god bring us food every day? Mestigoit thinks you can cast a spell on game. Can you cast a good spell tomorrow as you did today? I mean, bring us beavers as well as moose?"

"I can ask," Laforgue said. "But I do not know if my God will think us worthy of his blessings."

"Nicanis is a cunning old prick, isn't he?" Mestigoit said, prancing around in his usual irritating fashion. "He's not going to tell us anything, is he?"

"Just tell us where to get more moose," Neehatin said, laughing. "If you can do that, we'll follow you anywhere you want to go. Even past the Great Rapids. That's a promise, Nicanis. Talk to that god of yours, and if he brings me moose—oh, yes, and some beaver and a few fat birds as well—then I promise you I'll kiss his fucking toes as you do."

"My God can do more than find food," Laforgue said, but as he spoke he saw that Neehatin was no longer listening. He had turned away and now called out something to the women around the fires. One of the women took a piece of meat from a kettle, put it on a bark plate and brought it to the Algonkian leader. At once, he tore off a small strip and handed the remainder of the plate to Laforgue. He held up the strip of meat which he had torn off and said, "This is for your Hesu. Is that his name?"

"Jesus is his name," Laforgue said.

"Hee-sus. All right. Heesus, I give you this piece of moose and ask you for more." He threw the piece of meat into the fire, where it roasted and then shriveled in the flames. "Now, eat," he said, turning to Laforgue. "We will all eat our fucking faces full. Right?"

At that a great roar of joy went up from the men, women and children assembled around the kettles, and at once the women began ladling out pieces to all comers who proffered their empty bark plates. As Laforgue sat down beside the flames to consume his portion, dogs, frantic with hunger, barked and pushed at him, one sticking its snout right into the plate, upsetting the meat onto the snow. Hastily, Laforgue retrieved it. After ten days of eating only the foul-tasting sagamité, this half-cooked meat now seemed to him as fine as any beef he had eaten in Normandy. Famished, he wolfed it down and, following the example of the others, got up and went to the kettles for more. All around him were smiling faces and a noise of shouting, laughter, foul banter. Again, he was impressed by the way in which the Savages, although they must be as famished as he, did not jostle each other and seek out more than their share. Indeed, as he approached the kettles, the man in front of him turned and dumped on his plate the piece of meat he had pulled out for himself. Laforgue moved on into a throng of Savages, eating from his plate as he walked. He was searching for Daniel. Now is the time to speak with him; now, when all are occupied and before we lie down for the night. But as he walked, his ears began to ring. The heavy toll of the day's paddling, the freezing cold and the pain from the old injury to his foot all conspired to make him shiver as though he ran a fever. He remembered that he had not said his nightly office, remembered that in these moments of feasting he had thought of nothing but eating his fill. Why had he marveled just now that other men could become brutalized in these wilds? Was it any wonder that eating was the Savages' highest joy when, cast out from the sight of God, they dwelled here, in this harsh and unforgiving land, dependent as wild animals on finding prey? Would it ever be possible to convert such people? It is as though this country is far from the sun of God's warmth. Even I, who now beseech His aid, can only think of eating my fill, then brutishly huddling among other warm bodies in the smoking stench of tonight's habitation. My mind is fogged with pain and weariness. I can no longer think.

And then he saw Daniel, sitting among six or seven young hunters, licking his fingers as he finished gnawing on a bone. At once Laforgue went over and squatted down beside him. In the firelight the boy's features seemed to shine as though, like the Savages, he had greased his skin. He did not speak but resumed gnawing at the ragged fringe of meat which adhered to the bone.

"Why do you hide from me," Laforgue said. It was not a question, but an accusation.

Daniel stopped eating. He stared into the flames of the fire. "Because I am ashamed."

Laforgue felt his heart beat hard in his chest. If only he knew that I too have sinned, he might speak to me.

"I also am ashamed," Laforgue said. "I am ashamed for myself. Let him who is without sin cast the first stone. I can cast no stone."

"What are you talking about?" The boy kept looking into the fire. "You don't understand."

Laforgue bowed his head. "Daniel, I too have committed a sin of the flesh."

"You?" The boy turned to him for a moment, astonished. Then he laughed. "What sin did *you* commit, Father? Something you did long ago, in France?"

"No, no. A sin of intent. Here. With that girl."

Again the boy looked at him, a side glance, suspicious and confused. "My uncle does not like the Jesuits; he wanted me to go as an apprentice with the Récollet Fathers. The Jesuits lie for the greater glory of God, my uncle told me. The end justifies the means. One must never trust what they say."

"I am telling the truth."

"But why? To win me over, isn't that it?"

"We have sinned equally in the sight of God," Laforgue said. "Perhaps my sin is greater because I am a priest. Now we must ask His forgiveness and promise to amend our lives. I want you to kneel with me and say an act of contrition. And promise that we will avoid further temptation."

"Amen," the boy said sarcastically. "Father, don't you know that life isn't so simple for the rest of us? We are not Jesuits. God has not chosen us to be His special servants."

"God chose you to come with me," Laforgue said. "And now, Daniel—Daniel, listen to me. I am afraid. I am afraid of this country. I am afraid of this mission. I am afraid of what is happening here. I don't mean the ordinary dangers: starvation, capture, death. I mean the other, the greater danger. Perhaps it is heresy to say it, but in the last few days, as we go on, I know more and more that the devil rules this land. Belial rules here; he rules the hearts and minds of these poor people. Through them he seeks to wound Our Savior. Through them, and through our weakness. Through that girl, for instance."

"Woman is the devil's instrument, the fount of pollution," the boy said, chanting it mockingly. "Please, Father, I've heard it all before."

"That does not mean it is not true."

"It can be true or not true, it doesn't matter. I said I am ashamed. Do you know why? Because I have failed God, and because it means nothing to me."

"How can it mean nothing, since you feel ashamed?"

"Stop it," the boy said, in an angry whisper. "Don't try to trick me with a Jesuit's arguments. I am not going to give up this life, do you hear?"

"You are not going to give up that girl, you mean. What life are you talking about? This life—living like an animal?"

"Animals? The Savages are truer Christians than we will ever be. They have no ambitions. They think we are mean and foolish because we love possessions more than they do. They live for each other, they share everything, they do not become angry with each other, they forgive each other things which we French would never forgive."

"I know all that," Laforgue said. "I know it, and it fills me with shame. Their patience is extraordinary."

"It is more than patience. You do not know them as I do. Annuka tells me about the mysteries of this land and these forests. It is there that they find their spiritual strength. They think us blind and stupid. They say we are less intelligent than they are, because we ignore these mysteries."

"What mysteries?" Laforgue said. His ears rang. He had to strain to hear what the boy was saying.

"The mysteries of this world. They believe that all things have a soul: men, animals, fish, forests, rivers."

"That is because Belial rules here," Laforgue said. "The devil infects their minds, making them resist the truth of our teachings."

"What teachings?" the boy said. "Why should they believe in your world after death when they already have an afterworld of their own?"

"What are you talking about? They do not believe in

an afterworld. Father Brabant, who studied them for years, says they have no concept of an afterlife."

"He's wrong."

"So you know more than Father Brabant?"

"Yes, because they would never trust him. To them he is a Blackrobe, and all Blackrobes are sorcerers. They would not tell him of their world of the dead."

Laforgue stared at the angry young face in the firelight. Around them, the feasting Savages had begun to sing their monotonous chants of celebration. "What world?" Laforgue said.

"The world of the dead."

"And where is this world?"

"They believe that at night the dead see. They move about, animals and men, in the forests of night. The souls of men hunt the souls of animals, moving through forests made up of the souls of trees which have died."

"Is that what she told you?" Laforgue smiled. "But what childish reasoning! Do they believe that these dead souls eat and drink, as we do?"

The boy looked at him with scorn. "Is that harder to believe in than a paradise where we all sit on clouds and look at God? Or burn forever in the flames of hell?"

Laforgue felt his anger rise. He clenched his hands together. "So they have a world of the dead, a world of night when the dead come alive. And what do they do in the daytime, these dead things?"

"She said, in the daytime they are blind. The dead Savages sit like this, she said." Daniel crouched on the ground and put his elbows on his knees, his head between his hands, mimicking the posture which Laforgue had seen the Algonkin adopt when a sickness came upon them. "When night comes, they rise up," the boy said. "They go to the chase."

Laforgue shivered as with a fever. He felt cold sweat trickle down the back of his neck as the boy, squatting there like a Savage, repeated to him the foolish fantasies of these barbarians. "Forgive me," Laforgue said. "But do you realize what you are saying?"

"I am telling you what *they* believe. I did not say that I believe it. I am telling you that you will never truly convert them to your teachings."

"You wish to distract me," Laforgue said. "As the Evil One has distracted you and filled you with a lust, so strong that it drives out the fear you should feel now. The fear of losing your immortal soul."

"Why do I talk to you?" The boy jumped up and stood over Laforgue as though he would strike him.

"If you die tonight, in your state of mortal sin, you will find out that there *is* a hell," Laforgue said. "A hell for all eternity."

"Good night, Father," the boy said and, turning, went along the edge of the pit of smoking kettles, mingling with the crowd of jostling, chanting, feasting Savages. Laforgue did not follow him. Instead, his shivering increased until his whole body shook as if in a fever. His limbs ached and his stomach, sated with half-cooked food, became queasy, making him feel he would vomit. He rocked to and fro by the fire, staring at the flames, his mind confusedly remembering what had been discussed. If I become ill and unable to travel, the Savages will show me no kindness. Even to their own, when sick, they pretend indifference. Father Bourque warned that if I become ill I must conceal it from them. I must be strong. I should pray.

Shutting his eyes, he willed his weary mind to prayer but, instead, fell into a doze. He started, catching himself, as he almost tumbled headlong in the snow. All he could think of now was the time when, their feasting over, the Savages would crawl into their habitation and he could at last, amid warm bodies, find surcease from his fever and pain in long weary sleep. Tomorrow he must rise and paddle with the others. Tomorrow, they would journey on.

Neehatin woke. He stretched out his arm to the pouch in which, before sleeping, he had placed some scraps of meat, as was the custom after a feast. He looked at the rooftop opening of the habitation and knew that the sun had climbed the first wall of sky. He ate slowly, chewing the meat and spitting out gristle. Then he crawled past the huddled bodies of others and left the habitation. Some were already up. He saw the Blackrobe kneeling by the river, washing his neck and face. Chomina and Amantacha and Ougebemat were cutting hunting poles as he had told them to last night. He went to them.

"We will go down through the ravine to look for tracks," he said. "Then we will move to the high slopes. Are you ready for that, you silly cows?"

"You find us moose and we'll climb twenty fucking slopes," Amantacha said.

"Neehatin," said Ougebemat, "we have been talking. Tell me. Do you think the Blackrobe's spell brought moose to this island? Last winter and the winter before there were no moose here."

"There is a causeway on the far shore," Neehatin said. "At the end of summer, the water level is low there. A family of stupid moose might wander over here and then, when the water rose, find themselves blocked. No way back."

"What a wonderful fucking mind this man has," Ougebemat said, and all laughed good-naturedly. But they knew his explanation was the right one. And they prefer my explanation, Neehatin thought. They don't want to think they are eating moose brought here by the spell of a Norman sorcerer.

"So when do we start?" Chomina asked. Chomina looked at Neehatin with respect but no love.

"We'll start now," Neehatin said. "Better send the children on ahead to camp on the other side of the island. The women can follow them with the heavy bundles and kettles. We'll beach the canoes here."

"Have you told that fart of a Blackrobe?" Chomina asked. "He's going to shit himself."

"Fuck the Blackrobe," Neehatin said. "Leave him to me."

"If the children start now, they should reach camp well before dark," Ougebemat said. "It is only a half day's journey, even for the little ones."

"Give them some stuff to carry," Neehatin said. "Let the little fuckers get used to it." The others laughed. They loved their children, but he was right. They must be taught to carry.

"What about the Normans?" Chomina said.

"They come with us. I want to keep those cows in front of me, not behind me."

Neehatin left, then, and went down to the river. "Nicanis?" he called. The Blackrobe came to him, smiling, nodding his head as the Normans always did when they met you after the night's sleeping. The Blackrobe looked sick.

"Are you all right?" Neehatin asked. "You look as if you had shit yourself." He laughed and the Blackrobe laughed, but as always it was forced. He laughed as though his teeth hurt.

"Yes, I am well," the Blackrobe said. "It was good to eat that meat last night."

"And we'll find more today," Neehatin said. "There must be five moose in that family. We've only killed two. Now we'll go after the others."

"But surely we should go on," the Blackrobe said. "The snows have started. I am very worried. We must go on today."

"No, Nicanis. First we will kill moose and eat moose, and what we do not eat we will smoke and take with us. Then we will travel fast for many days."

The Blackrobe hesitated. Neehatin saw the sweat of a sick man on his brow. "Neehatin, my friend," the Blackrobe said, speaking, as always, like a little child who has just learned his first words. "If you must hunt today, I will stay here and rest."

"Fuck that," Neehatin said, laughing. "We're going to camp on the far slopes tonight. You're coming."

"But couldn't I stay here and wait for your return?"

Neehatin looked up at the sky. The sky gave no sign. Why did this sorcerer want to stay behind? Was there some danger he knew would overtake them? "No," Neehatin said. "I'll tell you what. Since you're so fucking tired, you won't have to carry a burden today. Mestigoit will be with you, and you'll come with us, with the hunters. Get your shoes on. I must go."

He did not wait for the Blackrobe to do any more complaining. The Normans always complained. They gave you good presents but then reminded you that they had given them. They worried about everything just like old women. They were full of shit. Neehatin went up the riverbank, calling, "Women with children, women with children."

Families were coming out of the habitation. He looked back at the river. The river went its way. It said nothing of danger ahead.

"Give them burdens," he said to the mothers. "Not too heavy. Make little sleds and have them drag them after themselves as you do. Start now. We will follow later. We are going to find moose."

He heard the sorcerer's chuckling laugh and turned to find the little man at his heels. "Did I hear you say moose?" the sorcerer said.

"Yes, moose. There must be at least three of them over on the farther slopes. I want you to travel in our rear. We will take Iwanchou with Chomina's men, but you will stay close to the Blackrobe. We are going to move fast, and that cow cannot use his shoes. If you see him start a sorcery, leave him and come to tell me. He is sick with the shaking sickness. Did you know that?"

The sorcerer smiled. "Of course I know it. Two nights ago, in the forest, the She Manitou smiled on him. The flesh-eater."

Neehatin felt alarm. "You saw Her?"

"Yes."

"Then why are *you* not sick?"

"I am a demon," said the sorcerer. "She will not harm one of Her own."

"You're a great little fart," Neehatin said, laughing, although in truth he was always uneasy when he spoke with Mestigoit. It was true that Mestigoit was said to be a demon who had entered a woman and had been born through her cunt. Perhaps he lied about seeing the She. "Are you sure you saw Her?" he asked again.

The hunchback smiled, showing teeth pointed like a dog's. "I saw. She did not look at me. She looked at the Blackrobe."

"Well, fuck it," Neehatin said, trying to joke. "That makes it easy, doesn't it?"

"Easy?" The wizened face no longer smiled.

"If She eats him in a night or two, we will not have to go as far as the Great Rapids. We will have gained our presents from Agnonha for nothing."

"There are no presents given by the Normans which are not paid for," the sorcerer said.

"What the fuck are you talking about?" Neehatin said, still trying to make a joke of it.

"I mean what I mean and you know what I mean," the sorcerer said. "We are two nights from the beginning of danger. The Blackrobe may not die. He is a sorcerer, a Norman sorcerer. And they are hard to kill."

"Normans shit and eat and bleed and die just like other men," Neehatin said. "Want to bet on it? I have two beaver skins who say if the She looked on him, he will not last two nights."

"I have no beaver skins," the sorcerer said. "I have this knife."

"My knife against yours, then, you little prick."

And, at last, the sorcerer laughed.

It had snowed again in the night. By the time the hunters reached the high ground on the far side of the ravine, the tracks of the moose which had escaped them yesterday were completely obliterated. But the snow was now deep, even on the high ground. Moose, which could run fast as deer on hard ground, were helpless in deep snow. Chomina took one slope, Neehatin the other. The moose could smell hunters from a great distance. As the Algonkin advanced, the moose would seek the shelter of trees to hide.

The hunters covered both slopes and then fanned out in a long line. The moose must have gone down to the far end of the island. The land narrowed there. The hunters moved their net all morning, walking on and on in their snowshoes over the deep soft snow. It was late afternoon when they saw tracks. The tracks were like long thin holes in the snow. The hunters stopped and smiled at each other. All were silent. The tracks led them toward a wooded place. Chomina moved his men into close formation as they approached the trees. Neehatin did likewise. Moving in a semicircle, the hunters entered the woods. The wooded place was not large. The hunters raised their long javelins and, silent, went through the dark spare aisles of trees. By now, the wind was in their faces. The wind was kind. The moose might not even scent them until they were close. But then, ahead, they saw a male and two female moose, blundering through the trees, plunging in panic, making for the open snow at the end of the woods.

The hunters began to run, swift on their unwieldy snowshoes. There was no longer a need for silence, so they began to yell in order to panic the moose. The moose blundered into the open, sinking to their bellies as their long thin legs plunged into the drifts. The hunters now closed the circle, moving closer their net of spears. Chomina saw that one of the females had turned and was now nearest to the Norman boy, Iwanchou. It was to Iwanchou that he gave the command to strike. The boy struck well, his javelin entering the moose's neck at a place where the blood ran thick. Within minutes, all three moose lay skewered; the male had plunged its antlers into a snowdrift. The hunters raised their javelins and shouted to each other.

Chomina, seeing Iwanchou with the others, went up to him and put his arm around him. "You silly pale prick," he said, laughing. "I think your mother was Algonkin."

The boy laughed. "Maybe she was," he said. "That would make me stupid like you. But that's all right. I like to hunt and eat just like the rest of you. Maybe I'll become Algonkian myself."

Chomina looked at him. He knew this boy was fucking Annuka. He had seen the presents he gave her, necklaces and other goods. "Why would you become one of us?" Chomina asked. "When you work for the Blackrobes in Québec, they say you eat every day. You build wooden habitations for them and you have no need to hunt."

"I like to hunt," the boy said. "I love you fuckers, don't you know that?"

"Better than the Blackrobes?"

"Yes."

"You're full of shit," Chomina said, laughing. "Come. Let's get these moose out of here."

The sun was low on the horizon when Mestigoit and Laforgue, moving in the wake of the hunters, saw them ahead, dragging their slaughtered prey. The moose had been cut into sections and placed on narrow makeshift sleds of wooden runners covered by peeled strips of bark. The hunters, harnessed like pack animals by cords bound around their foreheads, dragged these heavy sleds through the deep snows. Laforgue, half delirious from fever, wondered how the hunters could move their legs under this heavy burden. His own snowshoes had become weighted with snow, and each time he stumbled in a drift, it seemed as if someone beneath the snow pulled on his ankles as though to wrench them from their sockets.

When, at last, their caravan came to the new campsite, the women had already arrived, lit the fires and cut the poles for the night's habitation. The children, weary from their long journey, sat uncharacteristically listless on their bundles but now rose and ran yelling toward the hunters and their prey. Because of the deep snow, the habitation must be built in the true winter manner, and so, laying aside their harness, the Algonkian men removed their snowshoes and, using them as shovels, began to clear a large circle in the snow, digging into it to a depth of three feet. Even the hunchback helped in this work for, as Laforgue was to discover, it would take three hours in the shivering cold to prepare this place where they would sleep. The pit dug by the Savages made a white wall like the wall of a small house, surrounding the sleeping place on all sides except where a break was made for an entrance. Some twenty poles, which the women had already cut and trimmed from the surrounding woods, were then planted in the snow to form the scaffolding of a roof, converging loosely at the top. The long strips of bark, sewn together, which formed the roof of the previous habitations were now placed over this frame. The floor and walls of the habitation were then lined with small branches of fir, and a skin was draped over the entrance. Only when this work was finished, at a time when the sky was already dark, did the Algonkin return to the fires and begin to cook the slaughtered moose.

Laforgue, shivering although he sat close to the flames, was astonished to see that the Savages who had worked for hours in the freezing snow pit sweated on their return as though the night were warm. Merriment and the usual insults began as the first pieces of meat were thrown into the kettles. Laforgue, who had been reading his office by the light of the fire, sat apart. His hands, icy in their mittens, stung as though he were a schoolboy who had been caned. Indeed, there seemed no part of his body which did not suffer its own particular torment. He sat alone. He did not look for Daniel, nor did the boy come near him. All around him he heard the Savages shouting their obscenities, the dogs barking, the chants of the lugubrious Savage songs of triumph and the rattling sounds of the sorcerer's drum.

"Nicanis."

He looked up. Above him, holding a bark plate filled with meat, was Neehatin. "Eat," said Neehatin, handing him the plate. He took it, but his hands, frozen and stiff in their mittens, let the plate spill, the meat falling on the ground. At once, two dogs came bounding over. Neehatin kicked them away.

"Are you sick, Nicanis?"

"My hands are cold."

"Let me see." The leader squatted down and slipped off Laforgue's mitten. He felt his hand. "Shit," he said. "They *are* cold. Here." From his tunic he took his own mittens and put them on Laforgue's hands. The mittens were warm from the heat of his body. "I will take yours," he said. He laughed. "Nicanis, let me give you some advice."

"Advice?"

"You must not travel with us in winter. We are going to kill you."

Neehatin was smiling, and so Laforgue felt he must smile too. "I am stronger than you think," he said.

"A sick man on a sled is heavy baggage," Neehatin said. "If he's going to die anyway, why drag him along? Better to put a hatchet in his head." He laughed uproariously, throwing back his head, showing his perfect teeth.

"I'd better not get sick, then."

"Eat your meat," Neehatin said. "Tomorrow we will smoke what is left of these moose; then we'll go back to the canoes and continue our journey." He walked off with no farewells. Laforgue looked at the meat and felt he would vomit. Carefully, making sure he was not seen, he wrapped it in a cloth and hid it in his belongings. Then, feeling as though he would faint, he got up, left the fires and went to the newly built habitation.

When he crawled inside, the place was empty, save for two of the older women who tended the smoking fire. Laforgue lay down close to the fire, drawing his cloak around his shoulders. Although his face was seared by the heat of the flames, his back shivered from the cold of the snowpacked wall behind him. Huddled in a fetal crouch, he sought sleep.

At dawn her mother tugged on her hair, waking her. Together, they crawled toward the door. The other women who had been chosen last night were already outside and starting the fires. When the fires were burning well, her mother went to call her father. He came with six men. They took the male moose which had not been eaten last night. They removed all the bones, as was the custom, and, where the meat was too thick, slashed it with their knives so that the juice would come out. After that, the women helped to pound the carcass with stones, and at last the men trampled it underfoot to squeeze out the last of the juice. By then, the others were up. She saw Iwanchou standing nearby, pretending to watch the work. She did not look at him.

When they had finished trampling the carcass underfoot, the men took the sides of moose and stretched them on poles over the fire. The smoking began. Neehatin came out, eating scraps from last night's feast and calling the orders. The sleds were to be loaded and the children and women must start back across this island to the place where the canoes were beached. So we are going on, she thought. She looked for the Blackrobe and saw him sitting on a bundle of his belongings, peering, as he often did, at a small charm which he carried with him. It was covered in a black skin and was made of white strips of bark sewn together. On the white bark were signs painted with a black stick. Were they ornaments? She had asked Iwanchou, but he made some stupid joke. He said the Blackrobe heard men speak when he looked at the black signs on the bark. Now, as she watched the Blackrobe, she saw he had the shaking sickness. If the Blackrobe died, what would Iwanchou do? Where would he go? She felt afraid. Hurriedly she loaded her bark sled and then helped load the sled of her little brother. She went off with the first group, the younger women and children. The men were still smoking the moose. Later, they would fold it and bind it in packages and haul it to the canoes. As she left, she heard her father, Chomina, call out that he would form a party of hunters. There might be porcupine or beaver, he said. She heard Neehatin joke that her father pretended to hunt so that he would not have to carry his share of burdens. Her father did not like such jokes.

As she went along the edge of the trees, she heard the forest speak. She listened but did not catch it. She asked her little brother, Outiji, "Did you hear what it said?"

"It said there is a storm," her little brother told her. She did not know if she believed him. He was at an age when he wanted to be a man and always had an answer.

When they reached the canoes, the sun was still high. It was a cold winter sun, which did not melt the snow. Her mother told her to help reload the canoes. "But we are not paddling now, are we?" she said. "It's late."

"The bentback has told Neehatin we must go at once," her mother said.

The men, including the hunters, came into camp as the women began loading. They brought extra bundles and also the dried moose. When the canoes were loaded, Neehatin told them to put them in the water.

"Oh, shit," her cousin said. "That means we'll be building the habitation after the sun dies. What the fuck is going on?"

"Shut up," her aunt said. "Get in the canoe."

On the river, they began to sing; it passed the time. But Neehatin stood and called that they be silent. She looked back at the canoe where Iwanchou was the rear paddler. Did he know what that meant? Would anyone tell him? She saw the Blackrobe paddling in his awkward way. The bentback sorcerer sat facing him. Again, she felt afraid. A wind rushed up the river. It cried like a dying woman.

"I told you," her little brother said. "Here comes the storm."

It snowed. Not as it had snowed the days before, but a blinding wall of white driven by great northern winds, so that the air about them howled and swirled and the canoes stalled in the water like paper boats. They were forced to land. They landed on a thickly wooded riverbank, where the trees came down to the water's edge. They dragged the canoes through thick snow in which they sank up to their thighs before donning snowshoes. The storm lashed the trees, causing them to make a sound like cannon. The dogs, howling in discomfort, scampered up the snowbank and hid in the forest. But there was no real shelter, not even in the great vaults of birch and spruce. The Algonkin, with the weary tenacity of felons performing a penitential task, dragged out their birch-bark roofing, hacked at branches and in a makeshift yet deliberate way cleared a shallow space in the snow. Then, huddling in a human wall, they built a fire amid the swirling drifts. The poles were thrown up in a loose circle, and the birch bark was assembled and tied down to form a makeshift roof. By the time darkness came, all huddled around the fire in the insufficient habitation. Outside, the winter howled and the trees, groaning under the weight of snow, shook and swayed until heavy branches crashed into the white silence of the ground below. Toward dawn the storm died. At dawn a woman gave birth to a baby four months before its time. In the huddled confines of the habitation, the infant was brought forth amid the groans of wakened sleepers, its bloodied body, severed from the afterbirth, held up over the dying fire as its mother perfunctorily slapped it to see if it lived. It did not. She crawled to the entrance and went toward the forest where, high in a tree, away from the dogs, she laid the small slime-covered corpse in a crook between the branches. As she went back to the habitation, the Black-robe passed her. She thought he had come out to piss, but, as she watched, he went to the place where she had left the baby. He took down the corpse, put a handful of snow in his own mouth, then spit the snow water into his palm and trickled it over the tiny face. She heard him say something in the Norman tongue.

She watched the baby. It was dead. He took the corpse and put it back where she had laid it, high in the tree. He touched his hand to his brow, then in turn to each shoulder. He looked sick, as though he would fall down. She turned and went back into the habitation. When she crawled close to her husband, she told him what she had seen. Together they watched the Blackrobe crawl in again and lie down beside the sorcerer. Had the Blackrobe put a spell on her so that the child came before its time? She asked this of her husband, but he did not answer. She felt empty and weary and afraid. Her husband held her in his arms. Within a short time they heard the call to rise and go on.

Outside the habitation, Chomina passed a small piece of smoked meat to each man, woman and child. The habitation was disassembled and the canoes were dragged down to the river. As Laforgue helped, pulling a canoe, Daniel came up and took him aside.

"Are you ill, Father Paul?"

"I had a fever," Laforgue said. "But last night it broke. I am better now."

"It will be hard paddling," Daniel said. "I heard Ougebemat say that for four days they will be in an area of great danger. That means hostile Savages. They want to get through as quickly as they can."

"What people live in this part of the river?"

"I don't know. Father, I am sorry about what I said to

you. If we are going into danger, we must not be enemies."

"We are not enemies," Laforgue said. "But we must talk about these things. Nothing is more important than that."

"We cannot talk now. Besides, I don't know what to say." Suddenly the boy stared at Laforgue. "Father, what's the matter?"

"My ear," Laforgue said. He put his hand over his right ear, bent forward, then collapsed in the snow. Rolling over, he looked up at the boy. The boy's lips were moving. Oh, my God, Laforgue said to himself. Have I gone completely deaf? The ringing sound shut out all others as the boy helped him to his feet.

Then, as suddenly as it had started, the ringing ceased. Laforgue heard the boy ask, "Father Paul? Father Paul?"

"It's all right," Laforgue said. "I have these spells. They pass."

"You are ill. You are not fit to travel."

"I am stronger than you think," Laforgue said.

He heard the Savages calling his name. "Nicanis? Nicanis?"

"Don't try to paddle," the boy said. "It is too much for you. I will tell Neehatin that you are sick."

"No, you won't. I will paddle. Don't tell him." Laforgue turned and ran down to the waiting canoe, lifting his cassock as he waded into the icy water. When the canoe moved out, forming part of a snake which glided along the river, again he heard the telltale ringing. He looked at the sorcerer, who sat with the children on the bundles stacked in the middle of the canoe. The sorcerer was talking to the children, but Laforgue could not hear him. The ringing stopped. He heard voices, clearly, and the slap of his paddle in the water. It was as though some abscess in his ear had burst. He heard as he had not heard in weeks. And in that moment of deliverance, he saw Neehatin half rise in the canoe ahead and make a gesture with his hand. The

Savages fell silent. The stroke increased to a pace which made Laforgue break into a sweat. But the sweat was the sweat of toil, not fever. His fever had broken. His hearing seemed restored. *O Lord,* he prayed, *Thou hast given me back my ears and my strength. Thou hast shown me that through Thy hand, I am capable of feats I had not believed to be in this body of mine. If it be Thy wish that I suffer greater privations in the days ahead, I welcome it. Thou hast given me this cross for Thy honor and for the salvation of these poor barbarians. I thank Thee.*

And there, among the faint sounds of the river, the slap of paddles, the canoes gliding through the chill morning mists, he was filled with a strange exaltation. In France, in the cloister, after a long and painful night's vigil of prayer, or at humble or disgusting tasks in the kitchens and sickrooms of the Order, he had, on rare occasions, known this feeling. It was as though Paul Laforgue no longer existed on this earth but, instead, a body and mind made for Jesus did Jesus' will. And this morning that calm he had known in former days seemed as nothing compared with the exaltation he now felt in this wilderness, surrounded by Savages who drove on as though possessed. Everything that he did, everything that he suffered, he did and suffered as a Jesuit, for the greater glory of God. God had tested him and would test him further. God had restored his hearing to remind him he was not alone.

God is with me. God honors me with this task.

# 6

ON THE THIRD DAY OF THEIR RACE THROUGH THE PLACE of darkness, Neehatin saw the White Face Mountain. He had driven his people hard. That night, he asked men as well as women to help assemble the habitation. All moved like old ones, they were so weary from the paddling. But the habitation was well built. When the last of the smoked moose meat had served as the evening meal, all were drowsy before the fires. They would soon sleep. Neehatin beckoned to the senior men to lie close to him and brought out tobacco.

"Shit," said Amantacha. "Where did you find this?"

All were smiling. Tobacco was loved as much as food.

"I forgot it," Neehatin lied. "I put it among the beaver skins, and then I forgot it." He filled their pipes, then passed back the rest of the tobacco to the older women and the young men. He offered a pipeful to the young Norman, who refused, as did the Blackrobe. The sorcerer, smoking from a curved pipe of his own making, curled up like a child at Neehatin's feet as Neehatin peered across the smoking fires to make sure the Norman boy was not in hearing. Then he asked the sorcerer, "Do you tell me new things about my dream?"

"It has not yet been told to me," the sorcerer said.

"Then you do not yet know who is the fish?"

He wanted to press this little shit for an answer. For he knew the bentback. He would wait until Neehatin had spoken, then claim his wisdom for himself.

"No," said the sorcerer. "It has not yet been told to me who is the fish."

"When will you know?" Neehatin said. He wanted to be sure that all heard, including Chomina.

"It will come," said the sorcerer.

"Shit," said Ougebemat. He was happy. "This tobacco is good stuff."

"I am smoking," said old Awandouie. It was his way of saying thanks. The others said the "Ho, ho" of approval. Neehatin smiled. He was glad he had held this tobacco in reserve. They were grateful. They would heed his counsel.

"In the dream," Neehatin said, "the fish swam up to me and led me to the farther shore. Tomorrow night we will reach that shore."

"But who is the fish?" asked the bentback. "That is the question."

"You are the fish," Neehatin said. "That is why you did not know the answer."

"What are you talking about?" Chomina said. He lay on his back with his knees drawn up, sucking on his pipe with long grateful puffs.

"Mestigoit is the fish we have taken with us through the dark place. He has driven the demon out of the Blackrobe. The Blackrobe has lost his power. He cannot cast a spell on us any more."

"But how do you know?" Chomina said. He turned and looked at Neehatin as he said it.

"Today, as I paddled my canoe," Neehatin said, "the forest spoke. It said, *Mestigoit is the fish who helps us. He has saved us from danger,* it said." Neehatin looked down at the bentback curled up at his feet. "We must give you a good present, you little asshole," he said, and laughed.

"But we are still in the danger," Chomina warned.

"Not for long. Tomorrow night we reach the Great Rapids."

"The rapids are more than a night's paddling."

"Not so," Neehatin said. "We have passed the White Face Mountain. We are still in danger, but at the rapids we will leave the boy and the Blackrobe and send them on alone. We ourselves will cross the river to the other shore and go to the winter hunting place. We will be safe."

"Alone?" said old Awandouie. "The Normans will die. They will never manage the portage up the rapids."

"The Blackrobe is stronger than he looks," Neehatin said. "Last night in my dream he walked alone into a village in the Huron country."

"Some fucking dream," said Chomina, and the others laughed.

"I dreamed it," Neehatin said. He did not smile. In the smoky habitation a dog barked, a child cried. The senior men said nothing.

"He walked into a village," Neehatin said. "The village was empty. No people. No people at all."

Again, a dog barked.

"If you dreamed it, it will come to pass," said Ougebemat. "But will the Norman chief absolve us from our promise because you tell him you had a dream?"

"They gave us six fucking muskets and a little powder," Neehatin said. "And four axes and some awls. And beads and other shit."

"And two iron kettles," said Chomina.

"All right, two fucking kettles. Presents, good presents. All right. But, for that, in the last four days we came into the danger. We are still in it. Everyone here could die. Fuck the Normans. We will take them to the rapids. What more do they want?"

"We gave our word that day in the stone habitation of

Agnonha," Chomina said. "You and I, both. We said we would take them to the rapids, then send two men up the rapids with them and on to the place where they meet the Allumette. You know what that fucker Agnonha is like. He won't forget it if you try to screw him."

"Sometimes," Neehatin said, "I wonder if you think with your head or your ass. You tell me that if we leave them at the foot of the rapids, they are dead men. Now you tell me we should be afraid that these dead men will report back to Québec."

"That's right," Ougebemat said. "We will say we sent two men up with them. Who's to know the difference? Agnonha doesn't keep count of every fucking Algonkin. How could he?"

"And even if the Blackrobe survives to reach the Huron land," Amantacha said, "it will be another winter before he can send back any word to Québec."

"So we are agreed, then?" Neehatin asked. "We have risked enough for their fucking presents. We leave them at the rapids."

The others nodded. But not Chomina. "Shit," Chomina said. "I am not afraid of any Norman chief. You all know that. But the musket which Agnonha gave to me, I will give it to one of the young men if he will go up the rapids with the Blackrobe. It will only be a journey of—what—three nights? Then he can come down again, take a canoe and rejoin us in the winter hunting place."

"Easy. Nothing to it," Neehatin said, and laughed. "But I notice you don't want to go yourself."

"Asshole. I have a family," Chomina said. "I would have to take them with me up the rapids. That's why I don't want to go. But we gave a promise. We told Agnonha we would take Nicanis to the head of the rapids."

"Fuck the promise," Neehatin said. He looked around and saw uncertainty in some eyes. He looked at the sorcerer. The bentback hated Normans. "What do *you* say, Mestigoit?" he asked.

"I say we should follow the dream. The dream is stronger than any promise. You have dreamed that the Blackrobe walks alone in a Huron village. So he will walk there. Obey the dream."

The others gave the guttural of assent. Neehatin looked at the bentback and, for once, was glad he had brought him along. But Chomina took his pipe from his mouth and spat in the fire. "Now it is the rest of you who are thinking with your assholes," Chomina said. "The Blackrobe can only walk into that village with our help. Can you see that boy and the Blackrobe reaching the high place alone? Of course not. We must go with them. That is what the dream says. Don't you see?"

"I see that you are afraid of these wooden islanders," Neehatin said, smiling to negate the insult.

"I am not afraid," Chomina said. "But we have begun to need their trade. That is our undoing, and it will be our ending."

"We are not talking of that," Neehatin said. "I am saying that unless we dump the Blackrobe tomorrow night, every man, woman and child among us could die."

"I am not talking about risking all our lives," Chomina said. "I am talking about sending a young warrior who wants to earn a musket. That's what *I* am talking about."

"All right, I ask the council." Neehatin rolled over on his back and stared at the other faces. "Do we put this to the young men or not?"

"I say no. I say fuck the Normans," Ougebemat said. "What does Awandouie say?"

All looked now to the oldest man in council. He had lived sixty winters, maybe more. His was the memory of former dangers. "If Neehatin's dream sees the Blackrobe in a Huron village, then the Blackrobe will reach that village. In Neehatin's dream the village is empty. The Blackrobe walks alone. Not with Chomina, not with any of our men. Obey the dream."

Neehatin watched Chomina, then said, "Do all agree?"

"Just remember," Chomina said. "Agnonha will cut our balls off when he finds out about this." He laughed to show that he was joking. The other men laughed too but looked to Neehatin.

"Then we ditch the hairy ones tomorrow night," Neehatin said. "Are we agreed?"

"The council is agreed," said Awandouie.

---

It had ceased to snow. The freezing cold which had numbed Laforgue's feet these past two days was replaced by a mild breeze. The sun shone as though in this capricious wilderness the summer of flies and heat might again return to vanquish the approaching winter. Birds sang as the snake of canoes set off at its usual fast, gliding pace. Laforgue, paddling with an ease he would not have believed possible two weeks ago, felt a new vigor in his shoulders and arms. This morning, as the canoes were being loaded, Neehatin had said, "We will travel far today, Nicanis. But soon we will rest."

"How many days are we from the rapids?"

Neehatin thought for a moment. "Two nights, maybe less. We have made good time."

Shortly after noon, the silence of the paddlers was broken by a murmur of whispered excitement as the Savages looked down and saw ripples in the water. The hunchback, who, as usual, sat cross-legged on a heap of bundles facing Laforgue, bent to whisper in the priest's ear. "White water," the hunchback said. "We have traveled as fast as wet shit through a bumhole." He grinned in glee.

"What do you mean?"

"Shh," the hunchback said and looked with glittering eyes at the shore. "White water. Two hours. The rapids."

"But Neehatin said two nights."

"Shh." Again the hunchback peered at the shore as though afraid of being overheard. "Soon. Two hours. You'll see."

The canoes moved on. As was their custom the Savages did not stop to rest, and in early afternoon, as the sun began to dip in the sky, Laforgue saw myriad currents as they glided over stony shallows. Suddenly, Neehatin's canoe veered away. The other canoes balanced on the shallow rippling tide of river as Neehatin's craft went in to shore and the leader leaped out. He held a hatchet in one hand. Donning his snowshoes, he hurried across a thick carpet of snow, into a clearing. It was then that Laforgue saw signs of foot tracks and, in a circular place, cleared of snow, the remains of a fire. Neehatin went quickly to this dead fire, knelt, picked up charred embers, sniffed them, then looked about. In the other canoes, men, women and children, silent, stared at the shore as though they had seen something dread. Their leader, turning, ran back to the river and boarded his canoe, which at once swung out from shore. The other canoes, as though impatient to depart, circled in behind it. Swiftly, Neehatin's canoe forged again into its lead position. The paddlers bent to their task. The canoes fled on.

Laforgue, paddling, said a prayer. Was that fire a sign of the hostile Savages Daniel had spoken of two days back? The waters around them grew more turbulent. After less than an hour, Laforgue saw ahead, majestic in their white confusion, the Great Rapids of which Father Bourque had spoken. Here they would leave this band of Savages and, with two paddlers, portage to a higher point in the falls and continue their journey with two canoes. He looked over at Daniel's canoe. The boy, paddling at the prow, was staring about him, as though, like the Savages, he knew he ventured into a dangerous place. The canoes, stalled by the rapids, made slow progress until, at a widening of the river, Neehatin gave the signal to land.

All canoes were pulled up on the riverbank, but as soon as the Savages landed Laforgue noticed that they did not go about their usual tasks. Instead, mothers curbed their children, warning them to be quiet, and for once the unruly children seemed willing to obey. The dogs ran about sniffing, urinating on tree trunks, but when one of them attacked another and began to bark, one of the Savages at once felled it with a blow from his club. Laforgue saw Neehatin point to five of the hunters, who at once took up bows, arrows and hatchets and set off cautiously into the surrounding woods. Then the Algonkian leader went to the women and children. He spoke to them in low tones. At once, about half the women set about cutting pine branches for a habitation. The others did not assist. Laforgue saw Daniel, standing alone, staring at this scene. He went to the boy.

"What's happening? Do you know?"

"They are afraid," the boy said. "Something is worrying them. They will not talk to me. What are they doing down there at the canoes?"

"Those are our canoes," Laforgue said.

Among the beached canoes, three of the older women were moving bundles from one craft to another. "Those are our goods," Laforgue said.

Hurrying, he and Daniel went down to the canoes.

"What are you doing?" Daniel asked a woman.

"These are your things," the woman said. "We don't want to mix our shit with yours." She laughed, and the women with her laughed also.

"Come on," Daniel said, smiling at her. "Tell me what you're really doing."

"Ask Neehatin," the woman said.

Laforgue turned away. "Let's go. I will speak to Neehatin."

But as they went back up the riverbank they saw the Savages watching the forest. Through the trees, running lightly, came the five hunters whom Neehatin had dispatched. One of them held a large bird which he had killed with an arrow. He pulled the arrow clear as he handed the bird to Neehatin. The women who had cut branches for the habitation abruptly ceased their work. No one spoke. Ougebemat raised his hatchet and made a circular movement. Immediately, all the Algonkian men, women and children ran back to their boats, leaving Neehatin alone in the clearing with Daniel and Laforgue.

"What is happening?" Laforgue said to the Algonkian leader.

Neehatin smiled. He held out the freshly killed bird. "Here," he said. "This is for you. Tonight, you will eat. You will truly eat."

Laforgue did not take the bird. "You have not answered me," he said.

Neehatin threw the bird on the snow. "So you refuse my gift?" He no longer smiled.

"We do not refuse it," Daniel said and at once picked it up. "We thank you, Neehatin."

Laforgue turned and looked back at the canoes. The Savages were pushing them over the snow, going back down to the river. All but two canoes, those in which the Jesuit supplies were loaded.

"So," Laforgue said. "We have reached the rapids. Who are the paddlers who will take us on to the Huron lands?"

"What paddlers?" Neehatin said. "You don't need paddlers. Your sorcery will take you up the portage."

"You made a promise to Agnonha," Laforgue said. "Two men to guide us."

"You're full of shit, Nicanis," Neehatin said and laughed, a wild laugh, which he quickly curbed, looking back at the trees.

"You made a promise," Laforgue said again. "You gave your word."

"The branches are cut for your habitation and the ground is cleared," Neehatin said. "But do not camp here for more than one night. And throw out half of that shit you have in the canoes if you want to reach the upper rapids without going back and forth six or seven journeys." He turned away and walked down to the waiting canoes.

Laforgue watched him go. He remembered his days in the cloister, when he had read with excitement and dread of how Father Brabant had been abandoned at this point by Savages who had accepted presents and promised to accompany him. He felt a strange calm, the calm of knowing the worst.

Suddenly, without a word, Daniel ran down to the river, wading into the water, going toward Chomina's canoe. Laforgue saw the girl at the rear of the craft and Chomina's wife and little boy sitting in the center. Daniel spoke, not to the girl but to Chomina himself, whereupon Chomina shook his head and waved him off. At that moment, Neehatin reached his canoe, leaping into it like a cat. Chomina at once took up his paddle, and he and his men steered their craft out into the stream, leaving Daniel standing abandoned in the shallows. The canoes circled and turned downriver. Chomina's daughter did not look back. In a moment the canoes had rounded the bend in the river and were gone.

The boy, splashing in the shallows, climbed the riverbank, coming toward Laforgue. I will be gentle with him, Laforgue decided. I will pretend that he did not want to leave me. But, as he watched, the boy ran floundering in the snow toward the two canoes which had been left behind. In frantic, awkward haste he began to remove from one the bundles tied in skins which contained the provisions, mass vestments, books and other necessities for the Huron mission. When these bundles lay on the snow, the boy pushed the light craft down to the river and settled it in the water. He did not look at Laforgue but jumped in the canoe and paddled it out into the stream, circling, following the direction of the Algonkin, a solitary, driven figure, the light, half-empty canoe skimming like a flat stone over the shallow white waters of the rapids. In a moment he had reached the river bend.

Laforgue looked down at the dead bird at his feet, then at the pine branches cut for his night's habitation. He was alone.

It was still two hours to darkness. In the oilskin package which contained his map was a notebook in which Father Gulot and Father Brabant had set down their cautions and advice. Both priests had suffered abandonment and had survived. Laforgue, sitting on one of the bundles left in the snow by Daniel, opened the small book and read, in Father Gulot's neat handwriting, instructions on how to light a fire and protect it. In the same book Father Brabant had drawn a plan showing the construction of a simple shelter, and as Laforgue thumbed through the pages he decided that this would be his first task.

Working with surprising speed, he cleared a small patch of ground and laid down the branches already cut by the Algonkian women. He then erected a triangular covering on which he spread the sheets of birch bark which he found in the rear of the canoe. When he had finished, he lit a small fire and began to pluck the bird's feathers. He filled the kettle with handfuls of snow, planning to boil the bird. He did not think beyond each task but worked as he had seen the Savages work, with single-minded attention. He cleaned the bird, something which the Savages did not do, then put it in the boiling pot. He looked at the night sky, which was cloudy. He could not see a moon.

A light rain began to fall and, remembering that the bundles from the second canoe lay unprotected in the snow, he left his fire and dragged them back into the shelter of the forest. Tomorrow, when he traveled on, he would be unable to carry even a fraction of the contents of their two canoes up the long and arduous portages described by Father Brabant. He must take the minimum and bury or hide the rest until spring, when it could be reclaimed.

It was then, as he dragged the bundles into the forest, that he discovered at the base of a huge tree a space like a cave where the snow had not penetrated. The space was big enough to hold two men. It was dry and clean, covered with pine needles. He crawled into it. It was a cache where he might hide the mass vestments, the missals and the chalice, which he could no longer carry. In the morning he would rearrange all these things. He then realized that, weary as he was, he had no appetite for the bird now in the pot and that if he drew his heavy cloak about him in this sheltered cave he would sleep more snugly than in the rough habitation out there in the snows. Accordingly, he left the bundles by the tree trunk to mark the spot and returned to his fire, removing the kettle and setting it to one side. Then, taking his cloak and piling the other bundles beside the loaded canoe, he reentered the forest, found his cave under the tree trunk, crawled in and lay curled up in his cloak. He thought of Daniel and said a prayer. *O Lord, do not abandon him. Succor him as Thou has succored me.*

He slept. Outside his tree cave the night rainfall became a downpour, a rain which melted the snows, revealing again the earth's autumnal covering of leaves and moss. The noise of the rain did not rouse him, but sometime in the darkness of the hour before dawn, he was jerked into wakefulness by another sound. Voices.

Savages: close, very close. They have come back.

If they have come back, then Daniel is with them. Relief flooded him, making him feel almost faint. What were they saying? He crawled to the mouth of his cave, slipping off his cloak.

The voices spoke a strange dialect, kin to the Huron tongue.

"No, shit no. They wouldn't leave their peltries, would they?"

A second voice said, "Why would they build this shelter that wouldn't cover a dead hare?"

Cautiously he put his head out. The small guttering fire he had built had been replaced by a larger one.

Around it, eating from his kettle, sat five or six Savages, all males. On their knees or at their feet were clubs, hatchets and bows. In the firelight their faces gleamed with paint, colored red, yellow and blue. Their hair was cut and braided in strange patterns; they wore ornaments of teeth and shells.

"They are sorcerers," said a voice from outside the firelight, and at that moment two other Savages came up from the river. Behind their astonishing facial masks, their mouths were wide in laughter. One of them, the taller, was wearing, backward, the white mass vestments of silk and cloth of gold Laforgue was taking to the Huron mission. The sight of this Savage, his skull shaved, clothed in the blessed garments sewn for the mission by the nuns of the Abbaye aux Dames at Caen, seemed like a scene from some ugly dream. The other Savage who came up from the boats held out the precious flagon of sacramental wine.

"Norman drink," shouted one of those sitting at the fire. All rose, laughing, as the flagon was passed around. Although it was a two-gallon flagon, the Savages disposed of it in one round of swilling gulps.

"Norman sorcerers," said one of the strangers. "No Algonkin would carry this drink for days without sucking it down. They are Normans, these pricks."

"That's why they don't build a proper habitation," another said. "Blackrobes, I bet."

"Yes, Blackrobes."

"Then where are they? Did they have two canoes and take one of them? Or did they run off in the woods when they saw us coming?"

"Agariata, you are full of shit. How could they hear us or see us when we came up like shadows?"

"Then why did they leave their food and canoe?"

"Algonkin brought them here. That's what I think."

"Then where are those pricks of Algonkin?"

"Across the river, no?"

"Is there more of that fucking drink? I want more."

"Look in the canoe."

He heard them whooping, as they ran down to the riverbank, heard them talking down there, but not what they said. There was no more wine, he knew, and soon they came back. One of them was now wearing his spare cassock as a cloak. As they came back to the fire, the hideously painted Savage faces were solemn as icons. They spoke in low voices.

". . . and wrong, fucking wrong."

"Algonkin . . ."

"No, wait. Those pricks did not bury this stuff. Therefore they have carried other stuff up to the first portage stop. Tomorrow they will come down again and pick up this lot."

"We'll wait. . . ."

"Fucking right. At the fork we can see both the river and the trail."

He heard them approach. He ducked his head back down into his hiding place, heard their soft shoes on the rain-sodden leaves outside. The footsteps passed. All was silent. He lay, listening, but heard nothing. Two hours later, a cold sun rose over the river. Birds sang. Melting snow dripped from the branches overhead. Laforgue crept to the opening of his tree-trunk cave and peered out. There was no sign of the strange Savages, but he knew that they were out there, waiting. He was trapped.

# 7

NEEHATIN LOOKED BACK AND SAW THE NORMAN BOY, Iwanchou, in an empty canoe, gaining. Shit! He looked at his wife. She met his eye. She was the one who had said Annuka, Chomina's daughter, was fucking with this boy. And it was true. That is why he ran to Chomina's canoe. What will I do? If I let him come with us to the winter hunting place, we will have a witness who can tell Agnonha what we have done today. But if I put a hatchet in his head and someone betrays me, Agnonha will train his arquebuses on all the Algonkin until I come forward to confess. Then he will kill me. Shit! It's Chomina's fault. He made a friend of that boy. Now we must pay for that stupidity.

Iwanchou's canoe joined the snake. Neehatin turned and waved to the boy. He needed time. He looked at the forest but the forest was silent. He signaled to his wife to come to the rear of the canoe, and, as though she had been expecting this, she at once put up her paddle and crawled close. He bent to whisper. No one must know that he sought counsel from his woman.

"What do you see?"

She closed her eyes and rocked to and fro. "I don't see."

"Try. We are in shit."

"I know, I know."

She stopped rocking. She opened her eyes and looked at him. "Send the boy back."

"How can I? Even if I lift a hatchet to put in his skull, he will not go back now. He has left the Blackrobe. There is no going back."

"He will go back."

"Fuck off," Neehatin said, and laughed. He did not understand her, he never understood her, but he believed her. He had always been right to believe her.

She smiled. She crawled back down the canoe and, taking up her paddle, fell in with the others as they stroked. Neehatin rose and gave the signal for the fastest pace. He had just seen the beaver rock on the far shore. Soon they would leave the canoes and go inland. It was usually permitted to go through that place to reach the winter hunting. The enemy often allowed it. But not always.

When he came to the place of landing, he set his canoe in and passed out word that no one was to talk. The Norman boy disembarked with the others. Neehatin did not speak to him but did not stop him from helping as the people prepared sleds and loaded all their belongings. The canoes were carried on shore and placed in the higher forks of trees, then covered with cut branches. Chomina came up.

"What about this Iwanchou?" Chomina asked.

"What about him? You tell me. Your daughter is a bitch in heat, and he runs after her."

Chomina laughed as though this were a joke. "Shit," he said. "He came after us because he doesn't want to die. Who can blame him?"

"Let's go," Neehatin said. "We can talk when we're out of the corridor."

Amantacha came up and nodded to show his group

was ready. "If we see beaver or porcupine?" he whispered.

"Kill," Neehatin told him. "But don't delay and don't go out of the corridor."

Ougebemat came up. "Ready," he said.

The Norman boy now approached. Neehatin knew he waited his chance to speak. He pointed to the boy. "Go with Chomina. We will talk later."

"Neehatin?" the boy began.

"Quiet," Neehatin said. He turned away.

The people had made long sleds of bark, cut narrow because they must be dragged between the trees. Although the snow had half melted in this place, snowshoes were worn. To remain in the corridor, they must stay in the woods, bending down to pass under half fallen trees, stepping over large branches which had fallen on the ground. Even the children were burdened, but on this journey the men, not the women and children, went ahead. All were silent. Even the dogs seemed aware of the danger.

After the first hour, the party came into drifts of snow in which, despite snowshoes, they sank up to their knees. Neehatin gave the order that they rest. After some minutes they again set out. They saw no game, but when they were almost at the end of the corridor and coming toward the safe place, Amantacha's son found and killed a porcupine while Ougebemat, coming on a small river, found a beaver dam and killed eight before the beavers swam into a hiding place from which they could not be extricated. Neehatin reflected that there would be meat to supplement the sagamité tonight. Does that mean our fortunes have improved since we dumped the Blackrobe? Or is this a false moment of peace?

He looked up and saw, above the trees, the side of a small mountain. It meant that they had less than an hour to go. He signaled to Ougebemat and the others; then, whispering to Chomina to take the lead, he fell back, waiting until the women and children caught up.

As he watched the women approach through the trees, he saw his wife among them. She dragged a sled long as two men, the halter around her forehead straining as though it would break. Neehatin came up to her and, dragging his own sled, pulled a cord around hers to help her with her heavy burden.

"What do you see?" he asked in a low voice.

She shut her eyes and did not answer.

"Say it," he whispered. "Even it it's bad."

"Send Iwanchou back."

"Why?"

"I see him with blood on his face. Send him back."

"Blood?" His whisper seemed to echo in the surrounding forest. "Could it be blood caused by my hatchet?"

She shook her head. She trudged on beside him, silent, her breathing hoarse as a dog's as she dragged her sled through the snows. At last she looked up and saw the clear place beyond the trees, the end of the corridor, the place where they would be free to rest. She looked at her husband. "Now," she said. "Do it now. Send him back."

When they reached the safe place, the Algonkin threw down their burdens and, laughing, making their usual jokes, ran about in the snow, hopping like seabirds in their large round snowshoes. If the hunting was good in this place, they would not have to move for several days. In the next two months in the winter hunting place they could travel without fear of enemies. But there were some who did not take part in the general merriment. Chomina stood with his wife, watching the Norman boy as the boy spoke earnestly with Annuka, their daughter. Neehatin watched Chomina watch the boy.

"We will begin the habitation," Amantacha said.

"No," Neehatin said. "Call the senior men. We must talk."

"What is he saying to her?" Chomina asked his wife.

"He has put a spell on her," Chomina's wife said. "She wants us to take him as one of our family."

"It's not a spell, it's his prick," Chomina said, and laughed, although he was far from laughter.

The sorcerer came up to him. "Neehatin wants a council."

As the rest of the party went about the tasks for making camp, Neehatin led the senior men to a quiet spot. "The subject is the Norman," he told them.

"I have been thinking about that," Ougebemat said.

"I too," said Awandouie. "When the winter is over, Iwanchou will find his own people. He will say what we have done today. And we will be fucked. We will have Agnonha to deal with."

"Exactly," Neehatin said. "So what is your advice?"

"Send him back to the Blackrobe," said Amantacha.

"How can we do that? What if he does not go? What if he goes back down the great river and reaches Québec? As long as he is alive, he is a danger to us."

"Neehatin is right," said Ougebemat. "Let's put a hatchet in his head. Now."

"Whose hatchet?" Neehatin said.

"Yours. You are our leader."

"Mine? Fuck you. The man who puts a hatchet in Iwanchou's head is the man Agnonha will hunt down."

"Agnonha will never know," Amantacha said. "We are all friends here."

"Even so, Neehatin is right," old Awandouie cautioned. "Five winters from now, if some woman or child among us speaks with a loose tongue and tells what happened here, Neehatin is a dead man."

"Shit," said Ougebemat. "That's right."

"It's your fault," Neehatin said to Chomina. "That daughter of yours is why that young prick followed us."

"I see," Chomina said. "It is my fault that I have a daughter. But is it my fault that you broke our promise to Agnonha? If we had kept our word and sent two men up the rapids with the Blackrobe, we would be happy tonight."

"Would we? With two of our men up there on the portage? Two who might never come back?"

"We gave our word," Chomina said. "If we weren't going to keep our word, we shouldn't have taken Agnonha's presents. We have become as bad as the Normans themselves. All we think of is things. We have become greedy and stupid like the hairy ones."

"Yes, that is true," said Awandouie. "Perhaps that is how the Normans will destroy us. Not in war, but by a spell that makes us like them."

"That is shit," Neehatin said, and laughed to show he was not angry. "Look, you assholes, let's not have any bad words now. We have reached the hunting place. We are safe. We have meat to eat tonight. I'm going to send that boy back to Nicanis. I'll tell him that unless he leaves tomorrow, he'll get a present from me: a hatchet in his skull."

"But if he refuses to go," Amantacha said, "you're back in the shit. We've just said it's too risky to kill him."

"Wait," Chomina said. "I can solve this riddle."

Neehatin felt a twinge of alarm. Was this an attempt to take over his role as leader?

"I will go back with him," Chomina said.

"You're crazy," Ougebemat said. "That boy doesn't want to go back any more than you do."

"He wants to be part of my family," Chomina said. "I will go with my family, and he will follow us. We will find the Blackrobe and take them both to the top of the rapids, as promised. Annuka and my wife will help with the portages. When we reach the top of the rapids, I will have kept my promise to Agnonha. What the boy and the Blackrobe do after that is none of our business."

"But, fuck it," Ougebemat said. "You are one of us. Why should we let you risk your family for some fucking Normans?"

"Because I made a stupid promise through my own greed," Chomina said. "And now I am stupid enough to keep that promise. Let's get the kettles on. I am hungry. And after tomorrow, I see a few hungry days for me and mine."

"Well, Neehatin," old Awandouie asked. "What do you say to this?"

"I say Chomina has saved our fucking necks," Neehatin said, laughing. He embraced Chomina. As he hugged Chomina he thought of his wife's advice. We are doing what she said we must do. We are sending the boy back. She has the gift of seeing, all right. But who would have thought it would come out like this?

"Then are all agreed that Chomina make this journey?" Awandouie asked. "Those who do not agree, speak now."

No one spoke.

She watched Iwanchou as he worked with the other men, clearing ground for the habitation, using his snowshoe as a shovel, piling the cleared snow into a wall, as he had been taught by her people. As she watched him, she worked with the women on the edge of the clearing, cutting boughs and trimming them. He had not spoken to her since that moment when, heartsick, she paddled away, leaving him behind with the Blackrobe. Even then she had known that it was not finished between them.

Minutes later, when, paddling an empty canoe, he came into sight behind them, her mother asked, "Did you tell him to come?"

"No."

"You are sure?"

"Of course I am sure."

"Then don't speak to him when we land. If you do, we will be blamed."

So she had kept away, although it was as cruel as beating a child. If she did not go to him, he would not come to her. That was a promise between them, made long ago. But now, as the group of senior men came back from their meeting, she saw her father leave the others and go up to Iwanchou. Despite herself she stopped cutting branches and stood, trying to hear what was said. But they were too far away. She remembered what her father had said earlier, when Iwanchou had tried to board their canoe. "Go away. Go back to your own people." And Iwanchou had said, "You are my people now." It was then that he had looked at her. And it was then that she knew she could not give him up.

She set to work again, tying up a bundle of branches, then dragging it across the clearing. As she did this she was able to come closer to her father and Iwanchou. Iwanchou was smiling. Why? Surely the council had not agreed to let him stay? Even though she knew this could not be, her hopes rose, making her almost dizzy. He had a musket, which was something few men possessed. He could kill with it as none of them had yet learned to do. With his musket he would be a hunter whom all admired. He could be her husband.

But it was not until darkness, the habitation built and the kettles on the fires, that she learned the truth. They were going back. She, her father, her mother, her little brother, Outiji, and Iwanchou would go to the head of the rapids. There, her father said, they would leave Iwanchou and the Blackrobe and return to rejoin the people.

"But what if he follows us back down again? What if he will not stay with the Blackrobe?"

Her father laughed. "You'd like that, wouldn't you?" he said. "You put a spell on him, didn't you, Annuka?"

She said nothing.

"I promised Agnonha to take them to the head of the rapids," her father said. "What Iwanchou does after that is his business."

"But you like him?" she asked. "You said you liked him."

"What's the matter with you? You are beautiful. All the young men want to fuck with you. You can have anyone as a husband."

"The young men do not have muskets," she said.

Her father laughed. "You are full of shit, my girl," he said. "You think I am stupid, don't you? Maybe I am. I have been saying that you put a spell on him. It's the other way around. He has put a spell on you. What do you care about muskets?"

"A man with a musket is a good hunter, a good husband."

"Let us settle one point now," her father said. "He will *not* be your husband. Now, let's go eat. We will leave at first light tomorrow."

"May I speak to him?"

Her father laughed and, coming to her, embraced her. "Yes, you may speak to him," he said. "But listen to me. There are other men. Good men. Our men."

"It is you who is full of shit," she said and laughed to show him she was not angry.

"Go on, then," he said, smiling at her.

And so, with her father's permission, at last she could go up to Iwanchou, who sat near the kettles, not eating, but watching, waiting for her to come. As she went in his direction, he rose and left the light of the fires. In the darkness, outside the circle of feasting, she found him and kissed him. "Iwanchou," she said. "Iwanchou." For although she found it strange to say anyone's name like this, it was the Norman custom. He liked to hear her say his name.

"Annuka," he said, kissing her. "You've heard the news?"

"Yes."

"It is as if all my wishes are granted," he said. "If we can take Nicanis up the rapids, then, I think, he can go on alone."

"But you are going with him?"

He shook his head. "I spoke with your father," he said. "He told me that when he has taken us up the rapids, his promise to Agnonha is fulfilled. What I do after that is my affair, he said." He took her in his arms. "So everything is well," he said. "Come. Let's go in the woods for a while."

"No. The kettles are on. We must eat before all the meat is gone."

"I am hungry for you, not for food."

She laughed and pulled free of him. "Later," she said. "I want meat now. We will eat only sagamité in the days ahead."

# 8

A LYNX, MOVING AS THOUGH AT ANY MOMENT THE earth would shift beneath its paws, came with infinite caution into the clearing where last night's fire had been guttered by morning showers. Laforgue, who had waited since dawn, wondering if he dare venture outside his place of concealment, watched the lynx, his surrogate, as it moved closer to the empty kettle, its delicate nostrils leading it to the smell of food. Suddenly, the animal lifted its head, looking around as though it had heard something and was prepared to bolt. For a long moment it stood statue-still, then turned its head so that Laforgue could see its eyes, eyes which did not see him. Uneasy, as though threatened, the lynx crouched down, then cautiously began to make its way back in the direction from which it had come. As it did, Laforgue heard a noise like a sigh. The lynx stopped, transfixed, head thrown up. Vibrating like a harp string was a slender arrow embedded in its neck. At once, Laforgue ducked his head down into his hiding place. His ears, which a few days ago had been dulled by infection, now seemed to him like the ears of a Savage in their ability to detect the merest sound. When, again, he risked a look outside, a Savage, one of the strange painted faces of last night, bent over the lynx, removing the arrow. A second Savage crept from the trees and attached thongs to the dead animal's front paws. The first Savage lifted the animal up, placing it on the back of the one who had tied its paws. Both Savages moved away, going up the riverbank to the spot where the rapids, in a rush of white water, became unnavigable. Within seconds they were gone.

They are here and they are waiting. How long will they watch this place? How long before they decide to move on? They have killed a lynx and will want to eat it. For that, they must light a fire. If they light a fire, they will be sure to light it in some place where it cannot be seen. Where? They are waiting in a place where the trail from that first portage passes close by. They can also see the river. What will I do? What can I do?

The hours passed slowly. He watched the sun, fitfully present among high rolling clouds. He watched the river. For a time, he prayed. For a time he lay, staring at the little silver crucifix on the bead rosary his mother had given him on the day of his ordination as a priest. He thought of that day in the church of Saint Ouen, the solemn High Mass, the unseen choir singing the Kyrie high in the vaulted roof, his parents kneeling on prie-dieux just in front of the communion rail, their faces a mirror of their joy. How long ago that seemed, how odd, as though he had read of it in some book, or dreamed it, and now woke, half remembering what it was he dreamed. Would he ever again see Rouen, with its jumbled streets of crooked-timbered houses, the noisy, smelly fish markets he had played in as a child, or the ancient façade of Saint Ouen, its gable carved with the images of Judean kings and queens? An illimitable ocean separated him from that place, from that time; vertiginous walls of seas into which ships tumbled like paper boats. Was that other life a dream? Or was this a dream, this barbarous present in which he crouched in a hole beneath a tree trunk, alone, vulnerable as a lynx to an arrow in his throat?

Again, he crawled toward the opening and lifted his head into the light. He looked along the hidden path up which the Savages had dragged the lynx. He looked at the trees, high above the river. They are up there, hiding. They have lit no fire. They watch the trail and the river. Laforgue looked back at the river, curling into a bend. All was still. And then, closer, near the place where the Algonkin had landed yesterday, he saw two canoes drawn up on the riverbank. Coming up from them were Chomina, his wife and their little boy. Behind, his musket at the ready, as though to guard them, was Daniel. And lastly, the girl, Chomina's daughter. All of them looked around, looking for him.

At once Laforgue reached up from his hiding place and pulled himself to his feet. As he did, an eerie high-pitched yell struck into the silence. Ahead, he saw Chomina's party stop as if shot. Arrows hissed, some falling short, three finding a mark, one in Chomina's shoulder, one in his wife's neck, one in the bundle which his daughter carried on her back. At that moment Daniel's musket thundered. Seven painted Savages rushed out onto the trail, surrounding their victims, flailing at them with clubs. Laforgue saw Chomina turn to his wife as she fell, blood spurting from the arrow wound in her throat, saw Daniel on his knees, trying to protect his head and neck as the Savages with wild shrieks battered him down, saw the girl running with her little brother toward the canoes, saw four other Savages rush from the trees, pinioning her and tripping the child.

Laforgue stood, heart pounding. They had not seen him. Daniel's shot had felled one of the Savages, and now the Savage leader, wearing the mass vestments which he had donned last night, knelt by the fallen warrior, cradled him in his arms, then, with a cry of rage so terrible it made Laforgue quail, let the dead man fall back on the ground.

Rising, his silken robes bloodied from the dead man's wound, the Savage leader screamed to the others. Chomina's wife was dragged across the ground by one of her captors, while another ripped the arrow out of her neck. Laforgue saw them kick her and turn her over. The Savage leader, the embroidered gold cross on his vestments fouled with blood and dirt, uttered a second cry of rage, and at once the Savages fell on Chomina, Daniel and the girl, making them pass down a double line of warriors, each of whom struck at them with javelin or club. When Daniel, staggering, came in reach of the leader, the leader took a javelin, pulled Daniel's head back by his hair, then caught hold of Daniel's arm and held it up. With the point of his javelin he pierced Daniel's palm, laughing as the boy screamed in pain. Chomina, stumbling, fell to the ground. The Savages raised him up again, the better to beat him unconscious. The girl they punished with the staves of their javelins until they drew blood from her back and thighs. The little boy was the only member of the party they did not harm, one of them holding him by the hair as the child saw his mother bleeding from her dreadful arrow wound, his father bludgeoned senseless, his sister flayed. Again, the leader, brandishing Daniel's musket above his head, screamed an order. The Savages began to pass thongs over their captives' bodies, binding them, preparing to lead them to the canoes.

And in that moment, watching, Laforgue knew that Daniel, Chomina and Chomina's family all would die. And that he, if he crawled back into his hiding place, would escape their fate. But what is my life in the balance, if, by going forward now, I can confess Daniel, who is in a state of mortal sin, and, God willing, baptize the others before their last end?

He felt himself tremble. Deliberately slow, he began to walk toward the clearing. The painted Savages turned, their javelins poised, two of them threading their bows with arrows as he came toward the captives. The painted faces watched, impassive, as, pale and determined, a frail man in a long black robe, he knelt beside Chomina's wife and, wetting his fingers in the snow, began to say the words of baptism. He was too late. Tears came to his eyes as he saw her glazed pupils gaze past him at those heavens now forever denied her. Then, with a shriek of rage, the Savage leader came up behind him and clubbed him at the base of his skull. He fell forward, unconscious, and woke to hands passing thongs over his limbs. Within minutes, clubbed and bound, he stood with the others awaiting his fate.

The Savage strangers, silent now, loaded Laforgue's canoe with the remainder of the goods which Daniel earlier had strewn in the snow. Four warriors, coming from the trees, carried two canoes which Laforgue had not seen before, the canoes of the strangers. Within a minute all five canoes were launched in the waters of the lower rapids. With curses the painted Savages disposed of their captives, putting Daniel and Laforgue in one canoe and Chomina, his daughter and little son in the other. Then, with the Savage leader lifting his wet vestments up around his hips as he clambered aboard, and a second Savage, wearing Laforgue's spare cassock, pushing the leader's canoe to the front position, the strangers set out downriver. A light rain began to fall. Wincing, nursing his pierced hand, Daniel looked at Laforgue.

"We were coming back for you," he said.

"I know." Laforgue felt dizzy. The blow at the base of his skull had raised a large protrusion. "Your hand," he asked the boy. "Did they break the bones?"

"No, I don't think so."

"Chak, chak, chak, chak," said one of the painted faces, mimicking the French speech. Turning, he spat in Laforgue's face. "What is that dog talk, you hairy pig? What are you saying?"

"It is our tongue, the Norman tongue," Laforgue said. Again, pain stabbed at the base of his skull.

"We speak your tongue," Daniel said to the Savage. "What people are you? You speak like Hurons."

"Shut your hairy mouth," the Savage said. "If you cannot speak properly, then be silent, you prick."

The Savage then called to the two others who paddled at the rear of the canoe. "How is it that Normans can speak our tongue?"

"They talk like moose," one of the Savages said, laughing. "Algonkian moose. They will never sound like Iroquois."

"Fucking right."

*Iroquois.* Daniel looked at Laforgue. It was the danger Champlain had warned of. It was a sentence of death. Laforgue watched as Daniel, wincing, tried to lick his wounded hand. He leaned toward him. "Let me confess you," he whispered. "Say an act of contrition."

"Shut your fucking face," the Savage shouted, turning, striking Laforgue across the nose, making his nose bleed.

"Say the words to yourself," Laforgue whispered. "Not aloud."

Blood ran down his upper lip into his beard and mouth as he watched the boy close his eyes, watched his lips move in silent prayer. He felt a surge of joy. After a moment, Daniel opened his eyes, looked at him and nodded, as though to say he had finished. *"Ego te absolvo,"* Laforgue whispered, raising his hand in the sign of absolution. *"In nomine patris, et filii, et spiritus sancti."*

The Savage who had struck him did not look back, for the canoes were now skimming at speed over rocky shallows, moving closer to shore. Laforgue, blood spilling down his chin onto his neck, nodded to Daniel to show that he had finished.

"Thank you," the boy whispered. "Forgive me, Father."

"God is with us," Laforgue said. "It is He who forgives us."

After paddling less than an hour, the Savages abruptly swung back toward shore, landing a few leagues downriver from the place where the Algonkin had first made camp. Here they hid the canoes and their contents high in the trees, then roped together their prisoners. Shouting, cursing, beating them with javelin staves, they set off along a narrow track through the forest. Within minutes, Laforgue and Daniel heard cries ahead. Four Savage women came through the trees wearing necklaces of beads, their bodies naked to the waist as for a ceremonial feast. They carried bark platters containing strips of cooked meat which they gave to the returning warriors. Gleeful, they danced around the prisoners, pulling at Laforgue's beard, striking Annuka, her father and Daniel, calling out, "Let us caress them, let us caress them."

"Later," said the Savage leader, wolfing his meat and gesturing to the others to hasten on. And so, stumbling, bound, burdened, Chomina, his daughter and son, followed by Daniel and Laforgue, were led into an Iroquois village. Here were habitations of a sort Laforgue had never seen, dwellings laid out in a double row as in a village street with, at the end, a larger building, a communal house more than one hundred feet in length, built of strong saplings bent together to form an arched roof and covered with bark of oak and spruce. At the top of the arch was an open space to admit light and release the smoke of the fires.

As the warriors led their captives to this building, the party was surrounded by a large throng of men, women and children, all chanting at the tops of their voices. In the din Laforgue heard the beating of skin drums. At the entrance of the longhouse, a group of men, obviously leaders, stood waiting. They, like the warriors, had painted their faces. A few were heavily tattooed, their faces, backs and arms grotesquely traced in intricate arabesques. One of these tattooed figures, tall and gaunt, was adorned in such a profusion of colored shells and beads, and wore a beaver coat of such splendor, that Laforgue assumed him to be the paramount leader. It was to this man that the warriors led their prisoners.

"Normans," said the paramount chief.

"Traveling with Algonkin," said the leader of the hunters. He held out Daniel's musket. "Tarcha died of this."

The paramount leader took the musket eagerly, examined it, then pulled the trigger. There was no explosion. He shook it in vexation, then looked at Laforgue. "Bring them inside," he said to the hunters.

"Yes, Kiotsaeton."

The singing and drumming ceased. In a strange silence, the captives were led into the smoke-filled longhouse. Fires burned on the ground. Laforgue, looking up, saw rows of poles just under the vaulted roof. On them were suspended weapons, clothing, ornaments and skins. On a middle level were platforms running the length of the room and, as the captives were led to the fires, the villagers followed, scrambling up on these platforms to watch the spectacle.

"Strip them," said Kiotsaeton.

At once, all the prisoners, including the little boy, were stripped naked. A cheer went up into the rafters as the older women came forward, singing. They took firebrands from the smoking fire and approached the paramount chief.

"May we caress the captives?" asked one of the women.

"Caress them," said Kiotsaeton, "but carefully. We must make them last."

The women, gleeful, at once thrust their burning brands against the genitals of Chomina and Laforgue, causing them to double up in pain. They then burned Annuka's shoulder and thrust a flaming stick into Daniel's armpit. The crowd, wildly excited, yelled and shouted. "Make them sing, make them sing their songs."

"Sing," commanded Kiotsaeton. "Sing your war songs. And dance, you hairy dogs."

Savage hands pulled the two Frenchmen forward and amid kicks and shoves they were forced to perform a clumsy dance. "Sing," Daniel cried to Laforgue. "Sing or they will kill us."

*"Ave Maria,"* Laforgue sang hoarsely, the words of the hymn lost in the yells of the exultant Iroquois, *"gratia plena, Dominus tecum . . ."*

He looked and saw Daniel singing the hymn, his good hand clutching his armpit where he had been burned. Men and women now scrambled down from the platform and, going to the fires, took up hot coals on platters. These they sprinkled on the captives, all the while laughing and yelling in excitement. Then, as the captives writhed and shrank from these tortures, the leader issued a new command. At once all were silent. He pointed to Chomina. "Sing. Sing your war song." He pointed to Annuka. "Dance."

Impassive, not looking at his captors, Chomina began to sing a war chant in a loud defiant voice. His daughter shuffled in a circle in a primitive dance step. Laforgue stared at the girl, his eyes misted by pain. That slender body which had aroused his lust now filled him with an infinite pity as her shoulders and narrow loins were kicked and pummeled by bystanders each time she stumbled and fell. *Oh Lord,* he prayed. *Grant me the chance to baptize her. Grant her eternal peace.*

And then, suddenly, the girl collapsed on the ground.

The Savages fell silent; the only sound in the longhouse was Chomina's loud, monotonous war chant. Kiotsaeton and two other leaders went to the fires and spoke among themselves, then signaled to the waiting warriors. At once, a tall Savage, his head dyed red, his eyes horrid yellow circles, a strip of reddish fur hanging from a pigtail down his back, went up to Chomina's little boy, took him by the hair and, with a gesture callous as though he killed a fowl, swiftly slit his throat. Blood gurgled forth from the child's mouth. Daniel, anguished, tried to go toward him, but a Savage tripped him, spilling him on the ground. Chomina looked not at his dying son but up at the ceiling of the longhouse, singing a war chant as though he had seen nothing. And then, to his horror, Laforgue saw the child hacked to pieces with hatchets, its bloodied limbs thrown into a cooking kettle. He closed his eyes, as though unable to believe what he had witnessed.

Pandemonium filled the longhouse, a stamping, yelling, screaming din. The leader raised his hands for silence, then came up to Laforgue.

"Agnonha, who is Agnonha?"

"He is our leader, the leader of the French," Laforgue replied.

"Then you are a dead man, you hairy fool. Agnonha is the cunt who killed our people. You will die, but not today. You will die slowly. We will caress you and caress you again. Today, we will give you a first caress. Take his hand."

Two of the warriors at once seized and held Laforgue. Kiotsaeton took from his belt a razor-sharp clam shell. Taking Laforgue's left hand he pulled on the index finger; then, using the clam shell like a saw, cut to the bone. He sawed through the bone and pulled the skin and gristle free. He held up the finger joint. The crowd roared and cheered. He threw the piece of finger into the cooking kettle. In excruciating pain, Laforgue fell to his knees and then, in a scene so terrible that it surpassed horror or pity or forgiveness or rage, he saw three older women take from the cooking kettle the limbs of the dead child and pass them, parboiled, to the warriors who had captured Chomina's party. The warriors paraded up and down before Chomina and his daughter, eating the flesh as though it were succulent meat. Chomina stood, singing loudly, his eyes on the rafters. The girl vomited on the ground.

The women standing by the pot began to pass out parboiled flesh to other warriors. As they did, Kiotsaeton stepped forward and held up his arms. At once, the yelling died down.

"The prisoners must not die," Kiotsaeton shouted. "We will caress them again when the sun has risen. Give them food. Let the children caress them, but be careful. Give back their garments."

Surrounded by smiling, jeering Savages, the captives were thrown their clothes, forced to dress, then pushed and pulled outside the longhouse. Children danced ahead of them as they were led to a smaller dwelling where a fire burned on a pit of live coals. There, the villagers left them alone, save for one warrior with club and hatchet and four young and gleeful children. Exhausted, the captives lay down on the bare earth. The children circled them. One little girl giggled, her hand over her mouth, almost in a parody of embarrassment. "Take off your clothes," she said.

"Which ones?" the guard asked.

"Those two. The hairy ones."

"Take your fucking clothes off. Quick." The guard, raising his club, gave Laforgue and Daniel each a blow on the shoulder. Wearily, both men removed their garments and stood naked once again.

"Dance," cried a little boy. His companions, meanwhile, had gone to the rear of the habitation and returned now with sharpened sticks which they thrust into the flesh of the men's thighs.

Wearily, the captives began a shuffling dance.

"Sing," cried one child.

They began the Ave Maria.

"Be quiet," cried a second child.

They stopped singing. The first child, the one who had ordered them to sing, at once went to the fire and, picking up a burning brand, held it close to Daniel's penis. "I told you to sing," the child yelled.

Daniel began to sing.

"Stop!" cried the second child, approaching, also waving a burning brand. The guard laughed.

The little girl went up to Laforgue and pulled hard on his beard. "What is this fucking shit on your face?" she cried. "Are you a man or a hare?"

"All right, children," the guard said indulgently. "That's enough. We must let them rest. There will be more sport tomorrow. Now they must eat."

"We will eat them," cried a little boy.

"I will eat your foot," the little girl screamed, dropping a hot coal on Daniel's foot.

"And I will eat one of your hands," a second boy yelled.

"Now, children, now, children," said the guard, laughing. "Outside, go on."

Yelling, giggling, the children ran out of the habitation. The two men, awkwardly, again put on their clothes. The guard bound their hands behind their backs, bound their feet so that they could only shuffle in a hobbled step. He bound Chomina and Annuka in a similar fashion, pausing to put his hand under the girl's skirt and fondle her. Then he brought pieces of some corn biscuit.

"Eat," he said to the girl and gently held the biscuit to her lips. Like an automaton, the girl tried to chew, but vomited the biscuit on the floor. "Never mind," the guard said quietly. "Later I will give you another piece."

He then went to Chomina, who bit on the biscuit he offered as though he did not see him. The guard fed Laforgue and Daniel, then went back to the fire, where, squatting on his hunkers, he took out his pipe and began to smoke.

For the first time since the capture, Chomina seemed to rouse himself. He shuffled close to his daughter, and she laid her head in his lap. He sat, rocking, rocking. Daniel hobbled across the floor and lay at her feet, looking at her with agonized tenderness. At last, her sobbing and retching ceased and she said to her father, "These aren't men. They're wolves."

"No," Chomina said. "They are not wolves. They are men. They are afraid of each other."

Laforgue, lying on the floor, turned to listen. "What do you mean?" he asked.

"If an Iroquois sees another Iroquois show pity to a captive, he will make fun of him. The warrior must not show pity. Pity is a weakness."

"They are wolves," the girl said again.

"No, no." Chomina looked down at her. "Our people do the same if they capture enemies. So do the Montagnais and the Huron. An enemy must be made to cry out in pain. That is why they torture us. But, alone, the Iroquois is like you or me." He nodded to the guard, who sat, his back to them, puffing on his pipe. "He will not harm us."

"Will we die?" she asked.

Her father rocked her but did not reply.

"But why must we cry out?" Daniel whispered. "Why?"

"If they can make us cry out, it means we cannot resist them. If we do not weep and plead for mercy, it means that when we die misfortunes will come upon them."

"But if we do cry out," Laforgue said. "Does that mean that they stop the torture?"

Chomina looked at him. "Don't you understand? If you cry out, then, when you die, they will possess your spirit."

"But that's not true," Laforgue said. "If I die, I will go to paradise. You and your daughter will come with me to paradise if you let me baptize you. I can do it now."

"Is that the water sorcery?"

"Yes. And all my God asks of you is that you believe in Him."

"Leave me alone," Chomina said bitterly. "I saw you do the water sorcery to my wife. But she was dead when you did it. She could not believe in your god, because she had died already. And some nights ago you did it to a baby. But the baby was dead. The water sorcery will not bring me to paradise. The water sorcery kills."

"You are wrong," Laforgue said. "Chomina, I am not lying to you. I will always be grateful to you. I can never repay you for coming back. But if you let me baptize you I swear that when you die you will go to paradise."

"What paradise? A paradise for Normans?"

"No. For you. For all who are baptized."

"But my people are not baptized with this water sorcery. Therefore they are not in your paradise. Why would I want to go to a paradise where there are none of my people? No, I will die and go to another country where our dead have gone. There I will meet my wife and my son. Your God shits on me and mine. My wife is dead because of you. My son is in the stomachs of the Iroquois. And the Iroquois will kill me slowly, day after day. It is you Normans, not the Iroquois, who have destroyed me, you with your greed, you who do not share what you have, who offer presents of muskets and cloth and knives and kettles to make us greedy as you are. And I have become as you, greedy for things. And that is why I am here and why we will die together."

"You are right about our greed," Laforgue said. "But you are wrong about our God."

"Leave him," Daniel whispered. "Be quiet, Father."

And so they lay in the smoking habitation, silent, in pain, each alone in thought of what had happened that day and what lay ahead. In the opening of the roof, the sky darkened to night. And when, at last, Chomina saw that their guard was asleep, he began to whisper to his daughter. Daniel, licking the wound in his palm, heard their muted voices and crawled closer to listen. But as he did, Chomina turned and looked at him in the flames of the guttering fire, as though warning him to stay away.

It was much later when, exhausted from their wounds and sufferings, both Chomina and Laforgue slept, that Annuka, inching herself across the bare earth, came and lay, bound, against her bound lover. In the darkness, he could not see her face. "Annuka," he whispered. "Your father is right. I have destroyed you."

Her face came close. He felt her parched lips touch his cheek.

At sunset, in the long room, tobacco was handed around. The seven in council moved to the central fire, some lying down, some squatting on their haunches. Pipes were lit. In the background, dogs barked and children cried, but on the sleeping trestles above the council, men and women turned away, showing by their posture that they respected their leaders' need for private debate. Kiotsaeton, who had called the meeting, listened first to Agariata and then to Honatheniate. Both were council chiefs but not leaders in war. Both were skilled in argument and memory. Both spoke at length. By the time Honatheniate had finished, the council had smoked two pipes. Pulling his beaver robe open, for it was warm in the long room, Kiotsaeton spoke at last. First he made a summary of the arguments he had listened to, for this was the custom and proved that one had heard and understood. He made no judgments on the arguments. When he had finished, he asked merely, "Is this what all have heard?"

The council made sounds of assent.

"Then let me give you a different solution," Kiotsaeton said. "About the girl, there is no question that, as Agariata has said, she is the only female captive and, as such, must be offered as a gift to Areskoui, by burning at the stake. Are all agreed?"

All were agreed.

"As for her fucking dog of a father, we will not let him defy us. We will caress him day and night until he screams like a hare. We will cut strips of skin from his body, we will burn him with coals and remove his fingers one by one, until he can no longer protect or feed himself."

"Even so, he will not be easy," said one of the council. "I watched him. He did not even look at his fucking child as the warriors ate it."

"He is a stupid Algonkian prick," Kiotsaeton said. "We will bring Ontitarac to work on him. Ontitarac will make him scream and give us his spirit. Eh, Ontitarac?"

Ontitarac, old, tattooed from head to navel, opened his robe and pulled on his penis, grinning at the others. Everyone laughed.

"Now we come to the Normans," Kiotsaeton said. "And this is serious business. Do you know what those Normans mean to us? Especially the Blackrobe? Do you know what Agnonha will say in Québec when he hears that we have killed them?"

"I don't give a shit what Agnonha will say," said Agariata.

"Remember. The Blackrobe is a sorcerer," said Kiotsaeton.

"We are not afraid of any sorcerers, even a Blackrobe," said old Ontitarac defensively. "That is why I say caress them unto death. Both have already cried out. They are weak. When they die we will eat their hearts and own their powers."

Kiotsaeton spat onto the fire. It was his way of signaling that now he would tell what was really in his mind. The others were silent. "Two Normans are twenty muskets," he told the council.

"Twenty muskets?"

"From Agnonha."

"Agnonha," said Honatheniate, "that cunt, that hairy dog. Our enemy will die in shit before I trade with him."

"Twenty," said Kiotsaeton.

"The muskets kill only once," said a council member.

"No, they can kill many times," said Kiotsaeton. "The Normans kill with them, again and again. It is a thing that must be learned, like the bow and arrow."

"He is right," said Annentaes, who was a war chief and rarely spoke.

"Twenty muskets," said Kiotsaeton. "And I would also ask for ten French kettles, thirty of their steel knives and some wampum belts."

"Ask what you want," said Ontitarac. "I tell you what Agnonha will give. He will give death and vengeance from generation to generation. That is what that fuckpot will give. When the Mohawk killed a Norman, Agnonha sent his warriors with arquebuses to destroy their villages. He will not trade with them or treat with them now, eight winters after the death."

"Exactly," said Kiotsaeton. "Let me say that I, like Ontitarac, do not fear any Norman. Not even that fucker Agnonha. But twenty muskets. Twenty muskets. Think of it, you men."

"Wait," said Manitougache. "Why should the Normans give guns to us, their enemies? They do not like to give guns to any of the people, not even to the Algonkin who are their allies."

"True," said Agariata. "The Normans are not like the Dutchmen. Agnonha refused to trade, even when the Montagnais offered him fifty beaver peltries for each musket."

"He cannot let a Norman die," said Kiotsaeton. "Especially a Blackrobe. It is said the Blackrobes hold him in their power."

"The Blackrobes are the worst of sorcerers," said old Ontitarac. "I have heard they live in a separate habitation, always. When they live among the Huron they will not allow the Huron to sleep in their dwellings. In each of the Blackrobe habitations there is a special room. In that room, there is a small box placed on a high ledge. Inside the box there are pieces of a corpse which they brought from France. They say this corpse is the body of their god. They have secret ceremonies in which they eat little pieces of this fucking corpse."

"That is true," said another council member. "I have been told the same story. And by a Huron."

"I have heard another thing," said Honatheniate. "It is that the Blackrobes do not fuck. They never fuck. They do not fuck because it increases their powers as sorcerers."

There was an uneasy silence. "Well," said Kiotsaeton, "that proves what I said. Agnonha fears the Blackrobe sorcerers. He will not dare to let one die in our hands."

"You are right," said old Ontitarac. "He kisses their asses and fears their spells. I have heard the same story up and down the river many winters now."

"Twenty muskets and the other goods," Kiotsaeton said, and smiled at the council. "We will not have to bargain. We have all power on our side."

"But how can we get the muskets?" asked Honatheniate. "We would go to give up the Normans and walk into an ambush. You cannot deal with a fucking Norman leader like Agnonha. He is a liar and has always been one. He does not keep his word."

"We will deal through the Dutchmen who live on the farther shore," Kiotsaeton said. "We will send a messenger to their place and tell them to tell the Normans that we have two of their men. When the guns are given to the Dutchmen, we will give them the prisoners."

"I see a trap," said Agariata.

"It will be a trap that can kill only one of us," Kiotsaeton said. "One man can bring the two prisoners to the place of the Dutchmen. If the muskets are there, he will give them the prisoners. If not, or if there is some trap, he will kill the prisoners."

"And which man will volunteer to go into that fucking mess?" asked Agariata, smiling.

Kiotsaeton spat in the fire. "I am the man."

When the light in the roof opening of the prisoners' habitation signaled that a new day had begun, Chomina, still feigning sleep, rolled over and made a covert signal to his daughter. The guard had wakened and was lying by the embers of the fire, eating a piece of the corn biscuit left over from the night before. Chomina watched as Annuka got up and hobbled painfully to where the guard lay. Chomina spoke to the wolf, his reigning spirit. She must not fail. For if she fails, by tonight the Iroquois will have caressed me to a point where I can no longer use my hands. I still have my hands, Chomina told the wolf. With my hands I can be free. Still pretending sleep, he rolled over and looked at the Normans. Both lay as though in dreams, although the boy moaned from time to time.

Annuka, obeying her father, came up to the guard very slowly, head bent in a posture which offered him no threat.

"I want to shit," she said, in a low voice.

The guard smiled and chewed on his biscuit. "Well,

shit, then," he said. "Go over there. I don't want you to shit over me."

She held out her bound hands. "The cords are so tight," she said. "My hands are like the hands of a dead man. When I try to get down to shit, my ankles fail and I fall on my face. Help me."

He laughed. "Help you? I cannot shit for you, you silly cunt."

Tears came into her eyes. In her pain and fear it was not difficult for her to make tears. The guard was young. They are men, not wolves, her father had said. If no one sees him, he will not be afraid that he will be mocked. If no one sees him, he may show you mercy. Her father was right.

"Come here, pretty," the guard said. She came up close to him in tiny steps, her ankles chafing from the hobble. She felt his hands on her numbed wrists. Her bonds were loosened. "Go on," he said. "Do it there."

She hobbled to the place he had pointed out. As she went there, she flexed her numbed fingers and moved her wrists. She raised her skirt and showed him her bum. She knew he was watching her. She let him look at it; then, pretending she had finished, she hobbled back to him, smiling to show her gratitude.

He was sitting up now, and she saw to her excitement that he had loosened his clothes around his thighs and taken out a large stiff prick. He looked up at her, grinning. "Lie down, pretty," he said. "Wait." He came to her and knelt at her feet. "I cannot fuck you with your legs tied together," he whispered. He looked back at the Normans and at her father. All three seemed to sleep.

She felt herself tremble as though she would faint. He freed her ankles and, numbed, she fell on her knees. "It hurts," she said. "It was so tight."

The guard smiled. He massaged her ankles, then fondled her breasts. He signaled her to kneel so that he could put it in from behind.

"Wait," she said. "I am hungry. Can I first have a bite?"

That was something he understood. He grinned at her; then, still with a stiff prick sticking up against his belly, went to the platter and bent down to get the corn biscuit. As he turned his back she reached for the heavy club. It was so heavy, for a moment she thought she could not lift it above her head. But she remembered the warriors standing by the kettles as they wolfed Outiji's flesh. She whirled the club. He turned, quick as a deer, but as he did she smashed the heavy club full in his face, knocking him back into the dying fire. You must make sure, her father had said. If you have a chance, you must make sure, and at once. So she ran forward and, choking, sick, raised the heavy club again and battered his head until it was a pulp of blood and matted hair. She dropped the club. He made little noise. She vomited into the embers.

The Normans were awake, lying on their sides, as was her father, all of them watching her. "Quick," her father said. He had told her to untie him first.

She went to him, but as she passed Iwanchou she looked into his eyes. She stopped, bent over him and began to free his bonds.

"Annuka," her father called in a low, angry voice. "Stop that. Don't touch him. Come to me."

She looked back at her father. "We cannot leave them," she said.

"The Iroquois want them more than they want us," her father said. "And besides, he has an injured hand. Leave him alone."

"No," she said. She freed Iwanchou's hands, and he began to undo the cords which bound his feet. She went to her father and freed him. He was angry at her disobedience, but when his bonds were removed he stood and embraced her. Iwanchou was untying the Blackrobe. "All right," her father said. "Nicanis, conceal your robe under the clothes of the dead one. Remember, we too dead men if we are discovered. How many *raquettes* are there here?"

In addition to the snowshoes of the dead guard, they found several other pairs, stored on shelves which hung down from the roof. There were also heavy winter garments of moose hide which they used as cloaks. Chomina took the dead guard's knife and handed the hatchet to Laforgue and the club to Daniel. Then, with showshoes tied to his back and his head muffled in skins, he went to the opening of the habitation. "Wait," he said. He went out and in less than a minute was back. "The Iroquois sleep late. There is no snow, and we are minutes from the river. Cover your hairy faces and be quick."

Outside, the village had not yet wakened. A few dogs wandered in the street, searching for scraps of food. Smoke from dying fires came from the roofs of the dwellings, and in the distance, at the end of the village, could be seen tilled fields, now cleared of their autumnal harvest. Chomina looked up toward the council longhouse where three women squatted by the doorway, picking and eating each other's lice. The women did not see them. "Walk slowly," Chomina said. He took the arm of Laforgue, who was unsteady on his feet. They walked down the village street, coming to the trail which led to the river. Yesterday's snow had melted, leaving the ground wet and muddy. As they came to the last of the dwellings, they saw, sitting on a heap of firewood, two little boys playing a game with a wooden ball tied to a string, which they threw up in the air and attempted to catch in an attached wooden cup. The children paid them no attention, but, as Daniel passed, he recognized one of the boys as the child who had tormented him the day before. He sunk his head in the rough cape of skin so that he could barely see the ground in front of him and, despite himself, quickened his pace. But the children, intent on their game, did not look up, and within a minute the village was out of sight as hurrying now, moving at a run, Chomina went ahead. The landing place by the river was unguarded. Circling restlessly among the Iroquois canoes, Chomina found his own and the one used by Laforgue. Hidden in the nearby trees were paddles, portage ropes and cooking kettles, which he placed in each of the two canoes. As he finished, his daughter reached the clearing, and when, a moment later, Laforgue and Daniel entered the area, they saw the two, father and daughter, in a whispered, angry discussion.

"Do what I say."

"No!"

"Come on." Chomina took her arm and dragged her toward his canoe. At that moment Daniel ran up beside them.

"What is this?"

"Shh!" Chomina glanced up the path leading to the Iroquois village. "We are going back to our people. You two get in the other canoe. Hurry. The Iroquois will soon be awake."

"I told you," Annuka said to her father. "I will go in Iwanchou's canoe. Let go of me."

Chomina released her arm and turned away as though to leave. Suddenly, he turned back to face Daniel, and now, in his hand, was the guard's knife. "She's my daughter. She comes in my canoe."

"Do not listen to him," the girl said. "He plans to leave you both."

Chomina, with astonishing agility, leaped on Daniel, circling his neck with his arm, the knife which he held in his left hand laid across the boy's throat. Slowly, he turned Daniel around to face Annuka. "Get in my canoe. Now, or I will cut this Norman's throat."

The girl stared at him, then slowly, obeying, walked toward the river's edge. "Hurry!" her father said. "Do you want us to burn in their fires?"

All three had forgotten Laforgue, who moved up behind them quietly and pulled out the hatchet Chomina had given him. "Let go of him," he said. Chomina, caught by surprise, wheeled, turning to face Laforgue, and at that moment the boy broke Chomina's grip, tripping him, falling on him, his good hand closing on Chomina's knife arm. The priest, running up, stood over Chomina, menacing him with the hatchet. "Give me the knife!" Laforgue said.

Chomina, lying on his back, felt a sudden fear of this Blackrobe sorcerer who stood above him like a manitou, waiting to cleave his skull. He dropped the knife and the boy picked it up.

"No one is angry, Chomina," the priest said. "Now, let us all travel in one canoe."

"Where will we go?" Daniel asked.

"To our winter hunting place," Chomina said, scrambling to his feet. "But we must travel quickly. When they find us gone, they will guess where we went. It is the only place we can go now."

"No," said Laforgue. "We can go up the rapids."

"Nicanis is right," the girl said to her father. "They will not think of that. And the Iroquois of this place do not travel above the rapids."

Chomina, his eyes still on the path leading back to the village and danger, stood for a moment, undecided. Then he turned to his daughter. "Go with them. I will go south, alone."

"Come with us, Father. I am asking you."

Again, her father looked back at the path. "You leave me no fucking choice, do you?" he said. "If I let you go alone with these hairy fools, you are a dead woman, even if the Iroquois do not come upon you. All right. We will go up the rapids. But in two canoes. You and Iwanchou in one, Nicanis and I in the other."

"Right," Daniel said, and smiled. "Then we know that you will follow us."

"Come on," Chomina said. "Hurry." But as he went to the canoes, he paused and looked at his daughter. "Remember, if I am killed today, I am not angry with you. They have put a spell on you, these Normans. You are not to blame."

"You will not be killed," she said. "Look." She pointed to the sky. A file of geese flew in a straight line, passing overhead with a rush of wings. "They go north," she said. "It is a sign."

Chomina leaped into the first canoe, led them out into the ebb of the main current, then turned north. Peering ahead as he paddled, he said to Laforgue, "You are not so stupid as you look, Nicanis. But remember, there may be other Iroquois fuckers waiting for us near the rapids. We are still dead men."

In less than an hour they again reached the rushing currents which signaled the beginning of the rapids. They passed the scene of their capture. Several hundred yards farther on, the rapids became foaming white shallows. The canoes stalled. Chomina, wading in the water, tied portage ropes, and soon all four were in the rapids, hauling the canoes over slippery rocks, sometimes falling and bruising their knees, sometimes forced to carry the canoes and climb narrow trails beside the falls. No one spoke. Their bodies ached not only from toil but from the wounds and beatings inflicted on them, yet all the while they moved in a heightened, anxious state, waiting for the hiss of a stone-headed arrow or the killing cry of the enemy.

Here, at the falls, there was no snow on the ground. The weather in this limbo of seasons had vacillated back to a strange warmth, and soon, in their heavy winter clothing, the priest and Daniel were dripping with sweat. They toiled on until early evening, when suddenly Chomina recognized something. He beckoned and, carrying the canoes, they came into a place where the river widened into a great pool below a thunder of falls. Chomina put the canoes back in the water and skillfully navigated the falls, leading them into a sheltered place beneath the roaring waters. There, he disembarked and beached the canoes on a grassy knoll.

"Wait here," he said. They saw him crawl across some green-slimed rocks and reach down into a hole. A few minutes later, he came back with some pieces of dried eel and husks of corn. "Hurons went up this way and have not come back down," he said. "This is one of their caches. If we can find the others, we will have food for the next three nights. They picked this place because there is no need to build a shelter. It is warm here, under the waters."

In the roar of the falls, sustained talk was impossible. Weary, aching, spent, they ate their small meal and curled up beside each other, covering themselves with skins and bark. Before they slept, Laforgue washed and cleaned the pus and dirt which had accumulated in Daniel's pierced hand. All were in pain, the girl from the beating and the lacerations on her thighs, Chomina from the arrow wound in his back and the heavy blows which had raised ugly weals on his neck and shoulder, Laforgue from genital burns and the severed joint on his index finger.

Before lying down, Laforgue thought to read his breviary but realized that for the first time in his life as a priest this was no longer possible. Sewn into his cassock were the only possessions left to him, his rosary, the map, and Father Bourque's instructions. His breviary, like all else—mass vestments, missals, the sacred communion vessels—had been lost forever. Into his mind came a vision of the Iroquois leader, rising up, clad in sacrilege in silken white and gold, the embroidered gold cross on his breast bloodied and stained with dirt. Again, in the light of the cooking fires, he saw the warriors gleeful as devils, their white teeth tearing the parboiled flesh of Chomina's child.

He looked at Chomina. The Savage lay on his side, his cloak drawn up around his neck. His eyes, obsidian, opaque, were fixed on the rushing falls; his bruised and blood-clotted face was impassive as a head carved in stone. Less than twenty-four hours ago, this Savage had a wife, a son and an honored place among his people. Now he had seen both barbarous deaths, had watched his daughter batter in a man's skull and was, with her, fugitive in a wilderness where, at any moment, cannibal enemies might again attack. What is he thinking, Laforgue wondered, this man who lives his life in outer darkness, far from the sight of God? What consolation can he seek, he who knows nothing of God's mercy? And Daniel. What is in *his* mind tonight, he who has come so sudden to man's estate and to this nightmare vision of a world few men ever see?

Laforgue looked at the girl, who lay, her head nestled against Daniel's chest, her eyes closed, her face shut in as though she were a mystic deep in prayer. Yet she knew nothing of prayer; she, like her father, was far from the sight of God, knowing nothing of God's mercy.

But as these thoughts jumbled in Laforgue's mind, the word *mercy, mercy, mercy* repeated itself like a meaningless stammer in his brain. What mercy? If Our Lord tests me, if He tests Daniel, then He promises us something which repays us a thousandfold for any suffering, any danger, any death. But what does He offer to these others, what mercy does He show to these Savages who will never look on His face in paradise, these He has cast into outer darkness, in this land which is the donjon of the devil and all his kind?

# 9

TO REACH THE UPPER RIVER BEYOND THE RAPIDS, THEY traveled three days. Most of that time they spent inland, away from the water, carrying their canoes as they trudged along a path worn by countless Savage travelers, a path which climbed a steep hill and brought them to a view in which the Ottawa River stretched clear ahead. In those three days and nights Chomina barely broke silence. He seemed to come to life only when, each evening, he searched for caches in which other travelers had stored food. Gradually, the silence which enveloped him spread to the others as they toiled on from dawn to dusk, up steep inclines, through bush and bracken, their wounds now part of a generalized torment which, in a mixture of fatigue and pain, seemed to anesthetize them and force them on.

Laforgue brooded endlessly on the journey ahead. Without proper weapons to hunt game, without supplies of food or goods to trade with the Allumette nation which they would shortly encounter, without even a guide should Chomina decide to abandon them, he must somehow complete this dreadful journey. According to Father Bourque's instructions he was now some twelve days from his destination. He must travel north on the Ottawa and Mattawa for five days, then cross Lake Nipissing and find the smaller river which led to that great lake of which Father Brabant had written, "It is a great gentle sea of fresh water, so huge that no farther shore is ever in sight." He must travel south along the shores of this great lake until he reached the Ihonatiria mission. If it still existed. He no longer allowed himself the luxury of hope. He who all his life had put his trust in God now paddled silent behind a Savage, his mind empty of prayer. At night he lay down like an animal and slept without thought of his nightly devotions. It was as though in these last days of degradation, pain and horror, his mind had become numb to moral judgments. He saw Daniel lie in the arms of a Savage girl and felt no anger, no sense of sin. He moved, blind and uncaring, shut out from God's sight as though he, like Chomina, was condemned to live forever in the darkness of this land.

Three days after passing the head of the rapids, Chomina failed to find any further cache of food. Nothing was said. But on the morning of the fifth day, paddling, faint with hunger, suddenly Laforgue saw Chomina turn their canoe toward shore. Perhaps he had sighted hares or deer in the woods? As the canoe slipped into the shallows by the riverbank and Annuka and Daniel turned their craft to follow, Laforgue saw Chomina's face. The Savage, whose normal complexion was a brick red color, had now taken on a purplish hue. Suddenly, he leaned forward, his paddle trailing the water, his breathing hoarse and constricted. When they beached the canoe, he got out slowly and, shaking off Laforgue's helping arm, walked alone, up to the top of the bank.

"Are you ill?" Laforgue asked, but the Savage shook his head as though the question were an irrelevance. At the top of the bank he sat down heavily and gestured to Laforgue to sit beside him.

At that moment his daughter and Daniel came up, concerned. Chomina beckoned her to come close, then whispered something which Laforgue did not catch. At once, she took Daniel by the arm and walked him away. When they were out of earshot, Chomina, breathing heavily, looked at Laforgue. "Tell me, Nicanis. What does your dream say now?"

"I am too weary for dreams."

"But you *must* dream," Chomina said and clutched his chest as though in pain. "If you do not dream, how can you see the journey ahead?"

"I put my trust in God. He will decide what must happen to me."

For a long moment, Chomina said nothing. He squatted on the ground, his knees up, his head hanging down in a posture which recalled to Laforgue a madman he had seen in the days of his youth, squatting among the cluster of beggars outside the cathedral at Coutances, a figure so frightening in its dejection that Laforgue, coming from the church, would hurry past, eyes averted, his mind mumbling a prayer as though it were a spell to cast out the devil.

"Then your god has told you to go on?" Chomina said, at last.

"Yes."

"In two days you will be in the country of the Allumette. You will need their help. You have no food and nothing to give them in trade. How will you go on?"

"God will provide," Laforgue said, but the words were stones in his mouth.

"How? If he does not provide, my daughter will die. You, Nicanis, I understand. You Blackrobes welcome death. You think that, if you die, you will enter a Norman paradise. But if my daughter dies, she will go to the land of night."

"If she will accept our Lord," Laforgue began, but the

Savage, breathing heavily and in pain, silenced him with a gesture.

"That is no answer," Chomina said. "How can we believe you? You have not seen this paradise of which you speak. I have not seen our world of night, but I know it is no paradise. You have no sense, Nicanis. No man should welcome death."

"You are wrong," Laforgue said. "For us, it is this world which is the world of night."

"What shit you speak. Look around you. The sun, the forest, the animals. This is all we have. It is because you Normans are deaf and blind that you think this world is a world of darkness and the world of the dead is a world of light. We who can hear the forest and the river's warnings, we who speak with the animals and the fish and respect their bones, we know that is not the truth. If you have come here to change us, you are stupid. We know the truth. This world is a cruel place but it is the sunlight. And I grieve now, for I am leaving it."

Laforgue glanced sharply at Chomina. As he did, the Savage bowed his head, withdrawing into that posture of frightening dejection which recalled the madman of Coutances. Some paces away, the girl and Daniel sat silent, watching. And, at that moment, Laforgue heard a chorus of birds announce the limits of their territories. If snow had fallen here, it had not lasted on the ground, and even now in the first days of November the trees were a last blaze of crimson and yellow leaves. The world is our sunlight, Chomina says, and for him it is true. I am not permitted to baptize him against his will. Laforgue looked at the Savage, ill, suffering, waiting for death. And, despairing, thought of God's mercy denied him. I must not dwell on these things. It is the devil who puts such thoughts in my head. But is it the devil? What has happened to me? Why do I no longer pray?

"Chomina," he said. "We will prepare a bed for you and we will rest here until you are stronger."

"I will not grow stronger," Chomina said. "I am ill. I will not see one more night. Send my daughter to me and I will speak with her. Then, all of you, get in the canoe and go on. At once."

"No, no, we will stay with you."

"Hairy fucking fool," Chomina said, with the ghost of his usual smile, "send Annuka to me."

The Blackrobe was coming toward her. But she had already risen because the forest had warned her. And now as she walked across the ground that separated her from her father, she knew that the She Manitou waited in the trees. Trembling, she passed the trees and came to her father. Already, he had assumed the pose of those who live in the world of night, squatting, his head down, his arms folded across his chest. "Father," she said. He looked up; his eyes were glazed with a film of sickness. "Is it a wound?"

Her father shook his head. "This morning when I woke, blood was in my mouth. Also, I shit black and cannot stop it. It is over with me. When I paddled past this place, the She Manitou called."

"Have you seen Her?"

"No. But I will. And She will touch me before night comes."

She knelt beside him and put her hand on his shoulder. His body was like stone. "We will stay with you until then."

"No. I must be alone. I have dreamed this. As I brought the canoe into this place, it was as though I had come home. That rock there, that line of trees, even this mound where I sit, all of it has been in my dreams for many years. Often I have asked myself what this place means. But it is not granted to us to know what some dreams mean. If only I had known then that it was the dream of death. That I would die in a quiet place and alone. Think what a gift that would have been. I would have been brave. I would have been a great warrior."

"You are a great warrior," she said.

"No. I am stupid and greedy and blind as any Norman. Because of that my wife and son are dead and now you will be left alone here with these cripples."

"Iwanchou is my betrothed," she said. "He will not abandon me."

Her father bent over, coughed and spat blood on the ground. "There is one chance for you. For both of you. Leave the Blackrobe and go back to our people. You must travel at night. The Iroquois do not hunt at night. I told that to Neehatin, but he has no fucking sense. Iwanchou can learn how to use a bow. You can make a bow for him."

"His hand is injured," she said.

"The winter hunting place is only seven nights away. The Blackrobe must go on alone. That is Neehatin's dream for him."

"You said that Neehatin has no sense."

Her father ground his teeth in pain. "Do not argue with me! Do as I tell you."

"I will do it," she said.

"Good. Now, go and bring some pine branches. I want to lie down."

She did as he told her. She took the hunting knife and cut the branches. As she did, Iwanchou came to her. "Can I help?"

"No. Leave us."

She went back to her father. When she had arranged the branches in a pallet for him, he lay on them and looked up at the sky. The film over his eyes had thickened. Perhaps he no longer saw her. "Are you hungry?" she asked. "I can look for berries."

He shook his head. "Go. Put both canoes in the water. Let the Blackrobe travel alone in the second canoe. When you and Iwanchou reach the current, turn south. The Blackrobe is sick and paddles like a child. He will not be able to overtake you."

Tears burned her eyes. "I will stay with you," she said.

Slowly, her father turned his head and looked at her. "I lied to you," he said. "When I landed here, the She came from the woods and touched me. She is waiting. When we are alone, She will lead me quickly to the land of night."

Fear came upon her. It seemed to her that she heard the She Manitou crying in the trees.

"Go," her father said. She bent and embraced him. She wept.

"I weep too," her father said. "But I have no tears left."

She turned from him, then, and ran back to the place where the Normans waited. "Come," she told Iwanchou. "Launch the canoes. My father is dying. He must be alone."

"Can I speak with him?"

"No. We do not have farewells. Come with me."

But the Blackrobe, hearing this, at once rose and went over to her father. She hurried after him. "Come away," she said angrily.

"Chomina," said the Blackrobe, kneeling and joining his palms together. "Chomina, do you hear me? If you can hear me, please listen. My God loves you, as I do. If you will accept his love, he will admit you to paradise."

"Come away," she said. She pulled on the Blackrobe's hair, making him wince.

"Let me be," the Blackrobe said. "Let me at least say one prayer for him."

"You fucking sorcerer!" she screamed. "Leave him alone. Iwanchou? Help me!"

Iwanchou ran up.

"Take him away," she cried. "Let my father die in peace."

She heard them speak with each other in their tongue. Iwanchou then pushed and pulled the Blackrobe, moving him toward the place of the canoes. She looked at her father. He no longer saw her with the eyes of the land of day. He looked toward the trees and she knew that he was looking in the face of the Terrible One. In fear, she ran back to the Normans. "Quick," she said to Iwanchou. "Get in the canoes. Hurry, Nicanis!"

But the Blackrobe, ignoring her, knelt down again, his hands clasped, staring at the sky, his lips moving in some sorcery. She slapped his face. "Come. We must not be here when he dies. Get in the canoe."

He rose and came with her. She screamed to them to hurry as they dragged the canoes down into the river. She and Iwanchou got into one, the Blackrobe into the other. Paddling in hurried strokes, she moved into the main current, the Blackrobe in his canoe following behind. When the canoes stood well offshore, she looked back. Her father lay alone in the clearing, resting on the pallet of branches. But, as she watched, his spirit rose out of his body. The spirit of her dead father walked toward the trees, his hand in the She Manitou's hand.

The canoes stalled, riding the current. Daniel kept theirs moving in a circle so that Annuka could watch the shore. After a while, she turned to look at him. She said, "It is a rule with the Algonkin that no children shall lack parents. If I go back to them, they will give me a new family."

"I am your family," he told her.

"My father said we should go back to the winter hunting place. Come with me. Let Nicanis go on alone."

Daniel looked at the other canoe, at the priest who steered it. "I cannot leave him now."

Again she watched the shore. "I promised my father that I would go back. It is foretold in Neehatin's dream that Nicanis will enter a Huron village alone."

"Listen to me," Daniel said. "That dream cannot be

fulfilled if we leave him. Look at him. How can we leave him?"

"That sorcerer, what do I care?" she said. "You saw him just now with my father."

"That was foolish, yes," Daniel said. "But he wanted to help him, not to harm him."

She looked over at the priest, then said, "We two could travel by night on the river. It is only seven nights' journey."

"I cannot leave him, Annuka."

He saw the glitter of anger in her eyes. "Then love him. Love that sorcerer and go with him, since you love him more than you love me."

"You know that's not true."

"I know you are a Norman. My father was right. The Blackrobe has you in his spell. All right, let's change canoes."

"Annuka . . ."

She took up her paddle. "We will land at the next bend of the river. We can't land here. The She Manitou is in those trees. But you, you fool, you're too blind to know that."

Suddenly, anger filled him like a drunkenness. "Father Laforgue," he called. "Follow us. We're going to change canoes."

Angry, he stroked, not bothering to match his stroke to hers. She thinks I'm stupid, but it is she who is stupid, a stupid Savage who will go back down there to torture, death, to cannibals! Because a stupid Savage like Neehatin had a dream. All right. Let her go.

A few minutes later they beached both canoes out of sight of Chomina's body. Laforgue saw the girl take a cooking kettle from her canoe and put it in his. "Good idea," he said. "It's better that we travel in one canoe."

"I told you he was stupid," she said, not looking at Daniel.

"No more stupid than someone who goes back down among cannibals."

"Be quiet," she said. "Your voice isn't a man's voice but the squealing of a hare."

"What's wrong?" Laforgue asked. "Annuka, Daniel, what's wrong?"

"You know very well what's wrong." She burst into tears. "You put a spell on him. He loved me and you took away that love. You hairy shit. I loved him. I love him."

"Daniel," Laforgue said, turning to the boy. "Listen, do you want to go back down the rapids?"

"No, I don't," Daniel said, and Laforgue saw that he too was close to tears. "I don't. But I . . . I can't—I don't want to leave her."

"Talk, talk, talk," the girl said, angry and weeping. "What are you jabbering about?"

"We cannot let her go back alone," the priest told Daniel. "She has lost her family because of us. What am I to do? If I send you with her and you lie with her and do not convert her and marry her, then you will destroy your soul."

"If that is what worries you," Daniel said, "I promise you I will try to convert her."

"Then go with her."

Daniel hesitated, then said to the girl, "He wants me to go with you."

She stopped weeping. "And you, what do you want?"

"I want to be your husband. I will live with your people."

"I warn you," she said. "They won't treat you well."

"Then come with me to the Hurons," Daniel said. "We can live there. And Nicanis will marry us."

"Is that true?" she asked Laforgue.

Daniel looked at Laforgue and said, in French, "Tell her yes."

Laforgue looked at the girl. "Yes, it is true," he said. "You can live among us as his wife."

She turned and walked back to the river. She stood, staring downriver at the bend behind which her father's body lay. At last she turned back. She looked at Daniel and then at Laforgue. "I have decided," she said. "Now I am your family. We will go in one canoe."

# 10

On the morning of November 10, Casson and Vallier, two fur traders returning from the Huron country, came down from the Upper Lake into the Mattawa River with six Algonkian paddlers and four canoes, heavily laden with furs. They were excited and nervous, for they were two weeks behind plan and racing the approaching snows. Ahead, in a bend of the river, they saw a solitary canoe approach, its occupants paddling in a desultory fashion. Casson could not make out the nature of these strangers. "Nipissing?" he asked, touching the shoulder of his lead paddler.

"Blackrobe," the paddler said.

Shit, Casson said to himself. He was a Huguenot. "One of your Fathers," he called back to Vallier.

"Shit," said Vallier. "Let's tell him we're in a hurry."

But Casson, uneasy now, stared ahead. Why only one canoe? The Jesuits usually traveled with several canoes, all filled with mission supplies. Had the other paddlers run away?

As his men stroked swiftly, closing the gap, Casson saw that there was one Jesuit, a French boy and a Savage girl in the canoe. He touched his lead paddler and pointed to the girl.

"Algonkian," the paddler said.

The Jesuit began to wave at them, asking them to pull in to shore. Casson looked back, questioning Vallier. Vallier shrugged.

"Hallo. Hallo," the Jesuit called in a hoarse voice. "We need help."

Unwillingly, Casson gave the order to land. At that point, coming close to the solitary canoe, he saw that all three occupants had been beaten and wounded. His spine prickled. He looked again at the Jesuit and remembered him as one of those he had seen in the residence in Québec. The boy he did not know. As the Jesuit steered past him, Casson looked at the priest's hand on the paddle. The index finger was severed at the joint. Casson's paddlers saw it too.

"Iroquois," one said to the man behind him.

Shit, Casson thought. Now they will leave us. We'll be stuck here on the river with no paddlers and a fucking fortune in pelts.

He looked at the Jesuit's sickly face and monkish beard and felt a flush of anger. And then, as though to irritate him further, the Jesuit smiled at him and called in his hoarse voice, "It must have been Saint Joseph who sent you to us today."

Saint Joseph my ass, Casson thought, but forced a smile. The fucking Jesuits were the real rulers of this country. Champlain was completely under their thumb. He was like a priest himself, now, in his old age, lecturing everybody else on the importance of saving the Savages' immortal souls.

When the canoes had all been pulled clear of the water, Vallier said to the boy, "What happened to you?"

The boy looked at Vallier as though he did not understand.

"What happened?" Vallier said, again.

"We're starving," the boy said.

"There's some cooked sagamité in our kettles," Vallier told him and asked his paddlers to bring it up.

While they waited for the sagamité, the priest, the boy and the girl stood silent as animals, and when the kettle was placed near them they went at once to it, scooping up handfuls of the cold greasy sagamité and stuffing it into their mouths. But, after their first swallows, they ate slowly, in the manner of starving people, as though the act of eating was difficult for them.

"How long are you without food?" Vallier asked.

"Eight days," the boy said.

The Savage girl, eating, suddenly vomited on the ground. Still retching, she went back to the kettle and scooped up another handful of the sagamité. As she did, Casson's lead paddler came up to her. "What happened?" he said in the Algonkian tongue.

"Shut up," Casson said, in sudden rage, going to the girl as though he would hit her. He turned wildly, staring at the priest. "Don't tell them what happened," he said. "If we lose these paddlers we'll never get back to Québec."

The priest, masticating slowly, nodded, to show he understood, but at that moment Vallier's head paddler came up to the girl and said, "Was it Iroquois?"

"You shut up," Casson said again, turning back to the girl, raising his hand as though he would strike her. But as he did, the French boy, thin, bruised, wild-eyed, pulled a hunting knife from his belt and held it against Casson's cheek. "Are you fucking crazy?" Casson said to him.

"Wait," the priest said, coming forward, holding up his hands. "Are we all mad? You have saved our lives. Daniel, put away that knife."

"You tell her to keep her mouth shut, do you hear?" Casson said. "Vallier! Help me."

But as he spoke he saw that four of his paddlers had come up behind him. He felt them at his back, as though their hatchets might strike into his skull. He turned around, but they were not armed. Then, their leader, Karatisich, ignoring him, walked up to the Savage girl and said, in Algonkian, "Why are you with these hairy pigs? Are you their prisoner?"

"No." She pointed to the French boy. "He is my betrothed."

"And where are your people?"

"In the winter hunting place below the rapids."

"You came from there?"

"Look, Karatisich," Casson said, going between him and the girl. "We will give these people food and help, but we must leave at once. I have promised you extra presents if we reach Québec before the snows."

Karatisich pretended not to hear him. He looked at the girl. "Were your people killed?" he asked.

"Shut up," Casson screamed at the girl. He knew he had lost control, but he could not help it.

"Be quiet," Karatisich said to him, then told the girl, "Pay no attention to this hairy fool. What happened?"

"Iroquois," she said. "Below the rapids. They killed my mother and ate my small brother before our eyes. My father died eight days ago."

"How did you get away?"

"They took us to their village and began to caress us. They would have gone on until, at last, they burned and ate us. But on the first morning I killed the guard and we ran away."

"Is that true?" Vallier said to the priest, his eyes staring in fear. "Cannibals?"

The priest nodded. Vallier turned to Casson. "What are we going to do?"

"We go on, for Christ's sake," Casson shouted hysterically. "Come on, you've heard enough. Let's get them back in the canoes."

"We can give you a ten-day supply of sagamité," Vallier said to the priest. "That will take you through the upper lake and the small river to the inland sea. You will meet the Allumette on the upper lake. We will give you trade goods. You can have the Allumette guide you to the great lake."

"If you make a receipt, I will sign it," the priest said. "Our Superior will repay you in Québec. But, of course, there is no repayment for your kindness."

"Get the sagamité," Casson was shouting to his paddlers. "Bring the dried sagamité, now. Hurry."

"It will be dangerous," the priest said to Vallier. "But remember, you must travel at night. That was our mistake. The Iroquois do not hunt at night. Now, tell me. You have been in the Huron country?"

"We just came from there," Vallier said.

"Did you see any of our fathers?"

Vallier nodded. "We spoke with Father Brabant in Ossossané less than a month ago."

"Then he is alive?"

"He is alive, but one of the priests in the villages was killed," Vallier said. "It seems there is a sickness in many villages. The Savages haven't had this illness before, and they blame it on a sorcery of the Jesuits."

"Who was the priest who was killed?"

"Come on," Casson said, coming up. "Make out that paper and let's go."

"Wait a minute," Vallier said. He sat on a log and began to write out a receipt. "Who was the priest Father Brabant said was killed?" he asked Casson. "I don't remember his name, do you?"

"Of course I don't remember," Casson said, in great irritation.

"He was in one of the northern villages," Vallier told the priest.

"Ihonatiria?" the priest asked.

"Yes, that's right, that was the name."

The boy, who had been listening, came up to Vallier. "Why did they kill him?"

"I don't know. Father Brabant wasn't able to get up there. He was told of the killing by one of the Christian Savages." Vallier stopped. "Are you the priest they sent to replace him?"

"Yes."

"I wouldn't go there now, if I were you. Go to Ossossané and see Father Brabant first."

"But Ossossané is several days south of Ihonatiria," the priest said. "Isn't that so?"

"Six or seven days' paddling," Vallier said. "But what does that matter, if your life is at stake?"

"For Christ's sake, give me that goddamned receipt," Casson said. "You just sit there talking."

The priest turned to him. "My son," he said, in his hoarse voice. "Please, do not blaspheme."

"I am not of your faith," Casson said rudely and began to scribble the receipt.

"Father," said Vallier. "We are going into danger. Will you hear my confession?"

The priest at once went to him, putting his arm on Vallier's shoulder. Together they walked off toward the trees. Casson, finishing the receipt, watched in disgust as Vallier knelt and the priest, sitting on a rock, made the sign of the cross.

Casson saw that his paddlers were watching. He turned to the French boy. "Fuck it," he said. "Have they no sense? The fucking Savages think it's some sorcery against them. Kneeling and making those signs. Shit!"

But the French boy, ignoring this, asked, "What is this sickness up there in the Huron country? Do you know?"

"Fever." Casson looked at the Savage girl, who had come up and now stood near them. "Does the priest allow you to sleep with her?" he asked.

"Fuck you," the boy said. "Tell me. Are there Iroquois where we are going?"

"There are Iroquois in the Huron country, yes," Casson said. "They are killing the Hurons and driving them out." He looked over at the priest and Vallier. "Shit, what's keeping them? How many sins has he got to tell?"

"They won't be long," the boy said. He turned to the

girl and said in Algonkian, "Are you still sick? Is it better now that you have eaten?"

"It's better," she said.

Vallier and the priest returned. Casson handed over the receipt and the priest signed it. "I cannot tell you how grateful we are," he said. "When you reach Québec, will you tell Father Bourque that you saw us and that we are well?"

"*If* we get to Québec," Casson said. He called to the leader of his paddlers. "Karatisich? We are ready."

Karatisich stood, flexed his arms as though he had a cramp and then came over to Casson. He smiled and said, "We are going on, then. But we are all agreed. I have spoken to the others. We will not go below the rapids."

"You have been paid to go to Three Rivers," Casson said. "Are you a bunch of pissing women, then?" He laughed to show he was not giving offense.

"Will you protect us from the fucking Iroquois?" Karatisich asked. He, too, laughed to show he was not angry. "I think not. You Normans kill beavers, not warriors."

"We will travel at night," Vallier said. "There is no danger at night."

"What do you know about the danger?" Karatisich asked. "I told you. We will not go below the rapids." He walked away and called to the other paddlers. "I have told them. We will go now."

The four fur-laden canoes were put back in the water. The paddlers took their places as Casson and Vallier walked down to join them. The priest, the boy and the Savage girl stood beside the sacks of dried sagamité they had been given. "Thank you, and God bless you," the priest called.

As the canoes moved out into the main current, the traders turned to wave their fur caps in the air in a gesture of farewell. Impelled by the downrushing flow of the river, their craft skimmed at great speed over the water and, in less than a minute, had disappeared from sight.

Daniel, watching from the riverbank, his hand on Annuka's shoulder, thought, What if those are the last Frenchmen we will ever see? He looked around him. The river was again that desolate place of swirling currents, sudden winds and the strange creaking of the trees which lined the shore. A chill November dew covered the ground. He turned to her. Although she had just been physically sick, although her face was still discolored from the beatings she had suffered, he felt a familiar rush of joy. He looked into her brilliant dark eyes and, as always, saw there the self she had not given, that unpredictable Savage self, which judged him by rules and signs he did not understand. He looked down at the bags of sagamité. In six days we can reach the inland sea where the Hurons live. There we can marry. If my hand heals I can become a hunter. If not, I can live as the Hurons do by growing crops. But then, as though the man still stood beside him, he heard the voice of the trader. "Fever."

He turned to Laforgue. "Father, if there is fever in Ihonatiria, should we not go first to Ossossané and consult with Father Brabant?"

"I have been ordered to Ihonatiria," Laforgue said.

"He said one of the priests is dead."

"All the more reason to go there first."

"Tell me," Daniel said. "Do you ever have doubts?"

"About what?" The priest picked up the bags of sagamité and began to walk down to the canoes.

"About this journey."

"Yes, I have doubts," the priest said. "Now more than ever."

"Tell me about them," Daniel said.

The priest smiled. "It's better not to. Instead, look at this food. And these trade goods. We could say that God did not forsake us today."

And suddenly, as though to confirm his words, they heard Annuka call, "Look, look!"

Around a bend of the river came two canoes. In the canoes were Savages, paddling. The Savage in the lead canoe rose and made a sign of greeting.

"Allumette," Annuka said. "They will guide us." She began to wave. The Allumette leader waved back. His canoes moved toward the shore.

The Allumette controlled the Mattawa River. The following day, having been paid in advance by the trade goods in Laforgue's possession, they brought them to the Mattawa and, paddling relentlessly, reached the portage known to the French as La Vase, a twisting snake of river, mired in mud, through which the canoes must be dragged and carried. After an exhausting day in this maze, they reached Lake Nipissing. Heavy winds caused high waves as the Allumette led the priest's canoe across the fourteen miles of lake and into the small river described in Father Brabant's instructions. Here the canoes glided under high rocky banks in a two-day journey which ended when the Allumette leader pointed ahead, and, from the dark green color of the river, the canoes emerged into the clear waters of the great bay. From there, having said their farewells to their Allumette guides, and aided by prevailing winds, they rode the waves down the shore of the lake. At night they camped under pines which grew on barren orange-colored rocks. They rose each day just before dawn, while frost still covered the ground. It was a race, and they knew it. Until the midmorning sun warmed them, they paddled, their hands freezing, their shoulders wet with a penetrating dew. They ate sparingly, a mouthful of cold sagamité on starting, and cooked sagamité when they lit their nightly fire. On the fourth day, Laforgue, anxiously watching each configuration in the bay against the map he had been given, pointed to an inlet fed by a small river. "There," he said. "We go there."

"Are you sure?" Daniel asked.

"From the map, it seems right."

Annuka, staring at the shoreline, pointed. There, on the riverbank, was the remains of a small fire. "Huron," she said.

They landed. Annuka seemed nervous. She inspected the fire and said it was two days old. A chill wind turned to rain, and, although it was early afternoon, they built a shelter and lit a fire. "We are less than a day from Ihonatiria," Laforgue told Daniel.

"What did he say?"

"He said we are less than one day from the village," Daniel told her.

"Then tomorrow he must go on alone."

"We have only one canoe."

"He still must go on alone. You and I will come on foot."

"But that could take three days."

"He must enter the village alone."

"Well, we can go with him and wait outside the village."

"No." Suddenly she was angry. "You go with him and you destroy the prophecy. Don't be so stupid, Iwanchou. We will go on foot. In two nights we will reach the village. Nicanis will be there before us. And the dream will be obeyed."

"Daniel," Laforgue said. "Don't argue now. We have come this far together. Maybe she's right. I will take you upriver and, at noon, you can disembark. I will go on alone."

But the next morning when, as usual, they woke just before first light, Annuka would not get into the canoe. And so, waving a farewell, Laforgue, alone, paddled up the small river which led to the village of Ihonatiria.

As he rounded a bend and was gone, suddenly, Annuka began to tremble. Daniel put his arms around her but she pulled free. "What's wrong?" he said.

She shook her head, refusing to answer, then squatted on the ground near the dying fire. With a shiver of apprehension, he saw that she had adopted the posture of Chomina, head down, arms folded across her chest.

"Why do you sit like that?"

"Be quiet," she said. "They are all around us now. Their day is ending as ours begins."

"Who?"

"The dead. There are many here. There has been a sickness."

# TWO

# 11

THE MIRROR, OVAL IN SHAPE AND ENCASED IN A WOODEN frame, had been dropped last year by one of the Savage children whom he had taken as a pupil. Now it was cracked in a spider web of tiny sections, which split and altered his image as he moved in front of it. Reflected, the face which examined him from the web of slivered glass seemed the work of an indifferent caricaturist who had tinted his beard gray, enlarged and discolored his right eye and drawn the left side of his face in a lopsided, lifeless manner, the mouth's corner turned up in a stiff rictus which parodied a grin.

He looked in the mirror through no motive of fear or hope, or even of disgust. He studied the left side of his face as his brain issued the simple commands of speech. Speech came, but he was not sure that the sounds could be comprehended. With his good right arm, he steadied himself on the makeshift crutch and then, with great care, dragged himself through to the second room of this longhouse, which he and Father René Duval had partitioned off in sections to form the residence of the Jesuit mission of Ihonatiria.

The second room had been their kitchen and workroom and a classroom for the children they had taught. Now, its kettles and pans, its tables and rough benches seemed like exhibits in some museum of former times. Water which had leaked in under the loose doorjamb covered this part of the floor with a thin film of ice, making it necessary for him to hammer and crack it before he trusted his moribund body on its treacherous sheen. He moved to the large wooden chest in which the corn biscuit was stored. Each day he ate biscuit and drank water which was now bad-tasting, lying in a pail covered with a film of dead midges. He gave thanks before he ate, saying the words he had always said. When he had finished he sat for a long time, half listening for Joseph's footstep. But Joseph, whom he had christened as the first of his converts—even Joseph no longer came. It was as Joseph had predicted. No one would come any more into this house. The village waited for his death.

Today, straining to hear sounds, he thought of former days when he had striven for silence. The residence had been built inside the palisades erected by the village to protect the community against enemies, but he had asked that it be placed as far as possible from the other dwellings. He had asked this so that he and Father Duval would have quiet for their devotions and studies. He had not known until the fever came that, like so many of his requests, the Savages interpreted this as hostile behavior. The Savages distrusted privacy. In time of illness, noise and company were thought essential to drive out evil spirits. When the fever had first come upon him and then on Father Duval, the villagers had crowded in with advice, beating drums and offering ritual cures. He turned them away and asked for silence. It was a fever of a sort he had known in France, a fever brought on by a sudden chill. After fourteen days he was rid of it, and Father Duval, being younger and stronger, threw it off in half that time.

Then the fever spread. Unluckily, the first to die was a young woman who last year had refused their efforts to convert her. Her family said it was the Blackrobes' revenge. Since then more than thirty men, women and children had caught it and perished. At first, the village did not believe the young woman's family, and he and Father Duval had been welcome as they went about dispensing herbs and other simple medicament from their pharmacy. They were welcome because the Savages knew that they had thrown off the fever. No one else had done so. Therefore they must be sorcerers of strength. But at that time, he and Father Duval, seeking to baptize those who were about to die, had said in all innocence that baptism would lead their souls to heaven. The Savages reacted with alarm. They had hoped that baptism would cure the fever. Now, they said, the Blackrobes did not promise a cure but performed an act which led to the sick person's death.

That decision on the part of the Savages caused a council meeting. It took place, he thought, on the week when he suffered his second and crippling stroke. But he could not be sure. No, it must have been later than that. Yes, he remembered clearly the day he heard drums outside the residence and, on going to ask the cause, found Father Duval's body, his head split by an ax, thrown into the doorway. He had carried Father Duval into the small chapel, which was partitioned off next to the kitchen. It was as he laid the body down before the altar that he fell and lost consciousness. And woke to the bad paralysis on his left side. How long ago was that? He was not sure. If the stench from the chapel was any guide, it was many weeks ago. The smell had been dreadful for a while, but now it was much less pungent. He had dragged himself into the chapel several times. The host was still in the tabernacle. Christ was present and watched over poor Father Duval's remains.

On the day after his stroke, he had managed, with a

makeshift crutch, to go outside the residence. All hid from him. He called out, asking for someone to come and help him bury his dead. But no one came. A week later, Taretandé, the leader of the village, came with the senior men to visit him and told him that the warrior who had killed Father Duval had, next day, been stricken with the fever and had died. It was proof, Taretandé said, that the cure of the sickness lay in the Jesuits' hands. Taretandé asked him to forgive the village for the death of Father Duval. As a sign of his forgiveness, they asked him to lift the fever. When he told them there was nothing to forgive and that the fever was the will of God, they withdrew at once. Later, Joseph, coming to him under the cover of darkness, told him that the council had ordered that no one cross his path. It was said that he willed the death of the village but that their own sorcerers had striken him with the falling sickness and soon he would die. Meantime, the people waited. In his death they saw their deliverance.

Now, when he had finished his biscuit, he felt for his crutch and cautiously propped himself up, preparing to make the difficult journey across the kitchen to the chapel. He did not enter the chapel but, as usual, sat himself down just outside the doorway. From there he could see the statuette of the Virgin, which sat on a niche to the left of the altar. He could also see the tabernacle. The squeaking sound below the altar was the sound of mice. He prayed, as every morning, for the soul of Father Duval, a soul which did not need his prayers, he was sure, for Father Duval must now sit at the right hand of God in heaven, the first martyr of the Ihonatiria mission.

When he had finished his prayers, he allowed himself to think of Paris. He had been born forty-four years before in the Rue Saint Jacques, and now the Seine, the Île de la Cité, the markets of the Marais, the nave of the church of Saint-Germain-des-Près where as a boy he had dedicated his life to God, the streets, the sounds, the hawkers, the feast-day processions all paraded once again across the retina of his mind. Sometimes he heard the music of Palestrina played on his mother's spinet. And sometimes he saw his father's body, covered in black velvet, carried high on a bier through the crowded gravestones of the Cemetery of the Innocents to be buried with pomp and circumstance in the place where his father's father lay. At other times, as in a dream, he saw a grave marker in the Order's cemetery at Rheims, a marker which bore his name and this year's date: *Fernand Jerome, S.J., 1591–1635.* The stone marker was worn with age and greened with moss. A certain peace entered his reverie when he looked on this marker, evidence that he had lived and died. For in this emptiness, now that René Duval was dead, it was the aloneness of his fate which caused him, at night, to fall into a trembling as though his fever had returned. The Savages, once so noisy, were totally silent. Had they abandoned the village? Had they taken their dead and dying and moved to some other place? Perhaps he was surrounded by empty dwellings. Winter was at hand. Without a fire, he would perish of the cold.

But today, as he dozed in his accustomed place facing the small simple tabernacle on the altar which contained the body and blood of his Savior, he fancied that, in his reverie, someone called his name.

"Father Jerome? Father Jerome?"

It was a fancy, he was sure. The Savages did not use his French name. They called him Andehoua. But again, clearly, he seemed to hear it.

"Father Jerome?"

Stumbling, he hoisted himself up on his crutch and, warning himself to patience, began the careful trajectory toward the doorway of the residence. Again he heard his name. And then the voice, in French, called, "Father Duval? Are you there?"

On either side of Laforgue the dwellings seemed deserted, but wisps of smoke from the openings in the roofs of the habitations warned him that he was being watched. Occasionally a dog ran up to sniff at him, and twice he saw children peering at him from the skin-covered doorways, before some hand plucked them inside. He had left his canoe at the landing place. Some twenty other canoes were beached there. He walked on. He had almost covered the entire area enclosed by the palisades when he saw, ahead, a longhouse, built like the others but with a wooden doorway and, on its roof, a small wooden cross. At once, approaching it in excitement, he called out, "Father Jerome? Father Jerome?" There was no answer. He quickened his pace, going up to the door, his heart hammering in anxiety. "Father Jerome?"

He tried the latch. The doorway was not locked. Surely this must be the residence? He opened and peered in. "Father Duval? Are you there?" Inside, he was met by a foul charnel-house smell which made him gag. In the darkness of the interior, there moved, unsteadily, a tall bulky figure. It spoke in a voice like the hollow echo in a sea cave. "Are you . . . ?" it said. "Are you there? Do I really see you?"

Taretandé and Sangwati were in the fields when the messenger arrived. "A Blackrobe has come. He wears a long cloak and carries *raquettes* on his back. He has been beaten and his right hand lacks a finger. He came alone in a canoe."

"Where is he now?"

"He walked through the village. No one greeted him. He called out in the Norman tongue and all hid from him. He went to the Blackrobe's longhouse. He entered. Then I came here."

"And Ondesson, where is Ondesson?"

"I think they went to hunt."

"Find him," Taretandé said. "We must call the council. Join us by the river in the meeting place."

When the messenger had gone, Taretandé looked at

Sangwati. They were brothers, born of the same mother, and did not need to hide fear from each other.

"If another one has come, and alone, it is not natural," Taretandé said.

"They are sorcerers," said Sangwati.

"More than sorcerers, they are witches. They are not men but evil spirits."

"You were the one who said we should not kill Andehoua but let him be, as he is dying of the falling sickness."

"I know," said Taretandé. "Ondesson will hold it against me. He would have killed him as the other Blackrobe was killed. One hatchet stroke."

"But even if you had killed Andehoua," Sangwati said. "Who's to say this other fucker would not have come?"

"You are right," said Taretandé. "They are not men but evil spirits. What can we do against them?"

They had been working with ten other men and boys in the fields, but now they took their leave and went to join the council members in the meeting place. It was a clearing in the woods not far from the village. When Taretandé and his brother arrived, Ondesson and the seven other council members were already assembled. All had been told the news.

Ondesson was the war chief. In the past he had deferred to Taretandé, who was chief in council. But today it was as though Ondesson had prepared a war party and was ready to set out. As Taretandé and his brother entered the circle, Ondesson said, "There is one solution. Both Blackrobes must be killed."

"But, fuck it," said Sononkhianconc, who was the leading sorcerer of the village. "You kill one, another springs up. And remember that Otreouti, who killed the first one, himself sickened and died within three nights."

"We will not kill them with a hatchet," Ondesson said. "We will caress them until they scream and are filled with fear. We will tell them how many of our people they have killed with their sorcerers' sickness and why we must pay them with death. We will cut our necks and let their warm blood flow into our veins, so that we gain their powers. We will eat the fuckers' hearts as soon as they have died. We will cut off their heads, their hands and their feet."

"And when will we do this thing?" asked Sangwati.

"Now."

"And what if, like the warrior who killed the other Blackrobe, we sicken tomorrow, all of us die within three nights?" asked Taretandé. "For these are not men but evil spirits."

"They are men, fuck it," said Ondesson in a loud, warlike voice. "They will bleed like men and die like squealing hares. If you are afraid to come with us, then sit and shit yourself."

"I ask a vote," Taretandé said. "I am the council chief. We will have a vote. Who votes for death?"

Eight hands were raised. Then Sangwati, Taretandé's brother, raised his hand also.

"Well?" said Ondesson. "Are you with us?"

Taretandé raised his hand. "Yes," he said. "And as council leader it is I who will enter their stinking longhouse and tell them their fate."

"And how many days have you been alone?" Laforgue asked, when the older priest had finished.

Father Jerome did not answer. "First," he said, "you know what must be done."

"No, Father."

"The body is the temple of the Holy Ghost. That must be your first task."

"The body is in the chapel?" Laforgue asked.

"Yes. By the altar. Those are now the remains of a martyr of the Church."

Laforgue stared at the pale paralyzed face, the enlarged discolored eye, the heavy gray beard. He thought of a painting he had seen in the cathedral in Salamanca, a saint's face but with a look of madness.

"Day and night, I have wondered how I could inter his remains," the sick priest said. "So let that be your first task. Afterward, you must find the leaders of the village. You speak the Huron tongue?"

"Yes. Not as you do, but I have studied it for two years."

"We must speak with them once more. We must convince them that this fever is not our doing. The Savages are under the spell of their sorcerers. And the sorcerers speak against us. Now, go. You will find a shovel and an ax in the outer room. The floor of the chapel is of earth. We cannot have a coffin, but we can bury him in God's presence. When you have dug the grave and interred him, call me. I will say the prayers for the dead."

Laforgue rose and went to the outer room. The stench was less overpowering there. He took a shovel and an ax and went into the chapel. As he crossed the threshold he made the sign of the cross and genuflected to the altar. As he rose from his knees he saw, sprawled beneath the tabernacle, the corpse of Father Duval, an arm thrown out as in a grotesque gesture of welcome. The face was already in a state of putrescence.

He looked away, then forced himself to look again. This was, as Father Jerome had said, the body of a Christian martyr. He saw the matted hair, the skull split by a hatchet, the dried blood and congealed fluids. Quickly, he picked a burial place and began to hack at the earthen floor. He threw off his cloak and unbuttoned his cassock and, in the dreadful stench, working like a man possessed, within an hour he had dug a rough trench, six feet long by three feet wide. He went to the corpse and, taking it by the heels, dragged it toward the grave. As he did, to his horror he saw the head, already split, come apart at the base of the skull as though it would separate into two halves. But then, with a lurch, he pulled the body into the trench. He stood, panting, and wiped his brow with the cuff of his robe. As he did, he heard a sound behind him.

A Savage watched him from the doorway. The Savage wore a long beaver cloak over a tunic and leggings of deerskin. His face was painted black on one side, red on the other, and his hair, elaborately arranged, was cut short on the one side and fell in a long braid on the other. Around his neck he wore a ruff of feathers, and bead bracelets decorated both of his arms. He carried no weapon.

"Come with me, sorcerer," the Savage said. "And be quiet." He spoke in the Huron tongue. He beckoned, and Laforgue followed him out into the kitchen of the residence. There, Father Jerome stood, tottering on his makeshift crutch. "Take his arm," the Savage said to Laforgue. "Help him."

Laforgue went to the sick priest's assistance and together, slowly, they made their way to the front door of the residence. The door was open, and outside they could see several Savage men, painted and wearing robes of ceremony. The Savage who had come to fetch them signaled to these men.

"He is Taretandé," Father Jerome said, in French. "He is their leader."

The Savages at once surrounded the two priests. Drums began to beat. Men and women, children and dogs came suddenly from all the longhouses, in a din of noise and excitement. Yelling and screaming they marched with the priests toward the largest longhouse, the place of assembly.

Laforgue, half carrying the sick priest, made slow progress in the din. When they entered the longhouse, he felt the paralyzed body sag and become almost a dead weight. He looked at Father Jerome. The priest seemed to have fainted. "Father Jerome?"

The sick man rallied and opened his eyes. In the uproar Laforgue could not make out the words formed by the half-paralyzed mouth. He leaned toward the priest's lips and heard, "Did you—did you bury him?"

"It's begun," Laforgue said. "I will finish later."

Ahead, a tall, heavily built Savage stood with three others, painted for war. All three carried heavy clubs.

"Ondesson," said the sick priest, nodding to this Savage. "Ondesson, we must speak together."

"Shut your hairy face," the Savage said, and laughed. "Are we all assembled?"

A roar went up from the crowd. People scrambled up on the sleeping platforms as though taking their seats at a performance. Laforgue, remembering that other time of torture, in the longhouse of the Iroquois, felt himself tense. Was this a parley, or was it what he feared?

"Come! You!" shouted Ondesson, beckoning to Taretandé, the council leader. "Tell them."

Taretandé bowed to the war leader, as though in thanks, then turned to face Laforgue and Jerome.

"Fifty-three are dead," he said. "Men, women, children. Fifty-three you have killed, of our people. And every night more sicken and die. No one lives once this fever comes upon them. No one who is a man like other men." He pointed to Jerome. "But *you* lived. You and the other witch. Both of you had the fever and lived." He turned to the crowd. "Today, I went into their longhouse. I went into that place, shut off, where they keep pieces of a corpse in a little box, a corpse they brought from France. And what did I find? This new one, this new witch who came alone to this place, was there, digging in the ground. And in the place where this fuckpot dug, there were the guts and head and body of the one we killed. He was hiding him under the ground so that some new fucking spell can be made."

There was a silence; then, suddenly, men and women began to moan and cry as in pain or terror.

"These are not men," Taretandé said. "They are witches. They must be killed as a witch is killed."

A roar went up. Father Jerome raised his crutch, waving it as though asking permission to speak. But as he did, Ondesson, the war chief, banged suddenly on the ground with his club. "They are men and they will die like men! We will caress them. We will take strips of their flesh, roast it on the flames and make them eat it. We will remove their fingers, one by one. We will cut out their hearts and give their bowels to the dogs. We will cut off their heads and their hands and their feet."

"Wait!" Father Jerome managed, despite his hoarse paralyzed speech, to make the word sound clear above the din. At once, the yelling ceased. "You must not do this," the sick priest shouted. "If you do, God will punish you! Do you hear me? God will punish you!"

"Prepare the coals," said Ondesson. "We will start with the coals."

At that, the din began again, rising to pandemonium. Three women ran to the fires and scooped up hot coals on birch-bark platters. They presented the coals to Ondesson.

"Strip the prisoners," he commanded.

At that, two warriors ran up to the priests. As they began to pull at the cassocks, ripping the buttons, the light died in the longhouse as though someone had blown out a candle. All looked up at the openings in the roofs and saw a sky black as night. Inside, only the burning beds of coals dimly lit the faces and figures of those near to it. In the darkness, the crowd, like some great panting animal, fell silent in dreadful unease.

Laforgue turned to Father Jerome. "What is happening?" he whispered.

"Come," said the sick priest, as, jacking his crutch under his armpit, he hobbled toward the doorway of the longhouse. In the dim light of the fires, faces moved away, letting them pass. They walked slowly out into the village street and looked up. And as they did, the eclipse moved, the sun gradually reappearing from behind its circle of blackness. "It is an act of God," Father Jerome said hoarsely. "Our Lord has saved us. Blessed be Thy Name."

An eclipse of the sun, an act of God. Laforgue, looking up as the light returned to the heavens, knew that, indeed, this must be God's hand. But somehow no words of thanks came to his mind, no prayer of gratitude passed his lips. Could this be, like thunder and lightning, an accident of nature, which had happened at this hour? Of course not. But still he felt no sense of miracle. He turned. The Savages were now pouring out of the longhouse, staring up at the sky. Laforgue looked at Father Jerome. The sick priest's discolored right eye was bright with a strange luminescence.

"Father Paul," the sick priest said, "God has given us this grace, this opportunity. Now, we must use it for His glory."

"In what way, Father?"

"You will see," Father Jerome said. He called out, "Ondesson? Taretandé?"

The leaders came forward, unease plain as speech on their faces.

"You have seen," the sick priest said. "God—our God—has warned you. How dare you try to injure us, who are God's servants? We are going back now to our house to bury our dead. You have seen the hand of God. You must change your ways. If you do not, we cannot help you. That is all I have to say." He turned to Laforgue. "Come, Father Paul. Let us go back to the residence."

Laforgue took his arm. Slowly, they moved away, the crutch hitting like a slow drumbeat as the sick priest hauled himself over stony ground. The Savages stood, looking to their leaders. After a few moments, Taretandé made a sign. The villagers began to disperse.

*"Deus qui inter apostolicos sacerdos familium tuum. . . ."* Father Jerome, his paralyzed bulk looming over the small altar, began to recite aloud the prayer for a priest deceased. As he spoke he looked down at Father Duval's replacement, who knelt by the freshly covered grave. Soon the men of the village council would

return. He knew what he would say to them. This would be his final task: to reap a great harvest of souls.

Laforgue, listening to the Latin, stole a look at the sick man who recited the prayer. He thought of the rotting corpse beneath the ground and in his mind saw the skulls of saints long dead, venerated in sanctuaries as holy relics.

Is this the martyrdom, the glorious end I once desired with all my heart and all my soul? Why have I ceased to pray? What error has come upon me so that, today, that eclipse of the sun seemed to me a phenomenon which, were I to believe in it as the hand of God, would leave me in the same murk of superstition as the Savages themselves? I should ask Father Jerome to hear my confession. I should tell him my doubts and ask for absolution. But if I do, this holy man who is close to death will know I am utterly unfit to take his place.

When night came, Laforgue settled the ailing Jerome on his pallet and then, still sickened by the stench in the residence, went outside and stood looking at the Savage dwellings. He heard drumbeats and the cries of sorcerers, trying to drive out the evil spirits which they believed to be lodged in the bodies of the sick. Dogs barked. Above him the sky was clear and cold and filled with stars. The Savages have not yet come to kill us. If they do not come, then this will be my home. When Father Jerome dies I will be in charge here, my life's work to convert these Savages now dying of a fever against which they have no defense. The Savages will not come to kill me. God did not choose me to be a martyr. He knows I am unworthy of that fate.

# 12

THERE HAD BEEN NO FEVER IN TARETANDE'S HOUSE. But on the morning after the black sun darkened the sky, he woke to find that his new wife had begun to shiver and sweat. He rose at once and went to a sorcerer. But when he entered the sorcerer's house, the sorcerer's child was sick and a curing ritual was in progress. He went out and, walking through the village, heard drums and lamentations. He passed the hated longhouse where the Blackrobes were and saw their sign of crossed sticks on the roof. He remembered that the Blackrobes, in former days, made that sign with their hands and tried to teach it to the children. He remembered that, last spring, the Blackrobes had invited families with children into their longhouse and there had given the children presents of beads if the children would learn answers to questions which the Blackrobes taught about their god. He remembered that Aenons had warned that the Blackrobes did not speak of curing rituals to combat sickness, but of death and another life to which they wished to lead the people.

The Blackrobes spoke this way because they were the sorcerers of death. He thought of the black sun, which warned of their power. His new wife would die. Perhaps all of the people would die. Already, there was little fishing; the crops had rotted in some fields for want of harvesting. It had been a mistake to kill the first Blackrobe, for another had come alone, like a manitou, to replace him. The Blackrobes were devils of great power. We must treat with these fuckers. We have no choice.

It was as though, that morning, every man in the council had been touched by the same thought. Ondesson's son had shown signs of fever. Achisantaete's mother, who had had the fever four days, died during the night. Ondesson asked for a meeting.

"We must go to the Blackrobes," Ondesson said. "We must ask their help for a curing ritual to end this sickness. We must find out what it is that these sorcerers wish."

"The water sorcery for all of us," said Sononkhianconc. "That is what they will ask. And the water sorcery kills, just as the fever kills. They wish our deaths so that they can lead us into some fucking Norman place of the dead as their captives."

But Sononkhianconc was a sorcerer, and the council members knew that, as such, he was jealous of all other sorcerers.

"That could be," said Taretandé. "But at least let us speak with them."

It was decided. The council members walked through the village, watched by all. They went to the longhouse of the Blackrobes and Taretandé entered there. A few minutes later he came out with the old Blackrobe Andehoua, who had the falling sickness and walked with a stick. Behind them was the stranger Blackrobe, who had been found with the corpse of the dead one, performing some evil spell.

In the longhouse of the council, all sat. Tobacco was offered but, although it was the first time the council had invited them to a parley, the Blackrobes behaved not as normal men but as enemies. They said they did not smoke.

When he heard this, Taretandé laid aside his pipe. "I understand why you will not smoke with us," he said. "We did you a great wrong by killing one of you. Now we are willing to give many presents to right that wrong. Tell us what things you want from us."

He waited. "We do not take presents," the old Blackrobe said.

Taretandé felt himself begin to sweat. Had these sorcerers decided on death for all? Was there no talking to them? "We have come to you today because we are all agreed that you have the power to stop the fever. You are its masters. The village is dying and the sickness spreads. We now put ourselves in your hands. What must we do for you so that you will perform the curing ritual that will rid us of this sickness?"

As he spoke, he saw the old Blackrobe turn and whisper to the other one. Then the old Blackrobe raised his stick, signaling that he would speak. Taretandé bowed to him.

The sick old voice rose in a quaver of anger. "Yesterday, the sun went black. You have seen the hand of God, our God who is above us, who is the only Lord of heaven and earth. What must you do that you will be cured of this fever? You must serve our God, who is your God. If you will end this contagion, you must make a vow to do His will. Do you understand?"

"No," said Taretandé, and smiled, hoping by a joke to turn away wrath. "We don't understand because we are stupid cunts. You must tell us what you wish us to do."

"Very well," said the old Blackrobe. "You must make a public vow that if God ends this contagion, you will be baptized and keep His commandments."

"The water sorcery?" asked Sangwati. "For all?"

"Yes," said the Blackrobe.

"And what does your god command besides the water sorcery?"

"You must give up those practices which offend Him. You must not cast off your wives, but keep them for life. You must not eat human flesh. You must not attend curing rituals or feasts of gluttony in which you become sick with eating. Above all, you must give up your belief in dreams."

"But how can we do that?" asked a council member. "The dream tells us what to do."

"You will have no need of dreams to tell you right from wrong," the old Blackrobe said. "Our Lord will tell you. I have not long to live, but this priest of God who sits beside me will take my place and live among you. He will give you God's orders. Now, you must go back to your people and tell them what we have said. All must be baptized. And I wish this to happen soon. Until you come before me for baptism, the contagion will continue."

Aenons, who was aged and of great intelligence, now signaled that he wished to talk.

"We cannot do these things," Aenons said. He looked at the older Blackrobe. "Andehoua, I thought of you as my friend. But fuck it, don't you see? If we do these things and if we give up our belief in the dream, then the Huron life, the way we have always known, will end for us."

"You will have no need of your former life," the Blackrobe said. "You will have a new life, as Christians. You will worship the true God and forget these childish notions which now fill your heads. When you die you will go to paradise."

"I want to live, not to die," said Ondesson. "And I do not want to have a wife like a burden on my back when I no longer wish to live with her. You are Normans. Your ways are not our ways. Why do you not respect that we serve different gods and that we cannot live as you do?"

"Can we not agree to take the water sorcery and still

retain our ways?" asked Aenons. "If your god wants that, then we will work among our people so that all will take the water and be cured."

"Baptism is not a cure for the fever. It is not a cure for the body, but for the soul," the old Blackrobe said.

"Is it something, then, for our deaths, not for saving life?" asked Taretandé, and looked at the others.

"Yes," said the Blackrobe. "It will lead you to paradise, as I have said. But it may also help with the fever. For, if you do God's will, you may hope for his mercy. We will pray, night and day to God, asking him to take this sickness from you."

There was silence. Taretandé rose. Sweat ran down his face. "We will leave now," he said. The others rose also. They walked past the Blackrobes and out into the day. They went toward Ondesson's house. As they walked, they did not speak.

When the two priests returned to their residence it was almost noon. Laforgue settled Father Jerome on his pallet and, with him, recited the prayers of the Angelus. Then he went into the kitchen and made a broth of corn husks. As the broth simmered on the fire, Laforgue began to scrub the kitchen and clear it of dirt. When they had eaten he went into the chapel and cleaned and scoured the altar, replacing the rough altar cloth. He opened the tabernacle and saw a chalice and hosts within. When he had finished his work in the chapel, he went back to the sick man, who seemed to be asleep. But as Laforgue began to sweep the floor of the room, Father Jerome groaned and turned on his side.

"Are you all right, Father?"

"I have pains in my chest. Soon you will have to dig another grave."

"Don't say such things." Laforgue came to him and propped him up. "You are needed here. The Savages respect you."

The sick priest winced in pain. "Only God knows

what the Savages think," he said. "And we are waiting for their decision. In either case, I welcome it."

"What do you mean, Father?"

"Today, or tomorrow, they will come back," Father Jerome said. "Either they will give us a great harvest of souls or they will put us to death."

"A harvest of souls?"

"The baptisms."

"Tell me," Laforgue said. "What if we baptize them and they then die of fever? Those who survive will turn against us."

The sick priest smiled, a smile which, because of his paralyzed face, was strange as a gargoyle's pout. "Those who die baptized will go to heaven," he said. "As for the fever, you and I must pray tonight. We must ask God to spare them. If it is His will, the fever will leave them and we will have many Christians here."

"Father, that troubles me," Laforgue said. "Surely, if they now ask for baptism, it will only be because they fear to die."

"Or because they fear God," the sick priest said. "Alas, most Christians do not perform their duties because they love God, but because they fear Him. This fever is God's hand."

Laforgue looked at the paralyzed face. "God's hand?"

"Yes, yes! The fever is the tool given us to harvest these souls. If they ask for baptism, we must have a great public ceremony. And at once!"

"But surely it is our duty to instruct them in the Faith before we ask them to accept it?" Laforgue said.

"Of course! But we must not delay the baptisms." The sick priest's voice rose, almost to a shout. "Besides, it is permitted to baptize people without instruction if they are in danger of death. As are these people, Father. This sickness is killing them!"

"I am not easy with that thinking," Laforgue said. "It seems sophistic."

"It is not! The means are fair, if the end is good!"

* * *

That night in the village Annieouton, a sorcerer, performed a healing ritual with drum, shouting and dancing, on a young woman who was ill of fever. By morning, the young woman's fever had left her. The sorcerer at once spread about this news, claiming that he had cured her. But that morning, also for the first time, two other victims of the fever suddenly ceased to sweat and shake and woke, their brows cool, their bodies weak but cured. Both were Huron men who had become Christians some months before.

These events were discussed at noon in a meeting of the village council. Sononkhianconc, the leading sorcerer of Ihonatiria, claimed that his fellow sorcerer had effected a cure and that there was no longer need of the Blackrobes. But the council disagreed. It was pointed out that Annieouton had performed this ritual a dozen times in the past weeks and that all his other sufferers had died despite it.

"It is the Blackrobes who have done this," Taretandé said. "Why did it happen last night when it has never happened before? They have done it to prove to us again that we are in their power."

"But why was the fever lifted from the young woman while a sorcerer was present?"

"Perhaps they did it to mock our ways," said Taretandé. "I know one fucking thing. Annieouton's beating drums did not hurt. But it did not cure the woman. We must treat with these witches. My wife is dying. I want her to live."

The council then voted. It was agreed to assemble the village. Even those who tended the sick were asked to come. The council did not propose a referendum. It voted to inform the village of its decision and to ask for all to cooperate.

"Of course there will be some who will not take the water sorcery," said old Aenons. "I, for one, will not give up the dream."

"But, listen, you silly old prick," said Taretandé, trying to joke him out of it. "Why give up the dream? We will do as they say. We will take the water. Then we will see what we will do."

"If we make vows to give up the dream, to keep our wives, to let our enemies die an easy death and all the other stupid demands the Blackrobes make, it will be the end of us," Aenons said. "If we make the vows we must keep them. For, if their god is strong as they say, then he will know if we lie to him."

"It will be the end of us if we die of fever," Ondesson said.

"Then I will die of fever," Aenons said.

On the second night of their journey toward Ihonatiria, Annuka and Daniel, lying in a makeshift shelter, woke shivering with the cold. A heavy frost covered the ground, and at dawn they rose and continued on their journey. About an hour later, Annuka saw a path in the forest which told her they were close to a Huron settlement. She stopped, looked at Daniel and said, "Come here."

He had already, many times, plucked out most of his boyish beard to please her, but now she pulled at his chin and face until he groaned and slapped her away.

"Wait," she said. She took off his cap. She braided and arranged his hair in the Algonkian manner, then, taking out the purse of skins in which she stored her necklaces, she painted his face brown on the left side and blue on the right. She took away from him his woolen cap and his French breeches and left him dressed much in the manner of an Algonkian warrior.

"When we go in there," she said, "we will not ask for Nicanis. We will act as though we know nothing of him, until we discover what has become of him. Remember, you are my husband, and Algonkin. We have been lost and separated from our people, and we wish to stay for a time with these Hurons."

"And will they believe that I am not a Norman?" Daniel said, laughing.

She looked at him and smiled. "Don't you know, you fool? You have killed the Norman in you. Now you belong to me."

When Laforgue awoke on his third morning in Ihonatiria, he heard noise and shouting outside. He went to the door of the residence and, in the streets, saw many people going in and out of each other's houses, talking and arguing. The drumbeats of curing rituals had ceased. Laforgue went back into the kitchen and took some meal, crumbling it into a porridge for Father Jerome's breakfast. But when he went to see the sick man, Jerome had fallen off his pallet and lay helpless on the floor. "My other leg," the sick priest said, in an almost unintelligible moan. "I have no feeling."

Laforgue lifted him with difficulty and placed him on his pallet.

"You heard the noise outside?" the sick man asked.

"Yes, Father."

The sick priest caught his breath and rested for a moment. Then said, "If they bow their heads at sight of us, when they come here, it means they will kill us. Promise me . . ." He began to gasp.

"Yes, Father, what?"

"If we die, let us die with the name of Jesus on our lips."

"Yes, Father."

"And if it is the baptisms, let us perform them together."

"But will you be able to do that?"

"God will give me strength," Jerome said. "Listen."

Outside there was a great shout, then silence.

"Help me up," the sick priest said. "I will stand by the door." But he collapsed when set on his feet. "Very well. Put me down. Go to the door and wait. They will be coming soon."

Laforgue went through the residence and opened the wooden door. Outside, people stood in the streets, looking at him. Then, from one of the longhouses, three men appeared. They were Taretandé, the council chief, Ondesson, the war chief, and the sorcerer Sononkhianconc.

They walked toward him in silence. Laforgue waited. Would they bow their heads?

When they were within ten paces of him, they stopped. "Where is Andehoua?" asked Taretandé.

"He is inside."

"We want to speak to him."

"Come in, then," Laforgue said. "He cannot walk."

The three leaders entered the residence and followed Laforgue to the room where the sick priest lay. Cold sweat lent a silver sheen to his brow. His breathing was labored.

"We have decided," Taretandé said. "We will obey your god. Not all in the village are agreed, but the greatest number wish it."

"How many?" asked the sick priest.

"More than a hundred. And there are some who now say they do not wish it, but who will change when others in their family accept it. Besides, the cures of last night will make a difference."

The sick priest glanced at Laforgue. "God has seen fit to cure some of them," he said, in French.

He looked again at Taretandé.

"Do the people know what they must do? One wife, no human flesh, no curing rituals, the dream, all of it?"

"Yes," said Ondesson. "We told them! We've done every fucking thing you asked. Now, let's have the water. People are dying!"

"First, we must instruct those who will be baptized," Laforgue told Taretandé. "You must know who our God is and how you must serve him."

"There is no time for that," the sick priest said hoarsely. "We must do it now."

"You are right, Andehoua," Ondesson said. "We will do it today."

"Very well," said the sick priest. "We will start by baptizing those who are already ill with the fever. Assemble them outside this house. When we have finished, we will go on to those who do not have fever. First, the children. Then the others."

"I want to ask a question," said Sononkhianconc, the sorcerer. "Will those who do not take the water die of fever?"

"That is for God, not me, to decide," Father Jerome said.

"That is not an answer," Sononkhianconc said. "I have promised some of our people that I will ask you this question. Fuck it, I want an answer! Will they die?"

"I told you, I don't know," Father Jerome said. "But let me ask you. If you were our God, who would you spare? Your friend or your enemy?"

"*That* is an answer," said Sononkhianconc.

"Well," said Ondesson. "Let us get ready. First we will bring those who are ill of fever."

When the leaders had left the residence, Father Jerome told Laforgue, "When the time comes, let me be carried outside. We will need a kettle filled with water. We will baptize them one by one. Father, think of the joy of this day."

"I will get the kettle," Laforgue said. He went into the kitchen and, taking a cooking kettle, went out to the village well, which was close by a small river that wound around the edge of the village. As he walked through the village, he was aware of eyes on every side. People fell back at his approach and children ran inside the dwellings. For the first time in his life, he knew what it must feel like to be feared. When he reached the well, two women, washing clothes nearby, moved away at sight of him. He filled the kettle, and as he did a woman's voice whispered, "Nicanis?"

He turned, astonished. Standing by the palisades was

Annuka and a young man. At first, he did not realize that this young man, a beardless painted Savage, was Daniel.

"What have you done?" he said to Daniel, surprised.

"Please don't speak French," Daniel said. "What has happened? What is this assembly?"

"The village is going to be baptized. Why are you dressed like a Savage?"

"We were not sure if you were alive," Annuka said. "It's safer like this."

"They say you cured three sick people in the night," Daniel told him. "Is that why they are asking to be baptized?"

"Yes," Laforgue said. Suddenly, to his surprise, he began to weep.

"What's wrong, Father?" Daniel asked.

"If everyone is taking the water, I will take it too," Annuka said. She looked at Daniel. "And then we can marry."

"Father?" Daniel turned to Laforgue. "What do you say? Will you marry us?"

"Yes, yes," Laforgue said, wiping his eyes. "But I must go now." He walked away, carrying the water-filled kettle. Daniel has become a Savage. And I, what am I? Do I still have the right to challenge Jerome, who is strong in his faith, I who am an empty shell?

As he approached the residence he heard shouts and saw a young man running, pursued by two warriors armed with clubs. One of the warriors was Sangwati, the brother of the council leader. The warriors gained on their quarry and felled him about two hundred yards from the residence. They then looked back at Laforgue, who, alarmed, ran into the residence. He put down his kettle. "Father Jerome?"

There was no answer. He ran into the sick priest's room. On his knees, his shoulder leaning against the edge of a table, was Father Jerome. But as Laforgue came closer he saw that the body had been propped up against the table leg, and that a hatchet had split the head at the base of the skull.

As Laforgue stared at this sickening sight, he heard footsteps behind him. He turned in panic, expecting a hatchet blow. Ondesson and two other Savages came into the room. They carried hatchets.

"Wait," Ondesson said to the other Savages. He approached and looked down at the dead man. "The one who did this will not trouble you further," he said. "And if any others seek to injure you, we will protect you. Shit! Why didn't we remember that there are some in this village who have become mad with fear? I am sorry. We are all sorry. You mustn't think we are your enemies."

"I don't think that," Laforgue said.

"Then you will cure us? We are bringing the sick up now."

"The sick?" Laforgue said. He looked back at the dead priest. "Wait," he said. "I must think."

"Don't turn against us," Ondesson said. "I am asking you. Help us. We will obey your God."

"I must think!" Laforgue said. "Leave me."

There was a silence. Then Ondesson signaled to the other painted faces. All three went out through the kitchen and into the street. The wooden door was left open. In the quiet which followed their departure, Laforgue heard a faint buzzing noise and saw that flies had settled on the dead priest's face. With his hand he brushed them away. I must bury him. I will bury him beside Father Duval. I will ask Daniel to help me. I must pray for his soul.

But as he looked at the blood-clotted face and dead eyes, his mind stumbled again into thoughts of despair. What are these baptisms but a mockery of all the days of my belief, of all the teachings of the Church, of all the saintly stories we have read of saving barbarians for Christ? Why did Chomina die and go to outer darkness when this priest, fanatic for a harvest of souls, will pass through the portals of heaven, a saint and martyr?

What is my duty now, if not to follow the dictates of my conscience and refuse them baptism until they truly accept and worship Our Lord?

He turned and walked through the silent house into the dusty chapel, still sickly sweet with the smell of putrefaction. On the altar rested the small wooden box with a golden cross which contained the body and blood of Christ; beside it, the statuette of the Virgin, brought from France, painted in garish colors of pink, white and blue. He looked at the empty eyes of the statuette as though, in them, some hint might be given him of that mystery which is the silence of God. But the statuette was wooden, carved by men. The hosts in the tabernacle were bread, dubbed the body of Christ in a ritual strange as any performed by these Savages. God, whose wishes he had dedicated his life to fulfill, was, in this land of darkness, as distant as the pomp and magnificence of the Church in Rome. Here in this humble foolish chapel, rude as a child's drawing, a wooden box and a painted statuette could not restore his faith. Yet somehow he must try.

He knelt. He made the sign of the cross and then, as though he had never said the words before, he began to recite. *"I believe in God, the Father Almighty, Creator of heaven and earth, and in Jesus Christ, his only Son, Our Lord, Who was conceived of the Holy Ghost, born of the Virgin Mary, suffered—"*

He did not finish. Someone stood behind him. He turned and saw an old Savage in the doorway. "What are you saying in your tongue?" the Savage asked.

"I am speaking to my God."

"Is that little spirit there your god?" the old Savage said, pointing to the statuette.

"No."

"I am Aenons," the Savage said. "Shit, man, I was a good friend to Andehoua, and it grieves me that he was killed. But listen, Blackrobe. I am speaking against you today. You and your god do not suit our people. Your ways are not our ways. If we adopt them we will be neither Norman nor Huron. And soon our enemies will know our weakness and wipe us from the earth."

Laforgue did not answer. The old Savage turned and walked to the doorway of the residence. Laforgue saw him go out into the street where, already, the sick had been carried up to be baptized. He watched the old man move among the sick and their relatives, urging them to return to their homes. And as he stood in the doorway, a dozen men and women who had been sitting just outside the residence got up and came to him. One of them greeted him. "Father, we are the Christians here. We want to thank you for healing two of our family last night and for lifting the fever from three others today. Everyone has seen what you have done. That is why they come here now. Everyone knows we were right to worship Jesus. We thank you, Father."

"Three more were cured today?" Laforgue asked.

"Yes, yes, as you know. Tell me. Is it true that Andehoua was killed by a hatchet?"

"Yes."

"Then must we pray for him?"

Laforgue, unable to speak, nodded. He saw two other men join Aenons and go about shouting warnings. He heard them say again that, as Christians, the Huron people would lose their way and be destroyed. He turned and closed the door. He sat at the table and tried to still the sudden trembling of his body. Outside, the shouting increased. The door of the residence was pushed open. Silhouetted against the light he saw Taretandé, the council chief.

"May I enter?"

Laforgue rose. "Yes, come in."

The council leader walked into the kitchen and looked around as though afraid. He went to the doorway of the dead priest's room and stared at the kneeling figure. "Does this grieve you?" he said.

"Why do you ask?"

"Because there are some who say that you Blackrobes are not men but witches. And witches feel no grief."

"We are men," Laforgue said.

"Who can believe you? What sort of men are you? You don't come here, as other Normans do, to trade for furs. You ask to live with us in our villages, and yet you stay apart in this house. No one may sleep here and you hide your nakedness from us. Why? If you are men why do you not fuck women? Why do you keep a corpse in that room and eat it to give you strength? Why did you bring this sickness which was never seen here before? And why do you use it to kill us, if we refuse to bow down to your god?"

"We do not use it to kill you."

"No. The dead one, in there, Andehoua, didn't he tell us what we must do? That we must give up our ways? Well, we have told our people and they are agreed. We will do what you want, all the things you asked. All of them. That is what I came to tell you. We are ready. Baptize us."

"No," Laforgue said.

Taretandé sat down heavily at the table, facing Laforgue. "Why? Because we killed Andehoua?"

"No."

"Then why do you want us to die?"

"I do not want you to die."

"But without the water sorcery we will die."

"I didn't say that." Laforgue put his head in his hands and sat for a long moment, in silence. "The water sorcery will not cure you."

"Then what *will* cure us? Last night and this morning some have been cured. That is your doing, isn't it? Well, isn't it! Fuck it! Answer me!"

"It's not my doing," Laforgue said.

"Then why did it happen today? Why?"

There was a silence. "It—it was the will of God," Laforgue said.

"Your god?"

"Yes."

"Then we are ready," Taretandé said. "Our people

are waiting. You say you are a man and not a witch, and I believe you. I ask you now, are you our enemy?"

"No."

"Do you love us?"

"Yes."

"Then baptize us."

The council leader rose and went out of the house. In the street, the murmuring of the crowd grew louder. Laforgue got up and went into the chapel. He looked again at the blank eyes of the statuette and thought of the prayer half finished on his lips when Aenons came. Had that statement of belief in God any more meaning than Taretandé's promise to do God's will? What *was* God's will? He looked at the tabernacle. He felt the silence.

*Do you love us?*

*Yes.*

He went to the chest in which vestments were stored and took out a linen alb, pulling the long white smock-like garment over his black cassock. He took up a gold-embroidered stole and, from habit, touched his lips to it before putting it around his neck. He walked past the dead priest, going to the door.

Outside, a cold wind came from the great lake. Before him, huddled in the village street, were four rows of litters containing the sick. Behind them stood the children of the village, and behind the children were the men and women not yet stricken by fever. He saw, standing to his right, Taretandé and Ondesson, with the other members of the council. And, close by, he saw Daniel and Annuka. He signaled to Daniel, who came up at once.

"Take the kettle," Laforgue said. "Help me."

He faced the crowd. Slowly, he raised his fingers, making the sign of the cross, touching his brow, his chest, his right shoulder, then his left. All watched this sorcery. Then, with Daniel carrying the kettle, he went down to the first row of the sick. He took a small ladle from the kettle's rim, filled it and poured a trickle of water on a woman's fevered brow, saying in the Huron tongue, "I baptize you in the name of the Father, and of the Son, and of the Holy Spirit." The Savage woman stared up at him, sick, uncomprehending. He moved on, saying over and over the words to make them Christians and forgive their sins. Was this the will of God? Was this true baptism or a mockery? Would these children of darkness ever enter heaven?

He looked up at the sky. Soon, winter snows would cover this vast, empty land. Here, among these Savages, he would spend his life. He poured water on a sick brow, saying again the words of salvation. And a prayer came to him, a true prayer at last. *Spare them. Spare them, O Lord.*

*Do you love us?*

*Yes.*

## ABOUT THE AUTHOR

BRIAN MOORE has long been recognized as "one of the best novelists writing, never traveling the same ground twice" *(The Times,* London). He began his career in 1956 with *The Lonely Passion of Judith Hearne* and has followed it with sixteen novels that have won the admiration of critics and an ever-widening audience of readers. Among his notable achievements are *The Luck of Ginger Coffey, I Am Mary Dunne, The Doctor's Wife, The Mangan Inheritance,* and most recently, *Cold Heaven,* which prompted *The New Republic* to remark that "Book by book, Brian Moore has been building a body of work . . . as good as that of any novelist writing today in English."

In Great Britain he has received the W.H. Smith Prize for *Catholics* and the James Tait Black Memorial Award for *The Great Victorian Collection;* in Canada, the Quebec Literary Prize and the Governor-General's Award for Fiction (twice); in the United States, a fellowship from the Guggenheim Foundation, and a special award from the National Institute of Arts and Letters. He is a fellow of the Royal Society of Literature.

A citizen of Canada for many years, he was born in Belfast in 1921, educated at St. Malachy's College, and served with the British Ministry of War Transport in North Africa, Italy, and France during World War II. He and his wife, Jean, live much of the time in California, spending several months of each year in Canada, Ireland, England, and France.

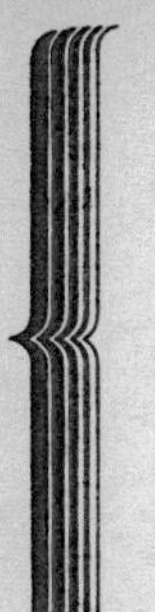

# BESTSELLING AUTHORS BRING YOU BESTSELLING FICTION... from Fawcett Books

**Available at your bookstore or use this coupon.**

____**RABBIT IS RICH, John Updike** 24548 4.95
Winner of the Pulitzer Prize, the American Book Award and the National Book Critics Circle Award in 1982. "Superb—the most important American novel I've read in years." —John Cheever.

____**THE BOOK OF LIGHTS, Chaim Potok** 24569 4.95
A national bestseller. The story of a young rabbinical student confounded by his times, who is drawn to the study of the Jewish mysticism known as Kabbalah.

____**THE COVENANT, James A. Michener** 21420 5.95
11 months on the *New York Times* Bestseller List. The best and the worst of two continents carve an empire out of the vast wilderness that is to become South Africa.

____**RIVER OF DEATH, Alistair MacLean** 20684 4.95
An SS officer, escaped to Brazil in the last hours of Hitler's Reich, builds a multimillion dollar empire. No one knows his secret past...except one man whose wife he murdered.

____**KANE & ABEL, Jeffrey Archer** 21018 4.95
8 months of the *New York Times* Bestsellers List. Spanning 60 years, the compelling story of two ruthless, powerful businessmen, born on the same day. Their driving passion is overshadowed only by their desire to destroy each other.

____**ANSWER AS A MAN, Taylor Caldwell** 20050 4.95
This bestselling novel reveals the life of Paul the Apostle and his life long struggle for Christianity. The story travels from Greece to Italy to Israel.

**FAWCETT MAIL SALES**
**Dept. TAF, 201 E. 50th St., New York, N.Y. 10022**

Please send me the FAWCETT BOOKS I have checked above. I am enclosing $..............(add $2.00 to cover postage and handling for the first book and 50¢ each additional book). Send check or money order—no cash or C.O.D.'s please. Prices are subject to change without notice. Valid in U.S. only. All orders are subject to availability of books.

Name________________________________________

Address______________________________________

City________________State__________Zip Code__________

20 Allow at least 4 weeks for delivery. TAF-4